CHAOS

CHAOS

Cydney Daemon

Author's Note

Despite being a fantasy, **CHAOS** is a series deeply rooted in reality.

It will deal with heavy topics at times. However, as someone who has worked in the mental health field and has personal experience with trauma, I will do my best to handle things with care and consideration. The QR code at the end of this note will take you to the page on my website that details any content advisories you may need. They will also be included in a highlight reel on my Instagram.

I have put in many hours, days, months, etc. of research into **CHAOS** so that I could do this story, this world, and these characters the utmost justice and treat them with the respect and dignity they deserve because to me characters are representations of real people. They are not perfect. They are flawed and multifaceted.

With that said, I want to note that there is a character who is Indigenous (Ojibwe) though she doesn't have a relationship with the community due to family history. I pulled from my own personal experiences as someone who is Ojibwe and doesn't have a relationship with her community due to family history. This in no way is meant to represent all Indigenous or Ojibwe people as we are not monoliths. For other characters, I also pulled from my personal experiences with mental health and trauma and my personal experiences as part of the LGBTQ+ community, and I also pulled from what I learned in my job in the mental health industry. Again, these are not meant as a representation of *all* people who fit these backgrounds or experiences.

For my other POC characters, I made sure to get assistance to ensure I am handling them respectfully, and I will do the same with all future books. That does not exempt me from being called out if someone finds any part of my work problematic in any way, and I respect that. I am only including this as my promise that I will always do my damndest to treat my characters and my audience with respect by doing my homework, educating myself, and seeking assistance from those who know better than me so I can avoid overstepping boundaries or causing harm to real people or communities. I take this very seriously.

I won't shy away from highlighting real issues because even if it is not part of the plot, to highlight one issue with purpose while ignoring other issues is ignorant, disrespectful, and incredibly harmful.

Thank you so much for picking up CHAOS. I really hope you enjoy this story. If you are interested, there is also a playlist at the back of the book, and you can find the playlist on YouTube as well.

Without further ado, I'll let the story begin with one reminder ...

All things are not as they seem.

x Cydney Daemon

Scan the QR code for Content Warnings

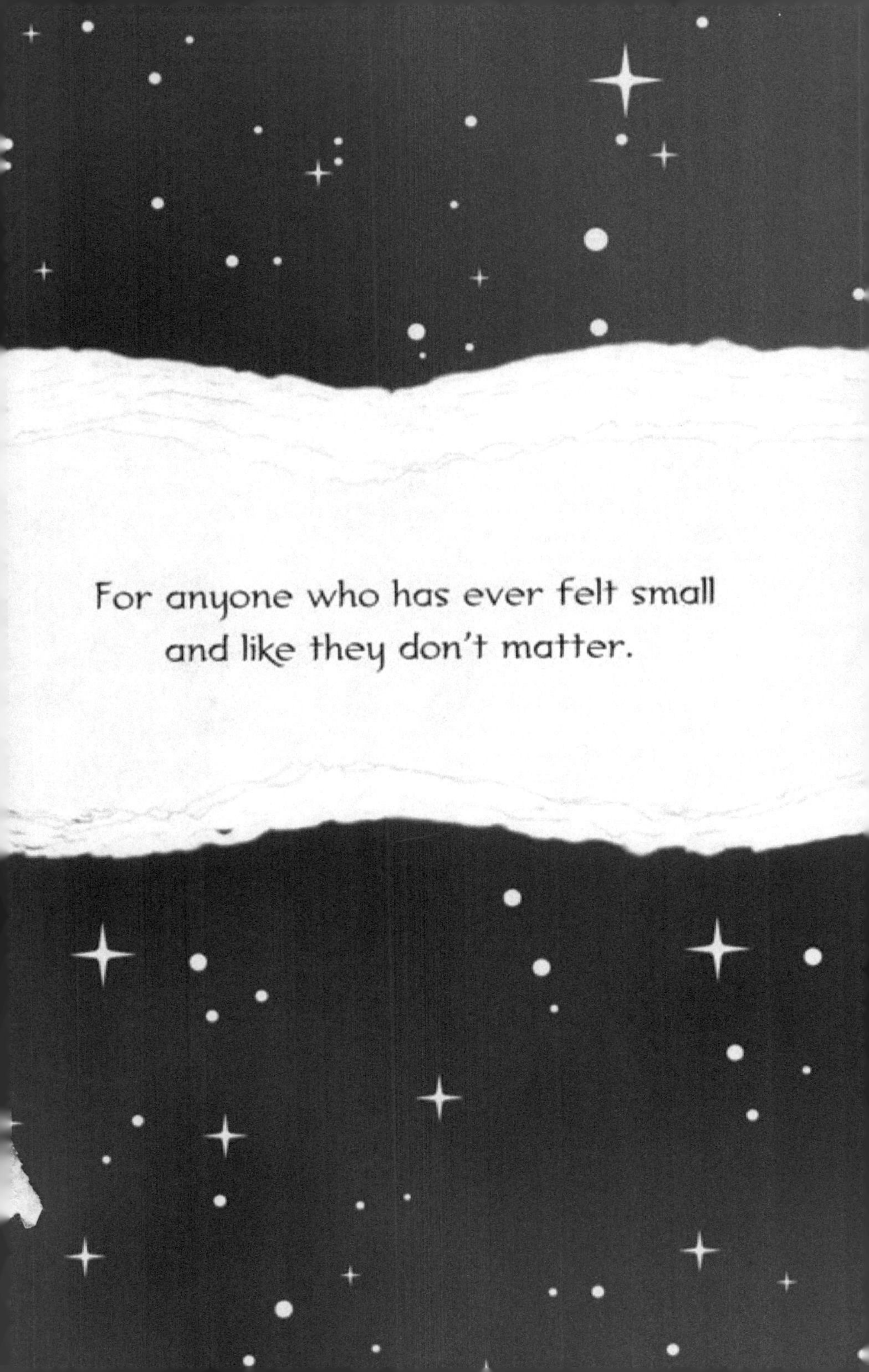
For anyone who has ever felt small
and like they don't matter.

CHAOS

Book 1 of 5

of the

CHAOS

series

I

September 1, 3699

Bitter pain wound her heart into a solid knot. Elsey Hallen bit her tongue and tried to breathe.

The pungent aroma of cabbage and pork choked the air from the room. For every note the cellist flubbed, she gritted her teeth. Her shchi remained untouched.

Surveying the room, Elsey noted every detail. Eight people around the table, herself included. Two exits—one on the far right and one on the left. Golden damask wallpaper. Cream crown molding. A gold chandelier trimmed in gleaming crystal. A string quartet in the—

"Elsey." The man across from her mother placed his elbows on the table. He rested his hard, flat chin on top of his folded hands.

Her striking blue-green eyes sliced to him.

Gray peppered Micha Adamson's slicked-back chestnut hair. His tailored navy suit hugged his wide shoulders, complementing his speckled robin's egg eyes. A crooked nose offset the features of his otherwise magazine-worthy face. He wore an arrogant sneer that seemed to fit with his prominent cheekbones and strong square jaw. Towering over the other attendees, his strapping build demanded recognition. His skin shone under the lights like raw pine treated with a layer of varnish.

"You always seem to be growing." Micha's stare lingered on the sweetheart neckline of her black velvet dress. "What are you now? Seventeen?"

"Yes." Her voice—like a crackling flame—carried an extra bite. "The same age as your son and daughter."

A pinch nipped her left side. Elsey jerked from her mother's grasp. Digging her black nails into her dress, she ignored the look she received from her father, Gregor, at the head of the table.

Micha's thin lips twisted up. "My last girlfriend was eighteen."

If Elsey had a weaker stomach, she would've vomited. "I'm not taking applications at this time, and I'd still pass on yours even if I were of legal age."

"What legal age? There are no laws dictating what I can and can't do." He burst into laughter, slamming his hand on the table. The dishes rattled. All eyes fixed on them. His gaze narrowed. "Don't worry. You've always been too willful for my liking."

The bitter pain knotted even tighter into her heart.

"Besides," he continued with a voice colder than frost, "what would a man want with a girl who looks like a jigsaw puzzle?"

Her face grew almost as scarlet as her long, voluminous curls. Every stare felt sharper. Elsey felt too aware of her appearance. The jagged line cutting from her forehead into her right brow. The deep hole creating a concave against her high cheekbone under her right eye before cutting into a sickle down her face. The pitted dip in her chin that forked at the end. The hollow stitch of skin at the left corner of her heart-shaped lips. The strained skin twisting around her left eye and slicing toward her jaw. The thick line carved along the valley of her left cheek. And underneath her long-sleeved dress and flesh-toned stockings, more scars—rough lines and gouges— defiled her entire body. Turning her creamy muted rose skin into a map of puckered and gnarled terrain.

Rage unfurled its wings in her chest. Burying all her pain in a shallow grave.

She gripped the table.

"Elsey," Gregor called in a warning.

She whirled on her parents.

Gregor's bold green eyes never left her. Like a feline waiting for the perfect opportunity to pounce on his prey. His close-shaved dark brown hair and tailored black suit contrasted his alabaster skin. Even with his meager height and size, he remained the imposing force in the room. Lips curled so it was difficult to tell whether he was smiling or holding back a secret.

Marnie, Elsey's mother, focused her cold blue-green eyes on Micha. Pearls adorned her fire-red hair and slender neck. Accenting her lavender chiffon gown. Her cool porcelain skin reflected the light. She didn't smile.

Elsey waited for Marnie's long silver nails to prick her side again. Nothing happened. Gregor shifted his attention to Micha.

Letting herself breathe, she continued her survey of the other people around the table.

No one sat across from Elsey or in the chair to her right. Reminding her of the discomfort her presence caused. A gentleman with thick black hair sat at the end of the table. His pallid, blemish-free complexion looked crisp against his smoke gray suit. His dark eyes locked on Elsey. A smile crept onto his small oval-shaped lips. Elsey averted her gaze to the couple sitting on either side of the man. A blonde woman with an artificial tan and a soft round face sat across from her husband. His stout frame hunched over the table. The light beamed off his pale ivory scalp as he shot looks at his wife's curves laced up in a blush silk gown. He spoke to the elderly woman on her right between spoonfuls of soup. The elderly woman looked out of place in her plain yellow dress. Her gray hair was pinned in a high bun, displaying her fair wrinkled face.

Elsey never bothered to learn anyone's names. She planned never to need them.

Buzzzzz. Buzzzzz. Elsey dug her phone from the leather jacket draping her chair. She held it to her chest so her mother wouldn't see Henry Adamson's name lighting up the screen.

"I told you not to bring your phone." Gregor glared.

Rolling her eyes, she grabbed her jacket. "I should take this."

The phone stopped vibrating by the time Elsey reached the alcove separating the VIP dining room from the main dining area of Staryy Dom—now closed due to the private party. A single buzz notified her of a voicemail.

"Hey, El. It's me, Henry." His caramel-smooth voice sounded thick and languid. "Can you come over? Or meet me somewhere? Please, I need to see you."

The whisper of an ache that might've once been familiar passed through her. She pulled on her jacket and typed a response. **Under the stars.**

Stepping into the shadow-heavy dining area, she spotted two

people huddled in a high-backed booth near the door. Elsey tried to crane her neck to glimpse their faces under the dull streetlight illuminating the front of the restaurant. She cursed herself for being short—even in combat boots.

"I'm telling you, Malini," a familiar deep resounding voice said.

Elsey froze down to her bones. *Fuck. Not her.*

The deep voice continued, "Henry's the one who found him and called me. They were friends."

Her breath escaped with a **woosh**. *Wesley Reed. They're talking about Henry. And Kade.* She glanced at her phone. Fuzz coated her thoughts. Memories attempted to surface.

"They were friends until me." Malini Nayak's shrill voice clawed Elsey's memories to pieces. "I can't make sense of it."

Wesley shook his head. "Hooking up with Henry won't give you answers."

A strange wave of pain pulsed inside Elsey's chest. Waking the constant bitter pain now twisting its claws into her tangled mess of a heart. She bit her tongue.

Wesley stood. His deep umber skin caught in the streetlight—shining like a burnished bronze statue. His black pants and white button-up defined his broad shoulders and toned muscles.

Malini curled in on herself. Her long black hair shielded her face. She sniffled.

"Look." Wesley sighed, rubbing his head. His low-cut fade brushed against his palm. "I'll get Jemma to—"

"I'm trying to figure out what happened to Kade!" Malini's head snapped up. Her hair fell back, exposing the black mascara and eyeliner smudging her warm olive-tan skin. She wiped her face and smeared the remnants on her smooth cheeks and the side of her aquiline nose.

"I'm at work!" Wesley held up his hands. "I don't have the luxury of time to spend chasing down leads. Taliyah is only eight. I have to take care of her."

"So, you're letting his killer get away?" She balled her hands. Tears slipped from her deep-set nebulous eyes. Traces of dark berry lipstick lingered on her plump lips.

"You don't understand!" He brought his hands to his rounded

face. "You have never had to work for anything in your life. I loved Kade, too. He took care of us when our parents died. But he's gone now, and it's all on me." He ticked a list of items off on his fingers. "My sister. My girlfriend. My job. Bills. Graduating. My life isn't just mine."

Elsey tensed. *I need to leave.*

Malini stared at the table. Chewing on her bottom lip like a wad of old gum. Tears dripped off her chin.

"Let me get Jemma out here." Wesley's shoulder slumped. "Or I can call Charlotte—"

"Hey, Wes—What the hell?" Another voice called from the kitchen.

Tightening her hands into fists, Elsey turned to find Jemma Soriano glaring at her. Jemma's blunt black bob accentuated her wide forehead and pointed chin. The light brought out the sunset hues in her ruddy brown skin. She wore black pants and a white button-up like Wesley. Her small bow-shaped lips bent with alarm, resonating in her hooded mahogany eyes.

Malini wiped a hand over her eyes, climbing from the booth. Her black hair appeared to shift between violet and deep blue under the light.

Glancing between the girls, Wesley snatched his apron off the table and looped it over his head.

Caution edged Jemma's mellow voice with a high-pitched falsetto. "Why are you eavesdropping on their conversation?"

"Please." Elsey rolled her eyes. "I'd have to give a fuck in the first place." Keeping her head high, she marched to the door.

Malini stepped in front of her. Black ink still smudged her face. A short violet dress cinched her tall, slender frame.

Remembering that Malini had been with Henry, a strange wave of pain flourished like nightshade crawling along Elsey's walls. She met Malini's wavering stare with her own like a sharpened blade.

Tension seized Wesley's shoulders. Keeping his smoky quartz eyes on them, he fiddled with his apron straps.

"What are you doing here?" Malini's voice shivered.

Elsey crossed her arms in front of her. "My father decided to celebrate something stupid, and I was dragged along as a trophy."

Wesley looked between Malini and Elsey. "Do your parents know you're leaving?"

Elsey's gaze cut to him. "Why do you care?"

A shiver slithered up his spine, suffocating the groan in his throat. Recalling the rumors that followed her, his eyes skimmed over her scars.

Malini narrowed her eyes. Her voice hardened. "What? Were you not allowed to murder any of the guests?"

Elsey shifted her gaze to her motorcycle tucked beneath the awning in front of the restaurant. The storm seething in her settled to an eerie calm. "Fuck off."

Shoving past Malini, Elsey stomped outside.

Smoke charred the air. Burning her eyes and nose. The valet waved from his barred plexiglass booth. She mounted her stripped-down, all-black street bike. The powerful V-twin engine roared to life.

Peeling onto Boyer Road, she searched the skyline to pick up the area of the fire. A siren blared. Signaling that someone could afford to pay the high price to save their life from flames.

HAL Tower stood tall against the smoldering backdrop. Like a gleaming onyx sentry watching over the humble peasants of Hallenwood. The tallest, most pristine building in the city hadn't been touched by the realities of the world.

A world most powered individuals saw fit to abandon and let waste away. A world born from chaos and pain. A world without any central government or any semblance of insurance.

The city might've succumbed to the rot and ruin eating at its heart if not for the tower. If not for her father.

Elsey looked away from the steel and glass effigy to her parentage.

A man dressed in rags leaned against a wall beside a long decrepit florist shop. His head hung against his chest. Her headlight caught the dark red slash on his shirt and the puddle around him. *Fuck.* She bit her tongue to cover the bitter twist of pain knotting deeper in her heart.

Litter drifted across the street on the autumn breeze blowing off the swell of the bay. Stray animals searched the night for any crumbs to stave off the ache of starvation. People huddled on corners. Beside burning cans. Inside boxes draped with newspaper. Screams crawled along the walls of darkened graffiti-stained alleys. Unmistakable pops and bangs covered dying gasps.

The growl of Elsey's motorcycle chewed up every sound before it could reach her ears.

Still, the bitter pain knotted tighter inside her. And still, she scanned every alley and every corner.

She passed floundering specialty stores—for hardware, crafts, sporting goods, and books—that struggled to keep their doors open and lights on. Thrift stores and consignment shops in questionable shopping strips or carved from abandoned houses. Mechanic shops and junkyards with vehicles stripped for spare parts now rusting away to decaying hunks of steel and plastic. The elementary and middle schools offering free education to all the children in the city due to the substantial funding from Gregor Hallen and all the wealthy people he collected around his table. Hallen Market—a massive two-story department store that served as the city's only grocery store and main supplier of household appliances and other necessities. The constant lights and zombie-like state of the employees stood as a reminder of the eternal desperation urging the city to keep going until all hope burned out.

Passing HAL Tower, she crossed the intersection of Boyer Road and Hallen Street. Shadows cloaked the marble columns and carved details of Hallenwood Museum. Soft white light backlit a statue atop the pediment of the gabled roof. A robed woman fashioned from gold. A spear clasped in her left hand. An owl with large round eyes in her upturned palm. Two of the city's banks stood at the same intersection as another reminder of the family that lay claim to most of the city. New Hallen Bank, the newest bank in the city, was owned and operated exclusively by HAL Corp. Freedom Financial was owned in a partnership between HAL Corp and the Boyer family conglomerate.

Boarded up businesses and abandoned houses decorated chunks of Boyer Road with the occasional turn leading to small housing communities, apartment complexes, or trailer parks. Storage facilities and factories sat back from the road with guards standing watch from protective booths.

Bedlam's neon blue and pink sign cast a disorienting glow over the street. Elsey veered into the alley between the dingy red brick club and Diamond Finance, a bank owned by the Hallen and Adamson families.

She stashed her motorcycle behind empty beer crates piled next to a dumpster. Her boots **clomped** over a metal grate beside a large dark stain coloring the pavement. Faint pulsing music fell behind her as she climbed the fire escape. An orange tabby with a mangled ear lounged in front of the only window. She continued until she reached the roof. Other than the weather-worn couch kept to the side and the door leading inside, the rooftop was bare. Using only the city view and the dim stars above for decoration.

A tall figure loomed over the front of the building. Staring down at the people cluttering the sidewalk. His black wool overcoat fluttered in the wind. His shiny black oxfords were crossed behind him. Concentrated smoke curled in front of him.

Elsey scrunched her nose. "The least you could do is put that thing out while I'm here."

"My apologies." Henry Adamson smirked, dropping his cigarette into the line of people below.

He tucked his hands in his pockets to steel himself against the buzzing warmth flushing his body. Feeling past his flask, cigarette case, and lighter. The faint rattle of pills in a plastic bottle carried across the rooftop. Alcohol and cigarettes clung to his amber musk cologne. His fingers brushed across a crumpled envelope and his cellphone in his other pocket.

Facing her, his heartbeat picked up while he stored her into his memory for later. Her red curls that fought the tie holding them back. The black velvet that draped her curves and stopped a couple of inches above her knees. The black combat boots she always wore. The clusters of bracelets always covering her wrists. Her soft features masked by countless scars.

His lips twitched. "You bail on a hot date for me?"

Stalking over to the couch, Elsey rolled her eyes. "I was at one of my father's stupid dinner parties. Your dad was there."

"Your father needs to keep better company." Henry leaned against the ledge.

The light breeze tousled his dirty blond hair. He cut a long, lean figure in black slacks and an emerald silk button-down. Above the streetlights and the hazy neon glow, his honeyed pine skin caught in the sliver of moonlight. Highlighting his strong square jaw and high cheekbones that often earned him bald stares of desire and worship.

"I'm surprised you came." His sapphire eyes twinkled like a clear starlit sky when they met hers. "We haven't been up here at the same time since—"

"I'm not sure why I did." She cut him off before she had to remember.

A net of unspoken questions hung over them. Tethering them in place.

Her eyes—a thousand shades of green spiked into rich cobalt—dug into him. His mouth dried like a desert. He pressed his fingers into the ridges along the bottle cap and listened to the rattle of salvation in his ears. He itched to feel it on his tongue and to see the colorful stars burst behind his eyes.

Taking a deep breath, he caught her toasted vanilla and honey scent blended with the smoke on the autumn wind like a campfire. He forced himself not to look away. "A few weeks ago, I was hanging out with Alex and his groupies downstairs. Alex and I had an argument that night. He was in my seating area with Victoria, Rachelle, and Brant. I was coming back after getting a refill, and I overheard him say something. I told him to fuck off, but they kept trying to talk to me."

She didn't interrupt, allowing him to continue with his natural flow until he reached his point.

"I got pissed and decided to leave. I was walking to the stairs when I saw this girl. She could barely even stand. A guy handed her another Red."

Reds, Red Deaths, Deaths, O's, or Orgasms—all slang for the little red pills created by Micha Adamson. With the ability to induce the mental and bodily sensations of a climax without any messy cleanup, the pills were given the name Petite Mort or Little Death. The rapid onset of terrible withdrawal symptoms endowed the name with another meaning and added to their highly addictive quality. The pills took off after their release to the public four years prior.

Their popularity showed no sign of stopping.

"I intervened and took her outside," Henry continued. "My dad came with his doctor. The doctor kept pumping her with the drug they use as an antidote. Her arm looked like a damn pincushion. He couldn't save her. I held her hand while my dad called his people. I felt this hot tingle enter my body. She died after that, and I've had little accidents ever since."

Elsey arched a brow. "Accidents?"

"The ground rumbling and cracking or the air getting heavier or thinner really fast. Some other things. Especially when I'm upset."

"That's impossible. You would've already had to have enough of a genetic base for the powers to be compatible."

"I'm sorry. I only understand simplified gibberish."

She stood, rolling her eyes again. "You would've already had to have powers because it would've been strong in your bloodline from a recent relative."

He pulled his hand from his pocket and lifted his index finger. "What about that other group you told me about before. The anomalies. Their parents don't always have powers."

"What you're describing is someone who is gifted powers, which can only occur if you are, in some way, compatible." She motioned with a hand to emphasize her words. "I've known you and Ana since we were nine. If either of you had powers, they would've shown."

"My mom was already sick when we moved here, maybe she didn't have the strength to use hers."

"Yours still would've shown."

"I swear I'm telling the truth."

She fell silent, pushing an escaped curl behind her ear.

"Thanks. I see you think so highly of me now." Henry spun around, resuming his stare into the crowd below.

Joining him, she put her back to the ledge. "You've changed a lot since we stopped being friends."

He glanced at her. The moon illuminated her hair and her eyes despite the smoke heavy on the atmosphere. Standing so close, he could see the faint freckles sprinkled over her face and over her scar-patterned skin. His heart shivered like a cord being plucked. "You ever think how remarkable it is that those two things coincided?"

Elsey shrugged.

Stealing another glance over her, one of her many bracelets caught his eye. A silver filigree star dangling between black and clear beads. The cord plucked again. A deep reverberating note sung in his chest. He grasped the pill bottle in his pocket. A faint rattle murmured beneath his fingers. "I have a proposition."

She squinted at him. "I'm going to go ahead and say, 'No.'"

"You don't even know what it is."

"I don't see how you'll change my mind."

He sighed. "I need to know how to control my abilities. It only makes sense for someone with abilities to teach me. Since you were born with yours—"

"Shouldn't your offer involve something to benefit both of us?" She lifted a brow.

A smirk curled the corner of his lips. "Isn't hanging with me benefit enough?"

She crossed her arms.

His shoulders deflated. He plucked at his heavy bottom lip, feeling the small scar usually left unnoticed. He looked at Elsey with a depth that was foreign to her. "You have my undying devotion."

The same whispering ache, like a tingling wave of heat, fluttered in her stomach. She stepped back. Waiting for him to smirk again.

"It's all I have left." He didn't smirk.

Buzzzzz. Elsey glanced at her phone. *Luci.* She looked back at Henry. "You're an addict. You're not even sober now. All you experienced could be some weird dreams or hallucinations from your dad's pills."

He groaned, pushing his hair back from his face.

"I have to go." Elsey started to turn.

"What if I can show you?"

"Then show me."

"I can't right now." His shoulders dropped. "There's too much in my system. I'm numb." He met her eyes, and his breath strangled in his throat. *Almost numb.*

She spun away.

"I'll show you tomorrow. I promise." He rushed headlong without thinking. "I'll stay as sober as I can all day. Just for you."

Elsey continued walking toward the fire escape.

"Hey, El." He stuffed his hands into his pockets. "We're not as bad as everyone thinks, are we?"

She hesitated. Her heart seemed to shudder against the breeze. "There are some sins we can't cleanse ourselves of so easily."

Memories and smoke burned her eyes. A distant high-pitched wail tore through her thoughts. "I need to go."

"Goodnight."

"'Night."

Henry watched her descend the fire escape. He pulled out his phone and scrolled to his old messages with Kade Reed. The individual messages he received that terrible night. A string of five messages. Just numbers.

2

3

0

7

8

Deep, sharp pain twisted in his stomach like a blade. He plucked a translucent green bottle from his pocket, preparing to silence the ache and any emotions that had been able to slip past his mask of perfection.

The roar of Elsey's motorcycle drew his eyes away from the numbers and the bottle containing a reprieve and source of his shame. His lips curled into a frown. Memories tugged at him. His promise to stay as sober as possible still fresh on his tongue.

His chest ached. Strained tension corded his throat. Guilt and shame laced his bones and seeped into his blood. Flooding him with a wave of painful emotions he hid with artificial happiness. All the thoughts he tried to keep at bay chipped away his fragile façade.

Watching Elsey drive away—back toward the direction she came from—Henry forced a deep breath into his lungs. *I'll try again tomorrow.* He opened his bottle and dropped two small red pills into his palm. *I'll do better tomorrow.*

He tossed the pills in his mouth. Retrieving his flask, he gulped the pills down with a swallow of whiskey and returned his attention to his phone. Letting the numbers burn into his mind.

The door slammed open.

Charlotte Marion jumped up. Sweat glistened on her tawny beige skin. Her silken espresso hair stuck to the damp spot on the back of her pink T-shirt. In a frenetic haze, she struggled to catch a solid breath. Gulping down a frenzy of air. Her body trembled. Her heart raced—caught in a tangle of not knowing whether to escape or act.

The light flipped on.

Landon, her dad, rushed to her side with his sienna eyes wide. His old windbreaker **swished** over his black security guard uniform.

"It's okay! Charlotte! It's okay. You're safe." He gripped her shoulders, training his voice to remain calm. "Breathe. Keep breathing. You're safe. You're in your room. Keep breathing."

Taking her hand, he guided it to the small silver bird charm encircling her throat.

Charlotte grasped the cold metal and inhaled a deep breath through her lips.

One … Two … Three … Four.

Holding the breath, she counted again.

One … Two … Three … Four.

She released the breath in a **woosh** of air while counting to eight. Repeating the steps, she continued to listen to her dad's voice.

"Look around your room. Find something to focus on."

She gave a nod and followed his suggestion. Searching for an anchor.

Running trophies and medals glinted from her shelves. A canvas tote—holding overused binders for the new school year—hung off the doorknob to her closet. Framed pictures lined her dresser. They were hazy from a distance, but she could recall them by memory: she and her dad in their old house in Brookhaven, Wesley hugging her before they'd begun dating, and her and her best friends—Malini and Jemma—sitting around a table in the library. A hint of fuchsia and teal from Anastasia Adamson's bright luxurious mane escaped the frame. Her cellphone and clock sat on top of her side table with a bible and daily devotional in a basket below. Wesley's favorite forest green hoodie draped the foot of her bed.

Charlotte motioned to the hoodie, and her dad passed it to her. She pulled the hoodie on over her shirt and breathed deeply. Wesley's fresh, crisp scent was weak on the fabric but enough to hold onto. She breathed again and rested her head against her thighs until her body calmed.

"I'm sorry for bursting in." Landon sat on the bed. "You were screaming."

"I was?" Sitting up, her soft, airy voice drooped with exhaustion. She swiped the sweat off her tapered forehead and rested her fingers under the peak of her cheekbone. Her clock read 9:55 P.M.

"Are you okay?"

"Yeah, it was another nightmare." She shot a betrayed glare at the dreamcatcher above her bed with her hazel eyes—a blend of jade and dried tobacco.

"Do you want to talk about it?" He watched her. "It used to help after your mom disappeared."

Charlotte sighed. *She didn't disappear. She left.*

Deciding she didn't have the energy to correct him, she fingered the tiny silver bird charm around her neck.

Images from her nightmare—from her reality—flooded her memory. The sharp, metallic odor of blood filled her nose. Blinking, she saw a gutted body. Her breath caught. Trapped in the cage of her chest. "How do you deal with it?"

His forehead creased with lines—hidden by thick black walnut hair. His warm taupe skin hid the age in his face. Darkened circles plagued his eyes. "With nightmares?"

Scraping at the skin beside her thumb, she shook her head. "The world. Everything happening."

"I don't think about it. If I do ..." His wide jaw tensed, and he glanced at the framed picture of him and Charlotte. He met her eyes. "You need me."

"Wes—" Dull pain throbbed in Charlotte's heart. "We both saw Kade's body. I can't stop thinking about it. I don't know how he's doing it. I feel so weak and helpless."

"It's not weak for it to affect you." Landon took her hand. "He just doesn't have the privilege of grieving."

A rigid lump rooted in her throat. Her voice wavered. "I'm *so* tired of living like this. I'm tired of being scared. I want to fix things."

"I know, Honey." He rubbed his calloused thumb over her knuckles. "Things are bad, but for some people, things might not seem all that different."

"The world is on fire." Charlotte gestured wide. "Someone should be *doing* something."

Frowning, he kissed her forehead. "I know."

Ping. Charlotte grabbed her phone from the nightstand. "I have to pick up Wes and Taliyah."

"I have to go back to work anyway. Hallen has me on a special assignment. I only came to get something to eat." He hugged her, kissing her forehead again. "I love you. Text me when you get back home, so I know you're safe."

"Of course." She squeezed him tight. "Love you."

The deafening *crack* of rapid gunfire covered the sound of her engine.

Elsey passed Trivia Reserve—the only bank in town not owned by HAL Corp or one of the other rich families in town. The constant flame from two torches on either side of the large black double doors flickered in the wind but didn't rise or extinguish. Carved into the marble frieze near the top of the building was a serpent eating its tail surrounding a maze of three connected whirls with two keys forming an X in the center.

She turned beside a street sign that lost its name some time ago to a coat of black spray paint that backed dripping red horns. A white van turned onto another street ahead. Passengers hung out the windows. Guns in hand. Ready for their next target.

Scattered protesters emerged from their shelter. Signs high and voices loud. Declaring the street home to a dungeon of sin. The mark—a large gray warehouse with **PURGATORY** painted on the side in bold black letters.

Elsey spared a glance for the teenagers corralling young children. Her gaze locked with a girl about her age with caramel-colored hair and dark green eyes.

Turning away, Elsey pulled into a small private lot behind the warehouse. She parked between a black full-size SUV and another motorcycle with a floral pattern painted on the fuel tank. A fading musty odor lingered around the vicinity. An emaciated dog barked at the open dumpster. Small hisses rose from the garbage heap. Jagged scratches ran down the back of the building and cut deep into the solid steel door.

She crossed the parking lot and let herself inside. Stepping into a black L-shaped hallway, bass-heavy music swallowed her. Elsey's heart pounded in time with the drums. Her skin prickled as if she were being stroked by the same deft hands that made the guitar sing.

"You're late." Luci's hollow monotone voice called from the black platform above. She sipped from a glass of undiluted absinthe. Crimson painted her perfect bow-shaped lips. A pronounced widow's peak and pointed chin emphasized her heart-shaped face. Black and silver ombre waves flowed down her back. Her terra-cotta skin shone under the low lights like fresh glazed clay. Loose black jeans and a black hooded jacket camouflaged her slim hourglass figure. Thick black liner rimmed her moss green eyes.

Elsey shrugged. "I got held up."

A door halfway down the hall flung open. Gene Doran strolled out of the small bathroom. His light golden-brown skin and thick stripe of rumberry hair cast in a bloody hue from the low red lights at his back. A thick black collar circled his neck. His full jaw and small forehead made him look younger than his nineteen years. A black sweater embroidered with flowers and baggy cargo pants stained with grease and oil masked his frame.

"Whoa!" His amber eyes widened. "What's with the wave of confusion, Little Fury?"

Elsey's brows pinched together. "I'm not confused."

His nose twitched. "And why do you smell like cigarettes?"

"*That's* why I didn't catch her scent!" A throaty voice sounded muffled behind the wall at the end of the hall. The wall slid open.

Tristan Doran's mountainous figure emerged from a dim stairwell. Light filtered past his broad shoulders and solid torso in a soft halo. He swept his long, thick dreadlocks aside, showing his high sweeping cheekbones and rounded jaw without obstruction.

Intricate swirling tattoos of obsidian ink scrawled over almost every inch of his deep rosy, brown skin. His patchwork jeans and bleach-patterned tee fit perfectly to his powerful legs and arms.

Flashing a smile with sharp canines, he strode into the hall with a book of crossword puzzles in hand. "Gene got us new ones earlier."

Tristan tossed the book her way and disappeared.

Elsey caught it with ease.

Appearing on the platform, Tristan wrapped his thick arms around Luci's waist. His fingers laced together over her stomach, showing the tattoos on his knuckles. GENE on his right hand. LOVE on his left. Luci leaned back and caught his uneven lips in a quick kiss.

Elsey motioned to the door leading outside. "There's a dog barking at your dumpster."

"Dammit, Tristan! You can't feed every stray." Gene took the steps by threes. Elsey followed at his heels.

Tristan arched a manicured brow. "Why not? We feed you." He stole the fight from Gene with a loud kiss smacked across his lips. Releasing Luci, he walked toward the red-carpeted stairs at the front of the platform. "Come on, we can't leave the others to run the bar."

"Fine." Gene pecked Luci on the lips before following Tristan down the stairs and through a gate where goths and punks cluttered the floor. "But don't think that lets you off the hook."

A laugh escaped Luci. She stood straighter, towering over Elsey despite being barefoot.

Elsey followed her across the platform into a room steeped in blood and gloom. Black wood paneling framed the crimson carpet stretched to every corner. An L-shaped sofa of the same bloody shade sat beyond the entrance. Luci's open laptop waited on a large coffee table that looked like an upside-down black oak tree with thick gnarled branches for legs.

Luci inhaled, watching Elsey grab a stack of black clothes from the sofa. "Cigarettes?"

"It's nothing."

"You've stayed away from him for what? Three years? Longer?"

"Mostly." Elsey clutched the clothes in her grip. "He wanted to talk about Kade."

Luci bristled. "Did you—"

"No," Elsey snapped.

Sitting across from her laptop, a silver tendril fell in Luci's face. "I just worry."

"Don't." Elsey spun around. Her boots thumped across the platform.

Luci drank from her glass, dulling the everlasting burn beneath her skin.

four

Smoke flavored the heavy breeze rolling off the bay.

Pulling up the hood of Wesley's sweater, Charlotte descended the rickety steps outside the trailer. She eyed the street. Clutching her travel mug, she ran to her navy mid-size SUV and locked the door behind her. She took a quick sip of her coffee, not giving herself a chance to savor the blend of caramel and coconut before setting the mug in her cup holder.

Squinting against the dark, she backed onto the street and followed the winding road out of the trailer park.

Burger wrappers and ember-colored leaves skittered across the road. She passed the abandoned police station and city hall. A dog missing chunks of fur chased an engorged rat into an alley.

She took a right onto Boyer Road. People stumbled off the sidewalk outside Bedlam. Delirious in the haze of liquor and drugs. Rapid gunfire from a distant street fractured the night. She glanced at the statue atop the museum for a reminder that the little owl in the golden woman's palm watched over her.

The city bus ahead of her turned onto Hallen Street—the main street connecting the high school across the bridge to the south up through the city and all the way to the grand estates of the wealthy to the north. HAL Tower threw a blanket of light over the night. Hiding the glow of the moon and stars.

Charlotte crossed the intersection, sticking to Boyer Road. Running east to west, it linked small residential districts, factories, and scattered social spots to businesses and essential institutions like the hospital and morgue.

The green awning of Staryy Dom pitched into a modest parking lot. Red brick bathed in the flickering glow of a streetlight threatening to give way to darkness. She circled the building. Yellow light beamed from the windows in the apartment above the restaurant. Butterflies took flight in her stomach. She gnawed on the inside of her cheek.

Wesley Reed stepped into the alley. Charlotte's gaze consumed his well-muscled physique. Honed by years of basic fight training. His eight-year-old sister, Taliyah, held his hand. Her backpack slung over his shoulder. Their matching dimpled grins at a shared joke enhanced their plump cheeks. The headlights shone off the pink beads in Taliyah's braids and the silver fuzzy coat covering her pink dress.

Charlotte watched Wesley lift his sister in the backseat. Her stomach flipped.

Wesley waited for Taliyah to buckle herself. "You situated, Kiddo?"

"Yes. Now, give me my stuff." Taliyah grabbed her bag and sat back. "Thank you for the ride, Miss Charlotte."

"She's so much nicer to you than she is to me." Wesley chuckled.

Charlotte's stomach did another flip. She smiled at Taliyah. "You're welcome. Are you ready to go back to school tomorrow?"

"No." Taliyah shook her head. The beads in her hair clicked against one another. She pulled a coloring book from her bag. "I'm just ready for Kade to come back."

Wesley climbed into the front seat. A chill breeze followed him, settling over the inside of the vehicle. The salty sharpness of sweat and boiled cabbage shaded his fresh, crisp scent.

Charlotte faced him. The ghost of his brother haunted his eyes. His full lips wavered between a frown and a smile.

Seeing her filled Wesley with a delicious ache preparing to silence the pain scraping at his heart. His throat tightened. He pulled her to him, pressing a soft kiss to her lips.

"Ew." Taliyah's sharp voice slaughtered the butterflies rising in Charlotte's chest. "Can we go home? I have school in the morning, you know."

Wesley chuckled, shoulders rumbling. He looked at his little sister. "I thought you didn't want to go to school."

Taliyah narrowed her eyes—the same brilliant fragments of copper as Kade. "It's better than watching you kiss."

He laughed again. Filling Charlotte with a warmth that tickled her insides.

Pulling onto Boyer Road, she squinted again.

Wesley's hand found hers. He studied her like he was preparing for a stimulating test. His forest green hoodie hung off her shoulder. Her jogging pants hugged her long legs—toned from years of training with her dad and running track at school. Her hair flowed to her midback, enticing him like a lure ready to snare his hands. Her warm, soft skin waiting to be caressed by more than just the necklace resting against the tender spots of her neck. Delicious warmth spread through him. Wesley shifted his thoughts before they could detour down a route they'd been avoiding.

Shivering against the chill clinging to the interior, he adjusted the vent pointed at him. Wesley turned back to Charlotte. He noticed her tightened gaze trained on the windshield. "Do you need me to drive?"

"No. I can see fine." Charlotte twisted her hand on the steering wheel. "Can we talk?"

He snagged her mug with his free hand and sipped her coffee. Contorting his face in disgust, he returned the mug to its spot. "About?"

"About the world." She looked at him.

"Oh no." He released her hand. "We've had this conversation at least five times."

Charlotte tossed her hand up. "If you would talk to Elsey—"

"Char, there's a reason she doesn't have any friends." His well-deep voice lowered. He thought over the incident at the restaurant. "Even your best friends are scared of her."

"But you knew her. You grew up together."

"I knew her in kindergarten. She's changed a lot since then."

"She can't be that bad." Charlotte glanced at him. "She wasn't around for—"

"She disappeared, Char. Twice."

"Both sets of her grandparents died."

"They were *murdered.*" Wesley narrowed his eyes.

"You don't believe those rumors, do you?" She twisted her hands on the steering wheel.

"I don't know." He took a deep breath. "I don't hate her, but she's not the same person I knew in kindergarten. We didn't even talk when she returned in 3rd grade. And I don't trust someone who lives in a glass castle and—"

"You don't have a problem with Malini." Charlotte peered through the thick smoke painted like cotton candy from Bedlam's lights.

"I *do* have a problem with her. I don't like rich people. But she's your friend and Kade's girlfriend." Watching someone stagger off the sidewalk in front of Bedlam, Wesley reached behind his seat to make sure Taliyah's door was locked. "I barely tolerated Henry whenever he hung out with Kade or stayed at our house."

"I miss Henry." Taliyah looked up from her coloring book. "What do you think he's doing?"

"Probably something stupid."

She jabbed him with a crayon. "Kade says not to be mean about him."

"It's not mean if it's true." Wesley chuckled until he saw the pointed look from Charlotte. He tossed up his hands. "It's not like you ever stood up for Elsey."

"No one has." Charlotte sighed. "Except Kade."

"What? Kade hated—" Wesley glanced at Taliyah. "—*hates* Elsey."

Charlotte pressed her lips together. The need to scrape at her thumb ate at her belly. She picked up her mug and swallowed a long drink.

Taliyah leaned forward. "Why does everyone hate Elsey?"

A streetlight flickered. Charlotte glanced up before turning. A shadow flitted across the roof of an apartment building.

"Because she's a—" Wesley halted his words when he received another glare from Charlotte. "She's just not a nice person."

"I don't have a problem with her." Returning her mug to the cupholder, Charlotte shot another glare at Wesley. "Your brother's just hardheaded. He could do a lot of good, if—"

"If I convinced her to join me on a crusade to save the world?"

He swiveled toward her. "She'd laugh in my face."

She smacked her hand against the steering wheel. "Well, someone needs to do something!"

"I get it. But she's not like us. I'm not even talking about powers." Wesley shook his head. "She's rich. Stupid rich. In a world on the edge of destruction. You cannot seriously believe she gives two shits about anyone other than herself."

"Hey!" Taliyah jabbed Wesley's shoulder again. "Kade says not to swear around me."

Wesley grimaced at the stab to his heart. He forced himself to keep a light tone. "He's not here to get onto me right now, is he?"

A crayon whipped past his face and smacked into the dashboard. "What the—"

Taliyah jutted her hand in the air. "I'm going to need that back."

Grabbing the crayon, he passed it to her. "Next time, don't throw it at me."

"I didn't throw it!"

He glanced at her. "Let me guess, it was one of your imaginary gremlin friends?"

"First of all," she said, pointing the crayon in his face. "Grizelda is not imaginary. Second, she's at home right now and probably eating your socks as we speak. They smell bad enough to attract her attention."

Wesley chuckled and faced forward again.

Chewing on the inside of her cheek, Charlotte looked at him. "Maybe if you showed Elsey what you can do—"

"No." His voice rose with a severity that sent waves of ice through them both. He sucked in a calming breath. "I told you, I don't want people knowing about my power. I showed you because I trust you. The information Kade has—It's safer to keep it to myself."

"Everyone knows the Hallens have powers." Charlotte tossed the words out with a flick of her hand.

"The Hallens aren't like me. They're not like *any* of us. They own practically everything in this city." He began ticking items off on his fingers. "Three out of four banks, three of the local TV channels, part of the schools, part of the hospital and fire department, all but six of the local radio stations, the museum, the department store.

Probably even more than we realize. Hell, they'd probably own *us* if they could."

Another crayon smacked Wesley in the side of the face. He tossed up his hands. "Hell is not a swear word!"

Taliyah snickered.

"Wes, you're being a bit dramatic." Charlotte's eyes cut to him and then returned to the road. "Without the banks, we'd have a hard time functioning. They keep the barest minimum of an economy functioning. And they pay the largest sum so the schools can remain open to the public. They instituted public programs for education on TV and the radio. They keep the news running. Where would we be without the Daily Death List? It's grim, but without that in place, most people wouldn't know what happened to their loved ones without checking the morgue every time someone didn't come home. And the museum would've closed without them taking it on. Everything they've been doing has been to help us not collapse into complete destitution like some of the places in the world already have."

"That's my point. The Hallens are untouchable. Even shi—*bad* people need them around. You can't rob a bank if there's no bank to rob." His brows arched, but he forced them to relax with his shoulders and tone. "Let's drop it. I don't want to spend our time talking about some rich, snobby family who thinks they're making our lives better while they hoard their billions behind the locked gates of their mansions."

Another streetlight flickered. Wesley and Charlotte looked up. A shadow darted across a rooftop. Leaping from one building to the next.

"What the hell is that?" Wesley echoed Charlotte's thoughts.

Charlotte's heart sprinted. She looked at the road. A scrawny man wearing an oversized jersey and baggy pants walked toward the abandoned police station. Another man in an oversized coat and ripped jeans followed him. Wesley watched the men while they drove closer. Charlotte looked at the roof. The shadow disappeared.

"Lock your door," Wesley commanded.

Her eyes flicked toward the men. A flash caught her headlights. The man in the oversized coat pulled out a knife. Charlotte's heart lurched. Wesley shouted something she didn't hear. She slammed on her breaks. Jumping out before Wesley could grab her.

Scrambling after Charlotte, Wesley shouted for Taliyah to stay put.

A short figure—dressed in head-to-toe black—leapt from the shadows between the police station and a dry cleaner. With the speed of a viper, the figure snatched the knife from the man's hand. A heavy combat boot swept his feet out from under him. His knees smashed against a pothole. **Crack.** The figure's fist slammed into the side of his head. He crumpled to the ground.

The scrawny man ran inside the police station.

The figure whirled toward Charlotte and Wesley. A black mask shielded the upper portion of their face. The flickering streetlight caught their blue-green eyes and the scars on the lower portion of their face.

Wesley recalled seeing the same scars moments earlier. Those same eyes, now, shining like a threat. Red hair, now fixed in a tight braided bun. His heart broke into a full sprint.

Charlotte gasped. "Elsey Hallen?"

"Go home." Elsey tucked the knife into the side of her boot. She checked the unconscious man's pulse and hoisted him over her shoulder like he weighed no more than a feather-stuffed pillow. She fixed the gaping, wide-eyed couple in a fiery glare. "Don't you dare tell anyone about this."

Elsey darted into the pitch darkness of an alley.

Charlotte moved forward.

Wesley grabbed her hand. His voice charged with urgency. "Char, let's go."

She remained cemented in place.

The dark figure reappeared on a rooftop and leapt to another building. Still holding a large unconscious lump across her shoulder.

The couple exchanged a wary look and returned to the SUV.

"That was Elsey?" Studying the rooftops, Taliyah shrugged. "She doesn't seem so bad."

August 24, 3699

Lightning split the heavy black clouds cloaking the night sky. A low rumble followed a few seconds after. Wind ripped through the trees outlining the small trailer park, sending loose leaves on a spiral across yards and the twisting road.

Parking in front of a small three-bedroom trailer, Charlotte and Wesley jumped out of the SUV and ran up the shaky front steps. Hoping to get inside before the sky released an unforgiving amount of rain. Charlotte clutched a bag of takeout from Wicked Noods. Struggling to pull up the hood of Wesley's sweater, Charlotte's hair whipped around her face. Wesley dug his keys from the pocket of his work pants, mumbling curses under his breath.

A flash of lightning tore through the sky, and thunder **boomed** a final warning. Opening the door, they rushed inside. Missing the torrent being unleashed.

The wind slammed the screen door closed behind them, eliciting a wince from Wesley. He shut the front door and glanced toward Taliyah's room at the end of the hall. The door stood open a crack.

"She's already asleep," Kade said, stepping out of his bedroom and into the kitchen. Despite being older, he was shorter and had a slimmer build than Wesley. Three thick black braids coiled to the back of his head. His broad forehead and the devastating sweep of his cheekbones looked like glossy twilit sable under the light. His eyes shone like radiant russet-tone diamonds. A small box was tucked under his arm along with his raincoat. He glanced at the screen of his cellphone before shoving it into the pocket of his cuffed dark wash jeans.

Wesley relaxed his shoulders and pivoted to Charlotte. "I'm going to change really quick."

She nodded and watched him walk down the hall to disappear in his bedroom.

"Hey, Char." Kade's voice dropped low. He focused on her, opening the center of his mind to see the shades of light pink and lemon-yellow filling her heart. Her caring and nervous energy coated his insides in a tingling fuzz.

"Yeah?" Already scraping at the side of her thumb, Charlotte set the bag of food on the coffee table situated in front of the gray dingy and threadbare sofa. Two equally ragged seafoam green armchairs sat on either side. Framed photographs of the three siblings inhabiting the home lined the wall behind the sofa and flowed into the kitchen, beside the small dining table, and up to Kade's bedroom door.

Kade set the box and his raincoat on the dining table and walked closer. He dropped his voice to a whisper. The bubbling of her anxiety filled his chest, quickening his heart rate. "Can you please not tell anyone what we talked about? About Elsey? Not Mal or Jemma. Not even Wes."

She stared at him, scrambling for the right words.

He lifted his hands and gestured quickly while he spoke, unable to quell the sea of their collective emotions churning inside him. "I know I already asked, but it's *really* important right now. I probably shouldn't have even talked to you about it, but I needed to talk to someone."

"It's okay." She grabbed his hands and squeezed, ignoring the sharp knife of guilt in her gut. "You can tell people yourself when you're ready."

"Thank you. I mean it." He offered a soft smile and pulled his hands back before returning to the dining table.

Wesley walked into the living room, now in burgundy sweatpants and a navy long-sleeved tee. Rubbing his head, he looked at Kade. "How was your evening?"

"It was all right. Mal came over for dinner, and we colored with Taliyah. She left a few minutes ago." Retrieving his phone, Kade looked at the screen before shoving it back in his pocket. He looked at his brother, noting the vibrant green and lemon-yellow radiating from Wesley's heart—colors Kade had learned to associate with Wesley's compassion and constant fear. "How was work?"

"Busy as hell." Wesley walked around the breakfast bar and opened the cabinet beside the sink. Grabbing two glasses, he crossed to the fridge to fill them with store-brand soda. "Thankfully, I don't have to deal with the customers."

"Jemma told me she got yelled at by a table because they didn't like the wine *they* chose." Charlotte unpacked the cardboard containers and flipped open the lids, seasoning the small open space with the blended aromas of sesame with chicken and mushroom and shrimp with garlic and peppers. She turned to Kade and motioned toward the food. "We have a lot, if you want to join us."

"If I get between Wes and his food, I'll lose a limb." Kade laughed, pulling his raincoat over his tan sweater. "Besides, I have an errand to run. Can you listen for Taliyah in case she wakes up?"

"What errand?" Wesley spun toward Kade. "It's after ten and pouring outside."

Kade scratched at the part between two of his braids. He focused on buttoning his raincoat, seeing Wesley's spikes of yellow in his mind's eye. Feeling the fear grip his throat and his heart. "I have to run these papers up to the office."

Charlotte pulled her keys from her pocket. "Do you want to borrow my car? My dad's home tonight. If there's an emergency, he can give us a ride anywhere."

"No." Tucking the small box under his arm, Kade passed through the living room to the front door. "It's fine."

"It's not fine." Wesley's stomach twisted. A memory called to him. *Sitting on the bottom bunk in the bedroom he shared with his brother, waiting for their parents to come home.* He shoved the memory aside before it could fully surface, like he always had for five years since their death. "You can't go out alone in the city at night!"

"Keep your voice down." Kade shot him a hard look. "You'll wake up Taliyah. I'm just running up to the office. The buses run all night. I'll catch one there."

Fiddling with the small silver bird around her neck, Charlotte looked between the brothers.

"Can't you wait until the morning?" Wesley rubbed his hand over his head.

"I won't be able to make it up there, and these papers are really important." Kade pulled his hood up. He looked at Wesley with a soft warmth filling his eyes. "Everything will be okay. I promise. Just watch Taliyah for me."

Wesley opened his mouth.

Kade raised his hand. His brother's fear clogged his throat. "Wes, please. Do you trust me?"

Pressing his lips together in a tight line, Wesley nodded. His stomach twisted sharper.

"Okay. Just stay here and watch Taliyah for me. Everything will be okay." Kade opened the front door. Pushing the screen door open, rain showered past the threshold. Stepping onto the first step, he paused and met his younger brother's face with tenderness in his eyes and a soft brilliance in his smile. "I love you, Wes."

Wesley pressed his teeth against his bottom lip. He nodded again. No words. His stomach continued to twist. *Don't go. Don't go. Please. Don't go.* He repeated the same words while he watched the door close.

"Wes," Charlotte called to him. Her forehead creased with deep lines. "Are you okay?"

"Yeah." He grabbed their drinks and joined her in the living room. "What movie do you want to watch tonight? You can pick anything you want from our collection."

She laughed and sat on the couch. "Your *collection* is only nine movies." She held up a hand to silence his rebuttal. "Documentaries don't count."

"I will never understand how you fell asleep during *Cosmos* or *Planet Earth*. They're classics, and they have so much fascinating and good—"

"*Back to the Future* or *Jurassic Park*." She waved her hand to the small entertainment center holding the TV. "Still classics. You can get your science fix to distract yourself, and I don't have to be bored to death."

"I don't really think of time travel as *science*. It isn't possible in that sense. Einstein proposed the idea of wormholes, but..."

Noticing her blank expression, he let his words drift off. "I'll put in *Jurassic Park.*"

"Whatever you feel like." She reached into the bag to grab their eating utensils. "I didn't sign up for extra school during the summer like you."

"Forge Institute's summer program isn't extra school."

"If you had to write papers and received grades, it's school."

He chuckled, turning to put the movie in.

Grabbing the remotes, Wesley sat next to her on the couch. He gave her a quick kiss on the lips and pulled his phone from his pocket to set next to his container. Silence settled over them.

Wesley kept his attention on the TV the best he could, but the twisting of his stomach prompted him to glance at the front door or his phone. His leg bounced in place until he finished his food and leaned back into the sofa. Charlotte closed her half-filled container and nestled against his chest. He ran his fingers through her hair and breathed in her nectar and sweet peach scent, filling him with a calm ease that remained with him until the credits rolled.

Riiiiing. Riiiiing. Wesley's phone lit up on the coffee table. Henry Adamson's name filled the screen. The sharp twist returned to Wesley's stomach.

Charlotte sat up and handed Wesley his phone. "Since when does Henry call you?"

"He doesn't." Wesley stared at the screen. "I've not heard from him since he and Kade stopped being friends."

She scratched at the side of her thumb. An uncomfortable ache crept into her belly.

Sucking in a deep breath, Wesley answered the phone. Wariness shaded the edges of his voice. "Henry?"

"Wes—Wes—I—" Henry spoke with quick gasping breaths. He sniffled. The roar of the thunder and the heavy rainfall echoed around him. Water soaked him through to the bone. No. Not only water. Blood. Blood and water. Blood painted his gray wool trousers and mauve linen button-down shirt. Blood covered his hands and face, streaked by the rain and his tears. Blood pooled in the alley, seeping toward the grate. Pouring from the body next to him. Choking down violent sobs, he took another gasping breath.

"I'm sorry. I didn't know. I tried. I tried to—I'm sorry."

"Henry, slow down." Wesley gripped his thigh. His heartbeat raced full speed toward the panic ready to tear him in two. "What happened? What's wrong?"

Henry sniffled again. He wiped at his tears. Streaking more blood over his face. The sharp metallic odor filled his nose, and he gagged. He stared at the face he knew by heart. Sobs ripped through him, and he slumped forward. The words left him in trembling shouts. "Kade's dead!"

Clunk! Wesley's phone hit the floor. He stared at the front door. Replaying—in tandem with Henry's words—the last moment it closed on his life. *No. No. No. Not again. No. No. No.*

"Wes?" Charlotte rested her hand on his arm. "What's wrong? What happened?"

He couldn't move. He couldn't speak. His mind replayed his torment on a loop. *Not again. Not again. No.*

Realizing she wouldn't get an answer, she picked up Wesley's phone and listened.

"I'm sorry! I'm sorry! I didn't know Kade was out here! I didn't know! I tried to stop the bleeding! I tried! I tried! I'm sorry!"

Charlotte's heart crashed into her stomach. She squeezed Wesley's arm. "Henry, are you outside Bedlam?"

Henry nodded. "Yeah. In the alley."

"We'll be right there. Don't leave." She hung up Wesley's phone and used it to call her dad. He answered on the second ring. "Dad, can you come over to Wesley's and watch Taliyah? There's been an emergency."

"Of course." He stood from the sofa and grabbed his windbreaker and an umbrella from the rack by the door. "What's wrong?"

She thought over her words, knowing how he'd react if he knew the truth. "Kade needs our help with something."

"Okay ..." Deep lines wrinkled his forehead. "I'll be right there."

"Thank you." Charlotte hung up. Jumping from the couch she ran down the hall to Wesley's bedroom. She grabbed his sneakers and a pair of mismatched socks from the laundry bin by the door.

She rushed into the living room and handed them to Wesley. "I need you to put these on. My dad's on his way."

Struggling to think past the loop he was stuck in, Wesley moved on autopilot. Putting the socks and shoes on without registering his actions.

Charlotte worked around him, clearing off the coffee table. The front door opened while she finished rinsing their glasses.

Wesley's heart leapt, hoping that the phone call was wrong. That it was all a cruel prank. That his brother would walk through that door and everything would stay how it was. Any piece of hope crumbled when he saw Charlotte's dad step inside.

Broken from his mental loop, Wesley stood and shoved his shaking hands in his front pockets.

Rushing from the kitchen, Charlotte pulled Wesley to the door. She glanced over her shoulder to her dad. "I love you. I'll tell you everything when we get back."

"I love you, too."

Wesley took the lead outside, running through the rain to the driver's side of Charlotte's SUV. She climbed in the passenger's seat. He tore out of the parking pad and sped through the trailer park—racing toward Bedlam. Neither spoke. No words could patch the gaping hole that had been gouged into his heart.

He parked outside Bedlam. The pink and blue lights tinted the rain cascading down the windshield. Wesley shoved his door open and ran toward the alley.

Charlotte started to follow him but stopped when she felt the rain soaking into the hoodie she still wore—Wesley's favorite hoodie. Recognizing blood would absorb and stain, she pulled the hoodie off and tossed it into the backseat and darted into the alley. The cold rain beat down, drenching her jeans and her butter-yellow T-shirt. Sticking her hair to her face and back.

Wesley didn't feel the rain. Not the wind. Or the cold. With one look at his brother's body. At his face. At his wide eyes gazing up into the sky. He didn't feel anything except earth-shattering pain ripping him into a million pieces. The fragments of composure he clung to erupted, bringing him to a collapse like a dying star.

He fell on top of Kade's body, holding him while gut-wrenching sobs tore free from him. Blood he'd never be able to wash away seeped into his clothes. His subconscious worked at reorganizing his new reality to find some way to accept the changes he'd have to make.

Shivering against the wind, Charlotte sat beside Henry.

Red stained his eyes. Blood streaked his face and hands despite the rain. His clothes would never be clean either. He pulled the flask from his pocket with shaky hands and held it to his lips for a second before dropping it to his lap, remembering that it was already empty. He dug in his pockets again and retrieved a bottle of small red pills. Tossing two on his tongue, he swallowed them dry.

"Charlotte," Henry spoke with a low, trembling voice. "Can you do me a favor and tell Malini? I don't want her to find out on the Daily Death List."

She nodded, but her attention remained fixed on Wesley's pain and her own tears as her heart shattered for him.

II

September 2, 3699

Traffic halted on the bridge. Remnants of smoke clung to the wind. The stench of Gregor's expensive warm spice cologne filled the black luxury limousine, agitating Elsey's waning headache. He looked even paler surrounded by the black interior of the car. His bold green eyes glanced at her. He put his hand in front of his curling lips and continued to speak into his phone in a quick, hushed tone.

With a sharp eye roll, Elsey looked out the tinted window to her right. The old prison sat on an island in the bay where lakes and masses of land had long been overtaken by the ocean due to climate change. She trained her gaze on the small, barred windows. The faint glow of lamplight shone in some of the rooms.

The constant bitter pain tightened in her heart.

Elsey adjusted her deconstructed vintage band tee, making sure the black mesh-covered cutout landed where her scars weren't too noticeable on the high slope of her chest. She rested her hands against the seat. Her heart began to race. Washed-out sapphire exploded before her mind's eye. Revealing a vision of two men walking through the rows of cars. Both carried handguns.

The vision disappeared.

She looked at her father and opened her mouth.

Gregor raised his hand.

Her pulse quickened again. Elsey's nails bit into the leather seat. Another burst of washed-out sapphire thrust her into another vision. The men opened a car door. They yanked a purse from a woman's hands. She resisted. The butt of a gun bashed her face. Blood sprayed from her nose and mouth.

Elsey ripped her consciousness away from the vision. She shifted forward.

Gregor held up his hand again.

The left window shattered. Glass sprayed over Elsey and Gregor. A gloved hand grabbed a fistful of Elsey's hair. Dragging her from the car. Scraping her back and legs along the shards of glass protruding from the frame. Glass tore through her flesh-toned stockings under her patched-work plaid skirt. She didn't scream. A bulky blond man with a crooked smile slammed her against the side of the car. He pointed a gun between her eyes.

A brunette man rounded the car. Two perpendicular scars brandished his right cheek. Another gun in hand. Leveled at Gregor through the busted window. "Get out of the car!"

Elsey assessed the situation with a glance. Two men—heads and weight above her. Two striker-fired semi-automatic pistols. She rolled her eyes. *Easy.*

The ground began rumbling. *What the fuck?*

The men staggered. "What the hell?"

Elsey spotted familiar sapphire eyes peering at the scene from the cracked window of a cherry roadster two lanes over. *He was telling the truth.*

The bridge continued to quake on top of steel support. Screams from other cars pierced the atmosphere. The scarred man lurched backward. Elsey choked as the air thickened. Slipping from around her to a concentrated density in front of her. The bulky blond coughed. His eyes bulged. He fell to his knees. Dropping his gun to claw at his throat.

She leapt forward. Her heavy combat boots landed on top of the choking man's head. Pushing forward, she kicked the armed man in the chest. Her boot connected with his ribs. **Crack!** He flew backward into the rusted bumper of a minivan. Elsey caught the gun when she landed. The ground stopped shaking. The atmosphere righted itself. Elsey released the magazine and zipped it in her jacket pocket.

Sputtering groans came from her side. The blond pulled himself to his feet. Forgetting his gun, he charged. Ducking low, he aimed to catch her in the stomach. Elsey jumped up. Kicking herself off the cherry roadster. She somersaulted over the brute's body. Grabbing his shirt, she tossed him like a softball. He flopped onto his back.

Eyes wide as a heavy boot slammed into his face, knocking him unconscious.

"Bitch!" A shout came from behind her.

Elsey glanced over her shoulder. The scarred man produced a four-inch switchblade from his jeans. He ran toward her.

She waited.

Closer.

Closer.

Closer.

Close enough she could smell his sweat.

He thrust the blade out. She grabbed his wrist with a speed and strength her size belied. Kicking his feet out from under him, she spun behind him. She pinned his arm against his back. Capturing his head, she bashed his face into the pavement. His body went limp. Elsey checked his pulse before tucking his knife into her pocket. She dragged both men by their shirts to the side of the bridge overlooking the prison.

Traipsing around her father's limo, her eyes locked with the sapphire eyes. Pushing aside her swirling questions, she collected the discarded firearms. She climbed into her father's car. Slipping her cellphone from her waiting charcoal rucksack, she sent a quick text to Luci. **Clean up on the bridge.**

She settled against the seat.

Gregor looked between Elsey and the window. "Fix it."

Her scowl deepened. Resting her hand against the door, Elsey reached into the recesses of her mind. Tugging at the vibrant blue tendril of power connecting her heart to her brain. The power flowed through her. She directed it toward the door. The shattered window pieced together until it looked untouched. A low hum rose from the depths of her mind. The pain in her heart held fast.

"Hurry up," Wesley called from the kitchen. He shoved a granola bar and a bag of chips into his sister's backpack. "Charlotte's waiting."

"Hold your cows!" Taliyah's voice carried down the hall from the small bathroom wedged between their bedrooms.

Wiping his hands on his faded jeans, his brow creased. "That's not the phrase."

"Kade isn't nearly as impatient as you." She strolled into the small living room. Grabbing her fuzzy jacket from the sofa, she pulled it on over her turquoise dress.

Sharp pain wound Wesley's stomach into a corkscrew. He glanced at the cluster of Kade's photographs hanging on the wall leading from the small dining nook into the living room. His eyes lingered on the picture closest to the shut door leading into Kade's bedroom—what used to be their parents' bedroom—off the kitchen. A portrait showing Kade with his lean, toned arms around his younger siblings. Wesley's thoughts drifted to the memory of the last time he saw his older brother alive, remembering all the things he never said.

"Wes!" Taliyah waved a hand in front of his face.

"Sorry." Wesley blinked before tears could brim. He noticed Taliyah kneeling on a stool in front of the counter. "Get down before you hurt yourself."

Waving him off, she grabbed her backpack and hopped off the stool. "Let's go, Grumpy."

"I'm not grumpy." He shoved a granola bar into the front pocket of his forest green hoodie. Wesley grabbed his backpack from the counter and hoisted it on his shoulders before picking up Taliyah.

Opening the front door, they trudged onto the porch of the small trailer. Someone screamed in the distance. Taliyah tightened her grasp on Wesley's shoulders.

"It's okay. I've got you." He held her tight, scanning the street. Nothing.

He carried Taliyah to Charlotte's SUV idling on the cracked parking pad. Once he made sure Taliyah was secure, he climbed in the front seat.

"Good morning." Charlotte set her travel mug in the cupholder. Warmth flushed her cheeks while he imbibed her. Her hair draped her shoulders, framing the low scoop of her cream long-sleeved top.

He slipped his hand into her hair, pulling her to him. His lips met hers. Her hands pressed against his chest.

"Can you not do that in front of me?" Taliyah ripped through the moment of intimacy. "I don't want to puke up my breakfast before I get to school."

Wesley looked at Taliyah. "Are you saying you want to puke it up *at* school?"

She shrugged. "Whatever gets me out of gym class."

Pulling onto the road, Charlotte brushed her hair behind her ear. "I always loved gym class."

"I know." Taliyah narrowed her eyes. "I heard enough about you checking out Wes in his stupid shorts."

Charlotte jerked toward Wesley. "You told her?"

"No." His shoulders trembled with his full, robust laugh. "I told Kade. She must've overheard."

Her cheeks burned. She kept her attention on the winding road carved through the trailer park. Stopping behind a school bus, she shot him a glare. "You were checking me out, too!"

"Damn straight!" He chuckled again.

"Guys," Taliyah leaned forward. "As much as I like hearing you talk about who has the nicest butt, I would like it more if you wait until I'm not in the car. Please and thank you."

"We'll try our best, Your Highness." Wesley glanced back, spotting a plate wrapped in foil sitting beside Taliyah. "What's that?"

Charlotte sipped her coffee, enjoying the caramel notes. "I have to swing by HAL Tower. My dad had to work through the night, so I thought I'd bring him some breakfast."

Wesley watched the people cluttering the streets. Darting in and out of alleys. A scrawny cat dodged a brawl on a street corner before it could get stepped on.

They drew nearer to the gleaming onyx monument to the Hallen family in the heart of the city. A sour taste filled Wesley's mouth. Ninety-six floors of black windows and metal topped with soft glowing letters, H-A-L, jutted into the sky. The black metal appeared to have an iridescent rainbow shift under the morning sun.

Turning into the expansive parking lot, Charlotte drove to the back of the building. She parked beside her dad's car—a small green sedan with a dent in the front fender.

She retrieved the plate from the backseat and dashed across the asphalt with the grace of a gazelle. Her periwinkle chiffon maxi skirt billowed around her legs. She pressed the buzzer beside the back entrance. A tall young man with dark chocolate hair and striking green eyes opened the door. His security uniform outlined his sinewy frame. His smooth, fair skin and unblemished oblong face gave no clue to his age.

"Morning, Charlotte." Reagan Bullard smiled.

"Hi, Reagan." Charlotte nodded to the plate in her hands. "I brought breakfast for my dad."

Charlotte entered the main security room. The black metal walls looked flat under the dim light. Her eyes went to the four rows of video screens lining the top panel of an expansive control desk in the center of the large room. Some of the screens showed areas in the city. Hallen Market. Hallenwood Bus Depot. Forge and Hallen Fire Department. Forge Institute. G were R Private Investigations and Security. The Square—the streets home to most of the city's restaurants like Staryy Dom and Arnie's Deli. Cleary Hospital. The four banks: Diamond, New Hallen, Trivia, and Freedom. Hallenwood Museum. Boyer Morgue. Pleasure Strip—a collection of most of the brothels and drug hot spots in the city. Hallenwood

Middle School and Hallenwood Elementary School.

A couple of screens showed rolling static. Screens showing outside and inside HAL Tower lined a separate panel below the first.

Her dad's windbreaker hung off one of the chairs. She set the plate of food in front of it.

"These are new." Her eyes remained on the videos of the city.

"They were installed a couple months ago. Part of something Mr. Hallen is calling the Sentry Project." Reagan nodded. "Someone already hacked into them. The cameras pointed at the dock have gone completely dark. The others keep blacking out, too."

Charlotte's mind sparked with realization. *It's her.*

The door opened, and Landon shuffled inside. His hair hung limp in his face. His eyes—sunken with heavy bags—lit up when he saw Charlotte. "What are you doing here?"

She pointed at the plate on the control panel. "I brought you breakfast."

"Thank you." He hugged her.

She squeezed him back. "You need to get some sleep, Dad."

"I know." Landon slumped in his chair. "I'll go home in a couple of hours and take a nap before I come back tonight."

Charlotte toyed with her silver bird charm. "You're working again tonight?"

He rested his face in his hands. "Hallen really needs me to work on this issue."

Her eyes shifted to the screens. Frowning, she planted a kiss on top of his head. "I love you. Get some sleep."

Cars filtered into the parking lot outside Hallenwood High School. Parking in front of the school next to his twin sister's sunny subcompact car, Henry spotted Elsey's hair like a flaming beacon. He watched her disappear inside. Her father's limousine pulled out of the first parking spot that was always reserved for her.

Henry swigged his flask. Burning warmth filled him. Scalding the darkness clutching his heart. A faint itch built under his skin. A resounding tap grew louder in his brain. He dropped a red pill on his tongue and swallowed. The tingling warmth spreading through him was dull—he'd grown too used to it over the years. It was enough to halt the pains of withdrawal for the moment he needed to function.

Climbing out, he pulled his black wool coat over his dark lavender cashmere sweater and gray pants. The breeze coming through the trees mussed his combed-back hair.

"What happened?" Anastasia nodded to the boot print marking the hood of his car. She finished tying her fuchsia and teal hair in spiraling pigtails. She had the same honeyed pine skin and structured square face as Henry, but her eyes were their dad's robin's egg blue. A baby pink quilted leather jacket and lemon sundress flattered her short, full-figured frame.

Thinking over what he witnessed, his eyes glimmered. "Something exciting."

"Oh no. I know that look." She grabbed her backpack. "What's their name?"

"What's whose name?" Jemma walked around her mother's black sedan parked on the other side of Anastasia. Her denim shirt dress highlighted her tall, slim build.

Standing on her tiptoes, Ana pecked Jemma on the lips and pointed with a charcoal-smudged hand. "Someone new left their mark on Henry."

"That won't end tragically at all." Jemma slipped her hand into Ana's, tugging her toward the school.

Henry retrieved his cigarette case—engraved with a jester's mask—and placed the first cigarette between his lips. His long, slender fingers lingered on the image. Fishing out his lighter, etched with a large scrolling $\mathcal{H}$, he lit his cigarette and breathed in. He followed his sister and her girlfriend up the two-tiered stairs. Passing a dark stain at the halfway point.

Catching the door before it could crash into his face, Henry crushed his cigarette against the frame. His sapphire eyes blazed with mischief when they settled on Elsey's scowl. She perched against the wall opposite the entrance. Her rucksack slung over her shoulder. Fresh cuts in her thighs and calves showed under her ripped stockings.

People shot bald stares her way. Some murmured behind their hands. Others didn't bother to hide. Slinging words her way.

"Ugly."

"Freak."

"Crazy."

"Stitches."—A nickname that took off her second day of freshman year after she'd arrived with a stitched-up gash from her forehead to her right brow, adding to her collection of scars.

She plunged her serrated glare into the leering classmates. They scattered. Her eyes landed on Henry.

His chest tightened.

"We need to talk." She pivoted and stalked up the steps.

"What's going on?" Anastasia glanced up at Henry.

"I'll tell you later." Henry followed Elsey's path to the breezeway above the cafeteria.

Her fingers skimmed over the railing, and her eyes darted to the cameras on the ceiling. A miniscule white light indicated they were operational. With a tug on the essence in the back of her mind, she sent a stream of power through the building to the cameras. The light went dark. She halted and spun on him, clenching her fists against the rising hum in her head.

Breathing her delicious scent, his lips curled into a sly smirk. He trained his eyes on hers. Resisting the temptation to dip his gaze to the dim glimpse of her ample bust revealed by the mesh-covered cutout in her shirt. "What*ever* could we need to talk about?"

"Cut the bullshit." She rolled her eyes, noting the hint of alcohol haunting the fringes of his scent. She glanced at the students rushing past them.

"You mean I *was* telling the truth last night?" He chuckled.

Elsey watched people drift around them. Staring at them. At her. Whispering. Talking. Her stomach churned with a familiar pang.

He tried to catch her eyes, but she kept eyeing the people around them. He stuffed his hands into his pockets. A pill bottle rattled. "El, I—"

"Henry, I hoped to run into you," a soft heady voice called.

Tensing, Henry pleaded with his eyes for Elsey not to leave.

The fresh, white floral scent of lilies of the valley blossomed in the air around them. A delicate beige hand with red-pointed nails slid over Henry's shoulder and down his arm. Victoria Boyer stepped around him. Thick golden hair cascaded over her shoulders in deep waves, framing her perfectly symmetrical oval face. The small sky-blue flowers on her white mini dress matched the shade of her eyes, and her brown knee-high heeled boots knocked her a few inches above average height. Red painted her full lips.

He kept his eyes on Elsey. Shaking Victoria's hand off, he didn't bother to hide the irritation in his voice. "Victoria, whatever you're here to offer, the answer is still, 'Not if we were the only two people left on earth.'"

Before she could retort, Alexander Cleary wedged himself in the narrow space between them and slung his arm around Victoria's shoulders. Alex's blond side-swept fringe and baby blue eyes added to his boyish appearance. Meeting Victoria's lips with a kiss, he moved her to his side. He stood a couple of inches shorter than Henry, but his chest and shoulders were broader and tapered to his lean, muscled physique.

Victoria wrapped her arms around his waist. She slid one hand down the front of his striped polo shirt to hook her index finger around the belt loop of his designer jeans.

Wiping the red lipstick from his lips, Alex fixed his sneer on Elsey. "Why are you talking to Stitches?"

Victoria giggled. Not bothering to hide behind her hand.

More laughs rose nearby where part of the golden couple's clique watched the display. Alex's younger brother, Brant, hovered at the edge with his nose in a book. Only his thick brown hair could be seen over the group around him. Rachelle Forge, Victoria's best friend, stood near the front, with her emerald eyes writing love notes on Alex's back. A pale green flowy dress with crocheted diamonds along the center reached her knees and showed off her lean, fit frame. At a glare from Victoria, she averted her gaze and chewed on a chunk of her pale blonde hair between her lips, cutting off her baby-doll face.

Heat flared inside Elsey. Her hands and feet tingled. *No. Not now.* Crossing her arms, she kept her expression flat. "I was asking Henry whether he needed a ride to Hell. I'd offer you one, but I hear your seat on the bus is already reserved."

Henry released a shameless laugh. He withdrew his flask from his pocket, motioning his kudos to Elsey and taking a swig.

Victoria spun on Elsey. Pink flushed her neck and face. "Don't you have villagers to terrorize?"

Elsey arched a sharp brow high. "Why? Is it your day off?" She returned her attention to Henry, letting her eyes burrow into his.

Squeezing Victoria tighter to his side, Alex looked up at Henry. "You're coming to my party tonight, right?"

"I'd rather test my gag reflex on a chainsaw." He lifted his index finger and tossed a side-eye at Alex. He noted his twisted scowl. "Keep in mind, if I offended your small-minded sensibilities, I meant to."

"Come on." Alex narrowed his eyes. "Everyone expects you to be there."

"Sorry, I don't go back to play in trash once I take it out." Henry dropped his flask to his pocket and found his pill bottle. Gripping it tight, he faced Alex. "Now, if you don't mind, I was attempting to talk with someone who *isn't* the human equivalent of a staph infection."

Alex cocked his head to the side. "If you don't go back to play in trash, then what I heard about you hooking up with Malini last night must've been a lie."

Henry's anger spiked with a twist of pain. He glanced at Elsey and opened his mouth.

"Speaking of the cheating poser." Victoria angled to peek between Henry and Alex.

Malini glided toward them in red strappy heels, standing almost as tall as Henry. Her raven black hair was pulled into a high ponytail. An oversized black cable knit cardigan that had belonged to Kade cloaked her leopard print blouse and black cigarette pants. A sharp black wing lined her eyes—still red from crying. She nibbled on her dark berry lips. Ragged nails—normally polished to perfection—tipped her fingers. Jemma trailed after, but Ana pulled her to a halt when she spotted Victoria.

Victoria's grip on Alex tightened. "She's letting herself go, isn't she?"

Another sharp pain twisted in Henry's belly. "Her boyfriend was murdered. That's going to leave a mark."

"Thanks for the reminder." Alex hooked his gaze into Malini, watching her stop beside Henry. "Sorry for your loss Mal, if you ever need a shoulder—"

"Yours aren't available," Victoria snapped. She dragged Alex toward their posse.

Snickering, Alex squeezed Victoria to him and planted a firm kiss on her lips. He wiped her lipstick off again and looked over his shoulder. "Talk later, Henry." He nodded toward Elsey. "Bye, Stitches."

Elsey kept her expression calm, but her nails bit into the sleeves of her jacket.

Aware that the chance for an intimate conversation had been destroyed, Henry locked his eyes with Elsey.

Malini's gaze waffled between them. Her voice trembled with a sharp lilt. "You two are talking again?"

Anger ate at Elsey's resolve. Forcing herself to maintain an unaffected expression, Elsey kept her attention on Henry. "Under the stars."

Watching Elsey stomp off, Henry's heart twisted into a quivering pretzel.

Malini put her back to Elsey's retreating form and looked at Henry. "Did you want to get together again tonight?"

"Can't." He smirked. "I already have plans."

Charlotte parked in one of the back rows, where the students who couldn't afford a premium spot had been resigned. Before she could open her door, Wesley pulled her to him.

He kissed her forehead, her cheeks, her chin, her throat, her collarbone. Her nails dug into his shoulders. Wesley buried his face in her hair. Her heart galloped. He traced kisses up her neck. Sticky sweet syrup coated her insides. She leaned her head back, giving him better access. Her eyes lolled to the side, and she glimpsed out the window.

Malini and Jemma weaved through the vehicles. Faces paler than usual, they muttered to each other. The duo halted in front of Charlotte's SUV, and Jemma waved. Tears tracked down Malini's cheeks.

Pushing against Wesley, she motioned toward her friends. "Something's wrong." She grabbed her canvas tote from the backseat and her mug before climbing out.

Groaning, Wesley opened his door and grabbed his backpack. "Not this again."

"What?" Charlotte tossed him a look over the hood of her SUV.

Wesley shut his door and rounded the vehicle. "Malini stopped by work last night to talk about her crazy conspiracy theories."

"They're not crazy." Jemma narrowed her eyes.

Charlotte focused on Wesley. "Why didn't you tell me?"

"I forgot." He glanced at Malini and Jemma. Turning to Charlotte, he lowered his voice. "After what happened last night."

"We don't care if you talk about having sex," Malini said.

Pink flushed Charlotte's cheeks. She tightened her grip on her mug. "We haven't—We're not—"

Wesley held up his hand. "Even if we were, this is the first moment we've had alone since Kade died."

Malini pointed at herself. "I'm trying to figure out what happened to him!"

"This world happened to him!" Wesley tossed up his hands.

"Someone killed him," Malini said between gritted teeth.

"You think sleeping with Henry will get him to confess?" Wesley struggled to steady his voice.

"You slept with Henry?" Charlotte's eyes widened.

"He's the one who found Kade." Jemma flexed her hand.

"Jemma, he's Ana's twin brother. How do you think she'd feel if—"

"He was talking to Elsey a few moments ago." Malini sniffled.

"What does that have to do with anything?" Wesley rested against the SUV.

Jemma leaned forward. "She's dangerous!"

"And she hates me," Malini said.

Wesley's gears turned, searching for any logical connection. "They used to be friends."

Charlotte glanced at Wesley. Facing Malini again, she spoke with a gentle ease. "We get that you want to find out who's responsible for Kade's death, but you're going about this wrong. This won't bring him back."

"Mal," Wesley said, training his voice to take on a calmer tone. "If I thought there was even the smallest chance of finding who killed him, nothing in this world would stop me until I had every answer. But we know the facts. It was an alley at midnight. His phone is gone. He was only found because it was Bedlam, and it's busy. If Henry hadn't been the one to find him, we would've found out from the Daily Death List."

"You mean *you* would have. Some of us still found out that way." Malini's voice frayed. She wiped her tears with the sleeve of Kade's sweater. Bits of mascara and eyeliner smudged her cheeks.

"Come on. You need to get cleaned up before class." Jemma put an arm around Malini's shoulders and led her away.

Wesley's jaw slackened.

Squeezing her eyes closed, Charlotte clutched her travel mug tight. "Henry asked me to tell her that night. I was so focused on helping you, I completely forgot."

"Shit." He sighed and rubbed the back of his neck. "I didn't know."

Charlotte faced Wesley. "Maybe we should tell them about Elsey?"

"Yeah, telling them that Elsey is running around at night beating people up will help the situation." He shook his head. "We don't even know what she was doing."

"You don't actually think she had something to do with it, do you?"

"I don't know." He gestured outward with his hands. "Where did she take that guy? What is she doing with him? What was she doing at all?"

Her brow creased with thin lines. "She stopped that guy from getting stabbed and maybe robbed."

"A big fish often thinks it's the top predator only to get eaten by a shark. It's predation." Wesley rubbed the back of his neck. "Or in this case, it's probably an example of the competitive exclusion principle in humans since I don't think she's eating them. It's a law that states—"

"Save the textbook talk." Charlotte pressed her hand to his chest. "I'm already dreading this return to school."

"I'm just saying, you know the rumors. You heard her threat last night."

She scratched the skin beside her thumb. "Have you spoken to Henry?"

"A couple of times since the funeral. He calls sometimes to see if we need anything."

"Has he always been like that with you guys? Offering to do things?"

"Yeah, it makes it hard to hate him."

"You hate him?"

"Not really. Henry's just rich and very, *very* privileged." Wesley leaned against the front of her vehicle. "He's exempt from any of the rules we have to deal with at school or anything else we have to deal with in life, and he leans into it by being extremely lazy. He gets handed everything he wants and gets away with everything. If he wants to go to college, all he'd have to do is tell his dad. But I've had to keep my grades up since middle school. If I mess up in one class, I risk losing the chance at a scholarship to Forge Institute. I'd be stuck working at Staryy Dom forever."

Sipping her coffee, her brow creased with thick lines. "Didn't he get his dad to pay for the funeral so Kade wouldn't be put in one of the communal graves?"

Wesley nodded, regret from his words already seeped into him. His mind flushed with all the memories of Henry showing up late at night covered in bruises and asking for a place to stay for a few days.

"Like I said, he does things that make it hard to hate him." Sighing, he shook his head to send the memories back to their untouched corner. "He's genuinely a good person, just a lazy idiot. And they were best friends up until they weren't."

He pressed his lips together and dropped his gaze to the ground. "They did argue a lot though about Henry's addiction and impulsivity … and Elsey. She was the big button. I don't know why. Maybe because Kade hates her."

Charlotte shifted on her feet, scraping harder at the side of her thumb. She noticed his use of the present tense when speaking about Kade away from Taliyah, but she didn't comment.

"I'd hear them argue about it. To be honest, their friendship started breaking down before Malini broke up with Henry." He saw her scraping at her thumb and took her hand. "I could tell things were getting weird. Henry came over for dinner a couple of times, and normally they'd talk and joke. Or Henry would get in weird moods and tell stories that he definitely shouldn't share in front of Taliyah." Wesley felt another flicker of regret for his comment about Henry's ability to ask his dad for anything. He shook it off.

"In the last few weeks, Henry and Kade were both really quiet. Once after dinner, I could hear them arguing in Kade's room. I couldn't make out much from my room, but her name was mentioned a few times. Then one day, they didn't even argue. Henry stopped by and wasn't even in Kade's room for more than five minutes before he left. He never returned except to take Kade to work or school. That stopped altogether when Mal started taking him."

Charlotte glanced toward the school. "Mal just wants to do something."

"I get that." Wesley sighed, pulling her into his arms. "But in this world, it would be impossible to find his killer. There are too many variables, and if I slip up, I could lose Taliyah, too."

"You don't give yourself enough credit." She buried her face in his chest.

The school bell rang. Taking the lead toward school, Wesley smothered her impending groan with a kiss.

The warning bell rang through the halls. Students rushed to reach their classrooms before the doors closed.

Elsey stashed her schoolwork in her rucksack and stole into the nearest bathroom. Waiting. Listening. Her fingers twisted around the straps of her bag. She caught her reflection in a mirror for the briefest second before jerking to face the door. Words replayed in her head while she waited for the last footfall to cease. *Ugly. Crazy. Freak. Stitches.* They played on a loop, becoming a haunting melody.

Silence settled beyond the door. Pulling her phone from her jacket pocket, she scrolled through her five contacts: Father, Gene, Henry, Luci, and Mother. She typed a quick, routine message to Luci. School rescue?

Leaving the bathroom, she walked up the short corridor to the front door.

The sky looked like it'd been painted white and gray by fresh smoke rising in the city. Descending the first row of stairs, she ignored the dark stain at the bottom before beginning down the second flight.

"Too good to spend the school day with us peasants?" A sharp voice asked behind her.

Elsey froze. Shoving down the dark chill that swept through her, she turned.

Malini glared down at her with bloodshot eyes. The early morning sun highlighted the tan hues of her smooth olive skin.

Elsey leaned against the railing. "I see you returned to your favorite hobby of not fucking off."

Malini took the last few steps. She towered over Elsey. Her

eyeliner had been wiped away, but a faint dark line smeared her lower lash line. "What was that with Henry?"

"He needed to talk to me." Elsey crossed her arms. "And not that it's any of your business, Henry came to me first."

Malini's glare darkened. Any fear she showed before was gone. "Why weren't you at Kade's funeral?"

"Why would I go?"

"Everyone else went. Even Henry."

"They were friends before you broke up with him for Kade." Elsey dropped her arms to her side. She gripped the railing. Ignoring the biting pain inside her chest, she narrowed her eyes. "Did Henry ever learn about you cheating on him with Kade?"

Malini's eyes widened. "How do you know about that?"

Hearing a vehicle approach, Elsey looked over her shoulder. A black full-size SUV with tinted windows rolled past and stopped. She faced Malini. "Why do you care that I wasn't at Kade's funeral?"

"I think it's suspicious."

Elsey read the implication etched into Malini's features. She looked at the stain at the bottom of the steps. Pure rage unraveled the essence inside her. She wrenched hard. The essence flooded through her. Into the railing. Into the ground. The stairs trembled. The cement cracked open. Chunks of stone jutted up between them. Knocking Malini down. The ground pieced itself together. The hum in the back of Elsey's mind became steadier.

She watched the fear twitch in Malini's murky eyes. "If I wanted revenge, I wouldn't go after a pawn. I'd take out the fucking queen."

Elsey stomped down the second flight of stairs.

"We're not done!" Malini stood and dusted off her clothes. "Do you hear me?"

Rolling her eyes, Elsey raised both her middle fingers in the air without sparing a backward glance. She slid into the passenger's seat of the SUV and shut the door.

"You're not supposed to use that power," Luci said. Her black and silver waves spilled over her ever-present black hooded jacket. Holes decorated her black jeans, but her black and white canvas sneakers were spotless.

"I'm fine." Elsey grabbed the duffle bag from the backseat. She tugged her combat boots off.

Luci pulled away from the school. "I thought you were sticking it out this year."

"I changed my mind." Elsey focused on rolling the ripped stockings off her scarred legs and pulling on a pair of black pants sewn from durable but pliable fabric. She tugged off her skirt.

"What happened this time?" Luci looked between Elsey and the road, turning out of the school parking lot.

"The usual." Elsey shrugged off her jacket and tugged her shirt over her head. She hurried to pull on a black long-sleeved top—sewn of the same fabric as her pants—to cover the deep scars gouging and knotting into her torso.

Luci sighed. "Whoever you beat up on the bridge was already gone."

Elsey pulled her boots on, tucking her pants inside. "I should've known that would happen."

"We can scan the cameras and see what comes up." Turning onto the bridge, the sun beamed through the windshield and cast Luci in a warm golden glaze.

"It will have to be later tonight." Elsey twisted her hair into a long braid. "I have to meet Henry after school."

"What?" Luci jerked toward Elsey.

Elsey kept her face flat. She secured her long braid in a tight bun. "He wants to talk."

"Be careful, please."

"He would never—"

"That's not what I mean."

"I know." Elsey rolled her eyes.

She opened the glove compartment and retrieved a small black earbud from the electronic panel built in the dashboard. Pulling her black mask from the duffle bag, she shoved all the clothes she shed inside. "Were you able to track that van last night?"

Luci left the bridge, passing the museum and HAL Tower. "No. They'll probably be out tonight though. They never miss a night."

Elsey zipped up the bag. She risked a glance at Luci. "It's really hard for me to get to them."

"No, Else. I'm not doing it." An orange light appeared to flicker under the surface of her green eyes.

"I know." Elsey stared at the mask in her lap, thinking about Henry and about what happened to Kade. "But maybe if I had someone to help me—"

"No." Luci squeezed the steering wheel until her knuckles turned white. "You would be putting other people at risk."

Elsey continued to stare at her mask.

"Did you take care of that situation from last night?" Luci asked as she turned off the main road.

"I handled it when it happened." Elsey sighed and looked up, scanning the street. "Charlotte and Wesley won't say anything."

"How can you be sure?" Luci looked for an alley away from prying eyes.

"Because I handled it. Okay?" Elsey averted her gaze before she could lock eyes on her reflection in the window. *Because they're afraid of me.*

Luci slowed the car at the sight of a tall, slim man in a sleeveless shirt brandishing a knife and chasing a woman across the street.

"Looks like this is my stop." Elsey slid her mask over her eyes and pressed the earbud in her ear. It lit up with a faint red light.

Elsey jumped out, running after the man and woman. Elsey caught the man's shirt. Yanking him off his feet, he sailed through the air. He hit the sidewalk. Her fist slammed into his face. He didn't get up.

"That was quick," Luci said through the earbud. She turned into an alley. "I'll leave the SUV here, so you can stash him until you can get to the island."

"Thanks." Elsey already focused on the woman to make sure she was okay.

Clinging to Wesley's hand, Charlotte let him lead the way to her third class. The headache pressing on her eyes increased at the anticipation of having to stare at another textbook with fuzzy letters and numbers. Students filtered into the nearing trigonometry classroom.

"Why don't I sit this one out? I can go to the nurse and get something for my head." Charlotte's gaze slid over the orange T-shirt outlining the muscles in his back. She breathed in a big whiff of his scent from his hoodie covering her like a protective blanket. Her tension eased enough to reduce the urge to scratch at her thumb.

Wesley tugged her forward, wrapping his arm around her waist. "Your head will continue hurting if there's strain on your eyes."

"My dad can't afford to get me glasses right now." She frowned. "He's still paying off our cars."

"Which is why, I said to let me help." He pulled her to a halt outside of the room. "Kade was one of Mr. Adamson's property assistants. I have enough of what he left to help pay for it."

"You and Taliyah need that money. If I took it and then you needed it for food or bills. Or what if Taliyah gets sick and—"

He smothered her words with a kiss.

Tingling warmth spread through her body and curled her toes. He broke the kiss before she could lean into him. Her eyes went to the graphic on his shirt—a faded image of an angry amino acid demanding someone's lunch money.

Wesley cupped her chin and smiled. "Can you at least put your worrying aside for tonight?"

She met his eyes of black smoke gazing at her with such bare heat, she felt it on her skin. The dimples in his full cheeks sent the butterflies in her stomach in a flurry.

"Whoa!" Jemma stopped next to the couple, adjusting her backpack on her shoulder. "If you two need a janitor's closet for some alone time, there's one by the art room on the second floor."

Charlotte's cheeks lit up. She struggled to think of something to say. Her eyes caught the passing group of students from the popular crowd, aware they were within earshot of Jemma's remark.

Henry waded through the group. He waved at Brant and took a slip of paper from Rachelle. Pulling his flask from his pocket, Henry paused beside Wesley. "There's also an empty classroom and a private bathroom by the teacher's lounge on the first floor. Or you can try the concession booth in the gym. And the backroom in the library."

Wesley tossed up his hands. "Is there a place in this building you haven't violated?"

"Give him time." Jemma flicked out her hand. "There's only so many classes he can skip in four years without his dad being notified."

"I'm glad you understand my plight." A smirk curled Henry's lips. "Now, if you'll excuse me, I must attend to my afternoon siesta."

Wesley watched Henry saunter into the classroom. "I'm surprised he knows what plight means."

"I'm not convinced he knows what any word means." Jemma failed to stifle her laugh. Pursing her lips, she stood straighter. "I'm sorry about this morning. I don't trust Elsey, and then with him ..."

Jemma eyed the doorway Henry disappeared through, flexing her fingers at her side. "Don't you think it's odd that they started talking again after Kade died? Henry and Mal broke up over a year ago, and they didn't speak once in that time."

Wesley shook his head. "Henry and Elsey were best friends when his family moved here from Ainsvale. He talked to her when the rest of us were either told not to or were afraid of her. Henry just lost his other best friend. He probably reached out to make things right."

"You're making them into monsters." Charlotte fiddled with the small silver bird hanging around her neck.

Jemma met Charlotte's eyes. "She's dangerous. She attacked Mal outside of school this morning."

"What?" Charlotte glanced up at Wesley. His mouth sat in a firm line.

"Mal tried to question her about why she wasn't at the funeral, and Elsey used her powers to knock Mal down." Jemma flexed her fingers again.

Wesley rubbed the back of his neck. Silencing the growing unease frosting over his stomach. "Did she do anything else?"

"No, but we know she's dangerous. She's killed people."

Charlotte shifted on her feet. "Those are rumors."

"She was found covered in her grandparents' blood. Her dad announced it to the world. Why are you defending her?" Jemma's hooded mahogany eyes narrowed on Charlotte. "You used to be scared of her, too. When you first—"

"I was new here." Charlotte's stomach twisted. Her eyes shifted between Wesley and Jemma. "I'm not saying I'm not scared of her. I just think she can't be as bad as everyone thinks. We don't have the whole story."

"What is all this anyway?" Wesley gestured out with his hands. "First, Malini thinks it's Henry. Now, she's accusing Elsey. Who's next?"

"We're just being cautious." Jemma held up her hands.

Charlotte scratched at the side of her thumb. "How would Ana feel if she knew you suspected Henry of something like this?"

"I'll do whatever I have to do to keep the people I love safe." Jemma walked around the couple and paused before entering the classroom. Eyes crinkling at the corners, she cast them a soft, concerned look. "Just be careful. Both of you. There's no way they're not involved somehow."

Waiting for her friend to pass the threshold, Charlotte leaned against Wesley's chest. "What are you thinking?"

"Not about them." His eyes shifted to her. Sweet warmth sizzled in his chest. Wrapping his arms around her, he kissed the top of her head.

The bell rang. The teacher, Mr. Karimi, peered into the hall. He shifted his thick-framed glasses on his narrow nose and motioned for Charlotte to join the rest of the class.

Frowning, Charlotte prepared herself for the impending headache. "I'll see you after class."

"Wait!" Wesley pulled her back. "You never answered about tonight!"

A small smile danced over her lips. She kissed him and twisted free from his grasp, laughing as she darted into the classroom.

The small two-bedroom trailer seemed more like a shoebox than a home. Mildew tinged the rusty brown paint and the small, weathered porch. Bars secured the windows.

Charlotte grabbed her canvas bag from the backseat and scanned her surroundings before running to the front door. Rushing inside, she slipped off her sandals and locked the door behind her.

"How was school?" Landon looked away from the sandwich he prepared at the counter in their small open kitchen.

"I have homework in psychology and trigonometry even though it was only the first day." She dropped her belongings onto the couch.

An old television sat against the opposite wall. A coffee table collected books about strong female figures throughout history. Framed pictures of Charlotte at various ages hung on the far wall around a painting of a grizzly bear in the forest. A woven rug covered the floor. Pictures that became another backdrop in the few years they'd lived there lined the short hallway leading to the bathroom and bedrooms.

"Well, it's your last year, so you won't have to deal with that much longer." He grabbed two glasses from the cabinet and filled them with water. Handing one glass to Charlotte, he sat at their two-seater table.

"Unless I'm able to get a scholarship." She sipped from her glass.

Landon nodded. "Have you decided on what you'd want to go for?"

She scratched at the raw flesh beside her thumb. "I just know I want to help people. I want to make a difference."

He focused on his food.

Charlotte sat down. Her thoughts spun. Words spilled from her before she realized she started speaking. "I always thought it was pointless before, but that night. Seeing Kade. Seeing how it affected Wes. That he doesn't even have a chance to grieve. I can't stomach it anymore. I need to do something."

Her memory of that night was relentless. Wesley crumbling over his brother's bloody and lifeless body was seared into her heart and mind. The morgue staff eventually arrived and took Kade. They commented on the severity of the attack. At least thirty-four stab wounds to his chest. He had defensive wounds. He fought for his life. Even with the rain, there would always be a stain on the pavement.

"I wish you hadn't seen that," Landon said.

"I think I needed to. It made everything more real." She let the scene play behind her eyes again.

"Honey, I know you want to help Wesley." He held her hand. "But nothing you do can take away his pain. Remember what it was like when your mom disappeared? I tried to say and do anything I could to make it better for you, but I couldn't. All I could do was be there for you. That's all you can do now."

Charlotte stared into her dad's eyes. She wanted to argue. To make him understand. *I can do more. Everyone can do more.*

Riiiiing. Riiiiing.

"One second." Landon pulled his cellphone from his pocket. "It's Hallen."

Charlotte drank from her glass, listening to her dad tell his boss he would return to the office soon.

He hung up the phone. "I have to go. It will probably be another late night. It's been rough trying to solve this problem."

She perked up. "With the cameras?"

"Keep that between us." He carried his dishes to the sink. "Hallen isn't ready for the city to know about the cameras until they're working properly."

"What's he planning? Reagan said something about the Sentry Project." Charlotte scraped at the skin by her thumb. "The cameras won't help on their own."

Landon shrugged. "I don't know. Maybe he's getting ready to do something like you've talked about."

She took a long drink from her glass. *But his daughter is already doing something.*

He wrapped her in a tight hug. "I love you."

"Love you, too." She squeezed him back. "Be careful."

Searing pain clenched Henry's stomach. Nails raked along the inside of his skin. He blinked through the tears threatening to bubble over. A hammer drove rusted spikes into his brain. Monsters hidden in darkness cackled. Rattling his soul. Talons dug into the dirt littering his mind. With enough light, he'd glimpse their faces. He'd remember things he preferred to leave buried.

He stared down at the wrinkled envelope in his hands, trying to keep all his attention on his penmanship of trained perfection etching a single name—*Elsey*. Focusing on the name, he reminded himself of his declaration that he'd stay as sober as possible. For her. *Ignore the pain.*

The ***tinkling*** sound of delicate metal drew his eyes up.

Alex swept the chain curtain aside and entered Henry's VIP seating area. "I'm late to my own party because of you."

Henry sat back on the turquoise velvet sofa and stuffed the envelope into his pocket. "I see you learned to take accountability for your own actions."

"All I said was that I don't feel comfortable when it's just the two of us." Sitting on the matching sofa across from Henry, Alex propped his shiny brown shoes on the mirrored table between them.

"For the millionth time, you unglazed donut, just because I'm pansexual doesn't mean I'm attracted to everyone." Henry shoved Alex's feet off the table. "Even if I did find you physically appealing, which I don't, you have the crusty personality of overbaked sourdough."

"That's not *why* I said that. What you overheard was taken out of context." Alex flung his hands up with listless energy. "You're one of my oldest friends. I wouldn't try to include you in everything if I had a problem with you being pansexual. Hell, I've seen you with girls, guys, and everyone in between. I've walked in on you in my pantry so often, I've started knocking to make sure it's not occupied. Even when it's only me and Brant home, and *he's* not bringing girls in there. I've done a shit ton of other things to help you."

"You've made comments before. About other things, too. Jokes about things with my dad and other stuff I trusted you with."

"I didn't know what I said was a problem. You never cared before."

"I'm not the only one you need to be concerned about hurting. People surround you all the time, and you have no idea if what you're saying could hurt them or not. I'm positive you even do it on purpose sometimes." Henry winced against the pain tightening in his stomach and scratching at his skin. "Besides, I was too blacked-out to give a fuck about much for a long time. I overlooked a lot of things I shouldn't have. I don't want to be that person anymore. I never did, but I'm changing now. I'm finally going after what I really want— what I've *always* wanted. I wouldn't even be fun at one of your parties anymore."

"Speaking of fun," Alex said with a smug grin. "Are you and Malini getting back together?"

"No, but leave her alone. She's grieving." Ignoring the sharp twist in his stomach, Henry narrowed his eyes. "And didn't you refer to her as trash this morning?"

"Why do you care? She cheated on you."

Shooting him a glare, Henry snatched his glass from the table. "It's kind of hard for me to believe you care when it was almost always with you." He took a sip. "I couldn't help but notice you didn't get with Mal after she dumped me."

"I tried." Alex shrugged. "She declined. Said she was happy with your friend ... or whatever he was to you."

The pain in Henry's stomach twisted at the mention of Kade.

He did his best to mimic the harsh stare Elsey had perfected. "Fuck off." He took another drink. "Just leave Mal alone. She's going through enough. I shouldn't have gotten with her either, but grief makes people do stupid things. Just let Victoria take care of your needs instead of seeking it elsewhere."

Alex's lips carved into a deep frown. "Henry, I'm *trying* to be nice."

"You and your girlfriend bully everyone, including my sister and your own brother." Leaning back on his sofa, Henry stared at Alex. "Maybe not all the time, but enough that I don't know who's the real you. You've always been like that ever since I first met you. I'm not sure you even know how to be nice. If you want to try, maybe ask your mom and stepdad to pay for the surgery you need to dislodge your head from your own ass?"

"That's a low blow, Henry, and you know it." Alex shook his head and stood. "After everything I've done for you—"

"Helping someone doesn't erase the pain you've caused. You know that first-hand." Henry tightened his grip around his glass. "Today, you called Elsey that shitty nickname your girlfriend made up. Twice. Do you think that didn't hurt her? The problem is, I really don't believe you care."

Alex opened his mouth but swallowed his words. He pushed through the curtain and disappeared in the crowd. Leaving Henry alone with his pain and crumbling resolve.

Forcing himself to take a deep breath, Henry took a long drink from his glass. The hammering in his brain dulled to a faint tap. His skin itched. The pain in his stomach held fast. The monsters crawled forward. He reached into his pocket. The pill bottle rattled. His thumb pressed into the ridges along the cap. He retrieved two pills. He took another breath. The pain held steady. The monsters inched closer.

Henry tossed the pills into his mouth and drained his glass. Drowning the monsters. Cauterizing raw untreated wounds. The tingling hum began at the center of his chest. Rushing through his body with a euphoric release. Bright colorful stars burst in his mind. Filling him with a buzzing warmth. Sounds dripped with tension at the edges. Thick brushstrokes painted the colors in his private seating area. The velvet sofa felt like thick fur beneath his fingertips. Taking a rigid breath, he waited for his brain and senses to adjust.

He pushed through the chain curtain. The strobing rainbow lights turned people into writhing bodies of shape and color. Heavy dance music flowed like a river inside his chest. He spotted his sister by the bar with Jemma at her side. They hadn't changed their clothes from earlier in the day. They huddled close together. The bar manager, Theo, tossed them a passing nod before disappearing behind a swinging door.

Edging the crowd, Henry stepped behind Ana. His arms outstretched, preparing to grab her from behind.

Ana spun around. A grin plastered on her square face. "You realize I could see you, right?"

"I always forget that's there." His eyes went to the mirrored wall behind the bar. Smirking, he placed his empty glass on the bar. A bartender refilled it.

Jemma cocked her head, scrutinizing Henry's perfectly constructed appearance. "Somehow, I doubt that."

He ignored her remark. "What are you up to?"

Grabbing an orange paper from the bar, Jemma handed it to Henry. "I'm still trying to convince her to enter."

Henry skimmed the flyer.

Fine Arts Competition

Open to young artists ages 14 through 18.

Artists of all styles welcome.

An exhibition showing all entered pieces will be held after the winner is announced.

Winner's piece will be permanently showcased in the Young Artists of Hallenwood exhibit at the Hallenwood Museum.

Deadline to enter: September 23, 3699.
Winner announcement: October 2, 3699.

Ana shook her head. "Kade said he'd enter his photography too since I was nervous, but now it feels wrong."

A hollow fissure widened in Henry's chest. Tucking his hand into his pocket, he found the bottle waiting for him. He itched for one more. "You should do it."

"But—"

Jemma slid her hand into Ana's, entwining their fingers. "Kade only offered so you wouldn't feel alone. He would want you to do it. Do you still have the pictures he planned to submit?"

Ana nodded.

Jemma looked at Henry. "Maybe you could talk to your dad? He's close with Mr. Hallen. Maybe they'd let Kade's pictures enter still? Maybe a tribute?"

"That's her department." Henry gestured to Ana. He took a long drink from his glass. Burying his monsters beneath a liquid grave. "When I talk to that bloated nut croissant it never ends well."

Ana shot Henry a hard glare.

"I'll support you either way." Jemma kissed Ana's temple. "But you've always wanted your art on that wall."

Ana looked at Henry again, waiting for his input. Her jaw went slack. "Elsey?"

Henry's heart slammed into his ribcage. He whirled. Elsey stood a couple feet from him. Her voluminous red curls parted over her shoulders, shielding her ears. A black long-sleeved shirt and matching black pants—made of some strange thick material—enveloped her short, curvy frame.

"What are you doing here?" Jemma's soft gaze turned to stone.

Setting the flyer on the bar, Henry smirked. "She's helping me with my plan for world domination."

"As you can guess, I'll have to do most of the heavy lifting." Elsey gestured to Henry. "He'll be there to look pretty."

"You think I'm pretty?" His lips bent into a full grin.

Ana held up her hands. "If you need help with marketing, I can make posters."

Henry pivoted toward his sister. "Ana, last time you drew me, you made my head five times bigger than my body."

"Forgive me for making it true to size."

Chuckling, he gestured toward Elsey. "We should go."

"It was nice seeing you, Elsey." Ana's eyes filled with the warmth of her smile. She looked between the quiet redhead and her twin brother. "We should all hang out again. Like old times."

Elsey spun around, pushing through the crowd without a word. Heading toward the back stairwell. Eyes followed her. She could hear whispers carve their disgust into her skin.

"Hey, wait up!" Henry caught up to her in no time with his long legs. A glass of whiskey still in hand.

"We were supposed to meet on the roof," she said without looking back.

"Sorry, I got distracted." He followed her down the hall that led to his loft and the rear of the building.

Elsey rolled her eyes. "I'm running behind schedule."

"What schedule?"

Not answering, she continued toward the stairwell at the end of the hallway.

"We can go in my apartment," he called after her.

"No."

"Have you eaten?"

She stopped. *Fuck.* "Fine."

He smirked.

Henry opened the door and allowed her to enter first. Following her inside, his eyes slid to her standing centimeters from him. His mouth dried. His chest tightened. *This was a bad idea.* Deciding it wasn't the best time to give her the envelope, he drained the rest of his glass and strode around her.

Elsey surveyed the room. Committing every inch to memory.

Dingy brick and plaster walls and aged hardwood floors encompassed the studio apartment. A rustic red couch floated in the center with a scarlet knitted blanket draping the back. Neither matched the oversized blue-green rug or the dark green throw pillows. A trigonometry textbook and a notebook sat on a beaten and worn coffee table along with an empty glass and a half-empty pill bottle. The bookshelf to the right overflowed with books, with a mix of various kinds of fiction, true crime, and Greek mythology. The top was being used as a makeshift bar—corralling decanters and half-empty bottles of liquor.

An orange tabby slinked through the single window overlooking the alley and hopped onto the tiny metal table collecting two mismatched chairs. A small kitchenette backed the wall across from the entrance.

The far side of the room collected a full-sized bed—left unmade—and two nightstands covered in scratches and signs of wear. Four empty pill bottles sat on the nightstand nearest to the corner. A tall dresser beside the bed held more scratches and dents. Six more empty pill bottles and an empty rum bottle cluttered the top. Two framed pictures sat in front of the mess. One looked like it might have an unmistakable shade of red. The door to a walk-in closet hung open to the left of the bed. A small bathroom stood on the same wall as the entrance, facing the bed and the dresser.

Elsey scanned everything again. The scratches and dents in his furniture. The tears in the sofa. Even the mangled ear of the cat, who was inspecting her in the same way she inspected the room.

She looked at Henry, walking over to greet the cat with a chin-scratch. Still dressed in his favorite expensive black wool overcoat that'd been a gift. In his designer sweater and trousers and his polished black oxfords. His hair combed back to show off his perfect chiseled jaw and cheekbones that looked hewn from polished Italian Botticino marble.

The boy and the apartment didn't appear to match.

He glanced over his shoulder, scratching the tabby behind the ear. He gestured between Elsey and the cat. "Elsey, meet Meow. Meow, this is Elsey."

Elsey arched a brow. "You named your cat Meow?"

"He's not mine. We're roomies. I asked him what his name was, and he said, 'Meow.' It seemed rude to call him anything else."

She gave a single nod.

Henry wandered to the fridge. It contained a pitcher of lemonade and a bottle of orange juice. *Fuck.* "This is a terrible time to realize I have not gone grocery shopping yet."

Her brows rose. "Henry Adamson goes grocery shopping?"

"It's fun." Turning to the counters, he retrieved a lone apple from a bowl. "I should've made sure I had food before trying to impress you with my homemaker skills." He tossed the apple and watched her hand shoot up to catch it as if by reflex. "What was that on the bridge?"

"My parents taught me self-defense." She took a bite from the apple. Her eyes never wavered from his.

"El." Smirking, he sat on the sofa—angled toward her with his elbow propped on the back and his long legs draped over the front. "There's a boot print on the side of my car."

"Oops." She shrugged. "I can have it cleaned."

"Don't bother. I consider it a badge of honor." He waited, leaning the side of his head against his hand.

Taking a bite of her apple, Elsey joined him on the couch and propped her boots on the edge of the coffee table. "For the past two years, *roughly*, I've been taking care of things in the city."

"Like a doctor or a hitman?"

"Depends."

"That's amazing!" His eyes glittered. "Why?"

"Somebody needed to." She took a final bite of her apple and looked around before settling with it in her hands. "How long have you had your powers?"

"A few weeks." He took the core from her. Their fingertips brushed. A shiver jolted through him. He pulled back and tossed the apple core in the bin beside his fridge. "Probably four or five. I don't know the exact date."

"Why did you wait so long to tell me?" Elsey dropped her gaze to focus on her hand and the wave of heat from his touch.

He watched her. His heart pumped faster in his chest. He followed the lines of her face. The soft features that most people didn't see under the scarred surface. The constellations of freckles waiting to be mapped. "We don't exactly talk anymore. Not except for brief messages every day or whenever we exchange gifts for holidays. And even then, we leave our presents on the rooftop for each other. You don't give me much of an option to talk to you for real."

She met his eyes. "What about my father's party? You asked me to dance. It was three weeks ago."

Henry plucked at his bottom lip. "And you cut the dance short and disappeared."

"You know why." Her eyes burned with deep anger that singed

her soul. "You and Malini—"

"Haven't been together for at least a year, El. You were my best friend before she and I ever dated. Now, we live entirely different lives. I get why it happened. At least to a degree. My mom died. Your grandparents—" Seeing her jaw tense, he thought of a different angle.

"Don't think I didn't want to tell you because I did. I—" He swallowed his words before they could escape. *This is going terribly.*

"Then why tell me now?" The whispering ache that she couldn't place flashed through her body. She tore her eyes away from his face to stare at the cat moving to the windowsill.

Glancing down, he shrugged. "I don't know. I just did."

She risked another peek at him, meeting his eyes. They held the same unfamiliar depth. She rustled through her thoughts. To find something cold to hold onto. To stave off that strange ache that left her unsettled. "You've been able to use your powers on your own. You can control them. Like on the bridge. Why did you ask me to train you?"

"Sometimes, things happen when I'm upset. When I found—" *Kade.* He shook his head. "I've been able to figure it out enough to force it to happen." His fingers returned to plucking his bottom lip. "So, does that mean I'm *something* else ... not human?"

"I don't know what it means. Maybe things aren't as cut and dry as I was taught. There's no doubting who your parents are."

Henry flinched at the reminder that he looked very much like his dad's son.

Deciding to get things over with, Elsey took a short breath. "I need your help with something."

"Anything." He smirked. "You have my undying devotion, remember?"

She rolled her eyes. "There's a van driving around, shooting up streets." She brushed a strand of hair out of her face. "With my offensive power, I have to get close enough to touch them. I've attempted to get close enough to the part of the road they're on, but they have guns. If you could use your power to cause that earthquake thing then it could throw them off balance and give me an in. Plus, you can do whatever that was with the air and that'd help, too."

"Done." He shrugged.

"What?" Her eyes widened. "Don't you want to think it over? It's dangerous."

"Are you trying to sweet-talk me?" He stood. "You need my help. That's all I need to know."

That strange ache passed through Elsey, making it past her mental blockade. She dug her nails into her palms. "Okay. Do you know how to fight or how to at least throw a decent punch?"

"El, I'm pretty sure the closest I've ever been to being in an actual fight was you punching me in the face when we first met." He chuckled.

The muscles by Elsey's mouth twitch upward. A **beep** sounded in her ear. "One second. I have to take this. I'll introduce you to Luci later."

He watched her tap something in her ear.

"Yes?" Elsey asked.

Luci flipped through four screens on her laptop—each showing twenty-five videos of the city. "I spotted the van." She paused to sip from her absinthe. "You need to get out there."

"Okay. We'll be on our way." The words slipped before Elsey could stop them.

"We? Who is 'we?'" Luci's voice turned sharp.

Elsey flinched. "I talked to Henry."

"Elsey!" She slammed her glass onto the coffee table. "What are you thinking? Oh my—!"

"Look, you can yell at me later. He has powers, and he agreed to help."

"He has powers?" Luci's voice rose an octave with each word. "Since when?"

"Later." Elsey pulled a plain black mask from her pocket and handed it to Henry. "Change into all black and put this on. We have to hurry. Just use your powers. Stay behind something so you're not targeted. I'll teach you how to fight later."

"He doesn't know how to fight?" Luci groaned, holding her face in her hands.

"Coordinates, please." She tapped her earbud before she could hear the string of swears she knew Luci would utter.

Henry took the mask and disappeared in his walk-in closet. Elsey twisted her hair into a braided bun. *Buzzzzz.* She retrieved her phone. The map of the city opened with a red dot moving through the streets.

"How do I look?" Henry asked when he appeared from his walk-in closet dressed in black slacks, a black long-sleeved button-up shirt, his black wool coat, and black oxfords. His sapphire eyes shone from beneath the mask covering the top portion of his face.

Elsey looked up at him. "Dashing." *Does he own any sensible clothes?*

nine

Wesley's eyes darted to the clock across from the prep table. 8:50 P.M. His heartbeat quickened with a sugar-sweet ache. Smiling, he returned his attention to his task—filling squares of thin dough with a mixture of ground pork, onion, garlic, salt, pepper, and dill.

Liev Kazlova shoved past the swinging door. Gray sprinkled his burnt raisin hair. Faint wrinkles crept into his khaki skin. A tub of dishes teetered in one hand. A soggy rag clutched in the other. "I really need to hire a new busboy."

Wesley glanced at his boss. "I told you, I could do it."

"And leave Stavros to do the prep for tomorrow?" Liev shuffled to the sink on his short stocky legs. A burly laugh rolled through his barrel chest. "All the pelmeni would fall apart before we even got to cook it."

"Hey, I do all right." A tall hook-nosed man washing dishes tossed up his hands. Soapy water splashed onto the counter.

"You can't even keep water in the sink." Wesley chuckled.

The door swung wide. Taliyah rushed into the room. A sheet of paper in hand. Galina Kazlova followed, wiping her delicate hands on an apron tied around her waist. Her broad shoulders and skin, like antique parchment, were accented by her blue floral dress.

Taliyah thrust the paper into Liev's hands. "I drew you a picture."

"Another one?" Liev looked at the image etched in crayon: people having a picnic in a field of flowers. "It's beautiful."

"We'll hang it with the others." Galina took the picture from her husband. She carried it to the door of the walk-in cooler—already decorated with numerous drawings from Taliyah.

Wesley twisted toward Galina. "Thank you for babysitting her."

"We've told you before that you don't have to thank us." Galina waved her hand. "We love watching her. Just let us know when you're on your way, and we'll make sure she's ready."

Taliyah hopped onto a stool opposite Wesley. "Their food is better than anything you make."

He looked at her with narrowed eyes. "I make the food here, too."

"You're a butt-face." She rolled her eyes, earning laughs from the other occupants in the kitchen.

"Our faces look similar." He shrugged. "I guess that makes you a butt-face, too."

"Nope. It's cute on me." Taliyah pointed at Wesley. "On you, it's a butt-face."

Stavros turned from the sink. "Can that be his new nickname? Jemma will love it."

Taliyah shot him a hard glare. "I'll kick you."

Galina stifled a laugh and took Taliyah's hand. "Come on, let's go upstairs. We'll watch some cartoons."

Laughing and shaking his head, Liev waved Wesley off. "Go wash up. It's about time for your shift to be over. I can finish these up."

Wesley washed and dried his hands.

Buzzzzz. He pulled his phone from his pocket, reading the single word from Charlotte. Here.

Wesley hid his smile until he was in the alley. Unbuttoning his white shirt, he rushed to the waiting SUV. His eyes landed on Charlotte wearing his hoodie over a pair of athletic shorts. His heart battered like footsteps on pavement. Wrapping his arm around her waist, he pulled her into him. His mouth crashed into hers. She slid her hands around the back of his neck. Their tongues tangled together. His free hand wound into her thick hair. He inhaled her sweet fruity scent.

She pulled away and gasped for air. Her fingers touched her lips, still tingling from the heat of his kiss.

He grinned and sat back. "Want to go to Golden Fleece? We can get a couple of gyros and sit in the parking lot."

Nodding, she pulled onto the street. "I'm taking the back way to avoid traffic though."

"Do you want me to drive?"

She tossed him a pointed look.

He raised his hands and let the tension dissipate. "Were you able to finish your homework?"

"All except a couple of problems. I keep getting the wrong answers." She gestured to her tote in the backseat. "I brought it with me."

"You brought homework on a date?" His brows rose.

"You explain things better than the teacher." She turned right, taking a shortcut through the Pleasure Strip to the backend of The Square. Sex workers walked the sidewalk and lounged on the porch of Decadence, the most popular brothel in the city.

"I don't mind." Wesley shrugged. "You usually hate when I—"

The ground trembled, knocking over metal trashcans and sending people running.

Tires **squealed**. A white van careened around the corner.

"What the hell?" Wesley braced his hands on the dashboard.

Charlotte struggled to keep her SUV upright. The ground rolled. A dark figure leapt down from a rooftop. Landing on the sidewalk in a half-crouch. The figure darted into the road. The van **screeched** to a halt. A man armed with a semi-automatic rifle tumbled out.

"Turn!" Wesley gestured toward the closest street. Another masked figure—dressed in head-to-toe black—stepped forward from the shadows. "Who the hell is that?"

Charlotte slammed on the brake. "We have to help them!"

He spun on her. Eyes bulging. "What? No!"

She flung her door open and jumped out.

"No!" He scrambled after her. "They have—"

A loud **pop** silenced his words. His heart hammered in his chest. He ran to grab Charlotte. He froze when he registered that the pop didn't sound like a gun discharge.

Elsey stood over a man on the ground. His arm twisted at an unnatural angle. His gun in her hand. She tucked the clip in her pocket.

Six armed men jumped from the back of the van. Firing at the sex workers screaming and running toward alleys and storefronts.

Another man jumped out from the front seat, pointing a gun at

Elsey. The man dropped his firearm. Clawing at his throat. Gasping for air. Elsey kicked off the front of the van. Her boot smashed into the side of his head. She snatched his gun when he fell to the ground.

Elsey tossed the disarmed gun to the side. She jumped on top of the van. "A little more rumbling please!"

Wesley glanced toward the second figure, catching him sip from a flask. "You've got to be kidding me! Char, we need to—" She ran around the left side of the van. His stomach lurched. "Shit!" He ran after her.

Charlotte charged at the first gunman. Leaping off the ground, she latched onto him. Locking her long legs around his neck and bashing her elbow into his head. He reeled back to grab her. Seizing his hand and giving it a sharp twist. A scream tore from his lips. She yanked the gun from his grasp with her free hand.

The nearest gunman spun around. He leveled the barrel of his gun at Charlotte. A metal trashcan lid wheeled through the air and **cracked** into the man's nose. Stumbling back, he landed on his ass. His gun crashed to the ground beside the trashcan lid. Blood dribbled over his top lip. He scrambled toward his weapon. A black non-skid sneaker came down on the gun. A hand lifted the trashcan lid. The metal alloy—now shifting to the same deep umber of Wesley's skin—appeared to roll over the hand. He glanced up to see the metal coating Wesley's entire body.

The man's heart stalled. His breath caught in his throat. All sound died away except his blood **dripping** onto the pavement. "Oh sh—"

Wesley jerked the man by his sweater. Tossing him into the side of the van. The man thudded to the ground again. He climbed to his feet and raised his fists. The world wouldn't stop spinning.

Stepping forward, Wesley caught sight of a dark figure running along the top of the van before focusing on his target.

Elsey dove off the back of the van toward two gunmen. She clamped onto the one on the left. Bracing her arm against his throat. She swiveled, kicking the second man in the head. He sprawled on the ground. Landing, she pulled the first man overhead. Slamming him into the ground. Neither moved. She turned to survey her next targets. Confusion flashed through her. She stopped.

Luci's hands froze above her keyboard. "What the fuck?"

Charlotte's long legs were wrapped around the neck of the man she faced. He grabbed a handful of her hair. She rolled into a forward flip. Forcing him to release her. She spun, moving with a speed and expertise that only came from someone who'd been trained how to fight at a young age. With footwork so perfect, she almost seemed to be performing a choreographed dance. Left to rely on his clunky movements and brute strength, his face grew redder with each hit she dodged. She swiped his feet out from under him. Slamming the heel of her hand into his chin. **Crack!** His teeth smacked together. His head flew back.

Wesley gripped a metal lid that he'd taken from a trashcan at the curb. His body now appeared to be made of the same shiny metal alloy. Blood dripped from his opponent's nose. Wesley slammed his fist into the man's cheek, making him wobble.

A shriek jolted Elsey's attention from her schoolmates.

One of the gunmen lay on the road. His flesh curled away from his muscles and bones. Blood painted the asphalt.

Elsey jerked toward Henry holding his hand outstretched in the air. "Don't kill him!"

"He was about to shoot you!" A dark warning laced Henry's smooth voice. He kept his eyes trained on the man on the ground.

Elsey charged forward.

"Wait!" Henry dropped his hand. The air corrected itself before she could step inside the affected radius.

Elsey halted at the dying man's side. He trembled, growing pale from the rapid blood loss.

"The serum!" Luci's eyes widened at the scene unfolding on her computer screen.

Elsey reached for her pocket.

The barrel of a gun pointed in her face. She peered at the last gunman. His finger twitched beside the trigger.

"Back up, Bitch." The man growled.

The bleeding man whimpered. The sounds of the other struggles had ceased. Charlotte and Wesley stood on the other side of the street beside their unconscious opponents. Their hearts thundered in their ears.

"I said, 'Back up!'" The barrel of the gun pointed between Elsey's eyes.

"Drop the gun." She stared up at him with brazen defiance. "Or I'll wipe my boots off on your face."

"I thought they exterminated your kind." His finger twitched again. "The troublemakers at least."

Rage-fueled flames licked at her heart.

"Stay calm," Luci said, watching Elsey's body go taut. Ready to strike. "Don't—"

She moved fast. Like a knife to the throat. Swift and lethal. More deadly weapon than teenage girl. Ripping the gun from the man's grasp with a twist before he could pull the trigger. Slamming her boot into his knee. His scream covered the crack. His knee caved in the wrong direction. She pivoted. Kicking him in the side of the head. He flopped onto the ground. Blood spilled from his lips.

Wesley and Charlotte exchanged an uneasy look. Henry took a long drink from his flask.

The torn man shuddered against a sharp breeze. Sobs racked his body.

Discarding the rifle, Elsey pulled a vial from her pocket. A bright green liquid shined under the streetlights. She removed the cap. The man pressed his lips together.

She raised her eyebrows. "If I wanted to kill you, I would've let my partner finish what he started."

The man parted his lips, drinking half of the strange viscous substance.

Wesley, Charlotte, and Henry stepped closer to watch. The man's wounds closed. He stopped bleeding.

"Sorry about this." Elsey tucked the vial into her pocket. She punched him in the side of the head. His eyes closed.

"What the hell?" Wesley tossed up his hands. "Why'd you do that?"

Elsey arched a brow. "Did you want the bastard to get up and start shooting again?"

"You don't know that he would do that!"

Hoisting the man over her shoulder, she carried him toward the van. "I also don't have time to persuade a grown-ass man to come quietly."

Charlotte swept her hands between Elsey and Henry. "Do either of you want to explain what is actually going on here?"

Henry looked at Elsey. He tucked his hands into his coat pockets. A pill bottle rattled.

Elsey groaned and plopped the unconscious man inside the van. "Help me load up the bodies in the van and follow me."

"No! No! Do not bring them here!"* Luci waved her arms in the air. *"What are you thinking? No, Elsey! No!"

"I don't have a choice!" Elsey yanked another unconscious man over her shoulder. "We'll handle it when we get there!"

Charlotte and Wesley watched Elsey talk to herself. With confusion carved into their faces, they looked at Henry. He shrugged and took another swig from his flask.

"Keep your mask on," Elsey said, slamming her door closed. "It would be a bitch for Luci to private all the cameras again."

Henry settled into the passenger's seat, swigging from his flask.

Backing onto the street, she shot a direct look at Henry. "Also, *you* don't kill people. Ever."

His brows knit together. "He had a gun pointed at you."

"I don't care." The words sounded sharper than she intended, but she didn't apologize.

He watched her. The way she kept all her focus ahead. The way her jaw tensed with each word. Thorns pricked his heart. His hand slid into his pocket. Thumb pressing into the ridges along the cap of his pill bottle. *One won't hurt.* Certain she couldn't hear the muffled rattle, he snagged two—

He remembered his earlier conversation with Alex. *I don't want to be that person anymore.*

Dropping the pills, he secured the lid. "Can I smoke?"

"Fine." She didn't look away from the road.

Henry retrieved his cigarette case and lighter. Rolling down his window, he rested a cigarette between his lips. He lit the tip and inhaled. An ease flushed his chest to hush his ache. Facing the window, smoke curled between his lips.

A beep sounded in Elsey's ear. She pressed the earbud.

Luci set her cellphone beside her laptop and kept her eyes on the screens. Watching the vehicles drive through the streets of Hallenwood. "I let Asher know that you may need some help bringing them inside because you're in a hurry. He and some of the others will be waiting for you."

"Thanks." She pressed the earbud again to silence Luci's impending lecture.

Henry exhaled a trail of smoke. He twisted toward Elsey. "Do you still play the cello?"

Her brow arched. "No. Why?"

"I remember you liked it." He shrugged. "And you were good."

She kept her eyes trained on the road. "It was only to teach me discipline."

Studying her, he inhaled on his cigarette. Henry exhaled toward the window again. "What's your favorite color? Is it still black?"

She looked at him. Eyes narrowed. "What are you doing?"

"Just trying to get to know you again."

Biting down on her tongue, she stared at the road. "No. It's not still black."

The froth of waves beating the craggy shore reached through the open window. Elsey turned onto the street bordering the bay.

"What is it?" He flicked ashes out the window and retrieved his flask. "You wear a lot of black. And red. Green. Mustard. Gray. Some white."

"I don't wear it." She glanced at him. Headlights from passing cars beamed off his face. His eyes glittered like stars laced into the night sky. She faced the road. Biting hard on her tongue to silence the strange whispering ache that pulsed from her center. "What's your favorite color?"

He gulped down the smoky burn of whiskey. Looking at her, he spoke with conviction, as if his entire existence came down to one word. "Red."

Elsey kept her eyes trained on the road. Her attention focused on the destination.

Henry puffed on the last of his cigarette. Exhaling he flicked the butt into the street. "Cats or dogs?"

Her shoulders bristled. She squeezed the steering wheel. Color drained from her hands. She didn't answer.

He drained the last drop of liquor from his flask. Letting it warm his body. Eyes never leaving her. Probing for a crack he might be able to pierce in her impenetrable shell. His eyes slipped to the bracelets encircling her wrists, landing on the silver filigree star surrounded by black and clear beads. "Are you still afraid of the dark?"

The words called her attention like a siren calling a sailor to his death at sea. Splintering through her resolve and setting her skin aflame. *Say no.* Streetlights flickered above. Her heartbeat stuttered. *Say no.* She peered into the black wall of infinite night stretching where the headlights couldn't yet reach. *Say no.* "Let's stop talking."

Henry attempted another swig from his flask only to remember that it was empty. He stared at the empty container with betrayal and contempt.

Silence filled the van for the rest of the drive. They turned into a large gravel lot ahead of the dock. Stray animals ran to the shaded corners for safety. Elsey parked the van next to a black full-size SUV. Charlotte pulled into the lot beside them. They congregated behind the van.

Elsey nodded toward the dock. "I have a boat waiting at the end of the dock. We'll load the men and take them over to the island."

Wesley's eyebrows shot up. "What? To the prison?"

"We call it North Star Island." She opened the backdoor.

"Since when?" Charlotte looked at the island in the bay. Silhouettes dotted the darkened shoreline.

Henry nodded toward Wesley and Charlotte. "They don't have masks."

Elsey hoisted an unconscious man over her shoulder. "Asher isn't a threat." She pivoted and walked toward the dock.

"Who's Asher?" The trio echoed after her.

Brow wrinkling, Wesley faced Henry. "What the hell is going on?"

"Wes," he said, cocking his head to the side. "I have never known what was going on in any moment of my life."

"Come on, Guys." Charlotte grabbed one of the unconscious men. Henry grabbed the man's shoulders, and they carried him to the dock. Wesley lifted one of the men in his arms like a baby and followed.

The group carried each unconscious man to the boat. When all eight men were loaded, Elsey directed them to sit. She steered the boat through black water reflecting a cloud-heavy sky.

Small lanterns sprung to life, illuminating a short dock jutting from the island. A slender man with rich ebony skin leaned on a dark oak cane etched with scales leading up to a detailed serpent's head. His tan pants and turquoise mosaic-patterned Hawaiian shirt didn't fit the environment. A thin silver chain hung around his neck and dipped beneath his shirt, hiding whatever trinket might dangle at the end. He directed five men and three women gathered behind him.

Asher looked over the teenagers accompanying Elsey. "I see things got complicated." His voice sounded rough like he'd gargled with nails.

"A heads-up would've been nice." Elsey rolled her eyes.

"Now," Asher's lips curled into a broad grin. "Where would you get the idea that I would know anything about this occurring?"

She narrowed her eyes. "Bastard."

His shoulders trembled with his croaky laugh.

Wesley, Charlotte, and Henry exchanged looks muddled in confusion.

Elsey glanced at her companions and nodded toward Asher. "This is Asher. North Star Island was his idea."

"Which is?" Wesley watched Asher step aside for his assistants as they heaved unconscious men into their arms.

"A community of rehabilitation and peace." Asher leaned back on his cane. "We have two doctors and a therapist. Apartments instead of cages. Paying jobs. A small farm, a greenhouse, and shops. No one is locked up against their will unless they've committed a crime that makes them a threat to the community."

Wesley's eyes widened. "How?"

Elsey shot Asher a pointed look, earning her a curt nod. Neither spoke.

Charlotte watched the assistants follow a trail tucked in a thick wooded area lit by more lanterns. "One commented about exterminating people with powers."

Henry fiddled with the pill bottle in his pocket. "Two of them pointed guns at Elsey."

"That's all?" Asher laughed again. He pulled a handkerchief from his back pocket and wiped his forehead. "I stabbed her when we first met. Probably would've done more damage if not for my leg."

"You stabbed her?" Charlotte and Henry asked in unison.

Wesley watched Elsey, recalling all the scars hidden under her clothes. "Why did you stab her?"

"Thought she was trying to rob me. I was living on the street, and it was night." He gestured toward the masked redhead with his handkerchief. "You try having that come at you in the dark and see how you react."

"We have to go." Elsey glanced at the mainland. "Let Hellfire know any supplies that are needed. I'll return soon."

Asher tucked his handkerchief in his pocket. He placed both hands on top of his cane and looked at Elsey. Another grin curled his lips. "Divine guidance?"

She stared at him.

"Be careful of your temper while treading dark waters." His shoulders began trembling with his laugh as soon as he finished speaking.

Elsey started the boat, raising her middle finger without casting him a second glance.

The trio exchanged confused glances—aware they were being left out of an inside joke.

Elsey steered the boat back to the mainland. She nodded toward the black SUV parked beside the van. "Follow us in the SUV."

Wesley held up his hands. "This is a lot of running around with very few answers."

"And you'll get them," Elsey snapped. "Believe me, I have questions of my own."

Wesley opened his mouth.

Charlotte grabbed his hand and pulled him toward her SUV. "We'll follow you."

Charlotte stared at the deep claw marks cutting into the steel door at the rear of the warehouse. "What is this place?"

"No idea." Wesley watched the modestly dressed crowd declaring the building a den of sin and debauchery.

A girl with caramel-colored hair eyed the vehicles from where she wrangled children at the back of the group. She looked vaguely familiar, but unable to place her face, Wesley ignored the attention and shoved open his door. "Let's get this over with."

Climbing out of the vehicle, Charlotte choked back a sharp breath against the tangy, musky odor lingering in the air. "What's that smell?"

Wesley pressed his work shirt against his nose.

Removing his mask, Henry strolled over to the couple. "Smells like cats battling it out in a turf war."

Elsey shoved her mask into her pocket and motioned everyone to follow her into the warehouse. Dim light filtered over them. A fierce thunder of intense pulsing bass, rhythmic pounding drums, powerfully raw guitar riffs, and a voice like a deep melodic growl made the building vibrate.

Henry looked around the black walls stretching down a hallway and the black stairwell reaching up to a platform. "I've heard about parties like this." He looked at Wesley and Charlotte. "You'll need masks if this is heading in that same direction."

Following Elsey to the platform, they glanced down the gated stairs shielding the floor where people clothed in various styles of alternative dress jumped and thrashed along with heavy music. Luci stood in the doorway of a room dripping with vampiric charm. Her thumbs poked through holes in the sleeves of her black hooded jacket. Her feet were bare beneath her black bootcut pants. An ember-colored spark seemed to flicker in her moss green eyes, narrowed at Elsey.

Luci's fist tightened around her glass of bright green absinthe. "What the hell were you thinking?"

"*I* don't even know what's happening!" Elsey gestured toward the den. "We don't need anyone overhearing."

Luci tapped her foot in place. Angling aside, she nodded to the room. "Everybody in."

Crossing the threshold, Charlotte and Wesley sat on the sofa. Henry eyed the bar cart in the corner.

Elsey slammed the door. "Everyone, this is Luci."

"No need for introductions." Luci held up her glass with her forefinger outstretched. "One, I don't care. Two, I already know who you are." Storming to the bar cart, she shoved a bottle of whiskey into Henry's hand. "If I have to deal with your presence, I'm not dealing with you having withdrawals, too."

Spinning the cap, Henry shot a suspicious glance at Elsey before addressing Luci. "How did you know my preference?"

"What preference?" Wesley scoffed. "Kade once told me he saw you drain a bottle of mouthwash in fifteen seconds because your flask was empty."

"It was a party. I wanted to make sure my breath was minty fresh." Henry upturned the bottle. Savoring the smooth burn.

"It was at an apartment." Wesley's eyes thinned to a questioning squint. "In broad daylight. Your dad was having the new tenants sign paperwork."

Henry held up a finger. "If I was there, it was a party."

Luci pointed at Wesley. "He has a point." She whirled on Elsey. "You brought an addict who can't fight to an all-out brawl with guns!"

"We were there, too." Charlotte leaned forward.

Luci spun. "And you weren't supposed to be!"

Elsey dropped her arms to her side. "They fought well."

"It doesn't matter, Else!" Luci slammed her glass of absinthe down on the coffee table. "You're the only one who can do this!"

"You don't know that!" Elsey threw her hands up. "I've been trying to stop them for months. I couldn't get close to that van without getting shot."

"You've been shot?" Henry stood straighter. He stared at Elsey's profile, taking in her rough edges, harsh lines, and smooth curves. He took another long swig from the bottle.

Wesley watched Elsey standing her ground. He recalled her taking out the man holding a gun to her face. "How long have you been doing this?"

"Maybe a couple of years." Elsey shrugged.

"How have you not been killed?" Charlotte looked her over, taking in most of the scars on her face like they were brand new and remembering the scars covering her body.

"She was made for this." Luci sneered.

"What does that mean?" Henry plucked at his bottom lip, distracting himself from the itch of need building under his skin.

Elsey shook her head. "It doesn't matter."

"Wait, the cameras." Charlotte jerked toward Luci. "You're behind the cameras being hacked?"

"How did you know about the cameras?" Luci sat across from her laptop.

Charlotte scratched at the side of her thumb. "My dad is the head of security at HAL Tower."

Wesley's brows rose. He faced Elsey. "So, your dad has no idea what you're doing?" He looked at his hands and ran through the calculations. "What you're doing—The prison and *everything*. It has to cost a lot."

Leaning against the wall, Elsey crossed her arms. "My father has so much money that he would never notice when small chunks go missing here and there."

Luci emptied her glass. "Rich people are idiots."

"I'll drink to that." Henry raised the bottle of whiskey before taking a long drink.

Elsey rolled her eyes. She focused on Charlotte. "Do you have powers, too?"

"No." Charlotte shook her head. "My dad taught me how to fight since I was a kid. He wanted to make sure I knew how to protect myself."

"Kade and I took basic fight training for the same reason and so we could protect our sister." Wesley narrowed his deep-set eyes at Henry again. "Since when do you have powers?"

Henry held up a finger and looked at Luci. "Can I smoke in here?"

"Only if you want me to rip out your lungs and show them to you." Luci returned to the bar cart to refill her glass.

Pointing at Luci, Henry turned to Elsey. "So, your friend is allowed to threaten murder?"

"We're not friends," Elsey snapped.

Luci brought her fresh glass of undiluted absinthe to her crimson lips. "There's not a word for what we are."

Holding out her hands, Charlotte addressed Henry. "Wes asked about your powers. How did you get them?"

"I tried to help a girl who overdosed on Reds. She gave me her powers before she died." Henry's lips dipped into a deep frown. He took a weighted gulp of whiskey before nodding to Wesley. "How'd you get yours?"

"Wait." Luci held up her glass. "This talk of you two having powers cannot leave this room. It's not safe."

Charlotte gestured toward Elsey. "Everyone knows Elsey and her family have powers, even if no one knows what they are."

"That's because they don't use them," Henry said with a glance at Elsey. "Not openly anyway." He stuffed his free hand in his pocket, extracting a faint rattle from his pill bottle.

Wesley frowned. "That man said people like us were exterminated. The troublemakers."

Elsey dug her nails into her arms. "My father is untouchable. He's not a troublemaker. He's useful."

"What about your mom?" Charlotte picked at her hands.

"My mother is considered harmless." Elsey locked her gaze on a far wall behind the sofa. "If she leaves the house, it's only for my father's parties and for the one hour every day when she meets him for lunch."

"And you?" Wesley rested his elbows on his knees. "There are rumors about you. That you—"

His words died when Elsey's barbed glare pierced him. Some part of him wanted to curl away. He didn't drop her gaze.

Charlotte's stomach knotted tight. She replayed the sound of the man's scream covering the snap of his kneecap. Swallowing hard, she looked at Elsey. "Are you considered harmless?"

Elsey's eyes ripped to Charlotte. "What do you think?"

Unfazed, Henry stared at the bottle in his hand.

Charlotte took a deep breath, forcing her mind to stay on topic instead of tangling in upsetting memories. "So that's what happened to people with powers? In school, they teach us that they abandoned the world. That they went into hiding because they stopped caring."

History, like rumors, changed depending on who told the story. Depending on what they lost or gained. Depending on where they stood in the moment and what privileges they'd reaped in the end. Depending on whether someone stood on their necks or whether their boots were stained with the blood of those they tried to break.

Schools and history books parroted the same story.

When people with special abilities became more prominent, they became the world's greatest crutch. Relying heavily on powered individuals to take care of even basic functions and needs, *normal* people grew too comfortable in their daily lives. Overlooking wounds instead of healing them. Ignoring holes left leaking and filling the hull of the ship. When the arrogance of those with powers became greater than their care for their vulnerable, powerless kin, they abandoned everyone. Like ripping a bandage off an infected wound. Like a sledgehammer decimating an already damaged wall. Releasing the flood to let everything fall to pieces.

History repeated itself to varying degrees at different points in time. And often, the truth was written in blood.

"People teach what they want us to believe." Wesley found a spot to stare at on the carpet.

Elsey shifted her gaze between Wesley and Charlotte to Henry. "Do any of you even know where our powers usually come from?"

Wesley and Charlotte shook their heads.

Henry shrugged. "I remember what you told me about the gods when we were younger. I searched more about it, but everything dismisses it as a fairytale."

"Wait." Wesley raised his hand. "Gods?"

"They're all dead now," Luci interjected, sinking into her spot on the sofa.

Charlotte's fingers touched the small silver bird necklace around her throat. "*They* were real?"

"A long time ago." Elsey settled back against the wall. "All of humankind is connected. They all came from the same place. All mythologies and belief systems got their start in the same place, too."

"Africa." Wesley nodded. "That's why there are similarities and parallels all over the world. What does that have to do with anything?"

"It wasn't just one culture borrowing from another," Elsey said. "The deities themselves moved from one area to another, taking whatever form the resident culture gifted them when they visited from their realms. Sometimes, only a handful moved between regions. Other times, one or two moved. When they stopped interacting with humans, it was believed they all died or abandoned us because we don't have any other records."

Charlotte clutched her bird charm. "We?"

Elsey fixed her stare on the far wall. "My parents and their families spent their lives studying our history. Being born like this, they have more information available to them than those born without powers."

"And they taught you?"

"Yes. They focused more on Greek mythology—"

Wesley snorted. "Figures."

"I'll tell you what I know." Shrugging, Elsey continued, "Essentially, everything that exists now or has ever existed all came from one source: Chaos. There's more to it than that. More steps involving reality, inevitability, time, and so on. But it all comes back to Chaos."

"Like the big bang?" Wesley asked. Peeking at Charlotte, he noted her unfocused gaze and knew her thoughts were turning inward.

Elsey gave a single nod. "That could be considered part of Chaos. An action caused by a primordial being. When Chaos settled on Gaia, or Earth, darkness and night were created. From darkness and night came light and day. Darkness and light couldn't coexist peacefully, so they created their own domains. Darkness created the Underworld, and light created the Aether."

Wesley shook his head. "Einstein's Theory of Special Relativity and the Michelson-Morley Experiment from the 1880s don't support the existence of the aether."

"I'm not talking about luminiferous aether." Elsey flicked her hand out, adding, "Though it may be possible that Aristotle, Newton, and the other classical scientists somehow caught a glimpse of the Aether, and that might be what led to their theories."

Henry dropped his eyes to his bottle of whiskey. "If there's a pop quiz later, I'm blaming you for my failing grade."

Elsey glanced at Henry. "I've explained the Aether to you before."

His eyes met hers. "The sources I've read all say it's the upper air that the gods breathed."

"That's because the sources humans use are stories by dead humans who wrote their own versions of ancient oral traditions, not firsthand knowledge."

"I also have an oral tradition," Henry smirked, boring his eyes into Elsey's. "But it'd probably make you blush."

A chuckle escaped Luci, drawing Elsey's harsh stare. She silenced herself with a drink from her glass.

Ignoring Henry's remark, Elsey turned to Wesley and Charlotte. "The Aether is another world that's parallel to ours, same with the Underworld. The Titans, Gods, and their creations lived in either realm and visited Gaia whenever they wanted. They also created the beings that exist here on Gaia, from the Humans to the Supernaturals."

Charlotte shook her head, bringing herself out of her reverie. "Supernaturals?"

Elsey nodded. "People with powers are categorized into four different types. Immortal, Sub Immortal, Mortal, and Unnatural. For each type, there are subcategories, which can branch into further subcategories."

"Okay, I'm beyond lost." Henry lifted his bottle of whiskey. "Can I get a simplified version of what everyone's talking about?"

Wesley lifted his upturned hand. "Like taxonomic ranks."

"I said *simplified.*" Groaning, Henry pushed his hair back from his face. "Anyone care to translate for those of us without working brains?"

Wesley pantomimed a ranking structure with his hands. "Domain, kingdom, phylum, class, order, family, genus, and species."

Henry nodded. "I'll be sure to remember that when it comes up on the quiz."

"It's not that complicated."

"You're talking to someone whose GPA basically says LOL."

Elsey rolled her eyes. "That's because you lack self-esteem and self-control, not because you lack intelligence."

Henry gripped the pill bottle in his pocket, feeling the cap imprint on his palm. "If you're going to strip me naked, at least have the decency to do it in private where we can have some fun."

She arched a brow, shifting her attention back to the conversation. "For the Immortals, they were classified as Gods and Titans. Sub Immortals were Demigods, Demi-Titans, Aetherals, and Erebals. Aetherals and Erebals came in a variety of beings. Witches, Vampires, Werewolves, Dem—"

Wesley raised his hands to halt her. "You're telling me that Vampires and Werewolves are real?"

"*Were*," Luci said, locking her eyes on Elsey. "They were hunted down and killed."

Elsey pulled her shoulders back but didn't speak.

Luci kept her eyes glued to Elsey. "The same thing will happen to anyone else here if word gets out about them."

Silence settled over the group. Weighted like a blanket of blood and darkness.

The door opened before anyone could speak.

Luci's eyes lit up like fireflies settling in the leaves of a tree.

Tristan stepped past the cracked door, revealing his towering mass. Scrolling tattoos trailed over his deep brown skin—covering his neck, arms, hands and disappearing under his spray-painted T-shirt and his black jeans stitched at the knees with dyed cord.

"The fuck?" Peering up at Tristan, Henry's eyes bulged. "Are your parents giants?"

Wesley resisted the urge to press his hand to his face. "Ignore him. He's not used to having to crane his neck to look at anyone but his dad."

"My point." Henry lifted a finger. "How tall are you and could you take the arrogant festering codpiece in a fight?"

"I don't fight." Tristan's eyes—dark as a midnight sky—gleamed with amusement. He pointed to Elsey. "Ask her."

"I said take him in a fight. Not take him to his grave." Henry dropped his finger. "Although … No, Henry. Ana would be upset. Okay. That's settled."

Everyone stared at him. He lifted the bottle of whiskey to his lips and pulled in a long drink.

"Well, whatever that was, consider me thoroughly entertained." Tristan shifted his attention to Luci. "Three things. First, someone closed the lid to the dumpster again. I fixed it, but remind the others to leave it open. Second, Gene's feeling woozy after dinner. I told him to come rest for a bit. I'll have someone else man the bar."

Luci nodded. "I'll be down to help soon."

"Thanks, Love." Tristan grinned, flashing sharp canines. Turning to Elsey, his grin widened. He put his hands together under his chin. "What page are you on?"

"Thirteen." She arched a brow. "You?"

"Ten. Dammit!" He pointed at Luci. "She distracted me."

"Hey! I distracted you, too!" Gene called before pushing the door open wider. The light warmed the golden tones in his soft brown skin. He adjusted the black collar at his throat. A black sweater with a floral skull stitched onto the front hung over his distressed cargo pants. Standing on his tiptoes, he yanked down on Tristan's shirt and planted a kiss on his lips.

Tristan cupped Gene's cheeks, deepening the kiss for a couple of sweet aching heartbeats.

The men broke apart. Gene waved at the others in the room while he traipsed over to Luci. Flopping onto the couch, Gene pecked Luci on the lips. He rested his head in her lap. "Don't mind me, my Little Hellfire."

"I'm only an inch shorter than you." Luci's free hand buried into his strip of rumberry hair.

"Every inch counts." Tristan smirked. He looked at the assembled group, pushing his thick locs over his shoulders. "Elsey, you're keeping strange company these days."

Gene began snoring before Tristan shut the door.

Rolling her eyes, Elsey resumed the discussion as though she hadn't been interrupted. "The Mortal category includes Hybrids, Diluteds, and Supernaturals. Supernaturals are also split into subtypes. More Witches, Vampires, Werewolves, and the like."

"Wait," Wesley shook his head and held up a hand. "What's the difference between a Supernatural Vampire and an Aetheral Vampire?"

"We don't know." Luci undercut her harsh tone with a sip of her absinthe.

Charlotte released her necklace and leaned against Wesley. "I don't like the sound of that term *Diluted.*"

Elsey nodded, dropping her arms to her sides. "It used to be an insult against the offspring of anyone who was part Supernatural, Aetheral, or Erebus and part human. The nicer term was Hybrid, but after so many generations with different beings and humans continued intermingling, it became more difficult uncover someone's origins."

"Why not use DNA?"

"It's about something more. The essence—"

"The what?" Wesley's brows rose high.

"The essence. Where our powers come from." Elsey motioned outward with a casual hand.

"What essence?"

"You don't have an essence?" She arched a brow. "It's something deep in you that connects your heart and your brain. It's always a color that's important to you."

"I have no idea what you're talking about." Wesley looked at Charlotte and then at Elsey. "When I want to use my power, I think of it, and it happens. I don't have a color or essence or whatever."

Keeping her brow raised, Elsey twisted toward Henry. "Do you have an essence?"

"Yep." He took another short drink from his bottle of whiskey. "At first, I thought I was finally losing my mind because I could feel it or ... *see* it in my head. But then it would fill my body when I would use a power, and I realized it was connected."

She nodded. "You're what they call Gifted. Someone dying in their last hour gifted their power to someone else—you. But like I told you, it can only occur with those who already have powers from their family line. Or that's what I've always been taught. It also accounts for people who kill to steal someone's power."

"What?" Charlotte's eyes widened.

Elsey sighed. "If a powered individual is killed, their powers can go to another compatible person nearby. If the person is murdered, their powers *and* memories typically go to the murderer, so long as they're a compatible fit. If someone dies a violent death and doesn't willfully give their powers away, their memories are attached to their powers."

"So, if Kade had powers …" Wesley paused, letting his words drift. He found a spot to stare at on the carpet. "After Kade died, weird things happened. Like what you guys saw. I'd touch something and my body would copy the atomic makeup. I had to go through Kade's room to find stuff for the funeral. He had a box hidden in his closet. There were all these articles and weird documents and papers. Some had pictures. I didn't look at all of it. I didn't need to. I got the gist. Keep my mouth shut, and I'd be safe."

Luci looked up from Gene's sleeping face. "Do you know where he got that information?"

"No idea. I put it back where I found it. Some of the stuff I saw made me sick." A shudder tore through him. "I have a strong stomach. You can ask Elsey. We were lab partners in AP Biology our freshman year. I didn't have a problem with the dissections. But *this* was something else."

Elsey bit her tongue. Luci rubbed her right wrist—covered by her jacket sleeve—against the sofa. Henry upturned his bottle, letting the whiskey drown any tasteless questions or comments. Charlotte chewed on the inside of her cheek. Wesley continued to stare at the spot on the carpet, focusing all his energy into keeping any images from materializing in his thoughts.

Luci spoke low, her eyes fixed on Gene. "Did your parents have powers?"

"No," Wesley said.

She looked up at him. "And you didn't have powers before?"

He shook his head. "I think I would've noticed if I did."

She shifted her attention to Elsey. "Another anomaly."

"What's an anomaly," Charlotte whispered to Wesley. "Not the definition, but—"

Pulling her hand free from Gene's hair, Luci grabbed her glass of absinthe. "Anomalies account for anyone who is seemingly born with abilities without known links to powers."

Elsey met Luci's gaze. "It would make sense with what I suspected about Kade."

Wesley, Charlotte, and Henry jerked toward Elsey. "What?"

Pulling her rucksack forward, Elsey opened the flap and retrieved a book of sheet music. She tugged a scrap of paper free from between the pages. A rough sketch in pen showed a figure eight on its side with two perpendicular lines bisecting the center. The line running north to south pointed to a dot with another dot on either side. She showed the symbol around the room. "Have any of you seen this symbol?"

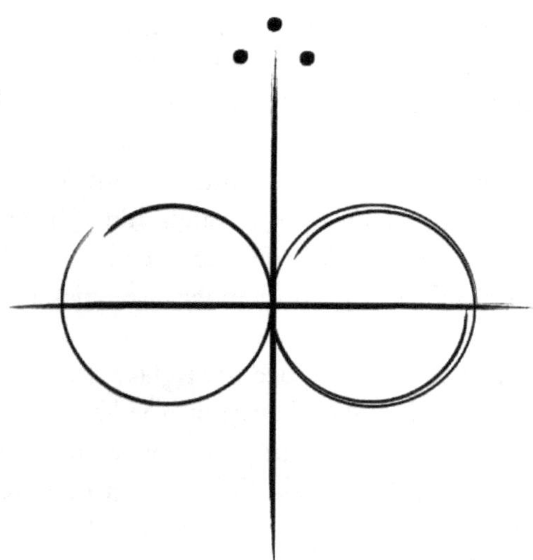

"No." Henry tightened his grip on the pill bottle in his pocket, the itch growing stronger by the second.

Charlotte stared at the symbol. She scratched hard at the side of her thumb.

When he experienced no spark of recognition, Wesley shook his head. "What does that have to do with Kade?"

"Elsey, don't," Luci warned.

Tossing the paper onto the coffee table, Elsey pointed at the symbol. "I should've told them when I found it. They might be able to help."

Wesley jumped up from the sofa, gesturing toward the paper. "What does that symbol have to do with my brother?"

Elsey met his stare. "It was stabbed into him."

"What?" His voice splintered like his heart was preparing to crumble to ash. He struggled to clear the starkness of reality from his thoughts. The gears in his brain spun faster, digging up questions and connecting dots. Emotions twisted and dug ragged nails into his soul.

"He was the seventh person I've found like that." Elsey continued. The harsh tones in her voice took on a hollow depth.

Charlotte leaned forward, slipping her hand into Wesley's. "What does it mean?"

"I don't know."

Wesley's pain coiled into a cocoon of confusion. "You weren't there when Henry found him."

"No," she said. "When I saw him listed on the Daily Death List the morning after it happened, I visited the morgue."

"So, you can find who did it?" Charlotte looked at Luci. "The cameras—"

Luci shook her head. "I tried, but—"

"You knew." Wesley's deep voice lowered with his loaded accusation. He stepped toward Elsey. His heart slammed against his ribs like a moth springing from the cocoon, drawn to the flames of anger growing in his stomach. "You had information about my brother's death, and you didn't tell me. Do you know how it's felt not knowing? Thinking it's impossible? Do you have any idea how guilty and helpless I've been feeling letting his murderer get away with it?"

Henry planted himself in front of Elsey. "Wes, she said she wanted to."

"I don't care! That doesn't make it right." Wesley pointed at Elsey. "She's out there being a damn hero every night! Well, where was she when Kade needed help? Huh? Where were you, Elsey? Where were you with your powers and that damn healing serum? He could still be here!"

"I'm only one person. I can't be everywhere at once." Elsey dug her nails into her palms. She glanced at Luci. "If I had more help, I could—"

"No," Luci slammed her glass on the coffee table. "Absolutely not."

"It makes sense." Charlotte leaned forward. Her hand went to the bird charm at her throat. Taking a deep breath, she looked at Elsey. "The world is falling apart. Someone needs to do something. Whether we like each other or not and regardless of anything that happened in the past, we all worked together tonight."

Elsey nodded. "Charlotte's right."

"The pretty boy doesn't know how to fight." Luci shot a hardened look at Henry.

"I can teach him."

"I didn't think there was a way to find out who killed my brother." Wesley pressed his lips together. He breathed deep, waiting for the ache burning his heart to settle. "If there is, I have to try. Whatever it takes."

Elsey opened the door. "I'll go talk to Tristan about making suits for everyone."

Luci opened her mouth, but Elsey slipped into the hall before she could respond. She fixed the closed door in a burning glare.

Slumping to the sofa, Wesley noticed the tension in his muscles. Like his body had been preparing his entire life for an attack. He settled his face in his hands.

Charlotte scooted closer, kissing the back of his neck. She rested her chin on his shoulder and rubbed consoling circles over his back.

Henry's eyes wandered from the couple to Luci. Her attention remained fixed on the door. He took a swig of whiskey before speaking. "How do you know Elsey?"

"None of your business," she said without moving.

A snort escaped Gene.

Henry, Wesley, and Charlotte glanced at him—wondering when he'd stopped snoring or if he'd even been asleep at all.

The door opened. Elsey looked at the assembled group. "Tristan said for everyone to come by sometime tomorrow, so he can get everyone's measurements. Everyone will also need proper shoes and masks. You can get those at the market. I know of a place where we can meet."

"Why not here?" Henry replaced the cap on his bottle of whiskey.

"No," Luci said without further explanation.

Charlotte slipped her hand into Wesley's and pulled him up with her. She turned to Elsey. "Do you need a ride home?"

"I'll catch a ride from someone here when I'm done for the evening." Elsey nodded toward Henry. "Could you drop him off though? Also, get my number from him."

Nodding, Charlotte let solemn silence envelop her and Wesley when they left the room.

Henry followed them, hoisting the half-empty bottle of whiskey over his head and pointing to it. "I'm taking this."

Elsey watched them descend the platform.

Gene rolled onto his back in Luci's lap. A smile tugged at the corner of his sharp lips.

"This is reckless and stupid." Luci's eyes bored into Elsey's back.

Looking over his shoulder before stepping outside, Henry's eyes locked with Elsey's. Her heart trembled with the whispering ache pulsating inside her. A faint smirk lingered on his lips. She bit her tongue.

"Can you get the communicators ready by Sunday," Elsey asked, watching the door shut.

"Yeah." Luci ignored Gene's growing amusement.

"Thanks."

III

September 3, 3699

Blinking against the heavy wind, Elsey scanned everything while Gene steered onto Hallen Street. The rumble of his motorcycle filled her ears. Neither spoke. Accepting the silence for what it was. His cellphone—mounted in a protective pouch on the gas tank—showed the clock in a continuous glow. 2:45 A.M.

Grains of sand dropped one-by-one in Elsey's mind to track the minutes she had left before arriving home.

The city fell to their back as they plunged into a thick line of trees carved by a winding road. Long, gated driveways led to palatial estates tucked behind dense trees and rolling hills. Cresting on the tallest hill, lay her father's land. Like a crown jewel in an already questionable display of excessive wealth amid desolation. High stone walls—lined with rows of imported Chinese juniper and grand fir trees—outlined the vast acreage. Spiked black iron gates with ornamental H's locked out prying eyes.

Gene veered to the left, cutting through the grass stretching past the walls of the estate and flowed under the walls. He stopped beside a tree with deep scratches raked through the bark.

Dismounting, Elsey adjusted her rucksack on her shoulders. "How pissed is Luci?"

"Don't worry about it." A smile crept on his lips. "Tristan is already thinking up ways he'll help her relax."

She faced the row of trees. Telling herself to step forward. Her feet didn't obey.

"You can always stay there, you know?" Gene leaned forward on his handlebars. "Purgatory is your home, too."

Her brain responded with a snap. Twisting the strange emotions eating at her heart into something solid she could push against. Letting her take the first step. "Thanks for the ride."

He bit back a sigh. "Try to get some sleep at least."

She followed a trail of trees gouged with deep scratches until she reached a gaping hole in the high stone wall along the property.

Beyond the wall, a thick forest of oak, maple, and weeping willows curtained a man-made stream that curved along the edge of the property. Her boots **thumped** as she crossed a low bridge over the stream. Sticking to the forest, she followed a path the cameras wouldn't be able to see.

Yellowing and merlot-colored crabapple trees adorned the spacious lawn surrounding a modern mansion. The walls of glass, opening the top two floors up to inspection, boasted a life without secrets. The solid stone walls of the first floor held the air of a private domain. The stream circled in a pool around the stairs—like a moat to deter those who saw it from afar—and dipped under the house where a motor kept it circulating. Flourishing crocus and gladiolus began to take the place of dying hibiscus and geraniums along the sides of the house and a concrete walkway that stretched over the pool. Orange-tipped yellow trailing begonias tumbled over the sides of the stairs like flowering flames.

Breaking from the forest, she walked the concrete path over the pool. She followed it to a door hidden behind the stairs. Elsey dipped her hand into the thorned branches of a lone rose shrub that never died. The branches curled outward, responding to her touch. Finding her hidden key, she let herself in the house through her father's study on the first floor.

The walls were so white they seemed to give off their own light. Her eyes went to the bookshelves lining the far wall. Worn books and various owl figurines overflowed the first three bookshelves. The fourth bookshelf tucked into the right corner held immaculate books with gold-leaf pages and a miniaturized version of the golden statue that topped the museum. A rosewood executive desk cut off the ornate print of a large, distressed graying rug. A painting of an olive tree hung in a gilded frame beside the single door on the right. The door to her bedroom was on the left beside a staircase leading to the top two floors.

Feeling her stomach grumble, Elsey remembered she'd only had an apple for dinner. She left her boots and rucksack by her bedroom door before heading upstairs, walking with soft steps.

The wall of windows in the living room made her feel like a puppet on display. She skirted between an orange mid-century modern sofa and a blue curved glass coffee table. The pristine surfaces and smudge-free glass making up the kitchen felt like a lie— seizing her muscles with armor-like tension.

Elsey selected a glass from the cabinet beside the sink and filled it with water from the filtered tap. Her thoughts raced through the events of the day. Beneath everything, a low hum continued to rattle her brain. She lifted the glass to her lips.

"You're late again." Her father spoke from the doorway leading to the dining room. His gray pajama bottoms and burgundy shirt looked too casual for him.

Elsey didn't move. "I was busy."

Gregor turned the light on. "Were you with him?"

"No, sir."

"You're lying to me."

She stared into her glass. "Prove it."

"You will not associate with Henry. Don't you understand?" He kept his voice low and soft—controlled. "I'm trying to protect you."

"He can't hurt me." Elsey took a long drink. "No one can hurt me anymore."

"Yes, they can. He will. Everyone will. They can't help it. It's what they do." Gregor strolled forward. Her fingers tightened around the glass when he continued to speak. "I'm the one who has kept you safe. You know what everyone thinks about you. He's no different. I have kept you safe and taken care of you despite everything. I'm the one who put you back together every time. I did that. No one else."

The glass fractured beneath her strained grasp. Bits of skin tore. She watched her blood stain the clear fragments and drip into the sink. "Congratulations on doing your job as a parent."

"What's this?" Marnie asked as she entered the kitchen from the living room. Her red curls were piled high. Her pink silk robe cinched her waist and hid the frilly nightgown draping her porcelain skin. "Elsey, were you out late again?"

"Yes, ma'am." Releasing the pieces of glass, she faced her parents. "I need to sleep. I have school in a few hours."

Marnie fixed her cold gaze on Elsey but let her step out of the room.

"Elsey." Gregor followed her into the living room. "We are not done with this conversation."

She halted on the top step.

"Tomorrow evening, if you're not home by seven o'clock sharp, you will be in serious trouble." He paused and let the weight of his words burrow into her. "Do you understand?"

"Yes." She glared at the stairs. A cold burning sensation flared to life in her heart.

Marnie cleared her throat. "Yes, what?"

"Yes, sir." Elsey clenched her hands into fists. "May I go now?"

"You may."

She descended to the study below. Dark plumes of rage and emotions she couldn't name roiled through her chest and threatened to consume her. Sharp pain buzzed in her brain. Her limbs went numb, like her body was not her own. Digging her nails into her fresh cuts, she took a deep breath. Elsey took another deep breath and held it, waiting for the mental pain to ease. When relief didn't come, she grabbed her belongings and entered her room.

Dark stone walls reflected the light but were too matte to reflect anything more. Black paint coated the two large windows, shielding the expansive backyard from view. Black cloth covered the mirror hanging over her large plain dresser. Her plain, nondescript nightstands were bare. Her bed was kept simple with black bedding and nothing else. A large black trunk and a simple black sofa sat a few feet away.

All too aware of the effect her presence had, she relegated her existence to the trunk in her room and the rucksack kept on her back. She kept herself tucked into darkened corners out of sight like a beast more afraid of the villagers and their pitchforks than they had any reason to be afraid of her.

Kneeling in front of the trunk, she grasped the heavy padlock and tugged on the essence in the back of her mind. The padlock opened.

The hum in her mind increased again.

Hidden under the top tray, lay cardboard boxes of various sizes, stacked in neat rows. Wrapping paper and ribbons had been folded in precise order and tucked against the sides of the trunk. A date—in black marker—had been written in immaculate penmanship on top of each box.

Elsey removed the lid of the largest box, pulling free a black throw blanket covered in shining silver stars. A card, left unopened and bearing her name in the same beautiful handwriting, lay at the bottom of the box.

Sitting on the couch, she pulled a book of crossword puzzles and a well-read book on Greek mythology from her rucksack. She flipped the book open to where an old, wrinkled photo of a Rottweiler marked her page. Her thumb and forefinger found the small heart that had been stitched into the corner of her blanket, absentmindedly rubbing the once vibrant blue threads. She let herself drift with the passages in her book.

And Zeus, upon receiving news of the prophecy, swallowed Metis to prevent the birth of the offspring believed to bring about his defeat. Metis had already conceived Pallas Athene, and she remained hidden inside Zeus—growing in wisdom. Athena continued to grow in strength and might, and upon receiving the arms of war, sprang forth from Zeus' head, pledging her loyalty to her father. Accepting the praise bestowed upon him, Zeus favored his daughter over all others.

The words filled her. The storm of emotion and pain diminished until she was left with the constant hum waiting under her thoughts.

two

The second bell rang through the school. Students rushed through the hall. Breaking with the crowd, Wesley ambled into his Environmental Studies class. The white brick walls and glaring lights couldn't seem to snap him out of his reverie. He found his assigned seat like a zombie wading through life teeming around him.

His mind continued driving on the same track. Reversing to that terrible night. He saw it over and over. Like a cursed television stuck on one channel. His older brother's body lying on the ground. A crimson pool so deep it looked black. The rain transformed the blood into a stream, flowing into the grate near the dumpster. His brother's warm eyes were now empty and lifeless. Staring wide as if his trapped spirit still watched the imprint of his murder.

Wesley's stomach knotted tighter, lodging a solid rock in his throat. His bottom lip quivered. He pressed his teeth against it. Everything seemed to blur with the sting of his eyes. He blinked up at the fluorescent lighting.

"Hey, Wes." Henry's smooth voice tore his moment of melancholy away. The unmistakable rattle of a pill bottle sounded with his every step. Spotting Brant Cleary sitting in the back corner, Henry gave a cordial wave but kept his attention on Wesley. The rusty shade of his long-sleeved merino wool polo peeked out beneath his overcoat.

Wesley released a heavy breath while Henry sauntered around the desks. "Which god did I anger for you to show up here?"

"Dionysus." Halting near Wesley, Henry pulled his flask from his coat pocket and took a long drink. "He thinks you need to have more fun."

"I have plenty of fun."

"Dying of the plague would be more fun than you."

Wesley scoffed and leaned back. His leg bounced in place under his desk. "I'm surprised you know what the plague is."

Henry shrugged. "I know it killed people, and that seems more fun than any of the boring stuff you do."

"You mean being responsible?" Wesley crossed his arms in front of him, gripping the long sleeves of his navy Henley.

"How dare you use such profanity in my presence."

"We just have different definitions of fun." The hint of a smile passed Wesley's lips. "Mine doesn't happen to include getting my stomach pumped."

Laughing, Henry took another drink from his flask. "I would be offended if the wind didn't feel like a rainbow right now."

"Henry," Wesley groaned. "Why are you here?"

"Funny that you think I need a reason to annoy you."

Wesley narrowed his eyes.

"Lucky for you, I do have a reason." Henry sat on top of the desk in front of Wesley, letting his shiny black oxfords rest in the seat. "I wanted to offer my bank account if you need assistance getting necessities, if you know what I mean."

"Thanks, but no." Wesley shook his head. "I can pay for myself."

"Of course." Henry nodded, dropping his flask in his pocket. "The offer still stands. For Charlotte, too."

Wesley's gaze shifted to Neil Jephson, another classmate, approaching.

Neil stopped beside Henry. "You're sitting on my desk."

Henry looked at Neil, letting his eyes roam over his short and bulky frame. He met Neil's sparkling green eyes with his classic smirk already at play. "Do you have a better place I could sit?"

Flipping open his binder, Neil jotted his number on the first piece of paper he could find. He ripped a good chunk off the class syllabus and handed it to Henry.

Wesley lifted his hands. "That has everything we need to know about the upcoming projects."

"Yeah, but I need *this* more." Neil motioned toward Henry.

Hopping off the desk, Henry lifted the slip of paper to his

forehead in a faux salute. "Good day, gentlemen."

"Henry." Wesley glared while Henry made his way to the front of the room. "This could've been a text!"

"But then how would I annoy you?" Henry pocketed the phone number and disappeared in the hall.

Groaning, Wesley looked up at the ceiling. *He's going to get us all killed.*

three

Scanning the protesters gathered outside Purgatory, Charlotte's mind wandered back to the discussion from the previous night. All her time attending church services with her dad now called into question. Her fingers fussed with the silver bird charm around her neck. Her thoughts tangled in a web of wonder.

"You've been quiet," Wesley said. He reached over to adjust his hoodie hanging off her shoulder, revealing the slim strap of her simple dusty pink flowy dress.

Glancing out her window to see the protestors, he spotted the girl with caramel-colored hair he noticed last night. She looked up from wrangling young children and watched the SUV pass. He still couldn't place her face. Dismissing the vague familiarity hovering in his mind as a coincidence, he focused his attention on Charlotte.

She tossed him a muted smile while turning into the parking lot behind the warehouse turned alternative club. "Just thinking."

He watched her release the bird charm she always wore. "About last night?"

She parked next to Henry's cherry roadster. Her eyes trailed over the private lot. The full-sized SUV was absent, and Elsey's motorcycle was parked beside another motorcycle with a floral gas tank. A gray cat ate from a bowl near the open dumpster. The scratches in the back walls and steel door appeared deeper in the daylight. She dug into her thoughts until she fell face forward down a dark tunnel. *What does it mean? Do I have to—*

Wesley took her hand, tugging her attention to him. "I know we don't have the same beliefs, but Kade and Taliyah went to church every Sunday. You can talk to me. I'll listen."

Charlotte chewed on the inside of her cheek. Searching his eyes— every smoke-colored wisp and every glimpse of bare soul she had memorized. Wading through the ghosts haunting his heart. Finding the comfort she always had with him. She dropped her gaze to their clasped hands and pulled forward all her strength to keep her voice from shaking. "I pray every night for my mom to come back. That she'll find us even though we moved, and she'll apologize and explain why she left. But now—They said God or the *gods* are dead. So, I just have to accept that she's never coming back? That I'll never know why she left or why she didn't want me?"

"Hey," his deep voice resonated with all the warmth of a plush blanket ready to wrap around her. He brought her hand to his lips. Pressing kisses to her fingertips. "You can believe whatever you believe. Just because they said something doesn't mean it's an absolute."

"But—"

"They don't know everything." He motioned toward the door and then to himself. "*I* don't know everything. Hell, none of this makes sense to me. Not even the stuff I've seen. If you believe in something, whether it matches what anyone says, you can keep believing it. We all need something to believe in. Whether that's a god, destiny, science, magic, or something else. It doesn't matter if it keeps you going. As long as you don't give up."

She met his eyes again. Sucking in a deep breath and swallowing the wad of emotion creeping up her throat. "What if it's wrong?"

"That's a gamble we're all taking." He shrugged. "Even me. Just because I believe in science doesn't mean all my beliefs are correct. I can read all the books and articles I want, but I won't know if I'm right until it's over. Until then, I have to keep going somehow. I have to hold onto what I believe. If you still believe in God, believe in him. Have faith or whatever it is you need. If you're not sure, that's okay. Just don't give up. Find something else you can believe in while you're figuring it out."

Charlotte remained silent, thinking over his words. Sifting through her life to find something, *anything*, she could believe.

"There are people who still need you. Your dad needs you." Wesley paused. His mind slid backward into the bottomless pit of his own pain. As the ache hooked its claws into him, he dug in his heels and wrenched himself free. He pressed another kiss to her fingertips. Meeting her hazel eyes, hoping that his voice wouldn't reveal how close he was to breaking. "*I* need you."

A delicious heat rose in her. She grasped it and held on, stapling it to her heart. Fixing this moment into her soul and holding onto him for all she had left. She pressed her lips to his. He buried his hand in her hair. Her hands slid over his chest, circling the nape of his neck. He sucked her bottom lip in between his. Shivers tickled her skin.

"Dammit, Tristan!" A voice shouted outside the vehicle.

The couple broke apart. They watched Gene run across the parking lot, shooing the cat by the dumpster.

The cat whirled on him—hissing and spitting.

A sound like the revving of a low motor rumbled through the lot, raising chill bumps on Charlotte and Wesley's arms.

The cat ran across the street to find shelter in another parking lot.

"What was that?" Charlotte rubbed her hands over her arms.

Wesley watched Gene bend down beside the floral-painted motorcycle. The sound replayed in his thoughts. Calling forth the memory of a project he completed in AP Biology his freshman year. He'd heard the sound before. Listened to it repeatedly so he could describe the difference between the territorial warnings of each big cat still inhabiting the planet. "It sounded like a Jaguar."

"What?" Charlotte spun toward him.

"When a jaguar wants to warn others away from his territory, they have this growl that's kind of like a disgruntled motor." He shook his head, dashing aside his growing suspicion. "It's probably nothing."

She watched Gene, thinking over everything Elsey and Luci revealed last night. "Let's ask."

"What? No!" Wesley reached for her arm, but she was already hopping out. Groaning, he shoved his door open. "Dammit, Char!"

Jogging across the parking lot, the handkerchief hem of her dress fluttered around her legs.

Without glancing up from the coolant tank that had his attention, Gene held his phone up for Charlotte to see the screen showing a paused video of a territorial jaguar growl.

Wesley halted next to Charlotte. "How did you know that's what she was coming to ask?"

"The video was loud." Gene shrugged, scrunching up the left sleeve of his knitted black and pink sweater. He pulled a pen from the pocket of his cargo pants and jotted something on his arm. Adjusting the thick collar around his neck, he walked around to Elsey's motorcycle and squatted to look at the coolant tank.

Charlotte scratched at the raw skin beside her thumb. "How was it so loud?"

"Luci works magic with technology. Figuratively speaking, of course." He wrote on his arm again and rolled his sleeve down before standing. "We like our music loud here, so she made some changes to our phones."

Wesley looked between Gene and the two motorcycles. "What are you doing to Elsey's motorcycle?"

"Why do you ask so many questions?" Gene walked toward the building, motioning them after him.

Charlotte and Wesley followed him into the blackened hallway. Two people—Henry's velvety smooth voice and Tristan's deep throaty voice—spoke somewhere deeper

"How do you know Elsey," Wesley asked, entwining his fingers with Charlotte's.

Leading them to the platform, Gene nodded to the side. "If she didn't tell you, you don't need to know."

"She doesn't talk to anyone."

"Then what do you call last night?" Gene rolled his eyes. He trudged down the red-carpeted stairs and nudged the gate open with his sandal.

Faint light shone from the empty stage and pit to the left. Upside-down chairs sat on top of tables near the front of the room. Sheer black curtains were pulled back from a lounge area to the right of the bar. Henry sat on a stool—one long leg dangled and the other sprawled over the stool at his side. Tristan loomed over the other side of the bar, filling in a crossword puzzle. A thick hair tie held his locs out of his face, and a fabric tape measure draped his broad shoulders. His mesh overlay button-up shirt was partially tucked into the front of his black jeans draped with chains.

Henry tossed a short wave their way but continued speaking to Tristan. "Please?"

"No." Tristan kept his attention on his crossword.

"Just one more."

"No."

"It won't even affect me."

Not looking up, Tristan scratched off a puzzle hint. "And if it does, you die or someone else dies. I'm not having that on my conscience."

"Tristan," Gene cut in. "Stop feeding strays!"

"No," he said, attention still fixed on his crossword.

"I'm serious! You know why it bothers me. If you keep doing it—"

"If you hurt any of them, I'll turn your pelt into a coat." Tristan's low voice held a note of intimidation.

Charlotte gaped. "You guys really threaten each other like that?"

Waving his hand, Gene walked around the bar. "His threats are as empty as a bag of hot air."

"A bag of hot air isn't empty." Wesley dropped Charlotte's hand and motioned while he explained. "Air is a form of matter. It's still taking up space, so nothing is actually emp...ty." Noticing everyone looking at him, he lowered his eyes and rubbed the back of his neck.

Tristan looked up. The dim light caught the high slope of his cheeks. "It was a joke."

"Well yeah, but it didn't make sense." He tossed out his hands. "Now, if he said your threats were as empty as Henry's head, that would make more sense. In that case, he defies the laws of physics."

Henry lifted a single finger. "I'm not empty. I drank a bottle of vodka and ate a salad."

Squinting, Gene twisted toward him. "That was a jar of olives."

"If it's a vegetable, it counts as a salad."

Wesley shook his head. "Olives are fruit."

"Fine." Henry shrugged, motioning with a hand while he spoke. "I ate a fruit salad and drank my vodka, and I didn't hear any complaints."

"There were many complaints." Tristan narrowed his eyes at

Henry. "From you."

"The point is, I didn't hear them."

"Where's Elsey?" Charlotte scanned the room again. Her eyes landed on textbooks for Humanities and Trigonometry at the end of the bar along with a familiar rucksack. "Is that her stuff?"

Tristan glanced at the textbooks. "It's not ours."

Forehead wrinkling, Wesley looked between Tristan and Gene. "How old are you guys?"

"Nineteen."

"Is Luci nineteen, too?"

Gene leaned against the wall behind the bar. "None of your business."

"How do three nineteen-year-olds own and run a successful business?"

"Also, none of your business."

Wesley advanced toward the textbooks and rucksack. "I've never once seen you guys at school, and you aren't Elsey's family."

Pouncing with speed like a flash of lightning, Tristan tore the books and rucksack off the bar. "I'll tell you the same thing I told your brother. Blood doesn't make a family."

Eyes bulging, Wesley took a step back. His stomach dropped like a penny tossed into a bottomless well. "You knew my brother?"

"We only met him once." Tristan handed the items to Gene, who shouldered the rucksack and tucked the books under his arm. He turned back to Wesley. "I'm sorry about him, by the way. I know what it's like to lose your family."

Wesley dropped his eyes to the bar. A hollow ache filled his chest. His thoughts drifted to all he believed he knew about Kade. The person he admired most. The person who made him feel like the world was a little safer. His eyes stung. Warmth enveloped his hand, and he glanced down to see Charlotte lacing her fingers through his.

A straining grunt sounded from the bar as Henry reached for a half-empty bottle of rum.

Tristan spun, slapping Henry's hand. He raised a finger like he was scolding a puppy for peeing on the floor. "No!"

"Pleeeease!" Groaning, Henry sagged over the bar. "My flask is empty. It's a long walk to my car. I'm going to die!"

"If you keep testing my patience, you definitely will."

"All right, Cuddles." Gene yanked Tristan toward him and gave him a soft kiss. "I'm going to check on Luci and get dinner started. Don't forget to give them the money."

"What money?" Charlotte's forehead creased.

"Elsey's paying for everything." Tristan pulled an envelope from his back pocket.

Wesley stared at the envelope. "You mean her dad is paying for it."

"Whatever way you want to look at it." Tristan tossed the envelope to the bar. "Nobody works for free, and everything is supplied. Elsey and I don't go to stores. Luci's busy. And Gene didn't feel like asking everyone's sizes and preferences, so you can do the shopping yourselves."

Henry lifted his finger. "They sell masks in the party section on the top floor of Hallen Market. A lot of different kinds, too. They have some great ones for a lot of different questionable situations." He paused, noticing everyone staring at him. "Or so I've heard."

four

Wesley weaved through the crowded entrance of Hallen Market to reach the escalator separating the grocery section from the appliance section. The envelope of cash felt like a block of uranium in his pocket.

Another complex factor adding to the destruction of the city. Bills with the image of the tower and Gregor Hallen's face etched in red and gray ink.

People teemed around him, bumping into him without apology. Like his existence was just something else taking up their space. His stomach wound into a slimy knot of disgust.

"Hey, Wes!" A musical voice called his attention.

Turning, he spotted Anastasia Adamson's fuchsia and teal hair like a beacon as she bounded toward him. The gold threads stitched into her knee-length dress shimmered under the harsh lights. Jemma, dressed in a pair of faded cut offs and an old T-shirt with the school logo, wasn't far behind. Her long strides kept pace with Ana's incessant energy. Malini trailed them at a sluggish pace, tugging Kade's cardigan to cover her long sunflower-printed dress. Her raven black hair hung around her face while she stared at the ground. Her teeth nibbled at her bottom lip.

"Where's Charlotte?" Jemma asked when they were within reach.

"She's babysitting Taliyah while I run some errands." Wesley glanced at Anastasia, wondering how much Henry divulged to his sister.

Jemma's brows knit together. "What—"

"Do you think I can watch Taliyah sometime?" A plea burned in Malini's reddened eyes. "I've not seen her since before . . . you know."

"I don't think that's a good idea." He pressed his lips together, trying to fight the urge to flee. "I haven't told her about Kade yet. I don't want her to hear it from someone who isn't me. And you've been …" —*unstable*— "… distraught."

Jemma's eyes widened. "What did you tell her to explain why he's not coming home?"

"I told her he went on a trip for work." Wesley rubbed the top of his head. "I don't know how to tell her yet. I can't take him from her."

"I promise not to mention anything." Malini's eyes bubbled up with fresh tears. She twisted the sleeves of Kade's cardigan in her hands. "I need something to hold onto. He loved her so much, and I didn't mind whenever she joined us on our dates. Please, it will just help me feel like maybe he's still here."

He pressed his teeth into his bottom lip to halt any pain rising to the surface. The truth of her need echoing his own burned deep in his heart. *What about what I need to feel like he's still here?*

Swallowing the temptation to yell, he shook his head. "I'm sorry. I can't. It's not about what will help you. I have to think about what's best for Taliyah. If you slip up and say something, it will hurt her. She's a little kid. I'm trying to give her the best chance at life. I don't know that I can do that if she realizes how much the world is ready to take from her."

Malini drew in a ragged breath and turned away, disappearing in the crowd.

Jemma narrowed her eyes at Wesley. "You can't handle her with kid gloves forever. The world is a cruel place."

"I know that." Wesley gestured wildly with his hands. "But I won't let my little sister think that she doesn't have a chance at making a better life for herself. I won't take that from her."

Silence breathed into the space for a handful of seconds before Ana stepped between them to address Jemma. "Can you let me talk to Wes alone?"

Jemma dropped her eyes to Ana. "Yeah, I'll go find Malini."

Ana stood on her toes and pecked Jemma on the lips. Once Jemma was out of earshot, she faced Wesley. "Why don't you tell her about what you found out about Elsey and trying to find who killed Kade?"

Groaning, he shuffled onto the escalator. "If Henry tells anyone else, I swear—"

"He only told me." Ana ascended to stand next to him, waving off his frustration. "So why aren't you telling her?"

He tossed his hand in the direction Malini disappeared in. "She's been acting erratic. Accusing everyone. Elsey. *Henry.*"

Ana laughed. "Henry doesn't have a murderous bone in his body."

Wesley glanced at her from the corner of his eye. He thought about the previous night. About the man lying on the ground in a pool of his own blood and flayed flesh. "And you're so sure you know him that well?"

"Better than he knows himself." Ana ambled off the escalator first with an exaggerated step. "How else do you think he made it this far?"

"What do you mean?" He stuffed his hands into the pocket of his hoodie, grazing the envelope of money. Pulling his hands free, he brushed them off on his jeans and led the way toward the party section.

"How many bottles do you think I've had to find and empty?" She picked at the hem of her dress. "Between Kade and me, and maybe Alex, we kept Henry from ending up in a ditch somewhere."

A hollow ache pulsed in Wesley's stomach. "You don't seem too bothered by Henry's drinking or drug use."

"He's an addict. Yelling, arguing, and fighting won't fix him. I've had to learn that the hard way." She glanced away when they passed the aisles of liquor. "The best I can do is try to keep him from destroying himself. Besides, when you know why someone is burying themselves, you can have a little more sympathy and a little less judgment."

He wound his way through shelves holding vast amounts of party supplies. "If it doesn't concern me, it's not my business."

"He's your teammate now. Whatever happens to him *is* your business."

Wesley's shoulders sagged. "Fine. Why does he do it?"

Ana tossed up a hand. "Our mom died. I thought you knew that."

"Both my parents died. And my brother."

"Everyone deals with their grief differently." She shrugged. "I have my art and Dad, but Henry—he's never handled his emotions well, and he doesn't get along with Dad at all. It doesn't help that he wasn't exactly planned, and admittedly, Dad did *not* take it well when Henry came out as pan. Dad realized his error and handled it better when I came out, but the damage was already done. Their relationship has never been good. It just got even worse after that. He even broke Dad's nose right before he decided to move out."

Wesley's brows rose. Again, he found himself recalling the countless times Henry would show up at his house covered in bruises and asking Kade if he could spend the night. Henry and Kade had never answered Wesley's questions. He'd grown accustomed to shoving the moments aside. Analyzing the memories cast Henry's addiction in a violent light. Wesley tossed Ana a side eye, wondering at her omission—whether it was on purpose or whether she knew as much as she proclaimed.

"I don't know what happened." Ana released the hem of her dress—the threads now frayed. "I came home to find Dad bleeding all over the place. A vase was smashed, and Henry was already gone. He left almost everything in his room."

Letting her words sit with him, Wesley shifted his attention to the wall of masks. Any mask he could've imagined stared back at him. Ones that covered the top half of the face—like the one Elsey wore. Ones that covered the eyes. Ones that covered the entire face. Lace ones. Plastic ones. Feathered ones. Animal-like ones. Plain ones.

"This one." Ana plucked one from the wall and passed it to him.

Wesley stared down at the mask. A plain black plastic mask meant to cover the entire face. Narrow eye sockets and a sealed mouth. A black sleeve covered the back to slip it over the head. It would conceal his identity entirely. Keep him safe. *Keep Taliyah safe.* He grabbed a second one for Charlotte.

Facing Ana, he saw her shifting on her feet and plucking at the hem of her dress again. "You didn't want to just talk about Malini and Henry, did you?"

She sucked in her bottom lip, thinking over her words carefully. "There's an art competition coming up. Kade was going to enter with me since I was nervous."

He nodded, glancing down at the masks. "He talked about it."

"He gave me his pictures and his application to submit with mine. Jemma thinks I should still submit them or see if Dad can get the museum to do a special tribute for him." Ana released the hem of her dress again to gesture with her hands. "I know how I'd feel if someone took something that belonged to my mom and used it without permission. It doesn't matter how long it's been since she died. Kade was your brother. That's your decision."

A cold tremor rose in the spot where Wesley stood. Goosebumps set over his skin despite his thick hoodie. A soft warmth wrapped around his heart, dulling the sting of loss. He rubbed the back of his neck. "Photography was the one thing he did for himself. He gave everything else he had to take care of the rest of us. He deserves a lot more than a wall in a museum, but if he wanted to share his art, I'll honor that."

"I'll talk to Dad." She nodded. "He really liked Kade. Maybe Henry went everywhere with Kade in the hopes that some of that would rub off on him."

Wesley let a sly smile tug his lips. "The last thing Henry needs is more people rubbing him in any way."

Lavender hues colored the sky. Leaves shaded honey gold and phoenix orange from native beech and birch trees scattered across the road. Henry followed Elsey past the high school. Past thick forest lined with dying foliage.

The buzzing effect from his last pills was muted. Waking the itch beneath his skin. Submitting to the sharp tap deep in his brain—drowning the rich dulcet harmony of a classical symphony playing through his radio. He tugged the pill bottle free from his coat pocket. Plopping a single red pill on his tongue, he reached under his seat for the fifth of whiskey he kept hidden. The smoky flavor burned away the monsters in his mind before they could rise. The itch and the tap died under the tingling warmth reclaiming him.

Nearing the edge of the city, a rusted mailbox lay in a ditch. Faded stickers flaked off the side. He could still read the name—**Yhu**.

Henry followed Elsey up a dirt road breaking the line of trees. They parked before a crumbling Victorian house surrounded by an overgrown yard. Nature took over the property some time ago.

The house's blue paint faded to green and blended with the mold growing on the sides. Chunks of a wrap-around porch rotted away. Steps collapsed into the dirt. Vines crawled over the sides of the house and claimed white pillars. Boards covered every window except the highest ones in a spire at the back. White gingerbread molding, now painted by weather and time, managed to remain intact as the single reminder of what the house might've been.

Henry climbed out of his car. The wind tugged his dirty blond hair combed back from his face. He faced Elsey. She shrugged out of her leather jacket and draped it on her motorcycle. A maze of stitched stars covered her distressed hi-low long-sleeve black tee. The ragged cuffs of her patched yellow corduroy pants reached past the thick soles of her combat boots and skimmed the ground.

Elsey arched an eyebrow at his plain burgundy V-neck, black sweatpants, and black sneakers. "I didn't know you owned sensible clothing."

"I prefer to look like I have my life together." He smirked.

His scent—alcohol and tobacco blended with amber musk—caught the air. Her scowl deepened. "You *smell* like someone who drove under the influence."

He held up a finger. "El, everything I do is under the influence."

Elsey crossed her arms. "You brought a flask to your first fight. You drank to and from Purgatory. I don't even know how many pills you took yesterday or today."

A deep frown twisted his lips. "I'm doing what I can to function."

"I know." She bit her tongue, pushing away the memory that haunted her heart before she had to relive it. "I know it's not easy. But if you're not careful you'll end up being the person I have to save. Again."

Silence fell over them like a weight, straining the unraveled threads between them with unspoken words.

Looking into her unreadable eyes, Henry steeled himself against the ache in his chest. He nodded to the house. "What is this place?"

She scanned the building and surrounding woods. "Someone I knew used to live here."

He stared at the golden halo surrounding her from the lowering sun. "Where are they now?"

"I don't know." She took in each crack inking the walls like scars veining flesh.

"Are we going inside?"

"Not yet. We'll practice out here." She stomped toward the far side of the overgrown yard. "I need to see what you can do, first. Show me your powers. Then, I'll teach you a few basic fighting moves."

Shedding his coat, he followed in her wake until he stood six feet away. He held up a hand. "Don't move. I don't know the range yet or if I can change it except for the choking thing."

Elsey nodded.

He focused on a line of trees to the left. Balling his hand into a fist, he reached into his mind to a scarlet vein of pulsing energy. He pulled it forward. It flowed to his fingertips. He opened his hand.

The air shuddered under his touch. Curling forward in a wave that bent the trees toward the ground. Snaps and pops echoed. Twisting his hand upward, he closed his fist. The wind **whooshed** back. Thinning with a speed that flayed the bark from the trees and ripped the remaining leaves from the branches. He dropped his hand to his side. Letting the energy inside him abate.

"And the choking?" Elsey watched the leaves spiraling on ribbons of air to the ground. "How do you do that?"

Henry shoved his hands in his pockets. He grasped for a pill bottle that wasn't there. "It's kind of a combination of the two. It thins but congregates it to a central point."

"So, your other power. Are you able to do more than cause earthquakes?"

He nodded. Tugging the energy forward again, he directed his gaze at a spot in the yard a couple of feet in front of him. The ground began to rumble. A crack slipped through the grass. Clumps of grass and loose dirt tumbled inside the widening gap. He felt for something solid to grasp. A boulder ripped through the earth and flung into the naked trees.

Elsey arched a brow.

"If you're impressed by that, you should see the other powers I have." A smirk curled his lips. "You don't need to teach me anything with those though. I'm an expert."

Her expression flattened, and she started walking to him. "It doesn't look like you need lessons with this either."

"That's not much." Henry swept his hand toward the boulder and crack in the earth. "And sometimes, things happen. Like the earthquakes. On the bridge, I didn't even mean to do it. I know you have powers, and your father does, too. But when that man pointed a gun at you, I lost it. If I was actually trying, I would've done more."

"Like when you tore that man's skin from his body last night?"

"I didn't mean to do it. I—"

"Lost control." She stopped with a foot left between them and crossed her arms. "There may be more you can do, but it sounds like that's not the problem. The problem is your emotions. You have to get them under control."

Taking a deep breath, he met her eyes. "How do you do it?"

"What makes you think I have mine under control any better than you?"

"I've not seen you use your powers since we were twelve." Recalling the incident on the bridge, he shoved his hands into his pockets. "Well, except your speed and strength, and you watered that down. But I saw you fix your father's car."

Elsey tucked a red curl around her ear. "I try not to use my powers unless I have no choice. That doesn't mean I have control. Even I slip up sometimes."

"How do you control yourself?"

"I find something real. Something to hold onto." Her eyes shifted over his shoulder. Fixing on the rudimentary unrefined blacked-out frame of her motorcycle. "Sometimes it doesn't work, but it's the only thing that's helped so far."

He searched her face. As though her harsh lines would tell him more than her words. As though he could dig secrets from her cracks like stones in the earth. "What if I don't have something to hold onto?"

"You do." Elsey looked at him. The strange haunting wave passed through her like a flare shot in a barren wasteland. She swallowed the flickering warmth growing in her chest. "You just need to find it."

The frayed threads laced tighter in the space between them. The weight continued to hold them in place.

Biting her tongue until she tasted copper, she dropped her arms to her side. "Hit me."

"What? No." He stepped back.

Elsey rolled her eyes. "I need to teach you how to fight. That means I need to know what I'm working with. You won't hurt me."

"And if I do?"

The muscle at the corner of her mouth twitched upward. "If you somehow *manage* to hurt me, I'll reward you."

Henry watched her lips twitch up with the hint of a smile before returning to a stubborn scowl. Lifting his brows, he smirked. "What kind of reward?"

Rolling her eyes, a clouded memory—too blurry for her to see—dragged a bold sense of daring to her surface. "If you manage to hurt me, I'll answer one of your questions."

"You've been answering my—" His eyes widened. "Oh, you mean a question about *you*."

She held her hands out to her side. "Now, are you going to hit me?"

He tossed his gaze up to the sky. "I can't believe I'm agreeing to this."

Henry balled his right hand into a fist and slammed it into her left arm. A small **hmp**, almost reminiscent of a laugh, escaped her.

"Okay, first, your thumb goes on the outside of your fist unless you want to break it." Elsey covered her mouth when her lips twitched more. Returning to her stoic expression, she pulled a thick hair tie from her wrist and pulled her hair back. "I have until Sunday to teach you enough for you to defend yourself. Let's get started."

SIX

Darkness felt heavy—like a living entity—as Elsey drove beyond the gates and followed the long driveway. The trees loomed overhead like fingers scraping the sky. The faint trickling of the stream murmured on the wind. Stars and the moon shone above, unobstructed by the absence of city lights. Any comfort they might've brought her slipped away the nearer she came to the glass house.

Steering to the right, she parked in the attached garage and let herself inside. She followed a long white hallway into her father's study. Her eyes found the fourth bookshelf again. Forcing her eyes away, she reached the door to her room. Her hand poised over the knob.

"Elsey, come upstairs." Marnie's voice called from the second floor.

Forcing back a groan, Elsey climbed the stairs.

She walked between the coffee table and the sofa. Her eyes went to the yard, lit by bright light shining from the walls of windows.

"You're tracking dirt on my rug!" Marnie gawked at Elsey from the open square arch to the kitchen. Her thick red curls were pulled in a tight, high bun. A floral A-line dress accented her small, delicate frame.

Elsey glanced down to see dirt and dried blood caked into the white fur blanketing the floor.

"Elsey." Gregor strolled to the arch, a glass of red wine in hand. A perfectly tailored black suit made him appear taller than he was. "You know the rule about your boots in this house."

Biting her tongue, Elsey pulled off her boots and set them aside.

She bent down and pressed a hand to the rug. Her stomach tangled into a ball. She tugged on the vibrant essence flowing in the back of her brain. It ran to her fingertips. The dirt and debris disappeared. The hum in her mind rose to a soft buzz. She blinked. Once. Twice. Nothing else changed. She stood and fixed her attention on her parents.

Shades of pink flushed Marnie's cheeks. "You made it just in time. Dinner is on the table."

Gregor led the way through the kitchen into the dining room. White light from the chandelier above touched every inch of the room, stopping any darkness from filtering through the wall of windows. A glass table sat in the center of the room with three place settings laid out. Seared pork chops, mashed potatoes, and roasted broccoli had been portioned on each plate. The lone glass of water designated Elsey's chair, which placed her back to the wall. Gregor sat across from Elsey, leaving the head of the table for Marnie.

"Dinner looks wonderful." Setting his glass by his plate, he kissed his wife's hand. "Just like you, Dear."

Elsey grimaced at the hunk of meat on her plate.

Gregor's lips curled higher when he noticed Elsey's expression. "Your mother went through a lot of effort to cook a nice meal for us. I expect you to eat it. There's no dog here for you to feed the pork chop too anymore."

Her stomach churned like an angered sea. She lifted her fork and speared a head of broccoli. Her skin itched under her parents' gaze. Elsey kept her eyes on her plate, eating only the broccoli and the potatoes. She listened to her parents. Cutting their pork chops and sipping on their wine. Even the slightest shift in their chairs filed away in her mind. Calculating the degree to which they turned their bodies. The move to pick up a utensil. The dotting of their napkins on their mouths.

The moment Gregor stopped, she peered at him through her long, scarlet lashes. Waiting for him to speak.

"Do you want to talk about your behavior now or in my study after dinner?"

"How about we don't talk at all?" Elsey slammed her teeth together, cursing her uncontrollable tongue.

Marnie's knife scraped across her plate, echoing into the glass room. Lifting the knife, she pointed it at Elsey. "We have been through this. You do *not* tell your father what to do."

"Yes, ma'am." Elsey lowered her gaze to her plate.

Gregor watched his wife and daughter over the rim of his wine glass. He swallowed and returned his glass to its place. "I called your school today."

Stabbing her fork into her mashed potatoes, she kept her eyes down. Her other hand gripped her thigh.

"It's the second day, and you haven't attended a single class." He kept his tone casual, only pausing to swallow a piece of broccoli. "Again."

Elsey dug her nails into her corduroy pants. "I collect my assignments and leave. I turn it all in the next day."

"We talked about this when we learned of this last year." He fixed his keen eyes on her. "You said you would attend your classes this year. You said you would stay at school with your peers."

"Why should I?" She jerked her head up. The waves in her stomach threatened to turn violent. "Nobody there likes me. I don't have friends."

"Not even Henry?"

She didn't move.

He pressed on, twirling his fork and shaking his head. "You're not at school, but you don't come home until three, sometimes four in the morning. Is that who you're with? Are you spending time with that *worthless* addict?"

Elsey's eyes widened against her efforts to maintain a flat expression. The sharp bite of rage flared inside her, but something colder chilled her bones. She didn't know whether to snap or to keep her lips sealed.

"You're talking to Henry?" Marnie's thin brows rose. "First, that wretched motorcycle and now you're talking to that drugged-up womanizer. Is that why you've been staying out all night? What's next, Elsey? Are you planning to run away?"

"Henry's not like that." Thorns of ice tore through Elsey's racing heart. "Besides, I'm not his type. He's not into ugly freaks like me."

"Do you think a boy like that cares?" Gregor tossed his napkin next to his plate and leaned forward. "You said you don't have friends. You talk to no one. You would be a victory for him to add to his growing list."

"You invite his father to every party you have!" Elsey let her fork **clank** to her plate. "You can't be sanctimonious when you let Micha brag about his last child bride to your daughter!"

Marnie pointed at Elsey. "You are out of line! You don't question our decisions. You are the child here."

"Did this start when you danced with him?" Gregor let his hands rest on the edge of the table, training all his concentration on Elsey's face.

"They danced together?" Marnie dropped her silverware and looked at Gregor. "When? Why did you let that happen?"

"It was at the benefit for the latest museum exhibit." Gregor twisted toward his wife. "You were speaking in private with Gravenor and Rowe about the Sentry Project at the time. He asked while I was talking to her. Donors were there. I didn't want to cause a scene."

Elsey bit her tongue and took a steadying breath. "I ditched him after only a few seconds. I told you, he's not interested in me."

"And yet you're still talking to him." Marnie tossed her hands up. "What else are you doing with him?"

"Nothing." Elsey's eyes widened and she sat back.

Marnie tapped her pastel pink nails against the tabletop. "You can't get preg—"

"Mother!" Elsey slammed her hands down. The glass rang with a sharp sound when her bracelets connected with the table. "I'm not doing *anything* with Henry! How many times do I have to tell you that he's not interested in me? He does not like me! He has never once asked me out on a date, hit on me, or asked me to go to bed with him! It's never been like that!"

"It's not him I'm concerned with." Gregor drew the attention back to him. He nodded to Elsey. "Do you like him?"

Elsey steeled herself under that strange wave of emotion flashing through her stomach, adding an extra edge to the frost chilling her. "No. I don't."

"Because if you have feelings for him, then—"

"I said, 'I don't!'" Elsey stood, shoving her chair. "You can't have feelings for anybody when you don't have a heart."

Without waiting to be dismissed, she stormed out.

"Elsey! Come here!" Marnie shouted.

"Just let her go. I'll deal with her later," Gregor said.

"Like you have been dealing with her?" Marnie snapped.

A loud **smack** echoed through the house, following Elsey into the living room.

Gregor's voice murmured low, "I'm sorry. I'm sorry."

Elsey snatched her boots beside the couch. Her hands and feet tingled, sweeping through her until she went numb. Her body felt foreign. Like she stood in the back of herself and someone else moved her limbs. Taking deep breaths, Elsey tried to count. A wave of dizziness crashed through her.

Blinking, she found herself in the garage—unable to remember the steps she'd taken to get there. She pushed through her thoughts to remember. All she found were locked doors barring her eyes from any memories that might fill in the gaping holes she'd been left with. Taunts and cruel remarks circled her, ravaging her soul. Her heart beat a vicious rampage.

She revved her motorcycle to life, silencing every harsh word digging fresh wounds into her mind. Elsey tore through the manicured lawn, cutting through the thick line of trees. She steered onto the small wooden bridge crossing the stream and shot through the hole in the wall. She continued toward the city. Searching for an escape—for something to hold onto.

August 31, 3696

The *tap-tap-tap* of Wesley's highlighter on the page echoed off the walls in his small bedroom. His other hand ran over his newly shaved head. Sitting at his desk facing the wall, he focused on re-reading the book he'd been given when he attended the summer program at Forge Institute.

Flipping the page, the paper caught the side of his finger with a sharp slice. He flinched. A drop of blood leaked from the tiny cut. He wiped it on his faded jeans and wrapped the cuff of his long-sleeved grape-colored shirt over his finger. He returned his attention to the words before him.

Kade traipsed in, carrying his black oversized cardigan in one hand and his socks and shoes in the other. Setting his shoes down, he pulled his cardigan on over his yellow T-shirt. "I'm taking Taliyah with me to go help the new neighbors. You want to go with us?"

"Nope." Wesley re-read the line he was on.

"You sure?" Kade sat down on the edge of Wesley's small twin bed to cuff the hem of his jeans and pull on his socks. He shoved his feet into his sneakers. Focusing on Wesley, he could see the dull red and lemon-yellow wrapping around the vibrant green of his heart—anger and fear smothering him. "She's in your grade. It'd be nice for her to know someone at school."

"She knows you, right?" Holding in a groan, he read the same line again.

"Wes," Kade sighed, eyeing his younger brother's back. "I know you feel uncomfortable around people, but you might feel better if you put yourself out there more."

"I don't feel *uncomfortable* or *scared* or whatever other words you want to use to describe it." Wesley dropped his highlighter to his book. He glanced at the clock on his bedside table. 9:20 A.M. *Once they're gone, I can focus.* "I have things I want to do, and they don't include dealing with drama or anything that comes along with people."

Hanging his head low, Kade pressed his hands against his forehead. He took a deep breath and looked up again. Wading through all the anger and anxiety rolling off Wesley. "What about how she feels attending a new school in a new city?"

Wesley tossed up his hand and fixed a glare on the tiny closet to his left. "That's not my problem."

"Come on. She probably feels alone and scared."

A sharp bite of anger flared in Wesley's stomach. He spun around in his chair to face his older brother. "You mean like how *you* and just about everyone else in this stupid city probably made Elsey feel before she disappeared?"

Kade's eyes widened. "Why are you bringing her up? She's been gone for—"

"I just don't like it when you preach to me about 'doing the right thing' when you've literally acted no better. It's hypocritical and annoying."

"Hey!" Kade's heavy brows knit together in a frustrated V. "I'm not trying to preach to you. I'm just saying maybe you could use some friends. That's all. You spend most of your time working or studying. You don't seem to enjoy spending all your time here around me and Taliyah, especially when Henry's over."

Wesley gripped the back of his chair and gestured with his free hand. "That's because Henry's annoying and has the I.Q. of an empty box of peanut brittle."

Kade shot him a hardened look but ignored the harsh remark. "It would be good for you to connect with people."

"Stop!" Blood boiling, Wesley tossed his hands up again. "Just stop! Stop acting like my fucking parent! You're my brother. You're only fifteen, Goddammit!"

"Watch it!" Kade motioned toward the hallway. Taking in a deep breath to calm himself, he pushed past the dull red anger pouring into him and urging him on. "I told you not to use that language when Taliyah's here."

"When is she not here?" Wesley gestured wildly. "Even when you're not here, she's here! I have to watch her and pretend like I'm an adult when I'm not! Why can't I be a normal teenager with a normal life? Maybe if you didn't boss me around and pretend you're my parent, I would enjoy being around you like I used to. I need you to be my brother, not my parent."

Kade squeezed his eyes closed and took another deep breath. He squelched the trembling ache bubbling up in his throat from his own pain. Exhaling, he stood and walked into the hall. "Come on, Taliyah! Let's go!"

"Coming!" Her bedroom door flung open, and she bounded out, wearing a pink puffy coat over a blue unicorn-printed dress. Her sneakers lit up with rainbow colors with each step, matching the barrettes clipped in her short braids. She clutched a green teddy bear dressed in a pink dress in one hand and a sparkling holographic bookbag in the other.

"You can't take Jeff with us." His emotions already began to calm with her joyous energy settling over him with the radiant white light glowing from her heart.

"I'm not." She marched into the room and shoved Jeff into Wesley's hands. "Watch him until I get back."

Kade pressed his hand to his forehead. "Taliyah, what do you say when asking Wes to do something?"

"Or else, Butt-face." She shot Wesley a hard look.

Wesley pressed his lips together, uncertain whether he should laugh or be annoyed.

"We'll keep working on it." Sighing, Kade ushered Taliyah out of the room. He glanced at Wesley. The same trembling ache radiated in his chest. "Make sure you eat some lunch."

"Whatever." Wesley put his back to his brother and plopped the teddy bear on his desk. He scanned his fingers for the paper cut he had received. Unable to find it, he dismissed it and fixed his attention on his book.

Time drifted around him.

Tension pulled his shoulders back and tightened his muscles. He pressed his teeth against his bottom lip. His foot bounced up and down.

Still, the tension wound him tighter.

He read line after line after line. Not taking in any information. The words just stood as a barrier to keep the rest of his thoughts at bay. He tapped his highlighter with rapid pace against the pages. His short hair brushed against his palm while he rubbed his head.

Nothing brought ease.

The tension continued to build. Rising until his body flushed with heat.

The front door **creaked** open.

"We're back!" Kade called, stepping into the room with a sleepy Taliyah in his arms. A slight film of sweat slicked his deep brown skin. "I'm putting her down for a nap. Did you eat?"

Wesley looked at his clock. 1:45 P.M. *Shit.* "Uh … yeah."

Kade stared at him and gave a short nod. "Sure, you did." He grabbed Taliyah's teddy bear off Wesley's desk. "I'll make a few grilled cheeses if you want some."

"Okay." He started to return his attention to his book and halted. The memory of their earlier argument twisted his stomach. "Hey, sorry about earlier."

Pausing in the doorway, Kade glanced over his shoulder. "It's all right." He offered a small smile. "I still love you."

Wesley pressed his lips together and nodded with a tight flat smile. He turned to his book. The tension eased in his shoulders, and his breathing softened. He was able to immerse himself in his studies, the words reaching him without any barrier.

Knock. Knock. The muffled sound reached out from the hall.

"Wes, can you get that?" Kade shouted from Taliyah's room.

"Yeah." Eyes not leaving the page, he carried his book and highlighter to the front door. He set his highlighter in the crevice of the spine and opened the door. Attention glued to the paragraph before him until he felt the light breeze on his face.

He glanced up, fixing his gaze on a girl about his age with eyes that collected all the browns and greens and ambers of a forest untouched by humanity. His heartbeat quickened—roaring in his ears. Sweat sprung up on his palms, slicking the cover of his book and sending it in a tumble toward the girl's feet.

"Oh no!" Her voice, soft and melodic like a bird's song, met his ears. She moved with a speed he didn't expect, catching his book and highlighter in an awkward hold. She flipped the book around, reading the cover—*The Biology of the Surface of the Cell*. Her smooth forehead creased with thick lines. "You're reading *this*? Your brother wasn't kidding."

He stared at her.

The wind made her thick, dark hair—tied in a high ponytail—dance. The sun warmed her beige tawny skin to a satin copper tan. Standing in white running shoes, she was only a handful of inches shorter than him. Neon green athletic shorts and a gray tank top showed off her toned, sinewy build.

"You're Wesley, right?" she asked, holding the book and highlighter out to him.

Realizing she had been talking to him, he scrambled to catch up. To push past the heavy dryness on his tongue as if he'd been sucking on a chunk of granite.

"Wesley am I, yes." *Shit! I sound like Yoda!* Blinking, he shook his head. "Sorry, I meant yes, I'm Wesley. Most people call me Wes though. Well, not most people. My brother and sister. And Henry. And the people at work ..." He continued to ramble on despite the protests in his mind. *Jesus Christ! Why can't I stop talking? Someone please shut me up!*

She stifled a laugh and motioned toward his book still in her hands.

"Oh right." A hint of red flushed his full, rounded baby face. He took his book and grasped it tight. "Thank you. I—" *No. Don't start rambling again. She'll think you're an idiot.* "Thank you."

"Sure thing." She nodded, scratching at the skin beside her thumb. "I'm Charlotte, by the way. I don't know if your brother told you about me. My dad and I just moved here."

Catching himself before he could go adrift, he forced himself to nod. The heavy dryness coated his tongue again. *What's wrong with me?*

"Anyway," she said, glancing past him toward the living room. "Is he here? He told me to stop by to get the information for the church he goes to."

Great. She goes to church. She's going to think I'm a heathen. Wesley shoved his thoughts aside so he could answer, but a sugar-coated web trapped every word he'd ever learned on his tongue.

Rushing from Taliyah's room, Kade halted—noticing the enamored gaze on Wesley's face. He balled up his hand and pressed it against his mouth, hiding his mischievous smile. He walked down the rest of the hall and moved to Wesley's side so he could see Charlotte. Pink and lemon-yellow swirled together in her heart, filling Kade with nervous energy and the warmth of kindness. "Hey, sorry about that. I see you two met."

"Yeah." Charlotte's eyes lingered on Wesley before shifting to Kade. "I was asking about that information for that church."

"Oh yes!" Kade shoved his hand in his pocket and retrieved a crumpled piece of paper. "I hope you don't mind; it's written in crayon. Taliyah was nice enough to let me borrow one with the stipulation that I demand you and your dad sit with us."

"Of course." She smiled and turned to Wesley. Her fingers went to the small silver bird charm encircling her neck. "Will I see you there, too?"

Wesley's deep-set eyes bulged. *Oh shit! No! What do I say?* All his words remained caught up in a tangled mess.

Kade nudged Wesley in the side with his elbow, attempting to jostle him into speaking. When his younger brother didn't talk, he faced Charlotte. "Wes doesn't go to church. But like I said earlier, you two are in the same grade, so you'll probably see a lot of each other."

Chewing on the inside of her cheek, she nodded and tucked the piece of paper in the pocket of her shorts before pulling out a pair of small headphones. "Well, thank you for the information." She motioned behind her. "I should go on my run."

"You can't," Wesley blurted. Eyes bulging again, he sucked in a deep breath and rubbed the back of his neck. "I mean, it's not safe to go running around here alone."

Charlotte looked at him, meeting his eyes with a spark glimmering in her eyes. "I appreciate the concern, but I promise I can take care of myself." She shrugged, eyeing him up and down. "You're welcome to join me though if you want."

He pulled in another deep breath and held it. Telling himself not to gawk. She flashed a small smile and trotted down the steps. He watched her break into a sprint. "I think I believe in God now."

"No, you don't." Kade shook his head. "And don't be blasphemous in this house."

Wesley darted down the hall and into his room. He tossed his textbook and highlighter on his bed and dug through his dresser. Changing into a pair of gym shorts and a navy T-shirt. He hurried into the hall, pulling on mismatched socks and his only pair of tennis shoes as he went.

Kade—still standing in front of the door—fought his smile. "What are you doing?"

"I've decided to take up running."

"You hate running. You hate all sports." Kade gestured outward with his hand. "The only exercise you even remotely like is fight training, and you haven't done that in two years."

"I don't know what you're talking about. I love running. And if I didn't before, I'm certain I'll love it now."

"Of course, you will." Kade nodded, losing all ability to contain his smile.

Wesley shoved the screen door open and ran down the steps, narrowly missing Henry, who was just starting up them. "Hi, Henry! Bye, Henry!"

Henry jerked back to watch Wesley run through the yard and cut onto the winding road. He whirled back toward Kade and lifted a finger. "Did he just use my name and not Idiot?"

"Forgive him. He's a bit distracted." Kade swept his hand up toward a distant point on the road. "I'm sure he'll make up for it later."

Following Kade's hand, Henry nodded with a smirk curling his lips. "I understand."

"No!" Kade pointed at Henry.

Henry spun around, continuing up the steps. "What?"

"This is the only person Wes has ever liked, at least in a way that is so painfully obvious. You will not ruin it for him."

"All I said was I understand." Henry shrugged, stepping into the trailer. "Besides, I have a new girlfriend."

"What?" Kade's thick eyebrows shot upward. "Since when?"

He shut the door and faced Henry, allowing him to see his heart and feel his emotions. Shades of blue and red coated in a thick layer of gray and black—passionate and positive energy swallowed by a bottomless pit of despair and darkness. Kade shoved the emotions out and closed off his mental bridge before they could swallow him whole.

"Since last night." Stuffing his hands into the pocket of his tailored trousers, Henry retrieved his flask and took a quick sip. He fished a bottle of pills from his pants. "Well, if you want to get technical, I've had once since—"

"No." Kade took the pill bottle from him before he could get it open. He lifted the hem of Henry's vermillion cashmere sweater and tucked the bottle back in Henry's pocket. "Put the flask away, too. Taliyah's home."

Henry took another swig and shoved the flask in his pocket. Speaking as though he hadn't been interrupted, he picked up where his train of thought diverged without finishing his previous thought. "Ana and I went to the museum where we ran into Jemma and Malini. The security guards followed us, waiting for me to accidentally knock over another priceless artifact someone stole in the name of pretending to care about preserving history. I'm never going to live that down. You bump into one pedestal and—"

"*Henry.*" Kade held up his hand.

"Oh right. Sorry." He paused for a second to jump back a few carts on his train of thought. "So, Malini and I started talking. She asked me out on a date. We took a bus up to The Square and got burritos. It was all very romantic, I assure you. She asked me if I wanted to be her boyfriend, and well, now I have a new girlfriend."

Kade wound the cuffs of his cardigan sleeves into his fists. "What about what we talked about?"

"What about it? Me having another girlfriend doesn't go against what we talked about." Henry stuffed his hands into his pockets, clutching the pill bottle and flask. "I told you, I wasn't happy. Now, I can be happy. Is that a problem?"

"No. It's just—" Kade silenced himself and glanced down the hall to Taliyah's room. Grabbing the sleeve of Henry's sweater, Kade steered him through the kitchen. "Let's go to my room to talk about this."

IV

September 4, 3699

One

B **uzzzz.** Elsey looked at her phone, expecting the message from Henry earlier—around the same time he usually messaged every day. **Good morning.**

She sent her typical reply—already prepared. **Morning.** That was it.

All previous messages were similar brief exchanges. Good morning texts. Good night texts. How are yous? Happy birthdays and holiday wishes always followed shortly by a simple three-word phrase: *Under the stars.*

There were times when it seemed like he might want to send more. Dots would appear as if he were writing a message only for them to stop without sending anything. There were times when she stared at the phone, debating whether she should say something. If she should take the risk. Like now with her eyes locked on that simple morning exchange. *Maybe I can—*

Halting her thoughts, she set her phone down and returned her attention to her book. She let her mind drift with the words while her thumb and forefinger rubbed the small heart stitched in the corner of her black throw blanket.

The morning sun burned into the black paint covering her windows.

She continued to tunnel deeper into the book, clinging to the words to hold her steady. Ignoring the strange feelings twisted with the bitter pain that plagued her heart.

As a young god, Ares had been captured by the Aloadae giants, Ephialtes and Otos—sons of Aloeus. They cast him in a jar and bound him in chains too strong for his weakened youth. For three months, he remained imprisoned, growing feeble with each passing day. Their stepmother, Eeriboia, discovered the young god and delivered word to the young messenger god, Hermes. Hermes freed the young god from his bindings, and Artemis and Apollo delivered the killing blows to Ephialtes and Otos to avenge their brother.

"Elsey," Marnie called before knocking on the door. "Time to get up for school."

"Yes, ma'am." Elsey stood.

She folded her blanket and placed it inside the waiting box, slipping the unopened card between the top fold. She closed the box and replaced the tray covering her stashed items. Sliding the padlock into place, she held the metal in her hand and tugged on the energy in the back of her mind. The padlock closed, barring anyone from being able to open it without her permission. She pulled on her leather jacket and grabbed her rucksack. Elsey retrieved her book and phone from her sofa and tucked them into her rucksack before leaving the room.

A rich aroma of almond and chocolate filled the air before she entered the kitchen. The news played in the background while her father poured an entire pot of coffee into an oversized travel mug. "Good morning. How did you sleep?"

"I didn't." She reached for the breadbox on the counter.

"I already fixed it for you." Placing the lid on his mug, he pointed toward the glass table to the side of the room. "Even used that vegan stuff you asked me to get. I don't know why you like it."

Her morning blueberry bagel topped with cream cheese waiting in her normal spot. A glass of water sat next to it.

Elsey crossed to the table. "Thank you, sir."

"You're welcome." Gregor took a drink from his mug and continued to watch her. "You returned late again last night."

Her shoulders stiffened. "I wasn't with him."

"Somehow," his lips curled up further as he said, "I think if I could read your mind, it would tell me otherwise."

She looked at him with every ounce of daring in her soul. "It's a good thing you don't have that ability."

"Is that a confession?"

"That's me telling you, it's none of your business." Elsey turned away from him and bit off a piece of her bagel.

His lips slipped to their normal position. "I'm the parent. Everything you do is my business."

Elsey didn't respond. Her attention focused on the flatscreen television fixed into the wall on the opposite side of the room.

The newscaster began to present the Daily Death List.

Lifeless faces scrolled along the right-hand side of the screen in a morbid display of who hadn't lived through the night. Some had names. Most didn't. Waiting for a heartbroken loved one to arrive at the morgue to identify and claim them after spotting them on the morning list.

Everyone watched it.

It didn't matter if they were missing a loved one. If they had a TV, they watched the list.

It was the morning reminder that everyone had. A reminder that life was not safe. The city was not safe.

And yet, Hallenwood——named for the founding family— prevailed as one of the safest in a world that was burning alive.

She counted as the faces scrolled by. A habit she'd developed long before she took to the streets. When the list had been in the triple digits.

Now, a little more than two years later, it dwindled to two digits. Still too many for her.

The constant pain twisting her heart in on itself reminded her.

Even one was too many.

The list ended with five less than usual. Seventy-five instead of eighty.

She told herself it was worth the loss of sleep. It was worth the risks that might come with her actions.

"Have you noticed the list shrinking?" Gregor sipped from his mug.

The muscle beside her mouth twitched. She stared at her empty plate. "Maybe it's the newest bank you opened. Your peasants now have a place to put all the money they don't have."

He turned his sharp gaze on her. "I expect you home by seven tonight or I'll take your motorcycle."

Elsey stood and carried her dishes to the sink. Hoisting her rucksack on her shoulders, she stormed past her father. "You can't take something you didn't give me."

"Heeeeenryyyyyy," Anastasia's lilting voice called through the shut door.

"It's open!" He pulled his berry cashmere sweater over his head.

The door **creaked** open and **clicked** shut. Ana's soft footsteps halted in the living room area.

"Be right there." Henry splashed water on his face. He glanced at the mirror over the sink. His reflection appeared more vivid. Like a three-dimensional rendering of himself popping out of the surface. The veins in his eyes appeared a brighter shade of red. A reminder that any pain and memories ravaging his mind, body, and soul were buried under the pills and liquor he'd consumed before even stepping out of bed.

Leaving the bathroom, Henry found his sister leaning against the sofa with Meow cuddled in her arms. Stray pieces of hair escaped her messy updo. A color-block sweater and hot pink jeans highlighted her full curves. Her flip-flops revealed her toe rings.

"Sorry," he said, shoving his keys and phone into the pockets of his black trousers. "I overslept."

"I'm used to it by now." Ana kissed Meow on the head and placed him on the couch. "Come on, I want to catch Elsey before classes start."

An ache fluttered in Henry's chest. He grabbed his overcoat and followed her.

The twins traipsed through Bedlam. Empty of any employees and partygoers, silence filled the building.

A chill hung in the air. Leaves skirted across the parking lot. They climbed into Ana's small yellow subcompact.

"Damn!" Henry's knees jammed into the dashboard, and he hurried to adjust it to a more comfortable distance. "Why is this seat so close?"

"I moved it up so I could fit supplies in the back." Ana cast him a side-eye and smirked. "It's not my fault you inherited Dad's giraffe legs."

He shoved his hands in the pockets of his coat, clutching the pill bottle waiting for him. Letting the silence speak for him. *We talked about this.*

Ana sucked in her bottom lip. She pulled out of the parking lot, following Boyer Road until reaching the museum. The sun glinted off the golden statue watching over the city. The morning light concealed the soft glow of HAL Tower's letters.

Turning onto Hallen Street, Ana headed south toward the bridge and the high school.

Henry kept his eyes fixed on the road. An ever-present rattle mumbled from his pockets.

Too many thoughts swirled in his head, too fast for him to find one to grasp. Shifting, he retrieved his flask and took a short sip. It didn't help. Darkness pushed against his mind, trying to force certain memories into view. He took another sip. Focusing only on the smoky sweetness of whiskey coating his tongue. On the burn slipping down his throat and filling his heart. Another sip. Another. Silence settled in him.

Rolling down the window, he breathed deep. Letting the crisp wind coming off the bay try to cleanse his forever-stained soul.

Ana tightened her grip on the steering wheel, thinking of some way to pull him back from the edge.

Turning into the school parking lot, Ana looked at him. "Do you think she'll go for it?"

"Of course. I wouldn't have told you otherwise."

"You better be right, or I'm blaming you."

"Spoken like the favorite child."

Shaking her head, Ana parked in her reserved spot. "Come on. Jemma's already inside."

Henry shoved open his door. He retrieved his cigarette case from his pocket and plucked one free at random. Lighting the cigarette, he trailed up the stairs after his sister. He noted the first parking space stood empty. Pulling a deep breath off his cigarette, he tried exhaling the tension clinging to him like a second skin.

Ana opened the door, passing through without waiting for him. Catching the door before it could slam shut in his face, he took a final drag off his cigarette. He dropped it to the ground and crushed it underfoot.

The school buzzed with life. Students rushed through the entrance, heading toward the cafeteria for a free breakfast or their lockers to gather supplies for class. Anastasia and Henry slipped through the crowd to reach Malini and Jemma standing near the bottom of the stairs.

Jemma spun around. Her silky black bob was pulled out of her face with silver barrettes. A tie-dye T-shirt dress brought out the warmth in her brown skin and eyes. Her ever-present flats did nothing to mask her height. She wrapped Ana in a tight hug, leaning down to place a firm kiss on her lips "Finally! I was worried something happened."

"Blame him." Ana motioned to Henry wandering past to lean against the wall. "He overslept."

"Sorry." He crossed his shiny black oxfords in front of him and smirked. "A little bird told me last night if she catches me driving under the influence again, she'll break my kneecaps, and I believe her."

"And it was easier to give up driving than your booze and pills?" Malini asked.

Henry glanced at his ex-girlfriend as if noticing her for the first time. She leaned against the stairwell leading to the second floor. Her long raven black hair hung in perfect ringlets over her shoulders. The same black sweater that once belonged to Kade covered the ruffled orange day dress hugging her slender body. The misty dark tones of her eyes were stained with a faint red hue from crying.

The small sting of guilt wrapped in a fresh coat of anger settled into his stomach. Pulling a bottle of pills from his pocket, he twisted the cap. "Seeing as the latter makes your presence more bearable, I'd say you should be thankful."

Red curls caught everyone's eye when Elsey strolled through the front door.

Henry dropped the pill bottle into his pocket and stood straight. His eyes devoured the black ripped jeans embracing her curves and the worn-out band tee peeking beneath her leather jacket.

With a glance at the assembled crowd, she pivoted—catching Henry's eyes for a single heartbeat—and headed toward the nearest hallway.

"Elsey!" Ana dropped Jemma's hand.

Stopping in her tracks, Elsey shot another look at Henry before turning around. She fixed her attention on Ana—not having to look up thanks to wearing combat boots and Ana being only a few inches taller.

Ana's eyes shined with her bright smile. "I'm not good with math or science, and I really don't want to fail. Henry suggested I ask you to tutor me since you're good at those subjects."

"What?" Jemma and Malini gasped.

Sipping from his flask, Henry watched in silence.

Elsey bit her tongue. She tightened her grip on the strap of her rucksack. "No."

"I told you she only cares about herself." Jemma crossed her arms and glared at Elsey.

Ana looked at Malini and Jemma. "You just don't know Elsey like Henry and me."

Malini tossed her head back and scoffed. "Henry doesn't know her as much as he would like."

Henry choked on his whiskey. He glared at his flask as if it betrayed him.

Elsey glanced at him, arching an eyebrow.

"It's not just about tutoring." Ana kept her attention on Elsey. "You and Henry are friends again. I want to be friends again, too."

"I don't have friends," Elsey said. Spinning away, Elsey avoided Henry's eyes and continued toward the hallway.

"You should stay away from her anyway. She's dangerous," Malini said.

Elsey stopped walking. Digging her nails into her palms, she pulled her shoulders back and forced the heat building in her chest to recede. "Ana, get my number from Henry."

Watching Elsey disappear down the hall, Henry retrieved a pill from his bottle and dropped it on his tongue. He looked at his sister. "I told you she'd agree to it."

three

"Why did I agree to this?" Wesley motioned toward the school. "It's pizza day in the cafeteria."

"We haven't gone running in a while." Charlotte pulled his green hoodie over her head and tossed it on the bench beside the track field. She straightened her pink tank top.

"I can't run with you in the morning anymore. I have to stay—" His words escaped him when he saw her jeans drop to the ground, revealing her short black gym shorts. Heat flushed his body. *Get a hold of yourself.* Forcing his eyes to her face, he gestured to his tattered jeans and gray and green long-sleeved raglan shirt. "I'm not even dressed to go running, and you have practice this afternoon. You don't even need to go running now."

She tied her hair in a high ponytail, accentuating her narrow forehead and high cheekbones. "It helps me clear my head." Sitting on the red synthetic rubber top of the track field, she stretched out to reach her toes. "You can go back and eat if you want, but I'm staying."

He watched her stretch from one side to the other. His mouth dried. His heart danced to a clumsy rhythm. His thoughts drifted to places he did his best to avoid, especially when they were alone. Sounds of birds and cars couldn't reach his ears. The sharp breeze couldn't compete with the fire kindling inside him.

Realizing he never replied, she noticed his eyes fixed on her. "Wes? Are you okay?"

Wesley forced out a hot breath and looked at the sky. "I'm fine." *Dammit. I'll just eat at work.* He took a few more deep breaths until his body calmed down. Dropping his gaze to her, he pulled his shirt overhead and tossed it on the bench. "Let's do this. But I get a head start."

She climbed to her feet, fighting not to stare at the hard muscles carved into his deep dark skin. Her eyes caught his as she took her normal spot on the track line up. A warm tingle spread through her.

He started the countdown. "Five … four … three …"

Charlotte looked at him. Heat rushed to her face. Smirking, she dashed away from the starting line. Chasing the heat from her body.

"Hey!" He tossed up his hands.

"Enjoy the view!"

Groaning, Wesley ran after her.

She had distance on him—and speed that had earned her medals and trophies.

He pushed himself to run faster. He kept his attention on her. Her long, toned legs. Her shorts. Her hair bobbing behind her.

His leg muscles screamed. His heart pounded. His lungs burned. He sucked in a deep breath.

Slowing to a jog, he sputtered a cough. "God, I hate running."

"What was that?" She called over her shoulder.

"I said, 'I think I'm dying!'" He flopped on the ground and waved her on. "You go on without me. Keep my hoodie to remember me by. Tell my sister I love her. Tell Jemma she can have my hours at work. Tell Henry he's a moron."

Charlotte walked over to him, placing her hands on her hips. Sweat beaded on her tawny skin. "You're a little dramatic, you know that?"

"I'm pretty sure I'm dead, so nothing you say can hurt me."

She gestured toward the track and the school. "If this is your idea of the afterlife, what does that say about you?"

He shielded his eyes from the sun and let his gaze roam over her once more. Meeting her eyes, the way the earthen shades popped in the sunlight left him mesmerized. "That I have great taste."

A fluttering ache traced through her at the sight of his dimpled grin. Unable to fight the burn from her cheeks, she reached down for his hand. "Come on. We'll walk until you get more—"

Wesley grabbed her waist and pulled her on top of him. His lips caught hers in a deep kiss. His tongue brushed over her bottom lip.

Her hands slipped over his bare chest. One clutched his shoulder. The other caressed his smooth skin, sending fiery tingles through him as her fingers trailed up to brush against the stubble of his short hair. Her tongue tangled with his.

He grasped her hips like he was holding onto a life raft. Knuckles paling, afraid to lose himself adrift in a sea of want. Resisting every temptation to let his hands wander to places he wanted to explore.

She shifted, eliciting a moan from him when her leg brushed against him.

Pulling back, Charlotte rested her forehead against his. "We can't."

"I know. I'm not ready for that either. Too big of a risk." Keeping his eyes closed, he breathed deep to try to calm himself. "It's just hard."

"I could tell."

"Not tha—" He smirked. "Well, yeah that, too."

She rolled off him and nestled into his side. He adjusted his arms to continue holding her against him.

Resting her head on his chest, her fingers traced the peaks and valleys defining his muscles.

"You're not helping."

"Sorry." She halted, flattening her hand against his chest.

He opened his eyes a sliver to glance at her. "I didn't say 'stop.'"

Giggling, she let her fingers resume dancing over his skin.

They lay in silence, listening to the wind drag leaves across the track. To cars passing on the distant road. To birds singing their autumn laments. Cuddled together in a rare moment of peace.

"Are you sure you don't mind me borrowing your car after school?"

"Of course not." Charlotte glanced up at him. "You have to pick up Taliyah and get to work somehow. My dad said he'd take off for lunch to pick me up, so I don't have to ask Jemma or Malini to stay after."

"I just wanted to be sure." Groaning, he sat up and rubbed his aching thighs. "My legs are going to feel like wet noodles."

"See," she said, sitting up beside him. "Cardio is just as important as fight training."

"I haven't been doing that either. I really need to get back to it. But—" Snaking an arm around her waist, he pulled her into his lap. He tugged her hair out of its ponytail. His smoke-filled eyes burned into hers. "I *hate* running. Always have."

Her heart shivered with butterflies taking flight in her stomach. She rested her arms around his shoulders. "Then why did you start running with me when we first met?"

Leaning in, he whispered the faintest kiss on her lips. "One guess."

The tingle from his kisses filled her body. Ensnaring his lips, she pulled him against her.

He buried one hand in her hair. The other held her around the waist, pressing her against him. Her fingernails dug into his back, driving his desires he fought to keep at bay.

The school bell blared over the campus. Breaking apart, they struggled to recover their breath.

four

Shades of black and gray curled across the midday horizon, like fingers of smoke scraping nails over the city to unleash its darkness.

Elsey could hear shouts from protesters as she leapt onto the roof of a building at the corner of the street. A man called above the other voices, declaring Purgatory the reason for the current hell the world was facing.

She tossed her eyes skyward and continued to her destination.

Nearing the rooftop of the renovated warehouse, she could see her motorcycle parked beside a small car like a beam of sunshine behind the building. Anastasia sat on the hood of her car. Her fuchsia and teal hair fell from her messy bun while she hunched over something in her lap.

Elsey jumped off the edge of the warehouse and landed on her feet.

Ana didn't lift her eyes from the sketchbook in her hands. A smirk, reminiscent of her twin's, curled her lips. "You always did have a flair for the dramatic. That's why you and Henry get along so well. He likes that sort of thing."

Arching a brow, Elsey slipped her mask off her eyes. "I'm going to talk with him about telling you about all this."

"Good luck with that." Ana scooted off the hood of her car. "My brother tells me everything. Well—" She closed her sketchbook and met Elsey's eyes without flinching. "There has only ever been one thing he hasn't said, but he doesn't have to."

Elsey recalled the ever-present rattle and scent of cigarettes and alcohol that announced Henry's presence.

Tucking her mask into her back pocket, she nodded toward the back entrance of Purgatory. "Inside."

Ana followed Elsey into Purgatory and up to the platform.

Luci hunched over her laptop on the red sofa in the den. Silver hair and dark red lipstick were the only hints of color to her all-black ensemble.

Tristan's boots were propped up on the coffee table with Gene's head resting in his lap. One thick arm slung over Gene's waist while he ran his fingers through Gene's hair with his other hand.

Gene almost seemed to purr. His hands were tucked into the long sleeves of his light orchid-colored sweater. He surveyed the radiant girl following Elsey. "And who's this ray of sunshine?"

"This is Ana." Elsey gestured between the group. "Ana, this is Gene, Tristan, and Luci."

Luci gave a curt nod. Tugging the sleeves of her black hooded jacket down over arms, she returned her attention to her computer.

Ana waved—her hand flecked with paint and smudged with charcoal. "Nice to meet you." Perking up, she focused her attention on Tristan. "Henry said you're the one making the suits or uniforms."

"I do more than that." Flashing a dazzling smile with his sharp canines glinting in the light, he nodded toward Elsey. "She is personally styled by Yours Truly. As am I." He gestured toward his outfit: a black long-sleeved tee with an embroidered image of a bat hanging in the center of a ribcage and a pair of black distressed jeans with pinstripe patches. Motioning toward Gene and Luci, he added, "They're both styled by thrift stores and bargain bins."

"Not true." Luci glanced up. "I wear your shirts."

"You'd get mad if I treated your clothes the way I treat mine." Gene kicked his legs on the sofa as if to emphasize the grease stains and writing scribbled on his army green cargo pants.

"Thanks for your consideration. *Liar.*" Tristan shot Gene a pointed look but let it fall with a rumbling chuckle. He gave a gentle pat to Gene's butt. "Come on. Let's get things ready for the evening"

Gene stood, revealing the graphic of a kitten in a floral bow tie on the front of his sweater. He kissed Luci on top of her head. Waiting for Tristan to join him, he twisted toward Ana. "Nice meeting you, Sunshine."

"You, too." She settled into their spot on the couch, folding her legs in front of her. She fixed her attention on Elsey. "I lied about needing tutoring."

"What?" Elsey balled her hands into fists.

"I needed an excuse because you won't talk to me."

Elsey's shoulders stiffened.

"It's been four years, Elsey." Ana frowned. "I know you and Henry were always closer, but I still want to be friends, too."

Elsey crossed her arms in front of her chest. "I wouldn't even be talking to Henry again if it wasn't for all this."

"That's a lie." Ana's eyes lit up with anger. "I told you, Henry tells me everything. You two kept in touch after you came back. It might not have been like before, but you talked. You text each other, checking on one another. He calls, and you answer. You buy each other gifts for birthdays and holidays. Even when he was dating Malini, you two talked in secret. I know it all. And then at the party, I saw you dance with him, but you didn't even say one word to me."

Elsey dug her nails into the sleeves of her shirt. "He texts me first. Always."

"Not the first time." Ana shook her head. "I know he snuck his number in your locker when you came back. You sent him a message with your number, and you've kept in touch ever since. I know. I'm the only one he's shown, but I've seen the messages. So, what is your problem with me?"

Taking a breath, Elsey searched for another excuse. "He made an effort."

"I did, too." She glared, hoping to prod the answer from Elsey. "Why him? Why not me, too? Just say it so I can—"

"I don't know!" Emotions Elsey couldn't name gripped her heart with hooked claws and threatened to drag her to her knees. "I don't know why. I just couldn't let him go. When I returned, I tried to let everything go. But for some reason, I couldn't let him go. I don't understand it, but I tried my hardest to let him go. I did. You saw the messages. All I give him are short answers. Whenever he calls, I listen in silence. When I leave him gifts, I never leave a note. I tried not to leave him gifts. I tell myself, 'Not this year. Not this holiday,' but still I leave one, unwrapped sitting on the sofa with as much detachment as I can. I've tried everything to purge him from me, and I can't. Somehow, someway, he dug himself into me, and I can't get him back out, and I don't know why."

Luci picked up her waiting glass of absinthe. She watched Elsey's eyes go to the far wall and Ana pick at her bright pants.

Replaying Elsey's words, Ana sucked in her bottom lip. She looked up at Elsey. "Do you mean you don't remember?"

"Remember what?" Meeting her gaze, Elsey shrugged. "I remember being friends with you and Henry and playing at your house. I remember your mom reading us stories and her knitting that blanket for Henry. I remember your dad making you come over to my house when your mom was getting worse. I remember thinking people cared about me, and then, I remember learning those people were dating people who hate me. That's what I remember."

Ana glanced over at Luci and back to Elsey. "That's it? Do you remember anything else?"

She shook her head. "I don't know what you're talking about."

Sucking in her bottom lip again, Ana stood. "Why do you want to let go of Henry?"

"Because I shouldn't have connections."

"And yet you're here." Ana gestured to Luci. "And now you have my brother and two other people on a team."

"That's different." Feeling the bite of her nails through her shirt, Elsey beat her emotions back with a fury that always kept her on her feet. "I don't have friends."

Ana's eyes blazed to life again. "Elsey, I want to be your friend. I have always wanted to be your friend. I understand that you feel hurt by me and Henry dating people who don't like you, but you didn't talk to me. You wanted nothing to do with me. You let *me* go. Do you think you're the only one who needed someone? Do you think you're the only one who has had to deal with bullies and rumors? Henry looks like a marble statue wished to be a real boy. It doesn't matter that he's fucked out of his mind ninety percent of the time or wouldn't know how to act normal if he had a gun to his head.

"People overlook it because of his face, because he's the epitome of society's standards of beauty, and because he's a guy. I don't get that same privilege. I'm not saying I think I'm ugly, but other people are not *nice* to me or about me. I've worked hard not to let it affect me, but it still hurts. You're not the only one who has had to deal with shit like that and who has felt alone. For the longest time, I've felt like only people who cared were Dad, Henry, and Jemma.

"I know that Jemma's scared of you, and I'm sorry about that. I've talked to her, but what do you want me to do? She loves me the way I am and doesn't make me feel like I'm not enough. And that's more than I can say for you."

Feeling the sour taste of guilt on her tongue, Elsey dropped her arms to her side. "She doesn't want you to have anything to do with me."

"Well, she's not the boss of me." Ana pressed her hand against her chest. "I make my own decisions."

Luci dropped her attention to her laptop. She watched the boxes showing the scenes for the different cameras in the city. Four dots— one green and three red—were in the bottom right corner. Her eyes went to Elsey and Ana. She took in Elsey's fists balled at her sides and her hardened gaze on the far wall. She watched Ana suck on her bottom lip and pick at the hem of her sweater. Again, she looked at her laptop screen, focusing on the dots in the corner. Glancing up at Ana, she set her glass down. "You can come help me while she's out with the team."

Ana clapped her hands together and grinned. "Really?"

Elsey whirled on Luci with a single brow arched. "Since when do you need help?"

"Since I have to be the eyes and ears of four people." Luci nodded to her laptop. "I can set her up with a laptop and half the cameras so we can both keep an eye on the city."

"Fine." Rolling her eyes, Elsey faced Ana. "If you want."

"Of course!" Ana turned to Luci. "Thank you!" She grabbed her sketchpad from the couch and jotted her number on the corner of a piece of paper. Tearing the slip off, she passed it to Luci. "I need to go, but message me when to be here."

Elsey waited until the door closed behind Ana before turning to Luci. "She won't be hanging out with me if she's helping you."

Luci pulled her phone from her pocket and rolled her eyes. "Oh no, I didn't even think of that."

Elsey narrowed her eyes. "What are you doing?"

"You can't control everything. If you're not careful you'll get them all killed."

Elsey tossed up her hands. "And you just brought her on to watch it happen. Why? So, she can blame me later?"

"Be real, Else." Shooting off a text to Ana, she set her phone down. "With your history, you were always going to be blamed."

"Fuck you."

"You know it's the truth. Even Henry thinks you're a killer. He said as much when he asked Tristan to fight his dad. They know the rumors. To them you're a murderer—a monster. You always will be to people like them." Luci lifted her glass, staring at the vibrant green drink. "Do you think that will change when they see what you really do? When they see what you're capable of? Even if it's to protect them, whether it's to shield them from the dark reality that lives in this city or to save their lives. When it comes down to it, you will *always* have the same stain on you that the rest of us hide. That stain doesn't wash out."

Elsey narrowed her eyes. "I don't know what you're playing at."

"Just trust me." She took a long drink before meeting Elsey's eyes. "All I have are this place, Tristan, Gene, and you. I won't lose you. Any of you."

"You worry too much about me." Elsey dropped her arms to her sides and spun toward the door.

Luci stared at her back. "Someone needs to."

five

Chugging what remained of her water bottle, Charlotte trudged out of the gym. The wind twisted her hair. Past the line of trees, she could see smoke curling into the clouds over the distant city.

Another fire turning someone's life to ash.

A car horn **bleated**, tearing her attention away before her thoughts could get caught in the embers. Her dad's small green car stopped beside her. She climbed in the front seat, dropping her tote onto the floorboard and Wesley's hoodie in her lap.

"How was practice?" he asked, turning around in the parking lot.

"Good." Feeling sweat cool on her skin, she closed the air vents pointed at her. "Did you get any sleep?"

"A little." He followed the road away from the school. The heavy bags under his eyes seemed to draw his face down.

"Any progress on the cameras?"

"Not yet." He shook his head. "I thought we were getting somewhere, but they all went offline the day before yesterday. We thought we finally got them all up and running, but then, Reagan and I noticed they were playing a day-long loop of the same day. We're back where we started."

Charlotte shifted in her seat to face him. "What are you going to do?"

"Hallen wants me to get with the security company that handles the stuff for Micha Adamson. Someone tried hacking into their cameras around the 25th."

She chewed on the inside of her cheek.

"Whoever it was, didn't get into the server." Merging onto the overpass crossing the bay, he pinched the bridge of his nose between his thumb and forefinger. "It doesn't make any sense. Hallen's system has even more encryption. The only way anyone should've been able to get into it would've been if they had access to the codes. The only people who have access are Hallen, his wife, and me."

Thinking of Elsey and Luci, her frown deepened. "So … more work?"

"A lot more."

Eyeing the island in the bay, her mind dashed along the broken path of her thoughts. Wandering between the rumors about Elsey's past and her and Wesley finding themselves entangled with her. "Oh, I might be out late with Wesley on Sunday. Our date didn't pan out the other night, so we're having a do-over."

He left the bridge behind and glanced at her. "How late?"

"I don't know." She shrugged, realizing she failed to ask Elsey how late she typically stayed out.

"You have school Monday."

"I know."

Turning beside the museum onto Boyer Road, he glanced at her again. "Do we need to talk about safe sex?"

"Dad!" She threw up her hands. Her cheeks burned hot. "We're not doing anything. We both want to wait, and he's too paranoid to even risk it."

"Okay, but if you two change your minds, I want you to be careful."

"Oh my goodness! We can't even afford the high cost of birth control on your salary."

"There are options besides pills and doctors."

Charlotte covered her face with Wesley's hoodie, muffling her words. "I'm going to die. Someone, please, end my suffering right now."

"It's an important conversation." He gestured outward with one hand. "I'd prefer if you guys didn't do it, but sometimes, it happens in the heat of the moment. I want you both to be safe. I can cover the cost of condoms."

She jerked up. "Oh my God!"

"But—"

"I will jump into traffic if you keep talking!" She pointed toward the cars passing on the opposite side of the road. "And don't you dare bring this up next time you see Wes!"

"I just want him to know—"

"He knows!"

Turning onto the road before he reached Bedlam, he held up his hand. "If I taught him and Kade how to drive, I can—"

"Dad! I will die if you mention it to him. They are probably picking my plot at the cemetery right now because of this conversation."

He shook his head, failing to hide a snorting laugh. "You're being a little overdramatic."

Charlotte narrowed her eyes. "I will be as dramatic as necessary if it gets you not to have the most mortifying conversation of my life with my boyfriend."

"Fine." Landon focused on the road. After three seconds of weighted silence, he fished his wallet from his back pocket. Shifting his attention between the road and his wallet, he retrieved a wad of cash.

She stared at the bills he pushed into her hand. "What's this for?"

"To buy what you need if you and Wesley *do* decide to … be intimate." Turning into the trailer park, he dropped his wallet in the center console.

"Dad—"

"Just take it." He held up his hand. "I trust you and him to be responsible, but I want you both to be protected if you're caught up in the moment. And if you need more, just ask. You don't have to tell me why, but if you need something, *anything*, then ask."

Playing with the silver bird charm around her neck, she continued to stare at the money. Her chest fluttered with a faint ache. She tucked the money into her canvas tote. "Thank you."

Parking in front of their trailer, he looked at her. "If you need anything, you can come to me. I'll always be here for you."

Charlotte leaned across the console and wrapped her dad in a tight hug. Fighting the tears burning her eyes. "I love you."

"Love you, too." Squeezing her back, he kissed her temple.

SIX

Elsey slammed her fist into Henry's chest.

Stumbling backward, Henry sputtered a cough. "I should've brought protection." He straightened, dusting off the navy V-neck he changed into for training. "Maybe some padding and a helmet."

"You won't have padding when you're in a real fight." Elsey stalked closer. Her boots whispered against the dry grass with each step. "The closest thing you'll have to protection are the clothes Tristan makes and me."

"I love that you didn't include my abilities in that list."

"If you want it, work for it."

He flashed his smirk. "It wouldn't be the first time I've heard those words."

She rolled her eyes. "I'm not even using a quarter of my strength."

"Thank you for that. I'd like my organs to remain in working order."

Elsey crossed her arms in front of her chest. "Then you should probably stop smoking and your other bad habits. There are probably better things to do with your time."

His eyes—glittering with mischief—leveled on her. "Well, I can think of at least one, but it can be expanded into many things."

She lifted a questioning brow.

He grinned and charged forward. She snatched him mid-run. Flipping him overhead before he realized his feet had left the ground. Henry landed on his back with a grunt. She circled him.

He watched her straighten her top. "Are you sure you're not trying to kill me?"

"If I were trying to kill you, you would already be dead." Elsey jutted a hand down to help him up. The lowering sun bloomed over her back, giving her rustic ruby curls the appearance of a wildfire.

Smirking, he grabbed her hand. Jerking her toward him. Hooking his foot behind her knee, he rolled them over. His eyes wandered the crude lines etching her soft features like terrain waiting to be explored. "We need to work on your communication. There's a softer way to tell someone you won't kill them."

"I have never been soft."

Stars glittered in his eyes. His smirk widened. He opened his mouth.

She wrapped her legs around his shoulders and flipped them forward. Landing on top of him, she straddled his chest and pinned his arms to his sides with her thighs. Her face lingered above his.

His eyes slid over her body but returned to her enthralling blue-green eyes. Warmth and a bone-deep fluttering ache pulsed inside him. "As wonderful as this position is for me, I think it would be best if we tabled it for a later date."

Lines scored the skin between her brows.

Buzzzzz. Elsey climbed off him and retrieved her phone lying on her jacket a few feet away. Turning off her alarm, she yanked on her jacket. "Practice is over. I have to leave soon."

"Okay." His voice sounded muffled.

She glanced back.

Henry lay face down. His head rested on his folded arms.

"What are you doing?"

"Just wanted to get closer to the earth. She's my new mistress now." He chuckled into his arms. "That sounded more perverted than I intended."

She arched a brow but spun to walk to her motorcycle.

"Hey, wait!" He jumped to his feet. Trotting past her, he grabbed his overcoat from the top of his car. "We only have one more day until Sunday. Do you think I'll be ready?"

"As ready as I can get you." She shrugged. "You can throw a basic punch and kick now at least."

"I *love* your confidence in me."

"You'll get better." Leaning against the side of his car, she crossed her arms. "We'll keep training. In the meantime, try to use your powers more and let the rest of us handle any hand-to-hand combat."

"You make it seem like I'm a damsel in distress." Pulling his cigarette case from his pocket, he selected one of three he had left before seeing her nose scrunch up. He replaced the cigarette and dropped the case into his pocket. "You know, if you have a problem with someone smoking, you probably shouldn't gift them a cigarette case."

"It's not a cigarette case."

"What?" He yanked the case from his pocket. "What the hell else could it be for?"

"It's an antique card case." She motioned toward the small silver box in his hand. "It was made in the 21st Century, but it looks like the maker modeled it after the ones women used in the mid to late 1800s. To be honest, though, I did assume you would apply it to your current use."

"Well, fuck me. I didn't expect that." He looked the case over before dropping it into his pocket again. "And what about the lighter? There's no way that could have any other use."

"Everyone should have a lighter or something to start a fire in case of emergencies."

Cocking his head to the side, a stray chunk of hair fell into his eyes. "Does that mean you also carry a lighter on you at all times?"

Her eyes lingered on the stray hair before meeting his eyes. "I don't need one."

"Ah," he said with a nod of understanding. He pushed his hair back from his face and leaned against his car. "You probably won't answer this, but why don't you use your powers anymore?"

Elsey balled her hands into fists. "I do use them."

"You know what I mean. You used to use them all the time like they were party tricks." His eyes met hers, aching to pry something— a hint of her—free. "Do you still have attacks when you use them? Is that why you stopped?"

Tearing her gaze away, she bit her tongue. Her armor of rage coated her in heavy fog to protect her from the flare of painful emotions she couldn't name. She stared at the abandoned Victorian house sitting in the overgrown yard. She felt his eyes crawling over her scarred face. A dark swell of emotion built under her armor, calling forth Luci's words like a curse. *Even Henry thinks you're a killer.* Her gaze cut to him. "Are you scared of me?"

"What?" His eyes widened, confused at the sudden shift in

conversation. His mouth dried. He fumbled for the right words. *No. Yes. No. It's not that.*

She gave a single nod, a mark she believed she understood his non-answer clearly. *I will always be stained.* Her stare became harsh and unwavering. "Why did you call me or try to reconnect with me?"

His heart quickened to a soul-rattling pace. Not leaving her gaze, his tongue felt heavy.

Elsey turned away. Her hollowed-out heart echoed in her voice. "I'll see you tomorrow, Henry."

He watched her close the gap to her motorcycle. A little piece of him splintered with each step. *Just tell her!* "El, wait!"

She halted but didn't face him. "What?"

"I—" He shoved his hands into his pockets. He grasped the bottle of pills as if touching the contents could ease the pain burning deep in his soul. "I need you."

She glanced at him over her shoulder, playing his words on a loop in her mind. The strange whispering ache hummed to life inside her. Questions and thoughts she couldn't entertain, battered against the locked doors in her brain.

The burn of her eyes seared his heart. A cold sweep of fear flooded him. Words tumbled from his lips. "—in my life. I need you in my life. We were best friends. After losing Ka—" He swallowed the rest of the name and shook his head. "I missed having you in my life."

Twisting away again, Elsey bit her tongue. She remained frozen in place.

"El," his voice was low, fracturing at the edges. "I *missed* you."

She squeezed her eyes closed against the ache flashing sparks inside of her. Shaking her head, she scraped all her emotions behind her shield of rage. "I have to go."

"But—"

"I'll see you tomorrow." She mounted her motorcycle and revved it to life before he could try again.

Slumping against the side of his car, he watched her tear out of the yard. Away from him. Away from their conversation. Away from all the unspoken words they continued to leave like the unraveled strands of broken hearts.

V

September 6, 3699

Tall trees, shedding their autumn leaves, loomed in the darkness on either side of them.

Charlotte glanced at Wesley. "I didn't know there was anything out this way except the road to Brookhaven."

Wesley rolled down his window. "Elsey said she borrowed a couple of lanterns from the island to mark where we needed to turn."

She leaned forward, squinting into the darkness. "Are you sure you want to do this?"

"I need to." He released a heavy breath, but his body still ached with anxiety. "I don't think I'll ever fully trust her or like her. She's not like us. For more reasons than the money and the privilege. But, if she can help find who killed Kade, I have to do this."

Faint light glowed in the distance.

The weight of what they were about to do settled into them.

They fell silent as they approached a dirt road tucked between the trees. Charlotte followed the trail into a large overgrown clearing surrounding an ominous run-down Victorian house.

Henry leaned against a weathered porch railing. Anastasia's yellow subcompact car sat in the yard, but the vibrant girl was nowhere to be seen.

Elsey stood behind a black SUV with her arms crossed. Her scarred pale pink skin looked severe against her all-black outfit. Her red hair had already been pinned in a tight braid coiled against her head. Despite her small stature compared to everyone else, she managed to look the most intimidating—like a gargoyle come to life to seek retribution.

"Hair up." Elsey gave Charlotte a hair tie and pins when the couple stepped out of the car. "Or you'll give them something to grab onto."

Charlotte took the hair tools and began to fix her hair in a tight bun. "Why is Ana's car here?"

"Because I'm here." A light voice called from the open door of the old house. Ana bounded onto the porch with a lantern in hand. Pastel splashes of pink and green decorated her long gauzy white maxi dress trailing the floor. "I was being nosy."

"What are you doing here?" Wesley looked from Ana to Henry.

Elsey opened the back door of the SUV and hefted a duffle bag onto her shoulder. "Ana will help Luci watch the cameras. There's four of us, and it will be hard for her to keep track of all of us, especially when we split up."

"It's also a good way for El to make sure I'm not behind the wheel of a vehicle," Henry added, sneaking a sip from his flask.

Wesley shot Elsey a hard look. "You brought on a new person without talking to us first."

She arched a brow.

"I understand why." He held out his hands. "But if we're going to be a team, you should consult with us before making a decision like that. Teams work together."

Elsey nodded. "Noted."

"So . . ." Ana held up the lit lantern, drawing the attention to her. "Does that mean I'm in?"

"Yeah." Wesley nodded. "But don't say anything to Jemma."

"Or Malini." Charlotte shot a look at Henry's slumped form before continuing, "She's not taking Kade's death well. If she knew Elsey and Henry were beating people up, I don't think it'd help."

Henry took a long drink from his flask, but he remained silent.

"No worries." Ana waved them off and disappeared in the house.

Everyone fell in line behind Elsey while they climbed the few groaning steps left. Elsey nudged the door wider with her boot for everyone to step inside.

Floorboards creaked beneath each step into a pitch-black hallway. Low light flickered to life when Elsey activated a cluster of small lanterns hanging in the narrow foyer. The light caught onto peeling wallpaper and framed pictures lining the hallway. Wesley, Charlotte, and Henry leaned in to get a better look.

A woman with white-blonde hair bobbed to her shoulders and close-set blue eyes that glittered with the smile on her small pink lips. Her straight nose and thin frame gave her the look of something ethereal. Her warmth radiated from each image. A tall man with pale golden skin and lean, muscular build. His thick black hair reached to his mid-back. A romantic sadness lived in his tapered round silver eyes. His large grin lit up his face, lifting his prominent cheekbones high. A small boy—at various stages of childhood but none older than five—with the silver eyes and thick black hair of his father and the small pink lips and straight nose of his mother. Happiness beamed from him in pictures of him running around in a lush yard or sitting with his father on a couch learning how to strum an acoustic guitar.

The trio let their eyes slip over each picture until they all released a collective gasp when they caught a shock of scarlet curls in one of the final pictures.

Charlotte grabbed a lantern from the wall.

They cluttered in closer.

A hollow concave in a high cheekbone before cutting deep into the side of her face. The tear of skin beside small heart-shaped lips holding a perpetual scowl. Fair pink skin already patterned with scars on her arms, legs, and chest. A haunted edge to captivating blue-green eyes.

"This is you?" Wesley twisted away from the picture to find Elsey standing apart from them.

Her shoulders stiffened under his gaze, but she nodded.

Glancing back at the wall, he looked at the young boy in the pictures. A slight hint of distant memories tickled his mind. "I think I remember him. Vaguely. Was he in kindergarten with us?"

She gripped her arms and gave a single nod. Spinning around, she passed through an archway to the left.

Wesley and Henry followed her, but Charlotte let her lantern slip over the wall. It lit a large kitchen that appeared stuck in time.

A chair sat a couple of inches from the large round table in the center. Empty dishes sat on the table and the counter beside the sink. A bottle of wine—uncorked—rested on the counter with an empty glass. More pictures of the couple and the boy posted to the fridge along with a drawing of a small handprint turned into a turkey. A highchair waited in the corner, perhaps forgotten to be put up as the boy grew or brought out for an expected new life.

Charlotte swallowed the anguish gnawing at her heart.

Her lantern swept over the wall beside a staircase and landed on the edge of a framed degree. She climbed the first two steps and looked closer at the document.

Adriel Yhu—Doctorate of Psychology (PsyD)

Descending the stairs, Charlotte walked through the archway the others disappeared through.

Scattered lanterns provided enough light to see the layer of dust covering the living room. Pillows and a blanket flowed off the cushioned seat built into a boarded-up window. Long dead red camellias, Juliet roses, and buttery peonies hung their mournful heads with dried sprigs of huckleberry in a crystal vase on the mantel. A high-backed armchair sat beside an ornately carved fireplace. A floral camelback sofa sat against the wall to the right across from a midnight blue Chesterfield. Open books of guitar tabs rested on a coffee table centered on a large watercolor rug woven with threads in various shades of blues and purples. An acoustic guitar leaned against the chesterfield with a pick lying next to it, waiting for the owner to continue playing.

Charlotte set her lantern on the coffee table and met Elsey's eyes. "What happened to the people here?"

Elsey's eyes settled on the guitar. "I don't know."

Stepping around the coffee table, Henry flopped into the chair beside the fireplace. He tossed one leg over the arm. "Who were they?"

"Adriel and Arella grew up with my father and mother in the city." Elsey crossed her arms in front of her. "I played with Carson when we would come over. Sometimes, Arella watched me if my grandparents couldn't."

Wesley rested the guitar against a wall, tucking the pick in the strings along the neck. He and Charlotte sat together on the Chesterfield.

Elsey stared at the open arch. "Where's Ana?"

"Coooomiiiiing!" The beam of a lantern danced along the walls and hardwood floors up the hallway behind the staircase. Ana appeared in the archway. "I really like the sunroom back there. It'd be a beautiful place to paint." She sat on the floral camelback, folding her legs under her.

Elsey took a breath that rasped into her raw heart. She dropped her duffle bag to the coffee table and unzipped it. "We'll meet here. Avoid Purgatory when you can. Luci, Tristan, and Gene help, but I keep their assistance to a minimum for their protection. I don't allow them to hold any of the healing serum or anything else that might connect them to what I do. Luci can wipe her connection to the cameras in the city with a button, so that's not a concern."

Elsey paused and glanced at everyone. "Everyone should think of a codename to use around other people. Try to make sure it's not something identifiable to you. Luci goes by Hellfire, and I use Fury."

She pulled small black cases from the duffle bag and passed them around. "These are your communicators. We have backup on the charger in Luci's SUV. If you need to talk, tap it once. If Luci or one of us needs to talk to you, a beep will sound in your ear. Tap it once to answer and listen, and it will allow you to talk until you either tap it again or until it detects silence. To keep the line open, tap it twice.

"When the line is open everyone can hear each other. Try to do it before a fight. That way if we're separated, we can hear what's happening and can minimize any risks of someone disappearing. To turn it off, long-press it. It never fully turns off though unless it's on the charger. That way if someone turns it off and there's an emergency, they can still be reached."

Pausing long enough to pass around stacks of black clothes to everyone except Ana, she continued, "These are your suits. They're made of a special anti-ballistic fabric to protect against stabs, slashes, and most gunfire. It's also waterproof and fire resistant. Your clothes won't catch fire unless exposed for a long enough period or the fire is burning over 1,000 degrees Fahrenheit. Tristan will make more when he has time. He's usually pretty quick since it's a basic pattern he follows once he has your measurements. He doesn't sew in any padding because it can hinder the full range of movement and can be harder to clean from sweat and other bodily fluids. Leave the suits here at the end of the night."

Charlotte rubbed the tough slippery material, recalling the similar feel of her dad's work uniform.

Elsey shifted topics while they checked over their new clothes. "Luci has control of most cameras in the city. If it's on a private server, like a residential area, she could access it, but it'd usually take too much time in the moment. She'll private all the cameras in a designated area when we're within reach. Only she will be able to see us then. Still, you always need to wear your masks. If people see your faces and recognize you, it would be a risk to you and anyone you care about.

"Minimizing risk is also why I knocked out the man I healed." Elsey directed her attention to Wesley and Charlotte. "You two weren't wearing masks. If he escaped, you guys would be in danger. Also, if he remained awake when I brought him to the island, depending on his loyalty to his employers, he could pose a risk to Asher and the others.

"On the island, first, they're treated for any injuries and then their threat levels are assessed. If someone is a threat, they're relegated to one of the rooms on the top three floors. They're assessed regularly and able to work with a therapist regardless of their threat level. If they're determined not to be a threat, they're allowed to join the community, or they may return home if they prefer. Alternatively, Asher allows them to bring their families over if they decide to stay. He's established this protocol, and I don't interfere unless he or his team require assistance. He contacts Luci whenever they need supplies, and I bring whatever they need."

Charlotte smoothed her fingers along her solid black mask. "What about the police station? When we first saw you, that man ran inside."

"A lot of homeless people stay there and in the city hall. I don't know much about it." Elsey glanced at the ground. "I've talked to some about the island, but a lot of the people are attached to the city."

"What about the healing serum?" Wesley leaned forward, resting his elbows on his knees.

Elsey retrieved three slim black cases and passed them around.

"We have one vial each. If someone is injured, give them a small sip. If the injury is large, they may need more of it. The serum does not heal scars or brain trauma. It also cannot revive the dead. Which brings me to my biggest point," she paused and focused a pointed look at Henry. "None of you are to kill people. Ever. I did not start doing this to add to the Daily Death List. But..."

Her gaze fixed on the far wall. Her voice became hollow, plagued with the empty darkness etched into her existence. "There are things that happen out there. Things worse than death. Things that cannot be erased or forgiven. Unless you remove your heart and soul, they will destroy you from the inside out. Nothing can prepare you for it.

"We'll operate on a strict basis. Let me assess a situation first. If I give the okay, we'll move in together. But—" She paused, waiting for them to understand the full weight of her next words. "If I tell you to walk, then you walk. I will take care of it myself."

A vile sickness twisted Wesley's stomach. "What will you do?"

"Whatever I have to."

Wesley noticed Elsey's eyes glaze over, as if she were staring into something the rest of them couldn't see.

Charlotte tore at the skin beside her thumb.

Ana sucked in her bottom lip and picked at the hem of her dress.

Fixing his eyes on the floor, Henry took a deep drink from his flask to drown any darkness before it could climb free from its bindings.

Shaking the ghosts from her mind, Elsey returned to the conversation. "Ultimately, we are in the business of helping people, not hurting them. Which also means, if someone's property is damaged while we're fighting, we'll repair it."

Each member breathed in the significance of what they were preparing to do like tinder about to ignite a flame.

"Have you decided on codenames?"

Wesley nodded and stared at the clothes in his hands, thinking of one of his favorite scientists and the future he wanted for himself and his sister. "Just."

"Sparrow." Charlotte fiddled with the silver bird around her neck. Her chest tightened with a hollow ache.

Ana lifted her hand. "I'll go by Pixy."

Silence fell over the room. Everyone turned toward Henry.

He met Elsey's eyes with his flask paused at his lips. "What?"

"Can his codename be Idiot?" Wesley groaned and stood.

"Have you even been paying attention?" Elsey faced Henry and crossed her arms.

He sipped from his flask and tucked it into his pocket before waving his hand. Pulling his leg back from the chair arm, he remained slumped. "Yeah, I got it. Keep our masks on. One tap to speak for a short time, two taps to talk longer, long-press to turn off. Take the bad guys to the island. Homeless people live at the old police station and city hall. Healing serum heals everything but scars, trauma, and death."

"And *don't* kill people." Elsey narrowed her eyes at him.

He gripped the arms of the chair and hoisted himself onto the rug. His items tumbled to the floor. "And what if you're in danger and that's the only way to save you?"

Her shoulders tensed. "Then you leave me."

"What?" Her words hit him like a slap to the face. The threads holding him steady began to unwind. "I'm not abandoning you!"

"Since when?" Her hands tightened into fists.

"I have *never* abandoned you, El." His voice was strained and low. "You're the one who abandoned me."

Elsey watched his eyes fill with a depth she couldn't grasp. Anger tangled with a flare of guilt blooming in her stomach.

"Is there something going on?" Charlotte's brows rose.

"Nothing." The word scraped Elsey's tongue like sandpaper. She whirled and grabbed her duffle bag. "We'll head out together until we feel comfortable splitting up. Henry, think of a codename."

"I already thought of one." He snatched his items from the floor. Standing, he stared at her with his soul burning in his eyes. "Eros."

Ana coughed into her cupped hand, drawing the attention to her. "Maybe you guys should go get ready."

Elsey hoisted her duffle bag onto her shoulder and stomped across the living room. "I'll wait outside."

A beep sounded in Elsey's ear. She tapped her communicator twice. "Yeah?"

"There's a van parked in front of Arnie's Deli," Luci said. She leaned over to show Ana how to zoom in on a camera panel.

"Arnie closes at 7." Ana followed Luci's instructions, filling her screen with the section of The Square showing Arnie's Deli. "The lights are off, but I can see movement inside."

Elsey turned off Boyer Road and parked on a side street.

"Wait here." Ignoring her masked companions—Henry in the passenger's seat and Wesley and Charlotte in the backseat, she climbed out of the SUV before anyone could respond.

She circled around the vehicle and slipped into an alley between a bakery and an Asian Fusion restaurant. Kicking herself off the lid of a dumpster, Elsey launched herself into the air and caught the edge of the bakery. She hoisted herself over the ledge.

She charged toward the edge of the building and bounded to the next roof.

Then the next.

The next.

Making her way over the roofs like an arrow hitting its mark.

She landed on Arnie's Deli with a **thump**. Crouching, Elsey pressed her hand to the roof. She dragged forward the pulsing thread of blue light in the back of her head. Washed-out sapphire burst before her mind's eye before revealing a darkened view of the building inside.

Two men poured gasoline on the floor and tables. Three men ransacked a backroom, tossing papers to the ground after skimming through them.

Rough shouts filled her ears. "Where is it? He has to be keeping it somewhere!"

Elsey let the vision fade. She walked toward the front of the building. A man sat in the driver's seat of the waiting van. Breaking her silence, she recapped the situation over the communicators.

"If a fire breaks out, Eros can smother it." Wesley motioned to Henry. "We'd need to evacuate the place first."

"Agreed. Come up the street, take care of the driver. I'll wait behind the building for us to move in together." Walking to the rear of the building, Elsey vaulted over the edge and landed on her feet in the dark alley. "Be mindful of firearms and blades. I didn't see any, but that doesn't mean they don't have them. And Hellfire—"

"Already searching for Arnie's address." Luci minimized her view of the cameras and commandeered HAL Corp's city grid database to start her search of local residences that might be attached to Arnie's name.

Taking Charlotte's hand, Wesley led her and Henry through the shadows—aware that three masked strangers walking the streets might induce panic in any passersby.

Tension seized his shoulders. The nearer they came to their destination, the faster his heart thudded in his chest. His mind remained on one fixed thought: his sister. Her dimpled grin. Her bubbly laugh. Her teasing remarks. Her warm copper eyes, so like his brother's. A lump formed in his throat. *If this goes wrong—*

Feeling Charlotte's hand tighten on his, he glanced over his shoulder.

Charlotte met his eyes—the only visible part of them beneath their masks. She squeezed his hand again, hoping he would understand her message. *It will be okay.*

Giving a short nod, Wesley squeezed her hand back. He looked past her, catching Henry tossing what looked like a small red pill into his mouth before swigging from his flask. Wesley stifled a groan.

The group stopped beside the restaurant before Arnie's Deli. Looming in the shadows, they watched the driver of the van bob his head to music they couldn't hear.

Wesley started forward, but Henry patted his shoulder.

"I've got this." Stepping off the chipped sidewalk, Henry strolled toward the van. He knocked on the driver's window.

The window rolled down, and he found himself faced with the confused expression of a scrawny teenager with greasy brown hair.

Henry's smirk widened. "Hello. I'm Eros, and I'll be your server this evening. Right or left?"

"Huh?" The boy's forehead hunched with thick lines.

"Right or left?" Henry lifted his hands, showing his closed fists as if he were hiding a prize.

"What are you doing?" Luci paused her search, leaning over to look at Ana's screen.

"Ummmm … left?" The boy pointed to Henry's fist.

"Good choice!" Henry reeled back and slammed his fist into the boy's jaw. The kid slumped over his seat. Henry jutted his fists into the air. "I did it! Good thing I don't have a strong hand."

"What?" Charlotte asked, following Wesley out of the shadows.

Wesley jabbed a finger toward Henry. "Don't you *dare* explain!"

Luci rolled her eyes. "He's saying he alternates between both hands when he's lonely, so they maintain equal strength."

"No. He really is ambidextrous." Ana struggled to silence her giggles. "He prefers writing with his right hand and holding things with his left hand."

Henry rounded the van and shot Wesley an amused look. "You guys are perverts."

"Guys, focus." Elsey gripped the knob on the back door, waiting for the right moment. "Can you get in the front?"

"Easy." Henry pulled on the scarlet tendril flowing through him. The air quivered. He whipped his arm out, sending a wave of air crashing through the tempered glass windows.

Small pieces of glass exploded inside the building. Screaming, the men dropped their gas cans and ducked under tables for cover.

"What the fuck was that?" Elsey snapped the knob in her hand.

"Dude, not cool!" Wesley swept a hand toward the men cowering under tables. "The glass could've embedded into them!"

Shrugging, Henry crossed the threshold of the shattered windows. "What I lack in subtlety, I make up for with a good time."

Charlotte opened the front door, motioning to it with her free hand. "That whole thing was unnecessary."

Wesley collected a piece of the broken tempered glass. His skin became shiny, tinted glass.

A dark-haired man with a chiseled jaw jumped up from his hiding spot, pulling a gun from his waistband.

Wesley shoved the table with his foot, knocking the man down. The gun *clanked* to the floor. The second man leapt at Wesley. A gust of wind caught him and smashed him into the wall. Both men climbed to their feet. One grabbed a chair. The other charged toward the gun.

Charlotte leapt onto a table and ran. She caught the charging man with a hard kick to the jaw.

Snatching her ankle, he pulled her down with him. He scrambled on top of her. Slamming a fist into her masked face.

Wesley grabbed his neck and threw him like a doll. A chair came down across the side of Wesley's head. Feeling nothing more than the pressure of the metal *dinging* off the tempered glass covering his body, he peered at the man wielding the chair.

Clutching the chair in shaky hands, he retreated.

Shouts and a scuffle rose from the rear of the deli. A bulky man burst through the swinging door to the hallway. He froze when he saw the scene.

Wesley yanked the chair from his opponent's grip and sent it flying into the menu board on the wall. The man lunged to the side. Pivoting on the ground, Charlotte kicked his leg. He thumped to the ground.

A gun skidded across the room under a table in the corner.

Another man knelt on the ground before Henry. He clawed at his throat and gasped for air. Henry rammed his knee into the man's chin. His head snapped back, and he fell to the floor.

The new man on the scene glanced at the swinging door. Taking in the grunts and pleas from the companions he abandoned. The *crack* of a bone breaking. The *thud* of something heavy hitting the floor. He looked at the fight before him. The door swung open, knocking him sideways. He spotted the gun under the table in the corner.

Another man stumbled from the hallway, clutching his arm to his chest. He halted. Eyes wide as Wesley sent one of his partners flying into the glass counter.

Elsey stepped out of the hall, tucking a gun she collected in her pocket. She seized the man before he could move. Spinning him around, she slammed him into the wall. She pinned him in place with her knee jammed into his groin and her hand around his throat. "What are you searching for?"

"None of your business," he wheezed. Releasing his broken wrist with a wince, he punched at her face.

Catching his fist, she twisted until he screamed. "I won't break any more bones if you answer my question."

"Fury!" Leaping to her feet, Charlotte approached from behind.

"Go to hell, Bitch!" The man gurgled and spit in Elsey's face.

Heat flared through Elsey's body. She tightened her grip, crushing the bones in his hand. A wail tore through the building. She slammed her fist into his face. His screams died. He slid to the floor.

"What the hell was that?" Wesley tossed up his hands. "Why did you—"

"He had information." Elsey wiped the man's spit from her face with her sleeve.

"And did you get it?" Charlotte stared at the slumped body. The sound of his snapping bones and paint-peeling scream continued to replay in her mind.

"He pissed me off."

"That's torture!" Wesley pointed at the unconscious man.

Henry's eyes narrowed, his voice taking on a dark note. "Just—"

"Are you seriously about to defend this?" Wesley swiveled on Henry, gesturing toward Elsey.

The metal *click* of a gun being cocked sounded from the corner.

POP!

"One move—" Elsey's voice cut through the room like a razor. "—and your insides become wall art."

Everyone turned. Elsey held a gun pointed at the bulky man in the corner. He stood frozen. Gun in hand—aimed at Wesley. Eyes locked on the still smoking hole in the wall beside his face.

Swallowing a visible gulp, he looked at Elsey. "You missed."

"Trust me." Elsey drew her arm over, pointing directly between his eyes. "I didn't."

With a swift downward stroke, she pulled the trigger. Shooting him in the leg. He dropped to the ground. Screaming. Gripping his thigh. Blood gushed between his hands.

"Fury!" Wesley and Charlotte echoed each other.

Elsey ignored them. Approaching the bleeding man, she trained the gun on his face. "If you didn't point a gun at my teammate, you wouldn't have to pick bullets out of your body."

"Fury! Stop!" Wesley struggled to fight the fear that she might pull the trigger and he'd see blood and brain matter paint the floor.

Charlotte's eyes darted around the room. To the men knocked unconscious by her, Wesley, and Henry. To the man with a broken wrist and shattered hand. To the hallway where she presumed another man lay unconscious—if not worse. She looked at Elsey looming over the bleeding man. Her heart raced so fast she worried it might break free from her ribcage.

Eyes wide, Henry watched without speaking. He shoved his hand in his pocket. A muffled rattle broke the silence.

Lowering her gun, Elsey retrieved a vial of serum. She tossed it in the man's lap. "Take a drink. I can't have your blood all over my ride."

"Are you crazy?" The man looked between the vial to Elsey. "I'm not drinking any kind of poison—"

"Why would I poison you when I could put a bullet in your brain?"

"I don't care!"

"Suit yourself." Elsey bashed her boot into the side of his head.

He fell backward. His head lolled. His hands went limp.

Rolling her eyes, Elsey pocketed the gun and knelt beside his body. She held the vial to his mouth and waited for a couple of drops to pass his lips. Tilting his head back and massaging his throat with her thumb, she waited for the serum to enter his system. The tissue and flesh knitted together, pushing the bullet from his leg and sealing his wound closed.

Elsey stood. She brushed past Charlotte to enter the hallway. Reappearing a handful of seconds later, she had a burly tattooed man slung over her shoulder. She gestured toward the unconscious men around the room. "Let's load them up in their van and take them to the SUV."

"What?" Wesley flung his hands up. "No! We need to talk about what just happened!"

"Later." Elsey cut her gaze to him. "They were searching for something. We need to get to Arnie's house now to make sure he's safe." She stormed past the team, carting the unconscious man to the van.

Wesley spun toward Henry. "Are you okay with this?"

Pulling his flask from his pocket, Henry shrugged. "If she found the person who murdered—"

Charlotte pulled her eyes from the unconscious bodies around the room. She watched Henry take another long drink from his flask—silencing himself before he could say the name they all knew was coming.

"Would you want her to be nice about it?" Henry stared at the man he knocked out. "I wouldn't."

three

The team parked across from a row of small houses. Yellow light streamed from the open door of a gray craftsman in the center. Dark red liquid dripped down the windows and stained the white lace curtains. Someone yelled inside.

"Fuck!" Elsey dashed across the street.

Charlotte ran at her heels. Wesley and Henry trailed after.

Elsey and Charlotte halted in the doorway.

A tall black-clad figure spun on them. A black mask—identical to the one Wesley and Charlotte wore—covered their entire face. The figure held a bloody knife in black-gloved hands. A dark mass soaked the front of the figure's shirt and pants.

"Oh my God!" Charlotte clamped a hand over her concealed mouth when she caught sight of Arnie Koch lying on the floor before the hallway. Blood poured from his torso and mixed with the blood of a woman lying a couple of inches away.

Charlotte stumbled onto the porch. Wesley caught her before she could trip. Henry walked past them. His stomach churned, and he turned back.

Elsey leapt toward the person holding the knife.

They darted out of her reach.

She jumped again, twisting in the air and kicking with her right foot.

The person dodged again, tripping on Arnie's body. They stumbled backward.

Elsey pounced.

They seized her with one hand and tossed her overhead.

She crashed into the dropped staircase leading to the attic. Pain racked her shoulder and her back. She didn't scream. Climbing to her feet, she chased the person through the backdoor into the small yard outlined by a six-foot fence.

The person glanced over their shoulder. Facing forward again, a chunk of fence exploded. Wood splinters swept around the person and aimed at Elsey.

"Fuck!" She dropped to the ground, flattening herself and shielding her face.

"What happened?" Luci flipped through the cameras on her screen, unable to find one that showed what was happening. "You're in a residential area. I can't see shit."

The wood pieces crashed to the ground, and Elsey looked up. The person disappeared down a dark alley. "They threw me like I weighed nothing, and they made the fence explode! That asswipe tried to impale me!"

Ana shot a wary look at Luci. "What did you see inside?"

"Arnie and his wife were butchered." Standing, Elsey squeezed her eyes shut. "Like the others."

Wesley ran outside, motioning toward the fence. "You let them get away!"

"I did not *let* them get away!" Elsey spun on him. "They have powers! I can't chase them down unprepared!"

Lights flipped on in the houses on either side of the yard.

"They might've killed Kade!"

Elsey shot a look at the windows of neighboring houses, noticing curtains moving aside. Snatching Wesley's wrist, she pulled him in the house.

She released him once the door was closed. "You said your brother's name. You don't know who might be listening. Whoever the hell that was could still be in earshot. If they were the person who killed Kade, it wouldn't be hard to make the connection to you. You are not the only one at risk. Your sister. Charlotte. Henry. You put everyone else at risk by being impulsive."

"It was a mistake." Wesley narrowed his eyes. Anger bubbled in his chest. "But I'm not the one risking lives by blowing up windows."

"I know that." She motioned down the hallway toward the front door. "I'll deal with him."

"And what about you? Huh?"

Luci set her glass beside her computer, preparing to diffuse the tension. "Wes—"

"Who deals with you?" He crossed his arms. "We're not the ones breaking bones and shooting people."

"That man pointed a gun at the back of *your* head." Elsey balled her hands into fists. "There was no guarantee that the glass you used was strong enough to stop a bullet. Did you want me to let him pull the trigger? Did you want me to gamble with your life?"

Ana covered her mouth with her hand.

"You fired again *after* the warning shot! That was excessive."

"Else—" Luci tried again.

"How is what I did any different from you throwing someone into a wall or a van? Or beating someone up when you're covered in metal?"

"I responded in a moment of action. When there was a threat." He pointed at her. "You shot someone *after* they stopped. That's abuse. You broke bones to get information. That's torture. There are numerous studies that say torture does not work. You're causing unnecessary trauma. If you cannot see how they are not the same, we have a serious problem."

"Guys," Ana said, pulling her hand from her mouth. "Maybe you should—"

"You're right. We do have a problem." She nodded. "They were searching for something Arnie had. Arnie was killed by someone else in the same way the others were killed. The same way your brother was killed. That's not a coincidence. I'm not handing out lollipops and hugs to murderers."

"I'm not asking you to." Wesley motioned out with his hands. "I'm asking you to treat them like people. That's what they are."

"People who killed Arnie and his wife. People who killed your brother. In cold blood."

"You didn't know they were connected to my brother's murder when we were at the restaurant." Unease filled him. His thoughts ran at a rapid pace to keep up with the situation. "Unless there's something you're not telling us."

Elsey dug her nails into her palms. "Your compassion is

admirable, but I'm treating them like what they are. Murderers. Unless in self-defense, a killer is a killer. Whether they aided or wielded the weapon themselves, their hands are still painted with blood. Playing a role in murder does something to a person. To take a life in cold blood is to forfeit a piece of your soul. I'm not asking you to do that. I told you before, it gets dark out here. And sometimes to do the right thing, you have to become a monster."

He pressed his teeth against his bottom lip. His stomach roiled with burning anger. Her words filled his mind, and he picked them apart. Analyzing everything. *A big fish often thinks it's the top predator only to get eaten by a shark.* His conscience tangled into a distorted web with the distinct feeling that his previous statement to Charlotte wasn't far off from the truth—that he was working with someone whose morals lived somewhere between gray and pitch black.

Luci and Ana exchanged a heavy look. They listened to the thick silence coming through the communicators.

Wesley took a short step toward Elsey. "We need their information to find out what's happening. We can't get information from a dead body." He pointed at her. "If you bloody your hands, you bloody all of ours. Same as them."

He dropped his hand, now pointing at the ground. "This is a team. Everything you do affects the rest of us. From now on, check with us before acting."

"I don't take orders." A threatening edge laced her tone. "From anyone."

"Neither do I." He ignored the shiver shaking through his chest and kept his gaze hard. "I don't care what the situation is, I won't become an accessory to murder or any of your monster bullshit."

"Fuck you." Elsey spat the words like a punch to the face. "Fuck you and everyone else who thinks they know me."

"I'm not try—"

Elsey stomped around him, heading toward the living room.

"All right." Luci took a deep breath. "Just take a breather. Focus on the situation."

The front door slammed open. Charlotte hurried inside.

Wesley rushed past Elsey, grabbing Charlotte before she could step in the pool of blood. He glanced toward the doorway to see

Henry walking up the steps rubbing his shin. "You were supposed to hold her!"

"She kicked me!" Henry continued to rub his shin.

Charlotte's eyes fell on the bodies and the blood seeping into the plush cream carpet. A shudder tore through her, and Wesley hugged her tight.

"I'll show you guys what to look for," Elsey said, stepping toward Arnie's body. She looked at her teammates. "If you think you can handle it. If you can't, that's fine. Just close the door and wait outside."

Henry exchanged a look with Wesley. They both nodded.

Charlotte took a ragged breath, inhaling Wesley's scent laced with the metallic odor of blood in the air. "I can do this. I have to."

Closing the door, Henry took a long drink from his flask.

Elsey unbuttoned the blood-soaked shirt covering Arnie's body to reveal his mangled chest. "It's hard to see at first through all the blood but look close."

She let her finger hover above the dead man's chest and traced a pattern, connecting the punctures like a puzzle. A figure eight up the length of the torso with symmetrical perpendicular lines bisecting the center. Three separate wounds lay on the left side of the symbol, one directly above and on either side of the line dividing the figure eight. The same symbol she previously showed them. "Sometimes, it's turned on its side across the stomach. Other times, it's like this, stretched along the torso."

Charlotte squinted and followed the pattern again. "What does it mean?"

"I don't know, but I guarantee you, his wife will have the same symbol." Elsey looked up at them. "They're the eighth and ninth ones that I've found so far."

Wesley looked between the two bodies. "How long ago did you find the first one?"

"Two years ago. A man in his thirties. He was in an abandoned building."

Henry's brows rose. "How did you find him?"

"I was looking for homeless people to give supplies to. It was before I decided to start doing more." She stood and tracked a bloody trail across the carpet in front of a soft pink couch up to the splatter on the window. "This blood isn't theirs."

"What?" Wesley released Charlotte and neared the back of the couch to get a better view. He looked at Arnie and his wife. "They were stabbed. That's from a slash."

"A big one."

"Maybe they fought and injured their attacker." Stooping next to Arnie's body, Wesley checked his hands. He noted a couple of nicks but nothing big enough to cause the splash of blood. He continued to look over the rest of the body.

Turning to the bookcase beside the television, Elsey rummaged through books and papers.

Henry tilted his head to the side. "What are you doing?"

"Looking for something that connects Arnie to that symbol." Elsey glanced over her shoulder. "Those men at the deli were after something he had hidden."

"Speaking of those men," Luci said, glancing up as Gene entered the room and set two plates of homemade cinnamon rolls on the coffee table for her and Ana. She paused her words long enough to give him a quick kiss. "If you're all in the house, who's supervising them?"

Ana mouthed a silent, "Thank you," before Gene left—closing the door behind him.

Tearing her eyes from the blood and the gouges in Arnie's torso, Charlotte raised her hand. "I'll go."

"Not alone," Wesley said.

"I'll be fine." She shot him a hard look before slipping outside and shutting the door.

Henry nodded to the stairs in the hall. "Why are the attic stairs down?"

Elsey glanced over her shoulder toward the hallway where the drop staircase rested on the carpet. "No idea."

"Finally, something for me to do besides stand around and judge the décor." Dropping his flask into his pocket, Henry traipsed through the house and climbed the stairs.

"Find anything?" Wesley stood and walked over to Arnie's wife.

"Not yet." Elsey shoved a heavy book of German poetry onto the shelf and shuffled through a volume on classic cocktails.

Wesley focused on Arnie's wife. Gray striped her honey-colored hair. Her plump cheeks and sharp nose gave her the appearance of a fairy. He closed the lids over her pale blue eyes. Picking up her left hand, he noted the blood and skin under her fingernails and a cut through her palm. He glanced at the blood splatters. *It's not enough to make that pattern.* "What's Arnie's wife's name? I don't feel right just calling her his wife."

"The only name associated with the address and the deli is Arnie's," Luci said.

"I've never seen anyone other than Arnie working at the deli." Ana leaned back on the sofa. **"He's not really open. He's nice but quiet."**

Elsey shelved the book she held, and she scanned the beige walls around the living room and the small open kitchen. No pictures. She faced Wesley. "Are either of them wearing wedding bands?"

"No, but most people can't afford rings nowadays." He lifted the woman's right hand out of the pool of blood. Turning it over, he swallowed hard. Muscle and bone peeked through the blood painting her arm where a rectangle chunk of flesh had been carved free. "Someone cut out the skin on her arm. Have you seen that before?"

"Yeah, I have." Biting her tongue, Elsey stared at the ragged hole in the woman's arm for where she stood. She shoved any memories out of sight. "That either happened after she was dead or someone else held her still."

"Hey, guys," Henry paused, sipping from his flask. **"There are beds up here. And blood."**

Elsey and Wesley climbed to the attic and found themselves in a small room stacked with oversized containers labeled for different holidays most people no longer celebrated. Part of the wall had been pulled away revealing another small room. Henry stood in the center of the room, flask in hand. Two cots sat on either side of him. A round window between the beds hung open. Blood splattered across the sheets of the cot to the left.

Wesley walked over to the bed on the right. He pulled back the blankets. A small amount of blood stained the corner. "The woman downstairs has a cut on her hand. She could've been sleeping here and tossed the blanket aside to jump to her feet."

Elsey studied the part of the wall that had been pulled away. A handle had been attached to the side facing in the room. "Arnie was hiding her here."

"And someone else." Henry pointed at the other cot. "That's too much to be from Arnie. There would be a trail leading downstairs."

Elsey crossed to the window and leaned out.

Blood dripped down the side of the house and a palm print marked the white paint on the edge of the roof. Faint whispers settled on her skin—beckoning her. She pressed her hand against the blood dripping down the window ledge. The essence surged inside her. Washed-out sapphire flashed in her mind.

Terror flooded her. Muffled shouts filled her ears. Dark, hazy images of two figures wrestling. Pain slashed across her chest. A woman screamed, telling someone else to run.

The dark, blurry images replayed. The scream.

Something like a name hung off the edge of the scream, but it had been cut off—muffled under a hand or a pillow. Pain again, slashed her chest.

Her breath slipped as she felt blood pour down her chest.

The scream again.

Again.

"Elsey!" Luci dropped her plate. Listening to Elsey choking for air. "Pull back! Pull back!"

Elsey's fingernails bit into the side of the window. The pain tore through her chest again. Followed by the scream splitting her eardrums. Blood—so much blood—she could feel it gushing from the gouge along her chest.

"What's happening?" Wesley watched Elsey, eyes wide as she trembled and choked. One hand pressed to her chest as if attempting to close a wound that wasn't there. The other still on the window.

Henry's flask *clanked* to the floor. He leapt forward, wrapping his arms around Elsey's waist and yanking her back from the window. He twisted her around to face him. She inhaled a sharp breath. He moved to cup her face. His smooth hands lighted on the deep scars carving the sides of her face, and she jerked out of his reach as though she'd been burned.

"Are you okay?" He watched her. "That's worse than—"

"I'm fine." Elsey dragged another loaded breath into her lungs.

"What happened?" Wesley grabbed Henry's flask from the floor. It lay in a puddle of whiskey. He handed it to Henry and watched him drop it into his pocket without a spare glance.

Digging her nails into her palms, Elsey stared at the ceiling. She waited until her heart began to settle. Until the scream swept to the corners of her mind and the pain felt like an itch along her skin.

Henry's heart shivered. His fingers ached to reach for her again. "She can see past events if she touches something that has strong emotions attached to it."

"It's connected to my ability to see things as they presently happen in a space." Elsey looked at Henry, meeting his eyes for a second before forcing her attention to Wesley. "Sometimes, it's only sounds or sensations. Sometimes, it's both. When the emotion is really intense, there can be images. The clarity of the image varies. Sometimes, it's hazy and dark like it was now. Other times, it's not. It's never as clear as when I touch something to see what's currently happening because the past is never clear. But I experience it like I would if I were there. I try to avoid it when I can."

Before either of them could ask anything more, she relayed the vision she experienced.

"There were two people staying here when they were attacked." Wesley nodded to the bed he investigated. "The other person got away and went out the window."

"And Arnie?" A buzzing ache built inside Henry's chest. Tucking his hands in his pockets, he grasped the waiting pill bottle. He tried to think about how long it had been since he'd taken one, but his thoughts kept drifting to the torment in Elsey's eyes when he pulled her from the window.

"He was probably killed first," Wesley said.

Elsey shook her head. "We don't know that. There was a shout. Someone was still alive before we entered."

"The shout could've been from the attacker."

"Who would they be shouting at? Nothing was disturbed. They weren't—"

Henry pulled a hand from his pocket and lifted his finger.

"Speaking as someone who's been caught in some very compromising positions before, are you positive that person was the killer?"

"They were holding a knife covered in blood!" Wesley tossed his hands in the air.

"And their clothes had blood on them," Elsey added.

"You say that as if you've never gotten blood on your clothes." Henry's brows pinched together.

"They were wearing a mask." Wesley crossed his arms in front of him.

"We're wearing masks." Henry dropped his eyes to Elsey. "And I have *been* caught in a compromising position or two while wearing a mask before. More embarrassing than you'd think."

"And yet you're bragging about it now." Wesley narrowed his eyes.

"Not bragging." Henry lifted his index finger. "Merely playing devil's advocate."

"The devil doesn't need an advocate," Luci replied, catching the smirk crossing Ana's lips. "Whoever it is, you guys need to be careful because they know you're out there. Get pictures of everything and leave. I'll send a message to the morgue to pick up the bodies, and I'll check their system later to see if they identified the woman."

"What system are you not controlling in this city? And can you give me all A's in school?" Henry smirked.

"I won't," Luci paused to sip from her drink. "But I will tell you that you should delete those photos that girl sent to your phone before someone else sees them."

Henry gaped. "I didn't ask for them. I swear. She just sent them."

Ana broke into a fit of giggles.

Wesley covered his mouth to stifle his laugh.

The muscle twitched beside Elsey's mouth. "She's teasing you. The only phone she has access to is mine."

"Not true. I also have access to Gene's. I would have access to Tristan's too if he didn't hate technology like the grandpa he is. But," Luci started—her voice carrying the dangerous edge of a hot-tipped blade. "I could hack your phone if I wanted to, Lover

Boy, so don't try me."

"Hellfire." Henry tightened his grip around the pill bottle in his pocket. "I have no idea what you're insinuating."

Elsey arched her brow and looked at Wesley. "What's going on?"

"Hell, if I know." He dropped his arms to his side. "I'll get pictures up here. You get the ones downstairs, then let's get out of here."

Tucking their masks in their pockets, everyone took a seat on the boat.

Elsey started the engine and began the trip across the bay. Water painted with the reflection of the night sky slapped against the sides.

Charlotte shifted closer to Wesley, leaning against his shoulder. She stared at the unconscious men piled on the floor of the boat.

Feeling her fidget beside him, Wesley noticed her scratching at the skin beside her thumbs. He pulled her into his lap and entwined their fingers together. He kissed the top of her head.

Henry watched Elsey steer through the water. The itch rose under his skin. He pulled his flask from his pocket and tipped it upward. A single drop landed on his tongue. *Fuck.* Returning it to his pocket, he found the bottle of pills waiting for him like a loyal friend. He popped the lid off and retrieved a single pill.

Elsey glanced at him.

He froze, waiting for her to speak.

She fixed her attention back on the dock jutting from the island.

Dropping his eyes to his pocket, he glimpsed the red pill in his hand. *Let it go. I don't want it. Just let it go.* Tapping pressure rose in the back of his head. Focusing on it would only bring it forward faster. The itch scraped at his carefully pieced together resolve. He closed the bottle with the pill tucked in his palm. *I'm so fucking pathetic.*

A deep frown bent his lips. He peered at Elsey. *I'm so sorry.* His throat tightened. *I'm really so, so sorry. For being me. For everything.* His chest burned. Taking a deep breath, he blinked to clear the faint mistiness from his eyes. He looked away from her and stared at the reflection of the moon and stars in the water. *I hate myself so fucking much.*

Reaching the dock, Elsey released the anchor.

"Evening, Okan." She nodded to the short stocky man waiting to assist. The dimming light from the sliver of moon still clinging to the sky cast shadows on his rich golden tan skin. "Where's Asher?"

Okan nodded toward the path cutting through the thick trees. "He didn't feel like making the trek."

Grabbing one of the unconscious men, Elsey looked at her teammates. "When we get them inside Asher can give you a proper introduction to the place."

Henry waited until everyone carried the bodies from the boat, leaving him with only one. The teenager who'd been driving the van. He put his back to the team. Leaning down, he tossed his waiting pill into his mouth and swallowed it dry. The warm buzz tingled his insides and curled his toes. Everything became brighter. More vivid than reality. Like he saw everything the way the universe was meant to be seen. He gave his mind another second to adjust before scooping the kid into his arms.

Joining the team on the dock, he followed close behind. They left the dock to begin following the path lit by small lanterns. Elsey took the lead, carrying one man on her shoulder and dragging the one she shot on the ground.

Faint musical chirps and squeaks called from the trees.

Wesley peered into the leaves. Glowing eyes bounced off the lanterns. "Are those bats?"

Elsey nodded. "They were here before Asher. There are also a couple flocks of vultures, but they're mostly active during the day."

"They help with the ecosystem." Okan—cradling the man with a broken wrist and broken hand like a baby—looked over his shoulder.

"Vultures are the best at maintaining a healthy environment." Wesley nodded. "There were programs a long time ago to try to revive their numbers since they were so endangered. The conservation groups are still doing what they can, but with no protections in place anymore and public perception, it's like they're fighting a losing battle."

Okan's brows rose. "You know about that stuff?"

Charlotte smiled and shot Wesley a pointed look. "Wes really likes science."

Wesley shrugged. "I prefer biology, but I like all branches."

"He has the highest GPA in school," Elsey announced.

His brow furrowed. "How do you know that?"

Elsey rolled her eyes but didn't respond.

Charlotte and Wesley exchanged a confused look.

A faint smile splayed across Henry's lips. His attention remained glued on the trees. He stared at the eyes glowing like fiery pinpricks in the darkness. "I like bats."

Stepping in a clearing, they found Asher sitting on a bench in front of a massive thirty-story building made of tan brick. Small lanterns dangling from posts beside the door burnished his bare scalp and ebony skin with a soft faint glow. His serpent-shaped cane rested on the bench beside him. He patted his broad forehead with a white cloth that matched his short-sleeved button-up shirt. Looking up from something clutched in his other hand, he slid whatever it was into the pocket of his khaki pants. His silver chain was absent around his neck.

Asher flashed them a grin. "Evening, Team."

The tinted glass doors opened, and a group of people rushed out with stretchers.

Elsey flopped both men she carried onto the first ones within reach. Okan copied her and began loading the rest of the unconscious men onto the other stretchers.

Moving aside to hold the door open, Elsey gestured toward the team. "I guess I should give a proper introduction this time. Asher, this is Henry Adamson, Charlotte Marion, and Wesley Reed."

Asher's wide-set soulful brown eyes landed on Wesley. "I'm sorry about your brother."

Jerking his attention away from the people wheeling the stretchers into the building, Wesley's eyes bulged. "You knew him?"

"No." Asher grabbed his cane and stood, nodding toward Elsey while he shoved his sweat rag into his pocket. "The Angry One brings us newspapers, and she managed to get the electricity working so we can watch TV."

"How did she do that?"

A mischievous smile spread over Asher's lips. "You mean, you don't know what she can do?"

Wesley and Charlotte exchanged another confused look.

Henry lifted a finger. "I do."

Rolling her eyes, Elsey motioned between the team and the door. "Inside."

Asher hobbled through the doorway. Chuckling, he paused to murmur low enough for Elsey to hear. "I'm going to have some fun with this."

The corner of her mouth twitched up before returning to her stone façade. She waited for everyone else to pass through before following.

"Holy cow!" Charlotte's mouth dropped open.

Wesley's eyes bulged again to the size of saucers.

Henry swiveled his head around like an owl gone mad.

With shops, cafes, and restaurants, the first floor stretched out like a giant indoor marketplace. People bustled around in clean clothes free from tears and scuffs. Children giggled and ran around freely with no more than a glance from adults watching over them. Sparkling lights strung over the streets and across the railings of the upper floor. No one inhaled smoke from long-burning fires. No one fought in dark corners. Blood didn't stain the street.

A young man carrying a basket of what appeared to be groceries ran up a set of stairs. Their eyes followed him to the floors above that were now lined with numbered doors instead of iron bars.

High above, a large glass ceiling opened the roof up to the night sky.

Elsey pivoted and stomped toward an elevator. "Watch them. I have to check the infirmary, and they need to get to know the place."

"Hey!" Asher tapped the ferrule of his cane against the cement floor. "I am not a babysitter!"

"Brag about stabbing me some more." She pressed the button for the twenty-sixth floor. Her eyes landed on him as the doors slid closed. The ghost of what might've been a smile flickered across her lips. "I'm sure they'll love that."

A full, croaky laugh tumbled over his lips until he caught the glare from Henry. Reaching up, he gripped Henry's shoulder. "That will not end well for you, Son."

"I have no idea *what* you're talking about." Henry grabbed for his flask in his pocket, remembering it was empty. "Do you happen to have a bottle of hard liquor anywhere? Hell, I'll even take a beer at this point."

Asher arched his fluffy brows. "We don't allow alcohol on the island."

"I never thought an island paradise would be my own personal hell."

Charlotte motioned toward the elevator. "Shouldn't someone go with Elsey to make sure she doesn't break any more of their bones?"

"She wouldn't do that." Asher nodded for them to follow him while he led them through the main thoroughfare. "Unless they try to run."

Wesley took Charlotte's hand in his, tangling their fingers together. "You're okay with her excessive violence?"

Asher shrugged. "What she does here is to keep this place and the people here safe. If you're not a threat, she won't treat you like one."

"So, you're not scared of her?" Charlotte couldn't silence the echo of screaming and bones snapping in her thoughts.

Another throaty laugh rumbled through Asher. "I once knew a man who supposedly turned the skin of his enemies into blankets, and I wasn't scared of him either." Glancing back, he caught the wide-eyed expression on Charlotte's and Wesley's faces. His smile grew, accentuating the rounded curve of his cheeks. "My advice? Be thankful she's on your side. I'm not saying I couldn't take her in a fight, but I'd rather not risk my life trying."

Wesley looked at Henry. "What about you?"

Henry whipped toward Wesley—away from the people mingling in shops and on sidewalks. "I'm sorry. I wasn't listening."

"Do you not listen to the rumors about Elsey?"

"I don't listen to the rumors about anybody. They'd only piss me off, and they're rarely true. I mean, what do the rumors say about me?"

"That you're a drug addict and an alcoholic."

Charlotte looked over. "That you once got locked in the pantry inside Alex Cleary's mansion during a party because you got distracted and forgot how to get out."

"Okay." Henry gave a single nod. "That is an accurate representation of me, but to be fair, no one needs a pantry that big."

"That you'll have sex with anything with legs," Wesley added.

"That one's a lie. Having legs is a very low standard." Henry lifted a finger. "I require them to be human, my age, consenting, and not related to me."

Faint laughter escaped Asher.

Wesley scoffed. "I still think your standards should be higher."

"Probably."

Asher pushed open the door to a café and moved aside for the others to enter. "We'll sit down to chat for a moment before we get on with the tour."

A tall broad-shouldered woman with burnished amber eyes and naturally tawny tan skin greeted them from behind a glass counter filled with pastries and breads. A crooked smile lit up the woman's face. Henna ringlets spilled from her updo and framed her round face. Different machines meant for various drinks lined the wall behind the counter. A few people sat around the tables and chairs, but a small seating area with a sofa and two low-slung armchairs remained empty.

"These are Elsey's new partners, I take it?" The woman behind the counter looked over the teenagers. She grabbed a mug and began filling it with coffee.

Nodding, Asher passed around introductions. "Idalia, here we have Wesley, Charlotte, and Henry. Kids, this is Idalia."

"Nice to meet you." Idalia set the coffee in front of Asher before picking up a pair of tongs to place two glazed donuts on a small plate. "Anything I can get for you?"

Charlotte eyed the machines against the wall, already feeling the warm buzz by being in the same vicinity. She pressed her hands together under her chin. "Can you make a caramel-mocha latte?"

"Char," Wesley looked at her. "It's late, and we still—"

"Coming up." Idalia motioned to the boys. "Anything else?"

Wesley's shoulders drooped. "No, thanks."

Henry scanned the drink machines. "Not unless you have something that can get me drunk."

Idalia rolled her eyes.

Turning toward Charlotte, Wesley motioned toward the seating area. "Go chill out, and I'll get your drink."

She pressed a quick kiss to his lips and made her way to the back of the café. Henry followed close. She sat in one of the low-slung chairs, and he collapsed onto the sofa.

Henry looked from Charlotte back toward Wesley. "You two are cute together."

"Thank you?" Narrowing her eyes, she angled her head to the side. "What is this? Don't you hit on girls?"

"I hit on all kinds of people." Henry pulled his flask from his pocket. He upturned it to try to shake another drop onto his tongue. "But not if they're not interested or in a monogamous relationship."

Charlotte watched him shoot his flask a look of contempt.

"What I mean is, you two balance each other." He gave up his pursuit, dropping his flask into his pocket. "You're both anxious as hell, but you're more anxious in moments of calm. He's more anxious in moments of action. He likes to think everything through and to have a reason for everything. When he can't, he doesn't know how to respond. You're that push he needs to be impulsive when the moment calls for it. He's always been like that, but he was always more careful than—"

Studying the distant look that filled his eyes, Charlotte recalled the same instance of him cutting himself off before saying the name. "You don't talk about Kade."

Henry jammed his hands into his pockets, grasping for the pill bottle. His stomach twisted with the sharp blade of guilt and something deeper that weighed down his heart. His thoughts spun with the idea of just *saying* it. "He called me that night."

"What?" Charlotte gasped.

"And text me." Henry waited for the weight to lift. For the knife to pull free. Nothing changed. *I thought confessions were supposed to be freeing.* Pulling his phone from his pocket, he opened to the text messages and passed his phone to Charlotte.

Her mind whirled with confusion. Five single texts. All single digits. Nothing else.

2

3

0

7

8

"What does it mean?" The final message had been received at 10:20 P.M.

Henry clutched his pill bottle tight. "I don't know." The blade twisted further in his stomach. The weight dragged his heart down.

"Why didn't you respond?"

"I was … um … *entertaining* Rachelle that night, so I wasn't paying attention to my phone until after she left."

She backed out of the conversation, snooping through the cluttered inbox of random unsaved numbers. In the mix, she saw messages he never answered from the popular kids at school. Alex demanding that Henry talk to him. Victoria telling Henry to call Alex. Rachelle asking whether he'd be attending a party. Brant saying he needed advice. He appeared to only be corresponding with two people: Elsey and Ana.

Backing out, she went to his call log. She found more unanswered calls from the popular crowd. She ignored them and scrolled until she found the date of Kade's death. The last call from Kade came through at 12:06 A.M on August 25th, 3699. Henry had called Wesley twenty minutes later.

Charlotte handed back his phone. "Have you searched the alley for Kade's phone?"

"Yeah. I haven't been able to find it anywhere." Pocketing his phone, Henry cast a look at Wesley and Asher heading toward them. "Do me a favor and don't tell Wes about the messages or the call. He'll hate me for not telling him sooner."

"You want me to—"

"What does Henry want you to do?" Wesley reached Charlotte's side and handed her a warm mug. He shot Henry a hard look.

"Give my number to her teammates." Henry grinned. "I'm expanding my reach."

"I hope you're being smarter about your reach than anything else in your life." Wesley took Charlotte's place in the chair while she perched in his lap. "The last thing the world needs is a bunch of

Henry's running around."

Henry lifted his hands, sweeping them wide. "The only way I could be more protected is if I wore a hazmat suit with a chastity belt."

"Can we please stop talking about this?" Keeping her eyes on her drink, Charlotte's cheeks burned to a bright hue. She felt too aware of her seating arrangement.

Chuckling, Asher sat in the vacant chair. He rested his cane against the side and balanced his plate of donuts on his left knee. "Perhaps we should discuss why you're here in the first place?"

Wesley turned to Asher. "How did this place get started?"

"I envisioned it."

"Envisioned it?" Wesley's brow furrowed. His eyes widened. "You have powers?"

"But you were homeless!" Charlotte jerked toward him.

Asher took a sip from his coffee. "Who told you that?"

"You did," the trio said in unison.

"Did I?" He took another sip. "I don't remember."

Wesley and Henry exchanged a questioning look.

"Well, having powers doesn't mean you get to have a home." He set his mug on the arm of his chair. "But yes, I have powers. Elsey found me in an abandoned building and intended to give me supplies. I didn't realize that though. When I saw that little thing coming at me in the dark, I thought she was about to attack me. Caught her off guard by stabbing her with the knife I had hidden in my shoe and sent her across the room with a blast."

Breaking off a piece of one of his donuts, another chuckle escaped him. "Little thing didn't even scream when she hit the wall. Just got up, called me a bastard, and broke my cane."

Henry smirked at the smooth finish of Asher's cane. "She fixed it, didn't she?"

"After she got out the anger and I realized why she was there, we apologized. Me for stabbing her. Her for scaring me shitless." Asher popped a piece of donut in his mouth, chewing and swallowing it before continuing. "We got to talking. She told me what she was doing even though I already put two and two together. I told her about my vision of this place, and she told me she could make it happen. I didn't believe her at first. Then, I saw what she could do. She took my broken cane, laid her hand on it, and like Jesus-fucking-Christ performing an old-timey miracle, the thing was whole again. Let me tell you, I about shit myself. I've seen powers. I have them. But that was something else. I had to see what else she could do.

"So, I asked her to bring me here. She touched something and it changed before my eyes. She changed things one-by-one with a single touch." Asher stared off, remembering what he witnessed.

A soft smile settled on Henry's lips. "She has the ability to change reality."

Charlotte's eyes widened. "If she can do that, why doesn't she fix the city and everything else? Why not the whole world?"

Asher shrugged. "I don't know. She took breaks between changing things. She'd change a few things and go away for a little while, and then, she'd come back and change some more. Maybe it doesn't work on a grand scale. We're talking about a girl. Not a god."

"She has attacks." Henry's gaze dropped to the floor. His smile now gone. "If she uses it too much. At least she did when we were younger. Kind of like what happens when she sees the past. Only worse. A lot worse. She tries not to use it."

Asher looked at Wesley and Charlotte. "I guess that answers how people are in the dark about her powers."

Wesley nodded. "I've never seen her use them. I heard things a couple of times, but really, it's all rumors. Same thing with her parents. But she said her dad is considered useful and her mom is considered harmless, so I guess they don't really use their powers either."

Charlotte chewed on the inside of her cheek. Her eyes fell to Asher's legs. She recalled the scars covering Elsey's entire body.

"She can't change herself, and she can't change other people. I asked her," Asher said.

"How did you know—"

"Look at everyone here." He motioned toward the people in the café and on the indoor street. "You think any of them haven't asked the same thing?"

Wesley looked from the people enjoying their quiet company to the people scurrying around amongst the shops. "So, everyone here knows who Elsey is?"

Asher nodded. "We wait until we know they're not a threat. Once they graduate from the assessment stage, if they decide to stay here, I tell them about her. If they decide to return to the city, they're advised on how they can seek assistance if needed so they can get a better life. We're a team. She keeps this place a secret and has sworn to protect it with her life. I do her the courtesy of not releasing people who would endanger what she's doing. And we have a code in case we're in danger so we can evacuate."

Charlotte scratched the skin beside her thumb, thinking over everything she'd seen so far. "You don't keep any boats on the dock."

"We have another dock around the side of the island." He jutted his pointed chin toward the side. "It keeps people from getting suspicious. Same reason we keep the bars on the windows, and we try to minimize the light getting out through those windows."

"If you're creating a better place here, why don't you want people to find it?" Wesley continued surveying the people wandering the street in peace.

"Because not all souls are lost by happenstance. Some people are lost because they want to be, and they feel like it's their right to drag other people down that path with them. They could decimate the community we've built." Asher motioned toward Charlotte's drink. "Finish up, and then I'll take you kids around and show you the farm, the greenhouse, and anything else you want to see."

"Will Elsey be joining us?" Henry still stared at the floor.

Taking a sip of his coffee, Asher watched Henry. "The probability is not zero."

Charlotte savored the taste of her latte and focused on Henry and Asher. "Does she have any other powers?"

Asher shrugged, popping another piece of donut in his mouth.

"She can feel death." Henry stretched out his legs and crossed his feet.

"What?" Charlotte and Wesley echoed each other.

"Death." He repeated. "And suffering."

Thinking of the haunting glare in Elsey's eyes, Wesley fought off an involuntary chill.

Charlotte stared at her mug. "That sounds terrible."

"It is," Elsey answered behind Wesley and Charlotte, causing them to jump. She walked around the seating area and leaned against the wall. She crossed her arms in front of her.

Taking note of Asher's nonchalance, Wesley focused on Elsey. "What does it feel like?"

"Painful." The bitter pain screwed Elsey's heart into a tighter ball. "Constant."

Charlotte sipped on her mug. Henry fiddled with the rattling bottle of pills in his pocket. Asher finished off his donuts and coffee without comment.

Wesley stared at the floor, sifting through the piles of disorganized information he'd been given in such a short span of time. "Do most people have multiple powers?" He motioned to Henry. "You have two. Asher mentioned visions and blasting so that's at least two. And Elsey, you have three, maybe more. I have only one."

"I've never met anyone with only one," Asher said, tossing a glance at Elsey.

"You're an anomaly." Elsey shrugged. "You're an outlier of the normal, so it's hard to know what to expect. But abilities usually progress as you get older and stronger. You could have more that haven't developed or shown yet. Or you could have ones you haven't noticed before."

Wesley looked between Asher and Elsey. "What is the norm?"

"Most people, *including* our Gifted friends—" Asher lifted his cane and gestured toward Henry with the serpent's head before continuing. "—show signs of having powers at a young age."

Wesley frowned. "I think I would've noticed if I transformed into metal or glass when I was a kid."

"And you'd be quick to notice and accept something else unusual?" Asher inclined his head. He stood from his chair and leaned on his cane. "Most people with analytical minds find a way to explain away anything odd until something happens that they can't explain with a simple answer. Like turning into metal or glass."

"What does that mean?" Wesley raised his hands. "What else would I be able to do?"

"I don't know. That's for you to figure out." Asher nodded toward the door. "Come on, let's get this tour under way before the Grouch burns a hole in the wall with her glare."

Whispers crawled over the walls, stretching out from the faded wallpaper. Gathering their secrets behind the old photographs of the house's missing residents. Beckoning her forward. Just a touch.

One.

Single.

Touch.

"You didn't change?" Henry's voice jolted Elsey.

She jerked her hand away from the wall. Jamming her hands into tight fists.

Studying her and the cluttered wall, Henry descended the **_creaking_** stairs.

"No." Elsey forced her eyes to focus on him. Hoping it would be enough to block out the whispers. "I'm going back out. I don't want you three to tire out on your first night."

He nodded, still glancing between her and the wall.

Doors **_squeaked_** open. Wesley approached the top of the stairs with Charlotte close behind. "Is there a way to get our hands on Arnie's stuff?"

"Probably." Elsey nodded. "After someone dies, if they live alone, their stuff is collected by one of the storage facilities until a loved one claims it."

"People usually have to pay money to get the stuff released." Henry leaned against the banister. "My dad owns one of the storage facilities."

Charlotte's lips twisted into a deep frown. "Nothing like extorting grieving loved ones out of their rent money."

Henry cocked his head to the side. "I see you're familiar with the disease-ridden ass ferret."

"Only what Malini's told me." Charlotte shrugged.

Wesley shifted his attention to Elsey. "There were tubs and boxes in the attic marked for holidays people don't celebrate anymore."

"El and I celebrate them." Henry pointed to Elsey.

"Rich people celebrate them." Wesley shot him a pointed look. "You don't buy presents you can't afford."

Henry lifted a finger. "I know for a fact that you and Taliyah got gifts on your birthdays and on Christmas."

Crossing his arms, Wesley glared at Henry. "How do you even know that?"

Charlotte swept a hand toward him. "He was glued to Kade like a second shadow for years."

Henry tucked his hands into his pockets, groping for his pill bottle. "I was his personal taxi for so long that my passenger's seat is still perfectly molded to his ass."

"Well, it was never a lot." Wesley pivoted back to Elsey. "Arnie might've run a deli and had a house, but he wasn't rolling in cash. I doubt he was celebrating anything."

"I'll see what Luci and I can do." Elsey nodded. "My father owns a few storage facilities, too. If Arnie's house falls in his jurisdiction, we should be able to make a visit."

Nodding, Wesley took Charlotte's hand and led her toward the door. "We need to leave. It's late, and we still have to pick up Taliyah."

Henry started to follow them. Elsey's hand shot up and grabbed his arm. He froze. His heart fluttered. She jerked her hand away just as fast, watching the door close behind Wesley and Charlotte.

"Sorry." She questioned her impulse and the strange need echoing in her brain.

"It's okay." His voice was barely more than a whisper. All the flirtatious retorts that flew to the front of his mind couldn't make the leap past his lips.

Elsey bit her tongue and swallowed hard. Pulling her sleeve over her hand, she picked up the nearest lantern. She faced Henry, meeting his eyes as her heart resounded with that strange ache she couldn't place. "I wanted to show you something."

"Okay." He followed her down the hall past the stairs.

Silence clung to the walls. Wallpaper peeled away, and paint flaked to the creaking floor. More pictures of the missing family hung along the walls. Doors hung open, leading to an office, a bathroom, and two bedrooms. The odor of long dead tulips clung to the air like a noxious perfume.

"Are you going to show me a dead body?" Unease inched its way into Henry's belly. "Because I've already seen two tonight, and I wasn't exactly thrilled about it."

"If a dead body were in this house, you would smell it."

"Again, we *really* need to work on your ability to comfort people."

"It's not a dead body."

"There, was that so hard?"

"You're just filling up the space with words because you're scared, aren't you?"

His heart fluttered again. "You know me so well."

"You never shut up when we were younger." She cast a look over her shoulder before stepping through an arch near the end of the hallway.

"I grew out of being clumsy, at least." He chuckled.

She stepped through an archway on the left.

Henry followed with his full attention hooked on Elsey, smacking his shoulder into the frame of the arch. "Fuck." He rubbed his shoulder and cast her a look. "You didn't see that."

The corner of her mouth twitched up. She looked away.

Focusing on their surroundings, he felt an ache tremble through him. The house ached with sadness, but this room held a deeper haunting energy. Somewhere between beautiful and unsettling.

Vines—once wild and overgrown now long dead, strung over every surface in the cylindrical room. Covering old chairs and tables. Draping and crawling along the floor. Claiming the boards over the large picture windows. All except the windows highest in the spire showing an unmarred view of the night sky glimmering with brilliant diamonds.

Elsey sat in the center of the room. Placing the lantern in front of her, she folded her hands in her lap.

"Do you come here often?" Henry sat beside her, angling to face her.

"No." She kept her eyes glued on the view above.

He looked up. A sliver of moon cast a resplendent glow that he couldn't recall witnessing in the city, not even from the Bedlam's rooftop. The sight recalled a faint memory he stored away for safekeeping in the locked chest of his mind.

A redhead—small for her age and patterned in scars—sat atop the walls that separated their families' properties. She almost seemed to laugh when he tried to scramble up to sit next to her and fell to the ground. His eye was still black and blue from her punching him earlier that same day. She reached down and yanked him onto the wall. They settled in together. The moon's glow hung over her like a halo. She pointed out the brightest stars and told him stories of mythological figures and creatures that earned their place in the sky. His throat tightened when she looked at him with a steadiness that made his heart tremble. Her voice—delicate but jagged—met his ears like music. "Your eyes have stars like the sky."

He swallowed the emotions rising in his chest and looked at her. Noticing her sleeves covering her hands, he looked around the room. "This is one of those places." He thought of her almost touching the wall in the front hall. "It calls to you. You could touch it and find out what happened."

Tightening her hands into fists, she looked at him. "I don't know if I could see what happened to them exactly, but I'd see something. And from the feeling I get, I don't know that it's something I could handle."

"If you need me to help you—"

"You're scared of me." Elsey jammed her nails into her palms and focused her attention on the stars.

Henry frowned. Gazing at her, he dragged the words forward. Hoping they'd come out right. "It's not you."

She didn't move.

"I'm not scared of you." Again, his voice was nothing more than a whisper. Pushing his hair back from his face, he forced himself to repeat it with every ounce of his soul. "El, I'm not scared of you."

Elsey looked at him, seeing his eyes take on that unfamiliar depth she couldn't place. "Then why are you always scared around me?"

"I don't know." *Liar.* He shoved his inner voice down. "For the first time in four years, you're hanging around me again. You're not acting like you can't stand to be in the same room as me. Even if it's only because you feel like you have to or maybe because you want to. I *want* things to at least get back to where they were before." He swallowed hard and continued, "I meant it when I said I need you in my life. I need you. You were my best friend. Even all these years later, I still think of you as my best friend. I tried replacing you with anyone else, but I couldn't. You have no idea what it's been like to go from what we were, especially in that last month, to us living like complete strangers."

"We leave each other gifts." She struggled to recall that last month, finding a locked door barring her memories from view. "We text each other."

"It's not the same." His heart screamed like a soprano determined to lose her voice. Pulling in a deep breath, he decided to dive as close to the truth as his heart would allow. "I *am* scared. I'm scared to say the wrong thing because if I do then even the little progress we've made will be erased."

Letting his words settle inside her cracked and crumbling walls, her eyes returned to the scene above. *Words are easier when I don't have to look at him.* "I still have attacks when I use my other power."

"I figured when Asher told us about the island."

She nodded but didn't reply.

Tugging more memories forward from the darkened corners of his mind, he plucked his bottom lip. "Do you remember that saying you used to tell yourself whenever it happened?"

She released her stare from the scene above and let her eyes settle on him. "Tame the war within."

He met her gaze. "Was it something your parents said when you had one of those episodes?"

Shaking her head, Elsey pulled her right sleeve and a cluster of bracelets up—enough to keep her scars covered while revealing a black leather bracelet covering half of her forearm. It was embossed with a sword wrapped in wild roses and backed by stars. A crimson crystal in the shape of a small teardrop was set into the hilt of the sword. Tight laces secured the bracelet to her wrist, and small, strange markings decorated the edges. Across the embossed detailing, someone had scratched the phrase Elsey spoke.

TAME THE WAR WITHIN

"I found this in a box of stuff my father kept locked up when I was younger. I didn't wear it when we were children because it was too big. I thought it would still be too big when I finally tried it on, but it fit me."

"Do you still say it to help you with your attacks?"

"Not anymore."

He watched her roll her sleeve and bracelets in place. A hollow ache dug at his stomach. "El, do you ever think we'll get back to the way we used to be?"

"I don't know." She lifted her eyes to the moon shining through the high windows. "I don't remember who I was then. I remember parts of you and Ana. But not all of it. I remember returning and ... you were with *her.*"

The ache flourished inside of him, gripping his heart in a tangle of thorns. "You weren't around. I needed someone. I didn't know you were coming back, but if I did—" Henry's mouth dried. He clutched his bottle of pills and fought the urge to toss a handful into his mouth. "It's over between her and me and ... I'm not with anyone now. It should've been over between me and her for a long time. I could never make her happy. I knew that every time she confessed to hooking up with someone else, even the time I caught her with my dad."

"What?" Elsey's brows rose.

He stared at his hands, avoiding her gaze. "One night, I went with Ana and Jemma to the museum because Ana wanted to look at the local artist's section. She wants to get up there someday. Mal didn't go with us, but I told her to meet me at the house. I was high out of my mind when we made the plans. Or else I wouldn't have suggested that. I went to pick up Mal so we could meet Ana and Jemma at a restaurant. Unfortunately, I walked into the living room before they could put their clothes back on."

Rage roiled inside Elsey. Eating away at the constant pain tormenting her heart. "I know it's probably not what you want to hear, but Malini's not at fault. Your dad is an adult. She's a minor."

"I know." Henry nodded. Pulling his legs up to his chest, he wrapped his arms around them. "That's why I didn't break up with her. I didn't blame her. What happened was my fault. I should've been more present, and I wasn't. I never was present with her. I don't blame her for seeking attention elsewhere or for breaking up with me. I don't really blame her for anything."

"Why?"

He forced himself to swallow hard, ignoring the monsters laughing in the back of his head. "I think I deserved it."

"Why?" She repeated the same word with a heaviness he wasn't sure was real or imagined.

His heartbeat surged to his ears.

The **creak** of the front door echoed through the house. Ana's lilting voice called, "Henry! Come on, it's late!"

He held out a hand to Elsey. "I have to go."

"Okay." She took his hand and let him pull her up with him.

Starting toward the archway, he paused. "Text me when you get home, so I know you're safe. I don't care how late it is. I just want to know you're safe."

Elsey struggled to unravel that mysterious depth shrouding his eyes and the strange ache plaguing her heart. She nodded. "You, too."

Listening to the front door close, she pulled the communicator from her pocket. She replaced it in her ear, giving it a tap. "I'm heading back out now."

"Maybe you should go home and get some sleep, too." *Luci stood at the bar cart, refilling her glass.*

Elsey tapped the communicator without reply and left the house.

The whiskey on his tongue burned away the feelings radiating inside him. Henry dropped the flask into the pocket of his black wool overcoat—a recent gift for his birthday in May. He kept his attention fixed on the road.

Stars blanketed the sky away from the city. Thick rows of trees lined the road, leading further into the hills where the wealthiest families lived.

Veering on a shaded road to the right, he followed it until he reached the iron gates barring entry to the walls surrounding his family's estate—separating the Adamson and Hallen properties. He pressed a button on his keychain and waited for the gates to roll open. His stomach churned with a violent flood of bile. He retrieved his flask and took another swig. Holding the burn on his tongue until he passed through the gates and drove up the long driveway.

The driveway circled around a fountain with cherubs pouring water from vases in front of a grossly oversized Greek revival mansion complete with white pillars, a wide staircase, and large double doors. Henry parked behind Malini's new violet sports car. Ignoring the slimy sting of bile raging in his stomach, he left his car and entered the house.

Light from the gold chandelier beamed off all the matching trimmings in the foyer. A large mirror in a gilded frame hung to the right across from an ornate black and gold entry table that collected a writing pad and a crystal vase of golden yellow sunflowers and soft white lilies. A gold banister edged the grand wraparound staircase leading to the second floor. Gold details accented the swinging doors to the right and left, leading to the kitchen and the living room respectively.

Muffled voices came from behind the door to the living room. Recognizing his dad's voice, Henry grasped the pill bottle in his coat pocket and pushed the door open. He froze. His eyes glued on the scene in front of him while his mind raced to catch up.

"Henry!" Malini yanked her teal floral dress off the back of the white sofa and held it up to cover her nude body. Red flushed her dark eyes as if she'd been crying.

"You're home sooner than I thought." Micha, Henry's dad, stood from the sofa—pulling his black slacks up. He left his belt undone.

Bile climbed up Henry's throat. "What the fuck is going on?"

Malini hurried to pull on her dress and scrambled off the couch. "Henry, I can explain."

"Yes," Micha boomed. He swept his hands wide, a grin curling his lips. "Explain how I found you crying on the couch about Henry ignoring you and spending all his time with Kade or too wasted to give you the attention you need." He fixed his haughty glare on Henry. "She was begging for someone to take care of—"

"Shut up! Shut the fuck up!" A knot of anger unwound in Henry's stomach, crawling over his insides and swallowing the sickness eating him alive.

Malini stared at him. Her voice wavered somewhere between certainty and worry. "Henry, I swear—"

Taking her trembling hand, he led her from the room. He gripped the pill bottle tight in his pocket with his other hand. Reminding himself to hold his anger at bay.

"Henry," she said, trying again when they barged into the foyer. She looked at the door swinging behind them, catching Micha's imposing figure and sharpened stare. Anything else she had been planning to say never came.

He opened the front door and pulled off his coat, draping it around her shoulders. "Wait for me. I'll be out in a moment."

Searching his eyes, she tugged his coat around her. "What are you going to do?"

"Don't worry about it." Giving her a gentle nudge outside, he shut the door behind her. Anger tore his resolve to confetti. Coating everything in a haze of red. Sending his heartbeat to a fiery gallop. All the darkness he struggled to contain swelled forward. Uncovering all the monsters he kept buried beneath layers of pills and alcohol. The vile slimy wave pushed against his anger.

The door to the living room swung open. Micha passed through, staring down at Henry with a twisted grin. "She wanted—"

"I don't fucking care what she wanted! She's fifteen! You say 'no!' Or are you still having a hard time understanding what that word means?" Beneath the darkness, his monsters began dragging the skeleton of his childhood to the light. He swallowed against the sharp sting of bile burning his throat. Urging himself on without the full realization of his actions, he clung to his anger so he wouldn't spew everything he'd eaten.

Henry snatched the crystal vase off the entry table and heaved it with all his strength. The vase smashed into his dad's face with a sickening but satisfying *crack*. Blood spurted down Micha's face. The vase crashed to the ground, scattering flowers and shards of crystal across the white marble floor. "Don't *ever* fucking touch her or anyone else again!"

Micha's face turned a shade of red almost as bright as the blood dribbling over his lips and chin. "You worthless piece of shit!" He closed the gap between them with long, quick strides before Henry had a chance to back up. His fist slammed into Henry's face. Again and again.

Pain shot through Henry's right eye and cheek. Biting back a yell, he fell backward. He tried to scurry away. His dad kicked him in the side. Another kick to the ribs. Another to his stomach. With each blow came more insults and derogatory remarks slung into him.

Again, Henry tried to crawl out of his dad's reach. He heard the leather belt whip through the air behind him. With a burst of adrenaline, he rushed forward. The belt missed him, *smacking* the floor where he had been seconds earlier.

Henry huddled beside the front door, hugging his long legs to his chest. Rocking back and forth to keep himself from shaking and collapsing into a mess. The pain registered in the recesses of his mind, but it wouldn't fully hit him until later. The only thing that mattered was making it through this moment with the hope it didn't turn worse.

"Look at yourself." Micha's words met his ears—cementing into his brain. "Cowering like a sissy. God, what a waste. You're so pathetic. You're the worst excuse for a son! You've been a curse to me ever since you were born! You make me sick! You stupid, disgusting disgrace! Get your shit and get out of my house!"

Henry couldn't stand. His body trembled with quaking nervous energy crumbling his fractured foundation. Reaffirming how weak and powerless he felt. He continued rocking back and forth. His dad's words replayed in his mind along with every other similar time he'd been there—feeling just as weak and powerless.

"Didn't you hear me, Moron?" Micha jabbed his finger toward the stairs. "I said, 'Get your shit and leave!'"

Swallowing hard, Henry forced himself to look up at his dad. "I'm not leaving without Ana."

"You think *she* cares about you?" Micha's harsh laugh echoed off the walls. "You really think anyone cares about you? Look at what happened. Your girlfriend cheats on you. Elsey has nothing to do with you. All your friends think you're annoying and stupid. They only talk to you because they feel sorry for you. You're so stupid and pathetic that you don't even see it. *No one* cares about you! I don't care about you. Ana doesn't care about you. Your mom didn't—"

"Shut up!" Henry's anger flared to life again. "Don't fucking talk about her!"

"Don't tell me what to do! You pathetic piece of shit!" Micha raised the belt in his hand, glaring down at Henry. "Get your shit and get out. Leave. I don't care where you go. Just get out of my house."

Henry stared up at his dad, feeling impossibly small. His chest hurt with his heart beating at such a rapid pace. His skeletons caught the light in his mind, showing just enough to make the bile climb up in his throat. Taking a deep breath, he climbed to his feet and walked around his dad. Giving him a wide berth. Keeping his hands in tight fists to stop himself from shaking.

Walking up the stairs, Henry took the hall to the left. The door to his sister's large yellow bedroom hung ajar. He glanced inside, wondering whether she'd know what happened. Thinking of all the nights he'd come to wake her from a heavy sleep for comfort after his monster had been tormenting him.

Everything almost always happened out of Ana's view. When she was away from the house or when she was sleeping. What she witnessed was easily dismissed. He'd talked back. He'd lied. He'd stayed out past curfew. He'd played a prank or was involved in some form of impulsive mischief. Henry had always had a habit of doing something to get himself into trouble. It was enough that she could continue to wear her rose-tinted glasses to shield her from the truth.

She didn't know the things that happened late at night when he would see his doorknob turn. Or the times the bruises would be so bad, he'd spend days at Kade's or Alex's out of sight until they were light enough to be passed off as another clumsy accident.

He'd always wished to tell her, but he knew he'd be turning her hero into a demon.

Or she wouldn't believe him at all.

An ache flared in his chest. He continued down the hall to his room.

He hated the sight of the dark blue walls that held every haunted secret. Every memory of him lying in bed, crying, and praying for anyone to listen and to make it stop. Not to let the doorknob turn. To make his monster go away. To make him stop breathing so he wouldn't feel the pain anymore.

He looked around the room.

Doors to his massive walk-in closet took up the wall on the left. Bookshelves surrounded the desk and seating area on the right. Matching nightstands and an oversized bed with blue and white bedding sat in the center. A blanket knitted from scarlet red yarn draped the foot of the bed.

Grabbing the blanket, he decided what else to take. What else he could fit in his small car. He walked over to his shelves and grabbed three worn-out books: *The Phantom of the Opera* and the collected works of both Hesiod and Homer. Pulling the top drawer from his nightstand, he flipped it upside down on the bed and found the small manila envelope he kept taped on the underside: hiding two pictures and a white crumpled envelope bearing Elsey's name. He stuffed the manila envelope in the cover of the writings of Hesiod and left.

Henry walked through the house. Keeping his thoughts forward, he ignored the memories screaming at him.

His dad watched him descend the stairs and cross the foyer. Henry's mind ticked away the seconds he had left. The chance the situation still had to go from bad to worse. His heartbeat quickened more. Drowning every sound before it reached his ears. He couldn't move—couldn't escape—fast enough.

The monsters roared in his mind. Memories jumped forward to the light.

Him praying to God to make that doorknob stop turning. Him screaming when every blow came from his dad's fist. Him crying in bed as he remembered the variety show of abuse and the threats to stay silent that had been seared into his brain on an endless replay. Him begging his mom not to die—not to leave him.

Vomit stung his tongue. Yanking the door open, the cool evening breeze splashed over him. Allowing him to swallow it down.

Slamming the door behind him, Henry descended the stairs.

Malini leaned against the side of his car. She looked at him with wide, red-stained eyes. "Henry, are you—"

"I'm fine." He halted out of her reach, remembering for the first time that his right eye and cheek were probably developing a dark bruise.

She shifted her attention to the items in his hands. "Why do you have that?"

"I'm moving." The words left him before he realized what he was saying, but he decided to let them live as the truth. To cover the full reality of the situation with a layer of agency and a false sense of the strength he never felt. Feeling the house behind him—the possibility of his dad's eyes and ears on him—he nodded to his car. "Let's talk in there."

Malini nodded and climbed in the passenger seat. Henry joined her, tucking his blanket and books on the dashboard. He faced forward.

"Where will you live?"

"I don't know yet. Maybe my car."

"There's no room in here." She noted the two seats, neither of which reclined. "You can come over. My mom won't—"

"No." He spoke firmly, but his voice dissolved into a strained hollowness. "I can't have you take care of me again. Not this time."

She bit her bottom lip and squeezed her eyes shut. "Henry, I know how it looks. I *know* I've cheated on you before, but I—"

"It's not your fault." Henry balled his hands into tight fists.

Malini opened her eyes. "What?"

"It's not. I know I haven't been the best boyfriend. I spend more time getting wasted and not being present with you or anyone else. If I didn't, you would never have looked for attention elsewhere. I'm sorry. I need to do better. I need to get clean and to make more of an effort. I'm sorry that I haven't really tried. I'll try from now on though. I promise."

"Henry, I know you have no reason to trust me after what I did before. What happened wasn't—" The memory of Micha's threatening glare made the words shrivel up. She squeezed her eyes closed.

"I'm not mad at you." Henry pivoted toward her. "It's my fault. If I wasn't so absentminded, I wouldn't have told you to meet me here. I would've picked you up from your house. I know how he is. I know he wouldn't have thought twice about taking advantage of you if you were upset, especially if it was because of me. It's on him and it's on me."

Opening her eyes again, Malini stared at him. Realizing the full weight of his misunderstanding of the situation.

His anger and frustration built up. He slammed his hand into the steering wheel. "I should've been paying attention. I took a handful of pills when we were making plans yesterday, and I didn't even think about what I was saying or what could happen. I know that doesn't make it okay. It makes it a thousand times worse because I should never have let that happen."

Taking her hand, he squeezed it. "I put you in that situation. I know that. I *know* that's why things aren't good between us and why you've looked for attention elsewhere. I know it's all my fault. I'm sorry. I promise I'll do better. I will."

Malini tightened her grip on his hand. Her stomach and heart tangled into a ball. All the words she wanted to say sat heavily on her tongue. The shades of black and purple and blue covering his cheek and swelling up his eye made her remember all the other times he had bruises and cuts on his body and face. Bruises she'd helped him learn to conceal with strategic makeup and lies. She recalled all the times she heard him blame himself for the abuse and say haunting and terrifying things about no longer wanting to exist.

The memories weighed down the words on her tongue.

She glanced at the mansion. A dark silhouette stood in the frosted windows beside the door. The silhouette of a man much taller and larger than Henry—who made him tremble and recoil in fear from years of beatings and threats. A shudder raced through her at the thought of her own experience with him and the glare that followed her out of the room. Her heart and stomach twisted further. She faced Henry. "I need to go home."

Henry nodded and pulled his hand back.

She slipped his coat off her shoulders and opened the door. "Let me know where you end up staying for the night."

Nodding again, he gave her a quick kiss. "Message me when you get home or if you need anything."

"I will." She climbed out of the vehicle and shut the door.

Henry watched her rush to her car and speed down the driveway. When the red glow of her taillights disappeared, he looked at the house. His dad's silhouette stood in the window.

A wave of sickness crashed over him. Spinning around, he shoved his car door open and jumped out in time to hunch over the fountain. He emptied the contents of his stomach into the constant flowing water. He heaved until there was nothing left.

Taking a deep breath, he climbed into the car. He dug under his seat, finding the bottle of whiskey he stashed there. He took a long drink to wash away the rancid taste of vomit. Starting his car, he tossed his blanket and books into the passenger's seat with his coat. He pushed the gas pedal to the floorboard, peeling out of the driveway without a backward glance.

VI

September 7, 3699

One

*The **snap** of her kneecaps filled Wesley's ears. Followed by her scream when she crumbled to the ground.*

"No!" His heart broke even as it pumped at a high speed. He rushed toward Charlotte, grabbing a discarded metal pipe. The metal coated his skin.

A masked person stepped over Charlotte. Charlotte grabbed the person's foot and twisted. The person spun and kicked her in the chest. Charlotte didn't loosen her grip. The person kicked again, delivering a blow to her ribs. Charlotte continued to hold fast.

Wesley brought the bar down over the person's throat from behind. He pressed down on their windpipe. They wrapped their hands around the bar. The metal slipped over their skin—just like it did for Wesley.

He strained to yank it free. To break the connection.

*The person gripped the bar tight, slamming their foot with full force into Charlotte's torso in quick succession. A series of sickening **cracks** rang out.*

Blood bubbled over Charlotte's lips. Her hands released the person's foot.

Wesley's chest tightened. A growl rose in his throat. He drove his knee into the back of the person's knee. Their knee buckled. Grabbing Wesley's shirt in one hand and holding the metal bar in the other, they swung forward with the momentum of the fall and heaved Wesley overhead.

His grip slipped off the bar, breaking his connection and returning his skin to normal. He soared through the air and—

Wesley jolted up in bed. His heart raced. He gasped for air and sucked in deep breaths. Leaning forward, he pressed his face into his hands.

The **snap** of her kneecaps. The **crack** of her ribs. The blood pouring from her lips. His mind played it over again and again. **Snap. Crack. Crack. Crack. Crack.** So much blood. Again and again. Blood.

Her blood. Her life. Beaten from her. Taken from her. In front of his eyes.

Cold flushed his body. His throat tightened. Like his body was deciding whether to cry or to give up breathing.

Riiiiiing. Riiiiiing. He jumped. Still unable to shake the sound of her bones breaking or the sight of her blood bubbling up over her lips.

The ringing continued. Fighting through the barrage of images, he grabbed his phone off his nightstand. Feeling his heart begin to splinter again when he looked at the screen and saw it was Charlotte's dad. *Something bad happened! No! Please! No!*

"Hello?" He hoped the shakiness in his voice could be mistaken for him having just woken up.

"Morning, Wes," Landon said. He sipped from a paper coffee cup and sat down at the control panel in the security office. "Can you do me a favor? I've been calling Charlotte to make sure she's awake for school, and she's not answering."

Wesley felt certain Landon could hear the cracking of his heart.

"She probably just overslept." Landon swiveled around at the sound of the back door opening, and he nodded a greeting to Reagan.

"Overslept." The word sounded like a lie. A hopeful lie waiting to rip him open and bleed him out.

"Yeah." He turned back to the control panel and sat his coffee aside. "Can you run over there really quick and make sure she's awake?"

Feeling the panic starting to rise again, he nodded then remembered that Landon couldn't see him. "Yeah. I'll head over there now."

"Thanks. Tell her to call me."

"Okay." He didn't hear the click from the call disconnecting. All he heard was the **snap** of her kneecaps and the **crack** of her ribs.

Yanking on the nearest pair of sweatpants and grabbing his keys from his nightstand, Wesley rushed from his room. He slammed opened the door to Taliyah's room. The gust of wind blew back the drawings lining the wall beside her bed.

Taliyah bolted up in bed. "What the heck is wrong with you?"

"I'll be back. Don't go anywhere, and don't answer the door for anyone." Without waiting for a response, he spun and ran through the hall.

Wesley slammed and locked the door behind him. He charged over his yard and through his neighbors' yards. His heart raced faster than his feet could match. The scenery around him dissolved to a blur of fall colors and tin houses. All he saw was the image of her. Lying on the ground. Blood bubbling over her lips. Those lips that he ached to kiss one more time. *Please. No. Don't take her from me. Please.*

He ran up her porch and unlocked her front door. The horrible sounds repeated in his ears. ***Snap. Crack. Crack. Crack. Crack.*** The sight of her blood forever stained his heart. He reached her bedroom door. The sounds came louder. Louder.

SNAP.
CRACK.
CRACK.
CRACK.
CRACK.

His heart prepared to shatter.

SNAP.
CRACK.
CRACK.
CRACK.
CRA—

Wesley shoved open the door.

Charlotte lay with her back to him. Her dark hair spilled over her pillow. He couldn't tell if she was breathing. He couldn't see if there was blood on her lips.

"Charlotte!" He ran forward, grabbing her shoulders. Pulling her up. "Charlotte!"

"What?" She screamed. "What's happening?"

"Oh my God!" Wesley wrapped his arms around her. Pressing her tight against him. "You're alive. You're alive. Thank God."

"I won't be if you keep squeezing me." She muffled against his bare chest.

"Sorry," he said, loosening his grip. He looked down at her in his arms. All the shades of earth and wood in her soft hazel eyes. Her tawny beige skin that felt so smooth under his fingers. The natural tan and pink tones of her sharp defined lips—free from any blood. The sounds still repeated on a loop in his brain. Struggling to slow his still fragile heart, he pressed his lips to hers.

Charlotte ran a hand over his chest, feeling his heart trying to break free from his body. She pushed away to straighten her tank top. Cuddling up behind him, she wrapped her arms around him and pressed her cheek against his shoulder. "Not that I don't appreciate the morning heart attack, but do you want to explain what this is all about?"

Wesley nodded. Swallowing his heart, he hoped it would make it down in one piece, but he knew it hadn't been in one piece for a long time. Everything that came after the loss of his parents was just one more chunk broken off.

"I had a nightmare." He stared at the floor, focusing on a patch of carpet to stop the memory from replaying. "The person from last night. They killed you. I tried to stop it, but—" He leaned forward, dropping his face to his hands again. His shoulders shook while he fought a dry sob.

Tightening her grasp around him, she peppered light kisses over his shoulders.

He closed his eyes. Her kisses filled him with a comforting warmth.

"It's okay." She smoothed her hand over one of his arms until she found his hand.

Wesley laced his fingers through hers. He kissed the back of her hand and held it to his cheek. He remained silent. He didn't have the words to explain how everything shifted. Turning the image of her fictional death into the very real death of his brother. Gluing the image of his brother's body to the forefront of his mind. Blood staining his thoughts in a way he would never get out.

"I'm okay." Charlotte spoke between her kisses on his skin. "I'm still here."

Breathing deep, he nodded and sat up. "I know." He kissed her hand again. "I know."

Charlotte pressed into his back. He turned, catching her lips in a deep kiss. Angling toward her on the bed, he swept her hair behind her shoulders and ran his fingers along her throat up to her jaw. Chills rose on her skin.

Wesley cradled her face against his hand. "I can't lose you, too."

"You won't." She smiled.

He forced a smile to his lips and told himself to believe her words. Not to believe in the devastating possibilities lurking around the corners. Pressing a quick kiss to her lips, he stood. "I have to go get ready for school and make sure Taliyah is getting ready. Your dad wants you to call him."

"You talked to him?" Charlotte's face paled. "What did he say?"

"Just that you probably overslept, and he wanted to see if I'd come make sure you woke up and called him." His brow furrowed. "Why?"

"No reason." Her cheeks burned red. Remembering her current state, she pulled the blanket tight around her lap. "You should go."

Realization dawned on him. His eyes widened. "Oh, are you—"

"Wes," she snapped, pointing at the door.

He rubbed the back of his neck and kept his face down, covering the blush heating his face while he backed out of the room and shut the door behind him.

Sharp *ticks* echoed on the floor. The smoky odor of bacon wafted through the house.

Hoisting her rucksack on her shoulder, Elsey entered the kitchen. Her scarlet curls spilled over her opposite shoulder, covering the front of her pistachio green skull-painted tee. The hem of her black frayed jeans skimmed the floor beneath her heavy boots.

Her mother hovered over the stove. Her pastel pink heels and mint A-line dress flattered the red curls piled on top of her head. Grease *popped* and *sizzled* in a frying pan. She flipped a pancake on a griddle. Pointing her spatula at the table, she didn't look up at Elsey. "Sit."

"I'm not a dog." Elsey bit her tongue. *Why can't I just shut my mouth?*

Marnie looked at her daughter with a stare that could turn a man to ice. "I will not tolerate your attitude in this house."

If she felt fear, it was torn to pieces by the sharpened claws of rage before it could clot her heart. "That sounds like a problem I can solve for both of us."

"Don't test me." She pointed her spatula at Elsey. "You know better."

Slamming her teeth on her tongue, Elsey stomped through the kitchen. She opened the fridge.

Marnie flipped more pancakes and turned the bacon before it could burn.

Elsey opened the small drawer where her dietary needs had been resigned.

It was empty.

Slamming the drawer, she whirled to face her mother. "Where's my food?"

"You will eat what we provide for you unless you can earn the right to make your own decisions." Marnie gave a curt nod to the side without looking at Elsey. "And considering your history, I don't ever see that happening."

Boiling heat rose inside Elsey's chest, tensing all her muscles until she felt about to burst into a flurry of flames.

Marnie kept her attention on the stove. "Did you stay at school yesterday?"

Elsey tightened her grip on the fridge's handle. The plastic and metal molded to the grooves between her fingers. She didn't reply.

"I figured as much." Marnie set her spatula aside and wiped her hands on a towel draped across her shoulder. "You are to be at your father's office in the tower at four o'clock sharp today."

"Again, I repeat. I am not a dog. I do not respond to commands." She slammed the door.

The metal hinges snapped with the force, and the fridge door **slammed** to the floor.

She stormed past her mother and into the living room.

"Elsey." Marnie's voice grew colder. Sharper.

Stabbing into Elsey's heart.

Stealing all the fight from her with a single shift in tone.

Her mind flickered in and out. Her body became foreign. Numb. Just a lifeless doll sitting behind haunted eyes.

"If you do not meet with Gregor at the scheduled time, there will be consequences." Marnie picked up her spatula and continued busying herself without sparing Elsey a glance. "Do I make myself clear?"

Glaring out the windows, Elsey fixed her eyes on a spot in the front yard. "Yes."

Marnie cleared her throat. "Yes, what?"

"Yes, ma'am."

"Good," Marnie said. She waved her hand in a shooing motion. "Now, you may leave."

Shoving down all the rage clawing its way to her surface, Elsey headed toward the stairs at the back of the room.

The numbing fog continued to block the front of her mind. Everything blurred together. Colors, sounds, lights, movement all became one blob of existence she could never unwind.

She awoke from the fog on her motorcycle, tearing down the heavy tree-lined street. A fire seared her heart to charred remains and entropy ate away at her soul as it melted to distant everlasting hum.

three

"Mr. Adamson," a distant voice called.

Henry snuggled his head deeper into his coat on the tabletop, blocking the noise. Keeping himself in the safety of his fantasy. *Sitting on the couch on his rooftop. Stars blanketing the sky. A curly strand of scarlet hair twisting through his fingers. The weight of her head resting on his leg. Comfortable silence. None of the unspoken words holding them down.*

"Mr. Adamson!" The voice sounded more agitated.

He struggled to suppress an annoyed groan. *Maybe if I don't move, he'll leave me alone.*

"Let me handle this," said a sharp female voice, he knew all too well.

Leave me alone. Leave me alone.

A chair **creaked**.

Malini wrapped Kade's chunky black cardigan around her to cover the cutout in her black blouse and pulled the back of her brown leather pencil skirt down to keep herself covered. Leaning over the table, she aimed and tossed her pencil. It **popped** him in the head. Dull pain shot through his skull.

"Ouch!" Rubbing where he'd been hit, Henry whipped around and shot her a glare. "What the hell?"

"I have been trying to get your attention for at least five minutes now, Mr. Adamson," Mr. Pruitt said from the front of the room. The fluorescent lights glinted off the bald spot he endeavored to conceal with a poorly constructed combover.

Henry pulled his coat into his lap. "You're exaggerating a bit there. It was really only like two minutes."

"So, you were just choosing to ignore me?"

"I prefer to think of it as saving you the trouble of having to dumb down the lecture." Henry shrugged. "What is it about anyway? The fall of ancient Rome?"

The teacher ignored the faint giggles erupting from other students. "This is physics, Mr. Adamson."

"Henry." He dug through his pockets for his flask, failing to keep the tension from his normally steady voice. "My name is Henry. Mr. Adamson is my dad. Maybe if you called me by my name, I would have listened to you the first time."

More giggles rose from the other students. Malini twisted her hands in the sleeves of Kade's cardigan. She looked between the teacher and her ex-boyfriend.

"Somehow, I doubt that." Mr. Pruitt crossed his arms, focusing on Henry's expensive cashmere sweater and tailored trousers. "Besides, isn't Henry your dad's middle name as well? He gives you everything you could ever want or need while most of your classmates have parents struggling to put food on their table. I think you should be a little more grateful for him."

Any giggles in the room died. People watched Henry. Malini held her breath.

Dark thoughts clawed their way through the wave of sickness and anger crashing over Henry. Shoving his chair, he jumped to his feet. He gripped his coat as if he were attempting to strangle the life from it.

"Sit down, Mr. Adamson." The teacher pointed at Henry's chair. "If not, I'll be forced to call your dad and explain your behavior today and the fact that this is the second time you've actually been in class despite this being the fifth day of school."

Forcing down a deep breath that did nothing to calm the sickness rising inside of him, he returned to his chair. Henry glared at the teacher, all light in his eyes turned to the fires of rage.

"Thank you." Mr. Pruitt nodded and swiveled to the board to continue his lecture.

"Henry," Malini whispered.

He kept his eyes forward. Glued to the teacher's back.

"Henry."

He didn't move.

"Henry."

"I'm ignoring you." He kept his voice low to avoid calling the teacher's attention to him.

"I need my pencil."

"You would have your pencil if you didn't throw it at me."

Her chair **creaked** again. She leaned over the table to speak in a lower tone. "I'll be missing a stiletto in a moment too if you—"

Snatching the pencil from the floor, Henry flung it on the table in front of her. "You're really making me extra thankful that we are not together anymore."

"Wait." She held up a hand to halt him. "Are you talking to Elsey?"

He lifted his hands. "Why?"

She brushed her long black hair behind her shoulder. "I'm just wondering."

"Mal, *you* broke up with *me*." His control slipped, and his voice rose. "Why the fuck does it matter to you?"

"Mr. Adamson!" The teacher slammed his fist down on his desk. "What have I said about swearing in my classroom?"

Henry tossed his hand toward the poster hanging beside the door. "If I can spell it out with the periodic table, I should be able to say it in a science class."

"Fine." Mr. Pruitt nodded toward the poster. "Without peeking, name one element whose symbol can be used to spell that word, and I'll let it pass."

Feeling eyes on him, Henry's cheeks burned bright. The sickness roiling in his stomach inched up his throat. Numbness ate at his anger. He needed to escape before the darkness tearing at his heart left him to bleed in front of an audience.

Henry shoved his chair and tossed his coat over his arm. Grabbing his textbook and binder he strolled toward the door.

The teacher eyed him. "Step out of this classroom, and I'll have no choice but to call your dad."

His anger bit back. He spun on his teacher. "For your information, my mom named me after *her* dad who was murdered a few weeks before my sister and I were born. The fact that it's my dad's middle name too means nothing. And that you appear to have a high view of my dad in any way, especially if you did any sort of research on him to know his middle name, makes me question your ability to be an ethical and respectable teacher."

Mr. Pruitt crossed his arms and looked Henry over. "Considering you partake in what you dad is most known for, I'd say you're hardly the person to be giving anyone a lecture on ethics or morality."

"Go fuck yourself." Henry yanked open the door and slammed it behind him.

Two steps from the door, the cold wave of nausea rushed him.

He broke into a sprint for the nearest bathroom. Locking the door to the last stall and dropping his stuff to the floor, he spun toward the toilet and vomited. Sharp pain clenched his stomach. His head pounded with the force of a jackhammer. He spewed again and again. Until his stomach emptied everything he'd eaten for breakfast and lunch. Until all he could do was dry heave nothingness into the air.

He pulled in a deep breath and held it. Releasing it, the pain in his stomach eased. Another deep breath, and he could shift away from the toilet. Henry flushed the toilet and sat back, continuing to breathe deep.

Wrapping an arm around his legs, he rocked back and forth. His other hand plucked at his bottom lip, grazing his faint scar. He stared at the bathroom graffiti scrawled over the door and the walls. Buried in the ugly clutter, he could spot numbers written in two distinct handwritings.

One immaculate and pristine. *3 … 0 … 1.*

One jagged and quick. **3 … 0 … 2.**

The sharp stinging ache of a knife twisting in his stomach started up again.

Grabbing his coat, he dug in his pockets to retrieve a bottle of pills and his flask. He didn't think. Just acted. Needing to stop the feelings. Needing to stop everything from eating him alive and turning him into the broken boy he kept hidden beneath a makeshift mask of perfection.

He swallowed a deep gulp of whiskey down with two … maybe three pills or more—he didn't count.

This place—this moment—was not for thinking. It was not for

feeling. It was only for numbing. For reburying the pieces of him that had already begun to peek out behind his mask.

The warm tingling buzz filled him to the brim. Letting him drift until he could focus on one thing. The only thing he ever clung to. His one piece of hope shining in a life of darkness.

Henry pulled his phone free from his pocket and opened his conversation with Elsey. He stared at the, 'Good morning,' messages they'd exchanged when he first woke up and the, 'Good night,' messages they'd exchanged when he went to bed. The messages they'd been exchanging ever since she appeared again four years ago—after she'd been missing for two years. His heart trembled with the reverberation of a bass string being plucked.

He began typing a new message. Hey. I just—

He backspaced, erasing it. He tried again. I'm not sca—

Again, he backspaced. Would you like to—

Backspace. We could—

Backspace.

Backspace. Backspace. Backspace.

Backing out of the conversation altogether, he leaned back. Staring at those stupid numbers on the wall. Taunting him while the knife in his gut twisted more.

Buzzzzz.

The bass string of his heart plucked again. Reverberating through his body. Rattling his soul.

He picked up his phone and saw the message from Elsey. You okay?

Remembering that she'd never texted first before, a faint lightness eased into him. I will be now. You?

Same as always. She responded quickly, as if she were waiting for his reply.

A smirk settled on his lips. Their conversations usually didn't last long, but he decided in an instant to take a leap. Quick question. What elements on the periodic table spell out fuck?

He tried to imagine the corner of her lips twitching up with her barely-there smile, but the hopefulness in the thought was too painful. He let the image go before it could fully form.

She responded quickly again. Florine. Uranium. Carbon. Potassium.

Why?

Questioning whether she was trying to continue their conversation, his pulse hammered a shaky beat. Again, the hopefulness sent a shot of pain to his heart. *Too much.* Panicked thoughts he couldn't grasp spun through his head.

He typed a quick message, ending the conversation. Just wondering. Thanks.

Setting his phone down, he held onto the moment. Clinging to it for a little piece of comfort.

Buzzzz.

He jerked his phone to his face, reading the single word Elsey sent in response. Anytime.

The thrum of the cord shook his heart to life. Sent it racing at a fast pace he didn't know how to stop. He clutched the moment tighter. Wondering what it meant. The spark of hope ignited and fanned alive, glowing brighter than he could ever remember.

The wind tore Charlotte's hair from her hands. Fighting to pull her hair in a high ponytail, she missed the chance to stifle a full yawn escaping her.

"You've been yawning a lot today." Jemma's brows rose. Her short black bob danced in the heavy breeze.

"And Wes was like a zombie at lunch." Malini corralled her hair on her shoulder. Red stained her eyes from crying. Any traces of eyeliner had been wiped away. "Did you two—"

"What? No!" Charlotte's cheeks burned bright. "I don't want to talk about that."

"You *never* want to talk about it." Jemma clutched her books to her chest, covering the front of her faded yellow tee. Her worn-out jeans were in desperate need of new patches.

"And I shouldn't have to." Charlotte released her ponytail, focusing on the nearing gym.

"You don't have to." Malini tugged Kade's cardigan around her. "We're just curious. Have you two at least talked about it?"

"Yes." Charlotte opened the door to the gym and let her friends enter first. Shoving her hands into the front pocket of Wesley's hoodie, she headed toward the locker rooms. "We've agreed to wait. I'm not ready for something like that."

"And he's okay with that?" Jemma asked. "Aren't guys usually annoying about pressuring girls into having sex when they don't want to?"

Malini shook her head. "A lot of guys can be, but Henry and Kade weren't."

"I can believe that about Kade, but Henry?"

Charlotte opened the door to the locker room and traipsed to her locker, praying that her friends would find another topic soon. A few of her teammates were still changing at their lockers. The rest were already waiting on the track.

"Henry has a lot of flaws. *A lot* of flaws, but he was good about that." Malini sat on the bench with Jemma while Charlotte changed out of her jeans. "If I ever said, 'No,' he just shrugged like it was no big deal. I don't know who he learned that from, but I guess whatever I didn't do, he realized he could handle on his own."

"Ew." Jemma's face screwed up in a sour pinch, and she covered her face with her hand. "That's my girlfriend's brother. I do not need to picture that."

Malini released a small laugh—a rarity since Kade's murder. "Nobody's telling you to."

Pulling on her running shorts, Charlotte glanced at Malini. "Did you ever apologize to Henry for cheating on him all those times?"

The smile disappeared off Malini's lips. She dropped her eyes to the floor, hunching forward.

"Why did you do that?" Jemma lifted her hands.

"I just wanted to know if she felt bad." Charlotte dropped Wesley's hoodie to the bench and changed out of her long-sleeved mauve T-shirt into an orange tank top. "Especially with the last time being with his best friend."

Malini jerked her head up. "How did you know about Kade? We didn't tell anyone we were together until after I broke up with Henry."

Chewing on the inside of her cheek, Charlotte faced her locker. *Dang it. Why did I say that?* She scrambled for an answer. For anything that would fit.

"Wesley probably guessed." Jemma flexed her fingers in her lap. "I mean, you spent a lot of time with Kade before you two became official. And if you were ever at his house together, Wes might've overheard something or came to his own conclusions."

"He did." Charlotte shut her locker door. "You know how he is. You give him a problem, and he'll come up with an answer."

Malini stared at her for a moment before giving a slow nod. "Yeah. We probably weren't as careful as we thought."

Passing Wesley's hoodie to Jemma, Charlotte nodded toward the door. "I have to get on the field. Thanks for staying to give me a ride."

"Of course. I'm not scheduled to go into work until later anyway." Jemma bundled Wesley's hoodie on top of her stuff. She and Malini followed Charlotte.

"To answer your question," Malini said, twisting her fingers in the sleeves of Kade's oversized cardigan. "I apologized to Henry for cheating on him when I did it, except for Kade. He doesn't know about that, and I'm not apologizing for that when he has something to do with Kade's death."

Shoving the gym door open, Charlotte looked at Malini. Ignoring the blistering wind on her skin. "You're still on about that?"

"Henry found Kade's body outside of Bedlam." Jemma glanced at Malini before facing Charlotte. "And I've been inside his apartment. He reads a lot of old true crime books. He could've gotten the idea in one of them."

"I didn't even know Henry knew how to read." A faint smile passed Charlotte's lips when she realized Wesley would've laughed at her joke.

"He reads a lot actually. All kinds of books." Malini brushed her hair from her face, still fighting the heavy breeze. "He doesn't own a TV."

"You two cannot be serious. It's Henry." Charlotte lifted her hands. "Reading is very different from actually murdering someone. What would even be his motive?"

Jemma motioned toward Malini. "She broke up with him for his best friend. I think that's a good reason."

"Malini." Charlotte gestured with her hands to emphasize her words. "You said Henry didn't even care if you wanted to have sex or not. We've been friends since I moved here. I spent a lot of time around Henry while you were with him. I don't know much about him, but he's always been laidback. A bit chaotic and annoying sometimes, but still laidback and good for some mild amusement. After you broke up with him, did he call you or harass you once?"

"No."

"Then, and, I'm not trying to be mean, he obviously didn't care all that much." Charlotte raised her hands. "So, why on earth would he care now, all of a sudden, to the point where he was driven to brutally murder his best friend?"

Malini chewed on her quivering bottom lip. She met Charlotte's gaze with intense, watery eyes. "He and Elsey are talking again. If she told him what happened—"

"Stop." Ice traced through Charlotte's blood. Dialing the chill from the wind up to a freezing point. "We agreed we wouldn't talk about that. They were accidents. Both of them."

"Do you think either of them care?" Jemma frowned. "He's always been loyal to her over everyone else. Probably even over Ana. If he did it, she helped."

"That doesn't make sense." Charlotte shook her head. "Kade had nothing to do with it. Why would she—or *they* go after Kade?"

"To get back at me." Malini motioned toward herself, tears threatening to spill down her cheeks. "It was my fault. Both times. I did it."

"Then she would come after *you*."

"She might still be planning that." Malini's voice lifted to a dangerously high pitch. "Kade was there the second time. He saw it, and he didn't do anything. Do you think she's forgotten that? Do you think she's forgotten what *I* did?"

Jemma wrapped an arm around Malini's shoulders. "It was an accident. You were scared."

"I'm *still* scared!" Malini's eyes grew wide. Tears spilled over her cheeks. "She doesn't see things like we do! She's dangerous! You've seen the way she looks at people! I know she killed him! It's the only thing that makes sense!"

"Marion!" A voice called from the track field.

Charlotte whirled to see her coach waving her down where the rest of her teammates waited. "Be right there!"

She twisted back toward her friends, lowering her voice. "We are done talking about this. We agreed that we would never bring it up. She hasn't come after anyone, and it's been years since both incidents. If she wanted to kill anyone for it, she wouldn't have waited so long, and it wouldn't have been Kade. It would've been the person responsible. It was wrong. We know that, but it was an accident. If people found out—"

"You mean, if Wesley found out." Jemma narrowed her eyes.

Scratching at the sides of her thumbs, Charlotte turned toward the field.

Her stomach knotted into a ball. She thought of Elsey's expression when asked whether she was considered harmless while they were at Purgatory. Like she was moments from ripping out Charlotte's throat.

Squeezing her eyes, she faced Malini. "Maybe we should apologize. Even though it was an accident, she still deserves an apology."

Malini spoke firmly despite her tears. "I'm not apologizing to Kade's murderer."

"You don't know—"

"She *has* killed people." Jemma's frown deepened to a scowl. "She killed her grandparents. Both sets."

"That's a rumor." Charlotte peeled a piece of raw stinging flesh from her thumb.

"There's almost always a little truth to every rumor. She was the only one there. They found her covered in their blood. Both times. Once, I could believe it was someone else, but two times? No. It was her. I don't care how old she was. She's a murderer." Jemma squeezed her books to her chest. "She's a monster. And anyone that would associate with her, knowing what she's done, is probably a monster, too. Even Henry."

Charlotte bit the inside of her cheek. She forced herself to nod toward the field. "I need to hurry up."

Jemma pointed toward the gym. "We'll sit inside."

"You're *so* supportive," Charlotte called over her shoulder.

"We'll be with you in spirit!"

Laughing, Charlotte descended toward the field. With each step, her mind slipped further into the previous night.

Screams peeled the raw nerves under her skin. She took her place on the line-up beside her teammates. Bones **snapped** in her ears. *Dear God, please make it stop.*

"Go!" The coach shouted.

Charlotte ran from the starting line, taking the lead above her teammates. She cut a path through the heavy wind slamming against her. Everything around her fell away, leaving only **screaming** and bones **snapping** and then Elsey's serrated glare before she pulled the trigger.

She's a murderer. She's a monster. Jemma's words branded themselves on her thoughts in bold red letters. *Anyone that would associate with her, knowing what she's done, is probably a monster, too.*

D*ing.*

Elsey looked up from where she sat on the floor of the elevator, directing her eyes to the matte black doors. She folded her legs up so the young man stepping on wouldn't be so close.

Dark brown hair fell into his face. A black security uniform clung to his muscular body. His pale skin could've been used as a glow stick. Heavy notes of bergamot and neroli filled the cramped space.

"Hold the elevator," called a silky-smooth voice that held a vague familiarity.

The young man pressed the button to stop the doors.

A breathless Alexander Cleary appeared in the doorway. Pausing to catch his breath, he brushed his fluffy blond bangs to the side. His navy pants and watercolor floral button-up appeared tailored to fit his toned frame and complemented the gleam in his baby blue eyes. He passed a yellow folder to the security guard. "I'm glad I caught you. Victoria and I just got here. Can you give this to your mom?"

"Sure thing." The security guard tucked the folder under his arm.

"Thanks." Alex started to turn away but halted when he noticed Elsey. "Oh, hey, Stit—" He squeezed his eyes closed for a second. He tried again with a smile. "Elsey. I don't see you here often."

She held his gaze, trying to determine whether this was a trap. "I avoid it whenever possible."

"Say no more." Alex held up a hand. "I stay away from my mom and stepdad's businesses, too." He tossed a squeamish glance at the security guard. "I do *not* like hospitals. Too much sickness and pain and death." A shiver visibly tore through him.

The security guard chuckled. "That explains why you and

Victoria aren't interning at the morgue with her grandmother either."

"Yeah, it was either here or with Micha Adamson." Alex nodded. "I'd rather get in another wreck than work for him. Anyway," he said and twisted toward Elsey. "It was nice seeing you. I have to get going."

Alex stepped out of the elevator, and the security guard pressed the button to close the doors.

Elsey dropped her attention to her crossword puzzle.

"You know, reading in cars or elevators can give you motion sickness," he said when the doors closed.

"Thanks for the advice, but I think I'll be fine." She kept her eyes on the page and filled in a section on her puzzle. "If I vomit, it'll probably be from that offensive cologne you must've bathed in."

The man laughed. "I don't like it either. It was a gift from my mom, and I didn't want to hurt her feelings."

Elsey nodded and filled in another word. "You here to escort me to my doom?"

"That's what you call meeting your dad?" He pressed the highest button on the elevator—**96**.

"That's what I call being summoned against my will."

"You make it sound like you're a demon." He laughed again.

Arching a brow, Elsey looked up. "You're new here, aren't you?"

"Something like that." He jutted his hand down. "I'm Reagan. I also work down at the museum sometimes."

She stared at his hand and looked him over again. "Elsey, but I assume you already knew that."

Reagan hesitated before pulling his hand back. Drumming his fingers on the yellow folder, he faced the panel and watched the light on the numbers shift as they moved up.

The elevator **dinged**.

Elsey jammed her puzzle book and pen into her rucksack. Slinging her rucksack on her shoulder, she stood and watched the doors slide open.

She entered a long white hallway. A door leading to the stairwell stood beside the elevator. Reagan followed her to another door at the end of the hall into a small waiting room.

Stark white walls and bright lights made the room look larger. A small white sofa sat against the wall to the right. Gregor's dark-haired secretary hunched over her desk to the left, typing something on her computer. A nameplate that read *Theresa* sat in front of her. Her sage green dress highlighted her light beige skin and her rust brown eyes. Elsey reached for the large double doors next to the desk.

"He's in a meeting," Theresa said, focusing on her screen.

"Hi, Mom." Reagan approached the desk. "I'm escorting Mr. Hallen's daughter to meet him."

Theresa lurched to her feet, knocking a stack of folders onto the floor. "Shit." She looked between Reagan and Elsey. "Of course, give me one second."

Elsey stooped and gathered the fallen folders.

They watched her for a second before rushing to take over. "It's okay. We can handle it."

She continued piling the folders into a neat stack and placed them on the desk. Without waiting to be invited or announced, Elsey pushed the double doors open and entered her father's office—earning a gasp from Theresa and Reagan.

"Whoever owns Trivia Reserve is still refusing—" Gregor's words cut off at the sight of his daughter barging into the office. "Elsey!"

"I was told four o'clock sharp." Elsey crossed her arms over her chest.

Floor-to-ceiling windows wrapped around two sides of the room, allowing bright light to fall over Gregor's desk and fill the expansive, open space. The remaining white walls were bare except for black doors leading to a private elevator. A table mounted with a model of the entire city sat on the far right with whiteboards and bulletin boards surrounding it. **THE SENTRY PROJECT** was scrawled in Gregor's precise handwriting at the top of an otherwise blank whiteboard.

"I'm in a meeting." Gregor motioned toward the people scattered around his desk. He wore one of his typical black suits.

Elsey glanced at the guests, recognizing everyone from her father's dinner party. The elderly woman, in a saffron dress and with her hair pulled into a high bun, sat in a chair opposite the large black oak desk. To her right sat the attractive gentleman with thick black hair and dark eyes. He appeared more casual than the others in slacks and an ocean blue V-neck. The tall, tanned woman—wearing a peach shift dress—leaned against the desk. Her short, stout husband stood beside her in a black and gray suit with a cigar perched between his lips. The woman's baby blue eyes kept moving to Micha Adamson standing near the windows behind the desk. Micha's large muscular body was outfitted in a charcoal suit and a white undershirt with three buttons left undone.

Gregor looked at Reagan and Theresa. "Why didn't you stop her? You know I'm in a meeting."

"I didn't let them." Elsey arched a brow. "Did you want them to restrain me?"

He met her eyes. "Of course not." His lips curled upward further. "It seems I'll have to cut this meeting short."

He addressed the older woman and the couple first, "Ms. Boyer and Mr. and Mrs. Cleary, I'll call you as soon as we're done here."

The black-haired gentleman stood and shook Gregor's hand. "I'll be busy, but someone can relay everything to me afterward."

"Of course, Forge." Gregor pivoted toward Micha. "Micha?"

Micha glanced at Elsey before nodding to Gregor. "Got it."

Everyone stared at Elsey as they walked around her to leave. Her stomach churned when Micha passed her.

"Close the doors," Gregor commanded before sitting.

Reagan shut the doors, closing himself in the waiting room.

Elsey stood behind the vacated chairs.

Gregor rested his elbows on the desktop. The light filtered around him like he was an almighty deity, making Elsey's scowl deepen. "I know we've had this conversation before, but I need you to take it seriously this time."

"I'm not associating with Henry."

"That's not what I'm talking about." Gregor narrowed his eyes. "I want you to join me here."

"No." She dug her nails into the sleeves of her leather jacket.

"I built this from the ground up. Everything we have and everything this city is, it's because of me." He spread his hands wide.

A sour taste stung her throat. "I don't want this."

"And what do you want?" Gregor waved his hand toward the

window. "Do you want me to leave them all to suffer?"

"You think what you're doing is saving anyone?" Her mind began sweeping through her knowledge of the streets, but she silenced her thoughts and kept her attention focused on her father.

"The numbers on the Daily Death List are decreasing." He jabbed his finger onto his desktop. "That's because of my initiatives. I'm pulling this city out of the ashes. I'm making it rise again. Just like I did with you."

Elsey slammed her teeth on her tongue hard enough for blood to fill her mouth. Her limbs tingled and went numb. She forced a deep breath into her lungs and held it.

"I took care of you when no one else cared." Gregor stood and pointed at himself. "I gave everything I had for you. I built a world for *you*."

"You haven't built shit!" The sour taste in her throat smoothed with a roaring anger that flared to life in her chest, slaughtering any attempt to silence herself. "Not for me. Not for anyone but yourself."

"Elsey." His tone deepened with a warning. "I have done everything in my power to give you everything, and all I ask is for you to stand by my side. To accept what I've done *for you*. To join me."

"No." Elsey spun on the heel of her combat boots and stomped toward the door.

"With every advantage and latitude you've been given in life over everyone else, you have shown no drive to do anything other than stay out all night with unsavory characters."

She halted. Her temper flared to a fine point. The essence corralled in the back of her mind surged. With a single touch, everything around her would crumble. She took another deep breath, forcing herself to suppress her power despite the ache for release. Knowing she was near the edge and with the wrong trigger, she'd slip and let go.

"Time is running out, Elsey." Gregor's voice returned to its calm, collected state. "If you do not make the correct decision, I won't be able to continue to indulge you."

Elsey fixed the double doors in a glare. Focusing on the constant pain twisting her heart into knots, she wrapped a tight grip around the straps of her rucksack.

"People die every day, and you sit behind bulletproof glass claiming to understand. As if you know what it means to scrape together money to feed your children. To fight for a chance to live. To die on the street." She balled her other hand into a fist, nails biting into her scarred palm. "I. *Feel.* It."

Taking another deep breath, she reached for the door.

"Elsey," Gregor said in a smooth tone. His lips curled higher. "You will return directly home and remain there for the rest of the evening. If you do not, you will be in serious trouble. Do you understand?"

"Yes, sir." She stormed out of the office.

Reagan jumped up from the white sofa in the waiting room. Micha stood from where he leaned over Theresa's desk. Elsey walked past both men into the hall. Reagan followed her.

Micha closed the gap quicker, stopping when he reached Elsey's side at the elevator.

"Take the stairs." She jammed the button to call the elevator. Slime-coated anger gripped her stomach, but she didn't glance his way.

He faced her. "Excuse me?"

"Take. The. Stairs."

He opened his mouth.

"If I wanted to share an enclosed space with a pig, I would go to a farm."

Micha narrowed his eyes. "What has Henry told you?"

"That is assuming Henry and I speak." Elsey looked up at him, taking in his towering size as if he were nothing but a roach. "You have enough stench on you to be mistaken for a pile of dung."

The elevator **dinged**, and the doors slid open. Micha pushed past her.

Elsey grabbed his wrist and twisted it behind his back. She seized his suit collar. He struggled to pull himself free. Dragging him toward the stairwell, she called to a gawking Reagan. "Hold the elevator."

She shoved Micha into the door to the stairwell, using his weight to push it open before releasing him at the top. He tumbled down the first flight and hit the wall. Shutting the door, Elsey jumped off the top step and landed in front of him. The stark white of the lights and walls washed out Micha's pale face while highlighting Elsey's miniscule size and hostile glower.

Grabbing the lapels of his suit jacket, she slammed him into the wall. He kicked out. She caught his leg underfoot and pressed her boot on top of his thigh until he flinched. "Stop fighting, or I'll use my full strength and turn your femur into a pile of dust."

He froze.

"You've always made my stomach sick." Elsey released his left lapel and wrapped her hand around the front of his throat. "And based on a rumor I heard about you and a teenage girl, I'm starting to wonder how accurate my instincts were."

She watched his robin's egg eyes to see him squirm inside. "I remember you being a religious man. If you still are, I suggest you start praying now because I will be digging. And if I find so much as a single touch out of place—"

Eyes narrowing, he strained to pull himself free. "You have no idea who—"

She smashed her fist into the concrete wall beside his face. Debris crumbled and dusted his suit. All the rage and power she fought back begged to be released. She tightened her hold on his throat. Letting her eyes burn the single moment into his memory. "I will not flinch when I rip your bones from your body, turn them into lawn ornaments, and use your skin as a rag to mop up your blood."

Micha choked out a strangled breath. "You should be careful of the threats you make, Little Girl. People might think you really are a murderer."

Rolling her eyes, Elsey released him. She turned and ascended the stairs.

He tossed a glance to the imprint her fist left in the wall. Pulling himself off the floor, Micha straightened his suit and held his head high. "Shouldn't you give me a deadline?"

"Death doesn't hand out due dates. She comes to collect when she's ready."

Cold air cut through Wesley's thin white button-up and black pants. He rubbed his hands together. His breath hung in the air. He moved toward the shelves, making room for the produce and meat that had been delivered moments ago.

Stavros entered the walk-in cooler, pulling on a thick brown jacket. "Where's your hoodie?"

"My girlfriend has it." Wesley cursed himself for forgetting to get it back.

"Cute." Stavros chuckled and passed a box of mushrooms to Wesley. "On any day but truck day."

Wesley shrugged. "She has anxiety. It helps her."

"Okay, I take back what I said." He gave Wesley another box of mushrooms. "But what about your anxiety?"

"What?" Wesley glanced at him. "I don't have anxiety."

"Sure, and I don't have a gambling problem."

Wesley took the last box of mushrooms and shoved it on top of the other two. "You wouldn't have a gambling problem if you would go home after work instead of going to the Pleasure Strip."

"But then how would I become a millionaire?" Stavros tossed up his hands.

Wesley chuckled, shaking his head. "You really think you'll become a millionaire? You think the Hallens and the Adamsons and the Clearys and all the other rich people will hand over their millions because someone hit a jackpot in one of their cash houses? They use them as traps to bleed you dry."

"Anyone ever tell you you're a *little* negative?" Stavros held up his index finger and thumb a centimeter apart to emphasize his statement before handing over a box of onions.

"My brother." Wesley pushed the box to the back of the shelf. He nodded to the side. "His best friend. His girlfriend. My girlfriend. Her friends. Her dad."

"See." Stavros flung his hands toward Wesley. "Anxiety. Maybe some depression, too."

"Can you stop diagnosing me and hand me another box?"

Stavros picked up another box of onions. "You do *not* like talking about your feelings."

"I'd rather stab myself in the eye with a rusty screwdriver." He shoved the box of onions on the shelf, pushing a little too hard and leaving a dent in the side.

"That's unhealthy." Stavros shoved boxes of meat over to grab a box of carrots.

Wesley jerked the box from Stavros's hands. "Thank you, *Doctor*, but if I do talk about them, I talk about them with Charlotte." He pushed the box onto the shelf, still leaving a dent. Recognizing the tension in his shoulders, he took a deep breath. "Can we talk about something else?"

"Sure." Stavros plopped another box of carrots into Wesley's hands. "You think we'll die from eating this stuff?"

"What?" Wesley looked at Stavros like he'd grown two extra heads.

"I mean," he motioned to the box. "It all comes from that science place, whatever it's called."

"Forge Institute."

"Yeah." He nodded. "Don't they grow it in labs? How do you know we don't all have some disease from eating lab meat?"

"Jesus." Wesley's brow furrowed. "And you say I'm negative."

He set the box of carrots on the shelf and twisted to take the next one. "No, we won't die from eating food from the lab. They've conducted countless tests, and they continue to run tests so they can make sure it's safe and to make any improvements. Besides, the next city or town that has working farms for crops and meat is kind of far. The real stuff is more expensive now because it's only available to the people who can afford it, that's why we only get it in when we have dinner parties for people with deep pockets. It's more cost effective to find ways to grow food locally, and it creates job opportunities for the people who live here."

"And how do you know all this?" Stavros shifted over to the boxes of cabbage.

"I've seen it." Wesley grabbed the first box from him. "And I've helped, kind of."

"Huh?"

"They have a summer program for students interested in science and math. I've done it the past four years. They allow you to work in different areas to decide which one suits you best."

"So," Stavros tapped his fingers on the side of another box of cabbage. "Does that mean you don't dislike Forge?"

Tension tightened Wesley's shoulders. He took the box of cabbage. "He's helping feed the city. He's facilitating important research at the—"

"He's a rich as hell pretty boy who named a school and research center after himself."

"The school and research center are the same place."

"My point still stands." Stavros handed over another box. "You're pretty open about your disdain for the wealthy people in the city. I get it. They're not my favorite either. But when the Hallens had that dinner party here a few nights ago, Forge was sitting at the table with them."

Wesley pressed his lips together. He turned away from Stavros, pushing the box onto the shelf. His mind fixed on the image of the leading scientist in the city sitting among the most elite families. Another image shoved his previous thought aside.

Blue-green eyes radiating with a haunting sharp glare, head-to-toe scars, a mouth that never smiled, and a temper that only promised fire and death for anyone that crossed her. Swallowing to fight off a shiver, he shook his head. "Sometimes, to make progress, you have to fight with the devil instead of against her."

Stavros glanced up from a stack of beets. "Sounds like you—"

The door yanked open, and Taliyah screamed. "WESLEY!"

Wesley covered his ears. "What the hell?"

"Liev said I could tell you that your shift was over." Grinning wide, her dimples highlighted her full cheeks. The dim light glinted off the silver threads in her striped dress. "That was payback for scaring me this morning."

"I think everyone in the restaurant heard you." Stavros dropped his hands from his ears and lifted a box.

Taliyah gave an exaggerated bow. The pink beads in her hair clicked against each other. "Thank you."

"Come on." Wesley took her hand and ushered her from the cooler. "Later, Stav."

Leading Taliyah through the kitchen, Wesley stooped to her level and gave her a hug. "Remember our secret?"

She nodded and squeezed him tighter. "Be careful, Big Idiot."

"I will." He kissed the side of her cheek. "I'll be back later to pick you up. Listen to Galina and Liev, okay?"

Taliyah pulled back. "I always listen to them."

"Oh, so it's only me you don't listen to?"

"Charlotte doesn't listen to you either."

"She doesn't have to." He chuckled. "She's my girlfriend, not my baby sister."

"I'm not a baby." Shooting him a glare, she kicked him in the shin.

Another chuckle rumbled free from him. "I have to go. I'll be back."

"Okay."

He started to stand.

Taliyah launched herself at him, wrapping her arms around him and burying her face in the crook of his neck. "I love you. Come back home or I'll beat you up."

"I will. I promise." A stabbing ache filled his heart. He held her tighter. Wesley kissed her cheek again. "I love you, too."

A stray chill brushed over them.

Taliyah released him and wiped her eyes, erasing any sign that she might've begun crying. "I'm going to watch cartoons."

"Okay." He stood and watched her bound away and dash through the door as Jemma shoved it open, side-stepping before she could collide with Taliyah.

"I hate waiting tables," Jemma announced to the bustling kitchen.

Sauce was already setting in to stain the front of her white button down from an earlier accident. Dried sauce crusted on her arms and hands. Part of the little makeup she wore had been scrubbed away in haste, leaving her neck a slightly different tone of sunset brown than her face.

She carried a stack of dishes to the sink. "Wes, switch with me. You can have my tips."

"And deal with customers? Hell, no!" His frustration flared, and he motioned his hands with his rant. "I fell for that once. You cannot pay me enough to explain the difference between solyanka and shchi to a hundred different tables ever again. It's on the menu. We don't even serve them on the same night. How is it so confusing?" He took a breath to calm himself and nodded toward the door. "Besides, it's the end of my shift."

She faced him, brows rising high. "You're leaving without Taliyah?"

Brushing dust off his shin, Wesley relayed his prepared lie. "Charlotte needs my help with homework, and we decided to squeeze it into another date."

"Uh-huh." Jemma's brows furrowed. "I don't remember her bringing any books home from school when I drove her home."

"It's a project." He waved off her curiosity. "She has to do research. You know how that gives her a headache."

Before Jemma could respond, Wesley rushed out the back door.

Darkness dripped from the sky onto the streets below. The soft white glow from HAL Tower did little to compensate for the wavering streetlights. Silence clung to the team in the SUV.

A high fence, wrapped in barbed wire, circled the sprawling compound of storage warehouses. They passed two men in plexiglass booths outside the front entrance. Both carried a rifle. If they had any other weapons, they were concealed beneath their security uniforms.

"There are two more guards at the rear entrance." Elsey turned at the end of the street, parking inside the fence of a defunct factory.

"How do you already know that?" Wesley asked from the backseat.

"I checked it out."

"When?" He eyed her profile, inspecting her for any slight twitch.

"Earlier." She shut off the engine and opened her door.

"Wes," Henry said with a warning tone. He fought to avoid wincing from the pounding inside his skull.

"Henry, chill." Ana leaned back on the red sofa, pulling the computer onto her lap. "He's not trying to be mean."

Luci hunched over her laptop, clicking away on her keyboard. The sleeves of her black zip-up jacket fell over her hands. "Give me one second to access the cameras. They're on the same system as the city cameras, so it won't take long."

Pulling their masks over their faces, Wesley and Charlotte climbed out and followed Elsey to the back of the SUV.

"We'll split up to cover both exits." Elsey crossed her arms over her chest. "Sparrow and I will take the back."

"No," Wesley said.

"I'll be fine." Charlotte balled her hands into fists, tucking her thumbs inside to stop herself from picking at the raw flesh. She replayed the conversation she had with Malini and Jemma. Unable to silence the deafening echo of bones breaking in her ears.

"It's not that." Wesley groaned. "That means I'm stuck with— Where the hell is Eros?"

"Be right there."

Henry pulled off his coat and hunched forward, clutching his head in his hands. He sat back against the seat. Feeling the scraping underneath his skin, Henry watched from the rearview mirror. His head throbbed. Stuffing his flask and pill bottle into his pants pocket, he dropped two pills on his tongue and swallowed them dry. The tingling hum rushed through his body, dulling all his pain. Bright flashes of colorful stars burst in his mind. Sounds took on a soggy quality—the edges dripping with tension. The night felt like a thick blanket on his skin. Shoving his door open, he gulped a steadying breath of air.

Strolling around the vehicle, Henry took large steps—as if he were wading through a stream flowing against him.

Elsey watched him but didn't speak.

"I'm in," Luci said, *stretching out her long legs under the branch-like legs of the coffee table. Black socks peeked out beneath the hems of her black jeans. She sent the video feeds to Ana's computer so they could both watch the cameras inside the compound and on the surrounding streets.*

Giving a single nod, Elsey spun around and walked toward the factory. Charlotte trotted after her.

Elsey glanced over her shoulder. "Can you hop rooftops?"

"I've never tried."

"Well, look at this as your first lesson. And if you fail, you just break all the bones in your body."

Charlotte's stomach lurched.

"Fury!" Wesley snapped. He grabbed a metal bar from a scrap

pile and led Henry away from the factory, moving in the shadows out of reach from the streetlights.

"I won't let her fall." Elsey rolled her eyes. Jumping onto a dumpster, she bounded onto the roof of the factory.

Wesley's nightmare still plagued his thoughts. "Don't let anything happen to her, or I swear—"

"I'll be okay. I can protect myself." Leaping up, Charlotte landed on the dumpster and hoisted herself onto the rooftop.

Turning to her companion, Elsey pulled the communicator from her ear. She motioned for Charlotte to do the same.

Charlotte's stomach lurched again. The snap of bones echoed in her mind. She replayed the conversation with Malini and Jemma. Taking a deep breath, she reminded herself: *If she wanted revenge, she'd go after the person responsible.* She reached beneath her mask and pulled the communicator from her ear.

Elsey looked over the factory parking lot, watching Henry and Wesley leave for the street. "What do you know about Malini and Henry's dad?"

Deep lines creased Charlotte's forehead under her mask. "What?"

"Last night, you mentioned that she told you about him. Did she ever mention anything happening with him while she was dating Henry?"

"No." Charlotte shook her head. "Why?"

"Do me a favor and ask." Elsey began putting her communicator back in.

"Wait!" Charlotte held up a hand. "What is this about? I don't even know what you're talking about. How do I know what to ask?"

"If she tells you, then you'll know."

Chewing on the inside of her cheek, Charlotte thought about her conversation with Malini and Jemma again. She opened her mouth to say the words she knew she should say. That she wanted to say. Nothing came out. Looking Elsey in the eye—avoiding her scars— an oil slick roiled around her stomach. The words she needed remained lost.

Elsey put the communicator in her ear before Charlotte could find them. Charlotte copied her, promising to try again later.

Putting her back to Charlotte, Elsey motioned toward the other buildings spreading over the factory grounds and butting up to the warehouses. "In the city, they try to maximize space, so the buildings are usually closer than the needed ten to twelve feet for a human to make a safe landing. You still need to be mindful of the distance though as well as any obstructions and size differentials between buildings so you can avoid broken bones or severe injury."

Charlotte's brows rose. "You don't consider broken bones, severe?"

Arching a brow, Elsey twisted. "You really want to ask my opinion on the severity of different injuries?"

Charlotte dropped her eyes to the rooftop.

"Besides, if it hurts you, that's all that matters." Elsey pointed toward a trail of six rooftops. "We'll follow that route to the warehouses. They're all roughly the same size as this building and at least three feet apart. You should still do a running start. And since you're human, your bones are more fragile, so do a tuck and roll when landing, it will reduce the risk of any damage. I'll go first, so I can catch you if you don't make it or if you slip. We also have the healing serum just in case."

Charlotte nodded. She watched Elsey bound to the next roof with targeted precision. Taking a deep breath, she sprinted across the rooftop and leapt. She landed beside Elsey with a metal *thunk*, rolling into a crouched position.

"Sparrow?" Wesley pulled Henry into an alley.

"I'm okay." Charlotte stood and followed Elsey to the next rooftop. Then the next and the next. Like two darts sailing toward their mark.

Stopping at the edge of the final roof, Elsey nodded toward the two guards sitting in plexiglass booths on either side of the entrance. "I'll get them to leave their booths."

Charlotte looked at her. "How?"

In response, Elsey vaulted through the air and landed on the roof of the nearest warehouse.

A heavy metallic *thud* jolted the guards up from their relaxed positions.

"Did you hear that?" Shouldering his rifle, the man on the right shuffled out of his booth and peered at the fenced in compound. "I don't see anything."

The man on the left followed him, pulling his keys and flashlight from his belt. "It's probably just another cat."

"That was heavier than a cat."

Another heavy ***thud***—like something hit the cement inside the compound.

"That was *definitely* not a cat."

The second man rolled his eyes and shoved his partner aside. "How would anything else even get in there?" Unlocking the gate, he clicked on his flashlight and crossed the threshold. "Stay here. I don't want you shooting the poor thing. Here, kitty, kitty."

Silence.

He swept his flashlight over the first row of units. Nothing. "Here, kitty, kitty. Come on out."

Silence.

Moving his light over to the left he saw something step backward. His heart skipped. Chuckling, he shook his head. "Come on, kitty. Let's get you out of here."

Silence.

He trekked further into the compound. Only his flashlight kept him from being swallowed by the darkness. Something darted across the cement a few feet in front of him. Something fast. Larger than a cat. Dressed in head-to-toe black. Maybe it was just a shadow. A shadow of what? His heart quickened. He could hear it in his ears. Feel the pulse pounding in his chest. The figure darted out again, halting at a distance. He couldn't see their face. Only the thick shape of darkness just out of reach of his flashlight.

"Halt! You're on private property!" He reached for his gun. His heart plummeted. Glancing down, he realized he left his weapon in his booth. "Shit." He looked up. The figure was gone. Stepping back, he adjusted his grip on the flashlight.

He swung around, hunting for anything in the dark. Nothing.

"Hello?" His voice shook. "Come out!"

Silence.

Heart in his throat, he whipped around and started toward the exit. His partner hovered at the gate, clutching his rifle to his chest. Another black-clothed figure ran out from behind a booth and launched at his partner's back.

"Look o—" Sharp pain cracked through his skull. Everything went black.

Elsey watched the guard flop to the ground. "Dumbass." She leaned down and collected his keys and flashlight.

"Did you really have to call him dumb?" Charlotte eased her unconscious victim to the ground and collected a flashlight from his belt.

"He assumed he heard a 130-pound cat, and his first thought was to leave his gun and his partner and to arm himself with keys and a flashlight." Elsey motioned toward the unconscious man. "If they still gave awards for stupidity, he would be in the running."

Henry's laugh carried through the communicators.

"As much as I hate to agree with her," *Wesley stifled a chuckle.*

"How are you guys doing over there?" Charlotte flicked on her flashlight and entered the compound.

"I have a plan," Wesley said, leaning out from a darkened alley to watch the guards at the front gate.

"Good luck with that." Henry waved off Wesley and left the alley. He walked up the center of the street.

Wesley tossed up his hands. "What the hell is wrong with you?"

"A lot." Henry shrugged. "But we don't have time to get into that right now."

Groaning, Wesley stuck to the shadows.

"I told you to be careful," *Ana scolded*

Henry moved into the guards' view. He nodded while they left their booths, guns in hand. "Greetings, Fellow Earthlings. I have come to request peaceful entry into your depository, and if you decline, my associates and I will have to take it by force. I assure you there will be no probing of any kind. You're not my type."

Luci sighed, pressing her fingers into her temples. "What the

hell are you doing?"

"I'm asking nicely."

Ana failed to hide a giggle.

The guards exchanged a look and turned to the masked teenager standing in the middle of the street. They burst into laughter. One of them leveled the barrel of his rifle at Henry.

Henry lifted a finger. "Okay, it's rude to point at people."

A metal pipe bashed into the back of the guard's head. He crumpled to the ground. The second guard wheeled on Wesley as he leapt from the darkness. Wesley slammed his fist into the man's stomach before he could lift his weapon. The man doubled over. Wesley drove his knee into the man's chin and cracked his elbow over his head. The man fell to the ground.

Henry lifted both his hands. "I told them I had associates. I don't know what they were thinking."

"Probably that your brain was replaced with soggy cornflakes." Wesley yanked the gate. The lock snapped and fell to the ground.

"You say that, but I provided a great distraction."

Stepping out of the shadows from the storage units, Charlotte muffled her laugh. The corner of Elsey's lips twitched upward before returning to her normal flat expression.

Unlocking the door to the office, Elsey led the team inside. "We need information on new arrivals." She and Charlotte moved to filing cabinets on either side of a large key rack.

Henry plopped into the rolling computer chair and swiveled around. "What day did Arnie die?"

"Yesterday." Wesley lifted his hands. "You were there."

"A lot has happened since then."

"Like what?" Twisting his face at the realization, Wesley waved his hands. "You know, what? No. It's you. I do not want to know what you could've possibly been doing with all your other time. There's not enough bleach left in the world to scrub my brain clean from whatever you're about to say."

"You don't have to scrub with bleach." Henry pulled his flask from his pocket.

"I know that." Wesley scoffed and shook his head.

Charlotte glanced at Henry. "But how would *you* know that?"

He took a quick sip. "Who do you think does my laundry and cleans my apartment?"

"Guys." Elsey raised a hand. "Focus."

Wesley shuffled through a stack of folders on the desk. He pulled out a folder dated September 6th, 3699. Flipping the folder open, he counted fifteen pages. A number and a name headed each page above an itemized list of everything in each unit. "I think I found it."

He skimmed the pages until he found Arnie's name. "Unit 372."

Grabbing the key, Elsey took the lead with Henry carrying the flashlight at her side. Wesley and Charlotte walked hand-in-hand behind them.

The metal door to the storage unit **shrieked** open. Henry shined the flashlight on the contents inside. Boxes, bags, and furniture piled high to the ceiling in the small space.

Wesley and Elsey shifted items around to make space for them to wade into the clutter.

"This is disturbing." Henry tucked his hand into his pocket, finding the pill bottle waiting for him. "Imagine when you're gone, all that's left of you is relegated to what can be packed into 100 square feet and left to collect dust."

"I'd rather not think about it." Charlotte moved a chair to read the writing on a box.

Lifting a stack of blankets, Wesley spotted a familiar label. "Found one."

Elsey took the second flashlight from Charlotte. "I'll bring the SUV closer. You guys start bringing out the boxes."

Turning on the flashlight, Elsey followed the rows of units to the front entrance and stepped onto the cracked sidewalk. She glanced at the unconscious men slumped on the ground before starting toward the factory yard. A person wearing a black mask over their whole face glided out of the shadows with easy, deliberate steps.

Elsey halted. She recalled the attacker in Arnie's house. Her argument with Wesley still burned in her mind. *We can't get answers from a dead body.*

The masked person bent down and pressed their bare hand to the asphalt. A **buzzing** sound from the streetlights rose to a **screech**. The lights burst, sending sparks and glass showering over the street. The metal posts **creaked** and plunged toward the ground.

"Elsey! Look out!" Ana shouted.

Elsey jumped and grabbed one of the poles coming toward her. Swinging herself forward, she vaulted through the air.

"What's happening?" Henry ran away from his post at the storage unit door. Wesley and Charlotte followed.

"Someone wearing a mask is attacking Elsey," Luci's hands flew over her keyboard while she rushed to scan the nearby streets. "They were hiding somewhere."

"They're using my power." Elsey whirled on her attacker. "Not well, I might add."

She launched toward them with a kick. The attacker caught her ankle. Elsey kicked her other foot up and connected with their chin.

The stumbled, dropping Elsey's ankle. They righted themselves before they could fall and threw a punch.

Elsey dodged. Twisting to the side and grabbing the attacker's head. Jerking their face down to connect with her knee. A **crunch** reverberated beneath their mask. The attacker grabbed Elsey's hand and twisted it back. They spun and swept Elsey's feet out from under her.

She dropped to the ground.

Charlotte and Wesley rushed past Henry.

"Fuck!" Henry pushed himself to run faster. "I'm coming, El!"

Her heart jolted with a trembling spark, shattering her ability to keep her self-control in check. Flooding her with unforgiving rage. Power surged through her. Her hands went to the asphalt. The asphalt melted to a boiling tar. She grabbed her attacker's hand and shoved it into the scalding substance.

Shrieking beneath their mask, they jerked backward.

The tar continued to heat under Elsey's touch. Flames burst to life on the surface. The fire raced toward the attacker. A low hum echoed in the back of Elsey's head. She gritted her teeth.

"What are you doing?" Luci yelled. "You can't use that power!"

The attacker scrambled away from the fire. Scraping the remnants of tar from their hand. They climbed to their feet and jumped. Elsey pushed her power into the fire and watched it rise in a wall to meet them.

They burst through the wall of flames. Untouched by the inferno.

"Fuck!" Elsey plunged her hand into the flaming tar pit.

The attacker landed on top of Elsey. Pulling up a handful of the molten tar, Elsey flung the burning fluid at her attacker's masked face. They ducked and grabbed Elsey's wrist. Pinning her hand into the burning tar.

Elsey bit her tongue and pushed her power outward. The fire died, and the molten tar returned to asphalt. The hum in her head grew louder. Her heart sputtered. Darkness flitted over her vision, like someone was changing the channel too fast and all she could catch were brief images of the scene before her.

The attacker slammed their fist into Elsey's face.

Bile swam in Elsey's stomach. A pale blue hue tinged her sight between moments of darkness. Voices sounded heavy and bogged down by water.

Elsey sucked in a deep breath and pushed past the hum. She jerked up and headbutted the attacker in the face.

They fell back.

Rising to her feet, Elsey heard Luci and Ana's garbled voices in her ear. She blinked against the thick darkness threatening to overtake her sight. The loud hum didn't cease.

The attacker stood and squared their shoulders. Stepping toward Elsey, they pulled back their fist. A firm hand grabbed their fist from behind and spun them around.

Wesley held onto them—his whole body coated in metal from the bar gripped in his other hand.

"Thank you for your help." A sharp lilt sounded with the person's muffled voice. Their skin took on the same metal alloy as his. They shoved him.

He sailed through the air and crashed into the metal light posts blocking the road.

"Just!" Charlotte scrambled over the fallen streetlights to reach Wesley's side.

The attacker's skin returned to normal. They turned toward Elsey.

"Get away from her." Henry ran around the posts, tucking his flask into his inner pocket.

They ignored him. Stepping back. Putting themself closer to Elsey.

Heat flushed Henry's heart, and he stretched out a hand. The atmosphere quivered. He pushed the atmosphere in around the attacker. Their hands shot forward. The atmosphere crushed around Henry, bringing him to his knees. He choked and scratched at his throat.

Leaping toward them, Charlotte landed in the crushing atmosphere and fell to the ground with a gasp.

"Sparrow!" Wesley jumped to his feet.

"Don't!" Elsey pressed her hands to the asphalt and pushed all her energy into her power. The asphalt melted and spread to encircle the attacker's feet.

Wailing, the attacker dropped their hands.

The atmosphere righted around Henry and Charlotte. They climbed to their feet and took heaving breaths.

The attacker pressed their hands to the tar, trying to counter Elsey's power.

Elsey ignored the increasing hum and the darkness flitting in and out faster over her eyesight. The asphalt hardened around the attacker's hands and ankles.

Standing on shaky legs, Elsey struggled to catch air. The hum overtook her hearing. Thick darkness coated her vision.

"Elsey!" Luci and Ana shouted.

She couldn't hear them.

Darkness stretched before her. A dim light flickered in a distance she couldn't measure.

Her breathe became raspy as her ribs splintered. What felt like blades cut deep into her stomach. Her skin burned as she felt flesh peel away from her muscle and bone, head-to-toe. Pain stabbed into her. Like a dull needle stitching her back together.

Refusing to scream, she gritted her teeth. Choking on tears she refused to release, she pressed her hands against her head.

Pressure pushed against her skull. Her brain throbbed.

Distant voices called her name. They spoke words she couldn't understand through the sound of blood rushing to her ears and her heartbeat hammering a war cry.

Other voices, familiar and hollow, echoed somewhere in her mind. She tried not to listen. But the words scraped at her, digging into the scars mutilating her heart. Her throat constricted. Her lungs burned. Her heart ached. Her knees wobbled and gave out.

Warmth encircled her back and pulled her hand from her face. It squeezed.

"It's okay." A familiar voice, like smooth caramel, broke through the haunting words sewing themselves into her skin. "You're not alone. I'm here. You're okay." The voice trembled. The warmth squeezed her hand. "I'm not letting you go."

The voice repeated their statement. "I'm not letting you go. I'm here. I'll stay as long as you need me. Even forever."

Something about the cracking voice reached her. "I'm never letting you go."

The words ripped at the frayed string lacing up her festering wounds and replaced it with a fresh golden thread. Stitch-by-stitch. The sentence repeated again. And again. Low. Almost a whisper. "I'm never letting you go. I promise. I'll never let you go again."

The warmth squeezed her hand.

She took a breath and swallowed the rock of tears climbing up her throat. She squeezed back. Another breath, and the pain eased.

Henry continued to hold Elsey's hand. All his attention focused on her and not on the attack around him—until he heard them screaming his name.

Ana shifted her attention away from Henry and Elsey. She jumped forward. "Guys! They got out!"

"What?" Charlotte twisted to find the masked figure running toward her.

Wesley scrambled toward the metal bar.

Darting out of the attacker's grasp, Charlotte spun on her heels.

Wesley lunged for the person with the metal bar raised in his fist. They met him halfway and grasped the bar. The metal alloy smoothed over their hand, transforming their tan skin into a thick layer of the same material.

He brought up his foot and kicked them in the chest when they yanked on the metal bar. The attacker flew backward. The bar *clanked* to the road.

Aiming to give Wesley time to reach the metal bar first, Charlotte launched toward the attacker.

They leapt to their feet and caught Charlotte's fist before it could connect with their face. Charlotte twisted and jammed her elbow into their throat. Releasing a choked cough into their mask, they tightened their grasp on Charlotte's fist. Digging rough nails into Charlotte's knuckles. They kicked Charlotte hard in the back of the knees.

Charlotte's legs collapsed. Her knees connected with the pavement. *Snap!*

"No!" Pain racked Wesley's heart when he heard the sound from his nightmare. Anger and fear urged him on instead of allowing him to stop and think. He snatched the metal bar from the street and ran forward.

The attacker stepped over Charlotte. She grabbed their foot and twisted. They spun and kicked her in the chest.

She didn't loosen her grip. They kicked again, delivering a blow to her ribs.

Charlotte continued to hold fast.

A metal bar came down over the attacker's throat from behind. Wesley pressed down on their windpipe.

Wrapping their hands around the bar, the metal coated the attacker's skin.

Wesley's nightmare flashed in his mind. He tried to yank the bar free to break the connection. They gripped the bar tight and slammed their foot with full force into Charlotte's torso in quick succession. *Crack. Crack. Crack. Crack.*

Sharp pain stabbed into Charlotte's chest. Blood bubbled up the back of her throat. Her hands released the attacker's foot.

Wesley's chest tightened. A growl rose in his throat. Panicking, he drove his knee into the back of the attacker's knee. Their knee buckled. Seizing Wesley's shirt in one hand and holding the metal bar in the other, they swung forward with the momentum of the fall and heaved Wesley overhead.

His grip slipped off the bar, breaking his connection and returning his skin to normal. He soared through the air and landed on the road with a **_crunch._**

Pain tore through him.

Warm blood poured from his head and his left arm. His muscles sagged.

He couldn't move.

"Henry! Henry!" Ana screamed. "Turn around!"

"Turn around!" Luci echoed.

Henry glanced over his shoulder. The attacker walked toward him and Elsey. Laying Elsey down, he turned. Keeping himself in front of her.

The ground trembled. Henry glared at the approaching threat. "You will not touch her."

A distorted laugh sounded beneath their mask. "I don't want to touch her. I want to kill her."

The ground quaked harder. Cracks split the road and trailed toward the attacker. Rocks flew up toward them.

Still clutching the bar, the attacker's skin returned to normal. They lifted their hand and curled their fingers inward. The atmosphere pressed in around Henry. The rocks fell to the settling ground as he gasped for air.

"Henry!" Ana's eyes widened. Her heart cracked.

The pressure on his throat was too dense for him to breathe. Focusing on the red pulse of energy in the back of his head, he let his knees give out.

He remained in front of Elsey's body.

He couldn't catch hold of the essence. He raked his nails across his neck, scratching at something he couldn't grab.

Ana screamed when the metal bar bashed into his face.

His high cheekbone caved in. Blood gushed from under his mask in every direction. Painting his hair and the bottom half of his face.

"Fuck!" Luci gasped beneath her hands.

The metal bar came down again. His straight nose **_cracked_** beneath his mask. His skin ripped.

More blood flowed free.

The pressure on his throat tightened. He couldn't scream. He fell backward. Landing on top of Elsey.

The attacker drove the metal pole through his stomach.

White hot pain seared Henry's body.

Ana's wail peeled away the darkness coating Elsey's sight. The metal bar pierced her chest, pinning Henry's body on top of hers. Her heart knotted tighter into a ball of sharp pain.

Blood pooled around Henry and Elsey.

Ana's eyes burned with tears streaking her face. Screams continued to fall from her lips.

"Elsey! Elsey!" Luci jolted off the sofa, the panicked fire in her chest burning her heart to ash. "Can you hear me? Elsey! Please! Anyone? Someone answer!"

The attacker turned and walked away.

Ana's screams drowned any sounds that may reach through the communicators. Tears poured from her eyes. She jumped up from the crimson sofa, the same color as her twin brother's blood now staining the street.

Luci caught her before she could bolt through the door. "Calm down."

"Calm down?" Ana jerked out of Luci's grasp. "My brother is dead!"

"No, he's not." Luci lifted her hands and kept her voice level despite the panic building in her mind.

The door flung open, letting in a barrage of deafening heavy metal.

Tristan and Gene rushed in. "What's happening?"

"Elsey and the others were attacked. Bad." Luci motioned to Tristan. "Can you stay with her and keep her calm? Don't look at the screens."

Gene took Ana's laptop and balanced it on his arm. His black rose-covered sweater protected his skin from the heat. He looked at the screen. "Holy shit! Are they—Is she—"

"No." Luci tossed up her hands. "Don't even think it. They're fine. They're fine. She. Is. Fine."

The chains hanging from Tristan's jeans *clanked* against the edge of the coffee table. He pulled Ana to the sofa. His locs shielded his face while he spoke to her in a low resounding murmur until her screams became trembling sobs. He used the sleeve of his distressed and stitched up asymmetrical black tee to dab at her tears.

"I'm heading down there. They have the healing serum on them."

Luci started toward the doorway.

"Love," Tristan kept his voice calm and unwavering. "You can't do what you're thinking. You have too much in your system."

Luci spun around. "I need to get to her! She needs me! I can feel her—"

"Uh ..." Gene glanced up from the laptop screen. "Can I get someone's communicator?"

nine

Wesley stared up at the sky. A blanket of darkness hovered over him. With the moon in its darkened phase, the only light came from the faint glow from HAL Tower. Pain filled every inch of his body. He couldn't focus on the sounds coming through the communicator.

His thoughts drifted through the attack. To every moment that played out exactly as it had in his nightmare. To his girlfriend dying on the road out of his reach. He wanted to turn toward her, but the pain was too much.

Still, the physical pain didn't compare to the pain of his heart crumbling to pieces.

Tears slipped from the corner of his eyes and trailed down the side of his face beneath his mask.

A cold breeze settled over him instead of passing by. He shivered, certain it would only be seconds now before he would be gone. *This is it. I'm going to die. Taliyah won't even know what happened.*

The thought jarred him.

The pieces of his heart still left intact dug in together. The cold stayed with him. Clinging to him like a memory. He remembered Taliyah hugging him before he left for the evening. Telling him to come home and wiping away tears before he could see her crying. *Come home or I'll beat you up.* Squeezing him tight. *I love you.*

Anger consumed his sadness. Any ability to accept defeat turned into nothing.

The cold still clung to him, but he shoved it away in his mind. Digging through his thoughts for something. *No. I can't die. Not now. Think, Wes. Think.*

He remembered the healing serum tucked in his pocket. *I just have to reach it.* He flexed his fingers on both hands. He noticed then that his pain wasn't as strong as it had been seconds before. He flexed his toes. His feet and legs didn't hurt like they had before. He shifted his arms. That's when he noticed—

"Wesley, can you hear me?" Gene stared down at the laptop in his hands, blinking fast. Unsure whether what he witnessed was real. "Wes—"

"I can hear you." Wesley's voice came out stronger than he expected. He lifted his arms off the ground. The bone that had ripped through his flesh earlier was now back in place. His skin was solid—unscathed. "What's happening?"

Luci watched the screen over Gene's shoulder. She glanced up at Ana and Tristan eyeing them from the sofa.

"You're healing," Gene said, watching Wesley's bones fix back together.

"I'm what?" Wesley could still feel the pain, but it wasn't as strong. Like a phantom hanging over him. He moved to feel his head, finding the gaping wound under his mask now closed as if nothing had ever happened. He pulled his mask off and gulped in a deep breath.

"Healing. A lot of different beings can do it. Some take longer than others." Gene scooted over to the coffee table and set the laptop next to Luci's—still keeping it out of view of Tristan and Ana. "Don't move too fast. It could take a moment for your brain to totally heal."

"Do you have the healing serum?" Luci asked, sitting next to Gene.

"Yeah." Wesley took a deep breath and sat up. Dizziness swam in his head. He looked at Charlotte's body. Faced away from him.

If she was breathing, it was too shallow for him to see.

His chest hurt, like his heart wanted to crumble. The cold air still wrapped around him, pushing him to act.

"Move slow, but get over to—"

"Do you hear that?" Wesley caught it underneath Luci's voice. A small faint sound. Almost like a whisper.

Gene and Luci held their breath. Listening close. Focusing. Until they heard it.

Low. A rasping whisper. "Please, don't die. Please, don't die. Just hold on. Please."

"Shit!" Wesley saw the metal bar impaling Henry and Elsey and pinning them to the road.

"Elsey?" Luci yelled.

She didn't respond. She repeated the same pleas. "Please, don't die. Just hold on. Please. Please, don't die."

"She's alive." Gene glanced at Tristan and Ana. "I think they're all still alive or else she wouldn't be repeating that. Wesley, just focus on one thing at a time. First, Charlotte and then the others. Move slow but not too slow."

Groaning against the memory of the pain hovering on his nerves, Wesley climbed to his feet. He pulled the vial of healing serum from his pocket and shuffled over to Charlotte. Stepping in front of her, his chest ached with more tears bubbling up.

Blood spilled out from her mask, trailing down her neck. Her eyes shifted to him.

He knelt at her side and lifted her head as gently as he could. He peeled her mask off, holding his breath at the sight of more blood. Putting the vial to her lips, he waited. He waited and he prayed to no one in particular. *Please. Let this work. Don't take her from me. Please.*

A bitter salty taste laced with pure sweetness coated her tongue. The flavor made the blood in her mouth taste even worse. She fought the urge to spit it out.

Her throat remained tight.

She told herself to stop focusing on the pain. To remember how to swallow.

Forcing the serum down, a warm tingle spread through her. Her bones dislodged from her organs and pieced themselves back together. Her organs patched themselves up.

Charlotte sat up.

Wesley pulled her into his lap and wrapped his arms around her. He pressed a kiss to her forehead, not bothering to wipe the tears and blood from his face. She clung to him, pressing her bloody face into his chest.

Elsey's whispers cut through the moment. "Hold on. Please hold on. Please. Don't die on me. Please."

Charlotte looked over Wesley's shoulder and saw Elsey and Henry. "Oh my goodness!"

Standing, Wesley pulled Charlotte up with him. "I need your help separating them."

"I don't know if—"

"I have to get that bar out of them." He took her hand.

Henry's eyelids looked heavy. His gaze unfocused. Blood poured from his mouth. Covering his face and throat. Splattering his hair. Eyes remaining on Henry, Elsey's whispers were barely audible outside of the communicators. Their hands tangled together, gripping each other until their knuckles lost all color.

Wesley motioned toward Henry. "I need you to hold down his shoulders."

Struggling not to gag, Charlotte circled Elsey and Henry. She knelt in their blood and followed Wesley's request.

"Sorry about this." Wesley wrapped his hands around the metal bar. "This is going to hurt." He yanked the bar free.

Releasing a gurgling yell, Henry winced at the stabbing, burning pain.

Elsey didn't scream. Her eyes never left Henry.

Wesley tossed the bar. It hit the ground with a metal **_clank._** He pulled Henry off Elsey's body and crouched on the ground with what was left of his vial of serum.

Charlotte dug her vial of serum from her pocket and pressed it to Elsey's lips.

Henry and Elsey drank. Their wounds repaired.

He scrutinized the taste for something similar he could compare it to. The closest was a blend of pennies and black licorice.

She focused on one thing. *This is my fault.*

Climbing to his feet, Henry watched Elsey.

She stood and tried wiping their collected blood from her hands onto her pants—already soaked through with their blood. Spinning around before anyone could speak, she marched into the storage compound and out of their view. Her fist connected with the first building within reach.

Flinching against the sound of Elsey repeatedly punching the metal building, Charlotte wrapped her arms around Wesley. He squeezed her tight.

Gene and Luci exchanged a knowing look.

"Can you guys collect those boxes still?" Luci asked. "We'll meet you all at the house."

"What about the rest of the night?" Henry continued to stare at the metal fence until Elsey appeared in the doorway. Fresh blood dripped from her knuckles onto the sidewalk.

"There won't be a rest of the night." Gene closed the laptop and followed Luci to the doorway. They both paused to give Tristan a quick kiss. "We'll be back."

"I'm coming, too." Ana jumped up from the sofa and walked ahead of them.

Focusing on a patch of dead grass behind Charlotte's SUV, Ana shoved her car into park. She sucked on her quivering bottom lip. Her thoughts replayed the attack. The metal bar bashing into Henry's face and being stabbed through his stomach would be etched into her mind forever.

Luci glanced at Gene dismounting Elsey's motorcycle. She faced Ana. "Are you okay?"

Ana didn't move.

Luci looked toward Gene. He met her eyes and shook his head. She returned her attention to Ana. "If you want to talk or don't want to be alone, we'll be sitting on the porch."

Nothing.

Sighing, Luci opened her door and strolled past Gene. He caught her hand and their fingers laced together.

They walked through the tall dying grass to reach the crumbling porch. She sat on the third step and waited for him to sit on the step below her. He pulled her arms around him and kissed the back of her hands.

She rested her chin on top of his head. Her eyes moved to Ana—now hunched over with her hands covering her face. "I didn't mean for it to happen this way. Will she be okay?"

Gene gave a small shrug. "I don't know, Love. I wish I could say, 'yes,' but she carries a lot of sadness and pain in her heart." He fixed his eyes on the overgrown driveway. "They all do really."

"They're all a little bit broken"

"We all are. In our own ways." He squeezed her hand and brought it back to his lips. "That's the thing about being broken though. Broken pieces can find ways to fit together to make something new—something more beautiful. Like we did."

Luci struggled to stifle a snort. "You start making motivational posters?"

"Fortune cookies, actually." He laughed. Feeling his stomach grumble, he nodded to the side. "Speaking of fortune cookies. I'm hungry."

"You're always hungry." She rolled her eyes.

"Tristan's hungry, too." Gene paused and adjusted the collar around his neck. "He asks if we can bring food back on the way home."

She pulled her hand free from his grasp and ran her fingers through the thick strip of hair running along the center of his scalp. "How can you two even think about food at a time like this?"

A smirk tugged at his lips. "I assure you, Tristan is thinking about a lot more than food. I can't guarantee it's appropriate either though."

Shaking her head, she smirked. "Tell Tristan, I'll give him something to eat later."

Gene broke into a fit of laughter.

Headlights beamed through the trees. A large, black SUV crept up the driveway. The stoic expressions of everyone inside mellowed Luci and Gene to the appropriate level.

Elsey parked behind Ana's car. She stared at the small yellow vehicle. Still not speaking since the attack. Blood soaked into her clothes and turned her hair an even deeper shade of red. Henry watched her. Dried blood streaked his chin and neck and matted in his hair.

Wesley and Charlotte exchanged uneasy glances. They'd both done their best to wipe the blood off them, but there were still traces only a good shower would cleanse.

No matter how much they scrubbed, the memories would last forever.

Wesley spotted Gene and Luci heading their way. He opened his door. "We'll get these boxes inside."

Charlotte followed him.

Silence settled between Elsey and Henry. They listened to the back hatch open and to the others carry the ten boxes they collected into the house.

Henry took a sip from his flask. He looked toward his sister's car. "I'm going to check on Ana."

A single nod. Elsey gripped the steering wheel tighter. Blood trailed over her hand. She refused to take more of the serum to heal the torn flesh on her knuckles. It distracted from the ache eating her blackened heart.

Henry reached for his door handle.

"Are you okay?" Elsey wasn't sure where the words came from, but it was too late to take them back. Too late to let the silent pain eat her alive.

He dropped his hand. "I don't know. If you're okay, then—"

"I felt everyone dying." The steering wheel molded to her hands. She tried to loosen her hold, but her muscles refused to listen. "I felt *you* dying. Again."

"El—"

"You can't die. *I* can't let you die." A strange lump lodged in her throat. A deep trembling ache pulsed inside her heart. "I need you to be okay."

"I'm okay." His eyes darted to Gene and Luci outside the vehicle, but he returned his attention to her. A lamenting note thrummed on his heartstrings. "I promise. I'm okay."

"No, you're not." Elsey shook her head. Digging for something to hold onto, she snatched up her anger and let it coat everything she felt but couldn't name. "Not if I'm around."

The note stopped. Replaced by a sharp cut. "What are you saying?"

"This is my fault." She squeezed the steering wheel tighter. It would need to be replaced.

His heart slammed in his chest with a reverberating shake. His tongue felt heavy. *This isn't how it's supposed to end.* "Please don't say what I think you're trying to say."

Elsey twisted toward him. She took in the face that haunted her dreams and distant, warmest memories. *I don't even know what I'm trying to say.*

She met his eyes. Stars—a little dimmer than usual—danced in pools of sapphire. A recent memory, yet to be consumed by the holes in her mind or locked behind a door, darted to the forefront. *If you manage to hurt me. I'll answer one of your questions.*

Feeling the steady burning ember that had replaced her whispering ache for him, she told herself it was the right thing to do. "My favorite color is blue."

"What?" His eyebrows hunched together.

"Not just any blue." The next words she wanted to say fell dead before reaching her tongue. Unable to claw past a barrier she'd erected some time ago. She took a deep breath. Some part of her shook deep in her bones. She settled for repeating it—hoping he'd understand. "My favorite color is blue."

Henry stared at her, unable to ignore the cracking of his heart. *Her favorite color is blue? Why is she*—The memory shoved its way to the front of his mind. *If you manage to hurt me. I'll answer one of your questions.* "But El, I didn't hurt you."

"No, but feeling you die did."

"Please, don't do this. Please." Panic rose in his chest. A chunk of bloody hair fell into his face. "We were making progress. We were talking again. I need you in my life. We were fixing things."

"I can't be the reason you die."

"You said you need me to be okay, right?" He shoved his hair back. "Well, I'm *only* okay when I'm around you. How am I supposed to be okay if you're not there?"

"You'll be alive." She snapped.

"And what's the point of that?" He tossed up his hands. "What's the point of being alive if I'm not happy? Please, I *need* you." Henry met her eyes again, praying she could grasp what he was trying to say. *I don't know how else to tell you!*

"Henry, I can't—"

"Elsey, please." He reached for her hand but stopped himself. He shoved his hands into his pockets, grabbing the pill bottle like it was a genie that could grant his most desperate wish. "Please just give me a chance, okay? Just one. Without the fighting and the training. I'll admit it. I used that as an excuse to get you back in my life. I didn't know any other way. I didn't think you'd agree to it, but I had to try. Because someday I might not get another chance, and I—" He stopped and took a breath.

"Then you had this going on." He nodded toward Gene and Luci, helping Wesley and Charlotte carry boxes into the house. "And you needed me. I wasn't about to turn you down. But I don't care what we do. I don't care if you want to just sit in silence and stare at each other."

"You don't know how to be silent."

"I would try." He pulled his hand from his pocket and motioned toward her. "See, you get me. Even little things like that. You've always seen me for who I am, and you've never made me feel like I'm less than or unworthy for it. When you're around, I don't feel it."

She arched a brow. A spark shot off the burning ember in her chest. "Feel what?"

"Broken." He shrugged and leaned against the door. "Even when you tease me, you do it without making me feel like I'm a worthless, stupid piece of shit. You don't say things like they're insults. You say them like they are just what they are. Pieces of me that you accept instead of finding me annoying like everyone else. You don't treat me like I'm a child or baby me or like you need to dance around things because you're worried that I'll go off the deep end. You treat me like I'm normal. Like there's nothing wrong with me. You always have. You let me be myself and there's no pressure to be anyone else, and that's fucking terrifying but it's also really comforting. And it's something that I need. I need you."

Biting her tongue, Elsey faced forward. A memory haunting the fringes of her mind attempted to pull forward. She shoved it back. Gripping her anger tight even as it started to fray.

Henry watched her, breathing in all the unraveled chords that still somehow bound them together. "You don't try to fix me."

The ember inside her chest burned hotter, like a flame about to spring to life. Elsey watched Ana step out of her car. Her hands balled into fists. Her shoulders shaking. Tears streaking her cheeks while sobs continued to escape her.

Elsey nodded toward Ana. "You should probably check on your sister."

Glancing toward Ana, Henry flinched at the flash of pain in his stomach. He faced Elsey. Still holding onto the moment for all the hope he had left. "Elsey, please. Just give me one chance. Can we please just try to be friends? Real friends. No fighting or training has to be involved. Just me and you hanging out. Trying to get back to where we were or maybe something better. I don't know. But just one chance. Tonight even. You can drive me home. I'll fix us something to eat, and we can hang out. And if you have a miserable time … if you hate it—if you hate me, then I'll let it go. I promise. But please, I'm asking for one chance. Just tonight. Please."

She didn't move. She didn't breathe. Biting harder on her tongue, she held onto her anger. Struggling to ignore the ember burning brighter.

"Think about it at least." He opened his door. Pausing, he turned back to her. He took a shaky breath. "I don't know if you heard me before … when you had your episode. But if you did. I meant it. I meant everything I said."

Elsey tasted blood on her tongue. She listened to him shut the door. Her anger slipped from her grasp while she watched him round the front of the vehicle. Recalling his voice speaking to her when she was trapped in the darkness. *I'm never letting you go. I promise. I'll never let you go again.*

Warmth radiated from the golden thread stitching up her heart. Igniting the ember burning in her chest.

Just a small flame—burning with every fiber of her soul.

Wesley trudged out of the house. Charlotte followed, catching his hand and holding it tight. She fought the faint shiver as the memory of almost dying glued itself over any other thought. He pulled her forward and wrapped his arm around her waist. Reminding himself she was okay. That he was okay. That he *healed.*

Hearing a car door shut, Wesley and Charlotte watched Henry round the front of the SUV.

Ana rushed into Henry's arms and buried her tear-streaked face into his chest.

He held her against him, resting his cheek on the top of her head.

"It's okay. I'm okay."

She spoke, but it was muffled by his bloodied shirt.

"What?" He pulled her back, wiping the blood and tears smeared on her face.

"I don't want you to do this anymore." Tears poured down her cheeks. Her body shook from heart-rattling sobs. "Please. If something happens—You can't do this anymore. If you die—"

"No one is doing this anymore," Elsey said, slamming the door to the SUV. "No one but me."

Wesley's shoulders tensed. "Excuse me?"

Luci and Gene watched from the doorway of the house.

Elsey faced Wesley. "I should've listened to Luci in the first place. I can't enlist someone else who doesn't know the first thing about fighting for their life and hope they'll pick it up along the way."

"You think I don't know anything about fighting for my life?" Releasing Charlotte, Wesley descended the porch. "I'm a black kid living in literal hell on earth! Even what little protection there was for people who look like me even a millennia ago are gone! As soon as I was old enough, my parents put me in a class to learn how to fight. Same for Kade. Because out here no one will have our backs if something happens, so we have to have our own."

"My dad did the same." Charlotte lifted her hand.

"See." Wesley motioned toward Charlotte. "You think it's rainbows and sunshine out here for us?"

"And did that help either of you tonight?" Elsey balled her hands into fists, fighting to keep her temper from flaring.

Wesley tossed up his hands. "I healed for Christ's sake!"

"Congratu-fucking-lations." Elsey rolled her eyes. "And how far does that stretch? Huh? Do you know how much damage you could theoretically take before it overloads your ability to regenerate cells?" Her eyes went to Luci and Gene shaking their heads. She looked back at Wesley. "What if more than your bones get broken? What if you get stabbed in the heart? What if your head gets cut off? Do you think you could grow a new one?"

"I don't know. I've never done it before, that I've noticed." He glanced at his hands and arms. "I've never had a bad injury before. I just figured any cuts and scrapes weren't that bad."

"You have someone counting on you to come home at the end of the day. You *all* do."

"You do, too," Henry interjected, still holding his sister tight against his side.

Ignoring him, Elsey pressed on. "I can't risk you getting—"

"You didn't have a problem with me risking my life before!" Wesley tossed up his hands again.

"I wasn't thinking about the consequences if it went bad." Elsey dug her nails into her palms, squeezing to distract herself from the pain knotting her heart tighter. "It's different when I can feel you dying."

"And what about you dying?" Charlotte moved to stand next to Wesley. "If Wes hadn't healed and wasn't there to heal us, you'd be dead."

"No, I wouldn't." Elsey shook her head. "There would be a dead body, but it wouldn't be mine. I was holding back with my powers and my strength because of his stupid self-righteous pleas for me to spare the lives of people who clearly don't give two shits whether the rest of us live or die."

Wesley gaped. "You're blaming me?"

"No, but if you hadn't brought your morality—"

"My morality is what keeps me human! You could use some."

"Wes." Henry released Ana, getting ready to step forward.

"Human? HA!" Elsey tossed out a forced exaggerated laugh. "As opposed to what? A monster? If that's what you want to call me, then fucking say it! But guess what! If I'm a monster, so are you. Because you're *not* human. Humans don't turn into metal or glass. They don't heal at a rapid pace from broken limbs and fractured skulls."

"Maybe I'm not human, but I'm not a monster like you." Wesley jabbed a finger in her direction. "I don't have a disregard for life. That's what separates us."

"A disregard for life? I feel death. Every second of every day. Every single moment of my goddamn life." The pain in Elsey's heart clawed its way free. "Right now, someone died. Someone who had a family. Friends. People who were waiting for them to come home or to see their face at school the next morning. They could've been like you. Could've been a kid raising their younger siblings. But now those siblings don't have anyone. Now, they starve and die or fight on the street like everyone else. It could've been a woman who said 'no' to a man who didn't want to hear it. Or a kid who was the punching bag for a parent with an anger problem. Or something even worse—things that can't be forgiven or erased or fixed."

Henry shifted on his feet, fumbling for the pills in his pocket.

Wesley swept his hand out. "Just because you feel death and suffering, you think that gives you the right to decide who gets to live or die?"

"No. I think it helps me do what needs to be done when other people can't." Elsey forced her hands to unclench. "I don't judge anyone for not being able to pull the trigger. It's not easy. It *shouldn't* be easy. It takes a piece of your soul. But if you're already missing a soul, it makes it a hell of a lot easier. And I won't hesitate to end that bitch next time I see them. I won't stop until they feel what I felt. You want me to let them live after they nearly killed Charlotte right in front of you?"

He shook his head to free himself from the image of blood pouring over Charlotte's lips. His anger rose at the cracks of her ribs echoing in his mind. "No."

Eyes wide, Charlotte jerked toward Wesley. Her own morals raised questions. The memory of the pain stabbed into her.

Wesley continued, "What they did—"

"Is the same thing that happens to everyone else! Just because it happened to someone you care about doesn't mean they're the only one who deserves to pay for it." Elsey narrowed her eyes. "You want to go down to the island and talk to the people there? You want to tell Idalia that I shouldn't have snapped the neck of the man holding her in his basement? How about Okan? You want to tell him that his wife shouldn't have died after beating him with a cast iron skillet for the third night in a row? Or the many, *many* kids I have had to rip from the grips of some rotten festering excuse for human flesh they called mom and dad who did things that will haunt them forever. You want to go tell them that I should've let their *actual* monsters live another day when they'll never get to know a day that's not eternal pain?"

Wesley pressed his lips into a firm line, fighting the mental images forming in his mind.

Ana picked at the hem of her dress.

Henry stared at Elsey. The ridges of the pill bottle cap imprinting into the palm of his hands.

Charlotte looked from Elsey to Luci and Gene still hovering in the doorframe. "You guys never mentioned—"

"I told you guys, 'Things get dark and when I say to walk, you fucking walk.' If I come out with a survivor, they're not a villain." Elsey crossed her arms in front of her chest. "Robbers and thieves are one thing. They're doing it to survive. Even some murderers. But when it comes to the ugly things no one wants to talk about. The monsters who hurt people because they can or because it gives them joy. No second chances." She focused on Wesley. "Yeah, Wes. Your opinion of me is right. I am a monster. I'm the most dangerous monster there is. I'm the monster that hunts other monsters. But I won't add your lives to my body count. From here, I work alone."

"Ahem!" Luci cleared her throat.

Gene rested his hands on his hips. "I wasn't aware that we didn't exist. Tristan will have an existential crisis when he hears this."

Rolling her eyes, Elsey looked at Luci and Gene. "*Correction.* I work with my original team."

"Much better." Gene ushered Luci out of the house and closed the door. "The boxes are in the living room."

Luci took Gene's hand, walking down the porch. "We'll come by tomorrow and search everything."

Elsey nodded toward the SUV. "Gene, you may need to replace the steering wheel. Someone warped it. Thanks for bringing my bike." She strolled through the dead grass toward her motorcycle. Taking a breath, the small flame in her chest quivered. "Henry, do you need a ride?"

He spun toward her, releasing his pill bottle. Feeling his heart thrum with a heavy note that sent chills through him. "Yes."

"But—" Ana watched him rush over to Elsey.

Henry's brows rose. "Can I drive it?"

"Never." Elsey mounted her bike.

Luci exchanged a look with Gene over the hood of their SUV.

Wesley kept his lips pressed together, staring at the spot where

Elsey had been standing. Her words and revelations weighed heavy in his chest. He tried to organize them alongside his beliefs and morals growing more fragile with each passing second. Charlotte stared at Wesley, warring with her own questions that left her unnerved. Ana sucked in her bottom lip and hugged her arms around her body.

Henry sat behind Elsey. He glanced at her waist. "Can I hold onto you?"

"Unless you want to fall off."

He leaned forward and wrapped his long, slim arms around her waist. The flame in her chest burned hotter. Sitting so close, he caught a whiff of her shampoo and conditioner under the odor of blood. The chord of his heart plucked harder, reverberating with a rich soulful note. She revved the engine to life. Racing off into the city, he pressed closer to her.

eleven

The wind tossed Henry's bloodied hair out of his face. He held onto Elsey's waist. Breathing in her blood-soaked autumn bonfire scent like it would solve all his problems.

They cut through the manicured lawn in front of the museum and turned onto Boyer Road. The golden statue atop the building stared down at them, passing her wicked judgment. Stray dogs and cats scattered from tipped over trashcans. People dressed in rags huddled against each other for warmth.

Closing in on Bedlam, drunken people staggered off the sidewalk and leaned against the brick wall by the door. Elsey veered into the alley and tucked her motorcycle behind the dumpster. They climbed off, and she walked toward the backdoor.

"Where are you going?" Henry called after her.

Elsey stopped and twisted, arching a brow. "You said you wanted to hang out?"

"Of course. I just didn't bring my keys because I thought Ana would bring me home."

She glanced up at the window.

"You know," he said, trying his hardest not to smirk. "There is a front door. You don't have to go in through the window like a burglar."

Biting her tongue, Elsey looked toward the front of the building. Where pink and blue neon lights painted the street. Where people hovered, waiting to be granted entry. A deep ache trembled through her. Her skin itched at the thought of their stares and whispers. "People will see us together."

He shrugged. "I don't mind if you don't."

She looked at Henry. Beyond the blood streaking his perfectly constructed appearance. To the face that caused so many people to swoon.

He pulled his hand from his rattling pocket and held it out to her. "Come on. It will only be a second, and I'll stay with you the entire time."

Alarm bells rang in her head. If she did this, there would be no going back. No erasing what happened. No escaping the consequences. Every risk screamed at her.

She nodded but didn't take his hand.

Dropping his hand, he led the way.

Eyes fell on them as soon as they moved into the light. Whispers passed through the crowd.

Keeping her head high, Elsey tried to ignore the stares and the words that laced the pulsing music escaping the door. The nearer they came to the entrance, her stomach wound into a tight knot. Rage dug its nails into her. She reached out and took Henry's hand, startling herself. He glanced at their hands and gave hers a squeeze. Nodding a greeting to the bouncer, Henry passed the threshold and led Elsey inside.

Rainbow lights strobed overhead, masking the true color of the blood on their faces. People watched them weave through the crowd. They exchanged comments over the music. Elsey kept her attention on Henry. Focused on the flame burning inside her.

They stopped by the bar. A broad-shouldered man with spiked brown hair and intense blue-gray eyes greeted them with a wide-eyed stare directed at Henry. "What the hell happened to you?"

Henry tossed up his free hand. "A gaggle of werewolves attacked me and stole my lunch money."

The man glanced at Elsey, locking with her gaze before turning to Henry with an amused smirk. "I'm pretty sure a group of werewolves is called a pack. At least in most fiction."

"It's not my fault they lack creativity." He gestured between Elsey and the man behind the bar. "Elsey, this is Theo. Manager of Bedlam and Landlord to Henry. Theo, this is my guardian angel, El—"

"I know who she is." Theo's eyes locked with Elsey's again. A warning glinted in her glare.

"Everyone does, but you didn't have to ruin my fun." Henry held up his finger. "Did I mention I forgot my keys?"

"One second." Theo disappeared behind a swinging door on the right. A bartender took his place without being summoned and set a glass of whiskey beside Henry.

Nodding to the bartender, Henry faced Elsey and took a short sip. "Theo keeps a spare for exactly this reason."

She focused on him, feeling the mirror behind the bar waiting for her to look. "I thought your dad was your landlord."

"The apartment is supposed to go to the manager, and Theo decided to sublet."

Theo hurried back and handed Henry a key.

Henry drained the glass before leading Elsey away. They walked through the crowded club to the hallway upstairs. Eyes followed them every step.

Reluctantly releasing Elsey's hand, he unlocked the door to his apartment. "Meow, I'm home. And I brought the Angel of Death with me."

The orange tabby lounged on the arm of the sofa. Henry scratched behind the cat's torn ear and emptied his pockets onto the beaten-up coffee table.

Silence filled the space while Elsey's eyes drifted over the small loft. Taking in everything again though it had already been committed to her memory. Her gaze landed on the bookcase, and she moved to get a better look. "It's not organized."

"Yes, it is." Tossing his overcoat onto the coach, he sat on the floor.

She sat next to him. Aware of how close they were.

Feeling her body heat, he took a steadying breath. He motioned to the books, explaining his organization system from the top row down. "These ones I haven't gotten to yet. These are ones I want to read at least once more before I find them a new home. And these are ones that I've read way too much and need to stop re-reading so I can actually make a dent in my reading list. But they're my favorites, so that will be a while."

Creases cracked the spine of every paperback. Folds lined the covers. A few hardcovers looked like they might separate from tattered pages. Even the topmost books. The books he had yet to read.

"All your books have been read before."

"I get most of them at thrift stores or used bookstores." He pointed to a pristine book on Greek mythology. "That's one of the few I bought new. Most are used and well-read. I like them that way. Books give everyone else a new life, so they should get to live a life of their own. The creases tell you how much someone opened it. A worn-out cover means someone loved it enough to read it until they couldn't read it anymore or they took the book on an adventure. A highlighted line means, 'I love this. I feel this. I never want to forget this.' Handwritten notes mean the reader felt they had something important to say. A dog-eared page means someone had to stop, and you can guess why. Maybe someone knocked on their door. Maybe they had a cake in the oven and the timer went off. Maybe they saw a robbery happening and decided to close the book and use it for a weapon. It's fun to think about the possibilities.

"They each have their own story about what they've been through, and it left a mark on them. If someone didn't take these books they'd be thrown away because they're not new or *pretty*, but they did what they were supposed to do. They shared their stories. They gave people new lives. And they were stained and ripped and folded and burned and forgotten. But that doesn't make them any less beautiful to me."

When he finished speaking, he realized she was staring at him. The chord in his heart plucked, shaking his soul awake. "What?"

She turned away. Taking in every scratched and battered surface and piece of furniture in the loft. The torn ear of the orange tabby knocking Henry's keys onto the floor. Back to the books with their lives scarring their covers and spines. A memory pried itself free from the locked door she'd tucked it behind for safe keeping.

The flame in her chest burned brighter, bringing the memory closer to the light. *Don't.* She pushed it away. *I can't. I can't. I. Can't.*

She shoved hard. Sending it into the darkness before she could see. Words slipped out of her mouth, not the words she wanted to say. The only thing she could say. "They're books."

Plucking his bottom lip, Henry looked at his collection—

uncertain if he understood. "Books have souls. They collect pieces of them. From the author and everyone who has ever read them. It's how they live on even if they're not around. People keep them in their hearts, and they tell other people about them. Or they carry them with them and remember that time they picked up a book and found themselves living as someone else. Even a book someone didn't like. Every read book is a mark that a person lived. They lived and breathed, and the words kept them going even when they may have felt like they couldn't. They kept on because they had to find out what happened next. And though it didn't fix anything. It didn't make the pain stop or the nightmares go away, it was enough to hold on a little bit longer. Books save people when no one else can—when no one else will."

He watched her stare at the books lining his shelves. The monsters hiding in the dark of his mind trembled. "Kind of like you."

Sparks shot off the flame in her chest with a strong aching wave. She bit her tongue. Feeling his gaze on her, she scanned the bookshelves and landed on a title that sounded vaguely familiar. *The Phantom of the Opera*. Pulling it off the shelf, she looked at the cover. A white mask used to cover the upper portion of a face was front and center.

"That's one of my favorites. I don't know how many times I've read it. It never ends the way I want." Henry smirked. "To be fair, I don't think I root for the person I'm supposed to."

She flipped through the pages. Examining all the highlighted lines and notes written in Henry's immaculate penmanship.

"You can borrow it if you want. You'd have to return it though," he said, waiting for her to look up at him. "That way I can read it again and see if the ending ever changes."

The corner of her mouth twitched up.

His heartbeat jumped. He wondered if she would do it. If she would understand why he was offering. If maybe, just maybe, he could convince her to take another piece of him with her when she left.

"One more thing. If I can make a suggestion …" He pulled another book off the shelf. A red cartoon devil's face stared back at

Elsey, underneath the title *Hell*. "When you start it, you will think it is absurd and bizarre and that I'm nuts for recommending it. But trust me. The absurdity is what makes it wonderful. And if you appreciate my sense of humor, you'll enjoy every second of it."

She opened to the first page, skimming lines that earned a *Ha!* written in the margin.

Still watching her, his heart thrummed with a warmth he was worried he'd never get to feel again. The low burn of kindling waiting to catch flame. He pushed his hair back from his face. Dried blood came away on his hands. "Is it okay if I take a shower? I can fix us something to eat once I get done."

"That's okay." She nodded.

"Do you want me to get you a washcloth to wipe away any blood?" Standing, he strolled around her toward his bathroom.

"Okay." She focused on the book. Letting it pull her in until he returned, holding a wet washcloth out to her.

"Also, I should probably ask if you need to borrow any clothes. I don't mind."

Scrubbing at her neck and hands, Elsey looked up at him. Confusion dampened the sparks from the flame in her chest. "I'm okay."

"Okay. If you change your mind, help yourself." He walked toward his dresser and collected a pair of plaid pajama bottoms and a red V-neck shirt. Heading to the bathroom, he nodded to the kitchenette. "You can also fix yourself something to drink. I should've offered earlier, but I got distracted and forgot. Basically, anything you want here is yours." He pressed his lips together before he could say anything else that could possibly ruin the moment. Taking a deep breath, he glanced at her. "Will you still be here when I get out?"

"I have no intention of leaving until I know you're okay."

"I'm okay."

"I have never seen someone be healed with the serum after being so close to death." Setting the washcloth aside, she met his eyes. "I'm staying until the morning. I need to make sure you're okay."

Heart quickening to a rapid pace, his tongue felt like he gargled with dirt. "You can stay as long as you want." He nodded toward the bathroom. "I'll be out soon."

Elsey dropped her attention to the book he chose for her. Letting the words pull her in and hold her in place.

Steam filled the tiny bathroom.

Wesley stepped out of the shower. Grabbing his towel from the rack, he patted himself dry. His mind played on a loop.

One thought.

I healed. I healed. I. Healed.

He pulled on green sweatpants and a white T-shirt. The thought continued. Relentless. He wiped the condensation from the mirror. His streaky reflection stared back.

I healed.

Picking up his toothbrush, he remembered Asher's words. *You'd be quick to notice and accept something unusual?*

He picked up the toothpaste.

Most people with analytical minds find a way to explain away anything odd . . .

He squeezed the toothpaste onto his toothbrush.

. . . until something happens that they can't explain with a simple answer.

With a shift in his thoughts, his cells copied the properties of the thermoplastic polypropylene—coating his body in plastic the same deep brown of his skin.

Like turning into metal or glass.

Shifting his thoughts back, his skin returned to normal. He continued through his routine and pushed through his memories. Seeking anything that resembled healing or—

"My nightmare!" He stared at his reflection, eyes bulging.

"What?" Taliyah's muffled voice called from her room on the other side of the wall.

"Nothing!" Spitting in the sink, he rinsed his mouth. He opened the door and left the bathroom.

Entering her room, he noticed the cooler temperature. "You're supposed to be asleep."

She looked up from the book in her lap. "We were reading a bedtime story."

"*We?*" Wesley walked over to her bed. "You and your imaginary Gremlin friend again?"

"She's not imaginary." Taliyah glared at him.

"Then why can't I see her?"

"Because she doesn't like your attitude."

Chuckling, he reached for her book. "You want me to read that to you?"

"I know how to read, Butthead." She pulled the book out of his reach.

"Kade always reads to you before bed."

"Are you Kade?"

He ignored the hollow ache in his heart. Taking the book, he pointed to the small pink clock beside her bed. "Well, do you know how to read time?"

"Yes." She nodded. "It says it's time for you to get out of my room."

"Sorry, I must've missed the Taliyah-specific classes in school. You'll just have to deal with it. Bedtime." He carried the book to her bookcase. His eyes lingered on the framed family portrait standing on top.

A two-year-old Taliyah cradled in their mom's arms. Their mom had the same round face and full dimpled cheeks as Wesley and Taliyah. Her warm shining copper eyes were exactly like Kade's. Their dad beamed with a large grin that reached his smoky eyes. He had the same high forehead and strong jaw as Kade. The brothers stood together in front. Arms tossed over each other's shoulders. Kade was slim and had a smile that lit up the world. Wesley was still small and awkward. Still shorter than Kade. It would stay that way until he turned fourteen and seemed to grow overnight, needing new shoes and pants almost daily.

It was the first family portrait taken on Kade's first camera. And the last family portrait taken before their parents died.

Seeing the picture, he remembered the box he'd found stashed in Kade's closet.

Replacing the book on Taliyah's shelf, he returned to her bedside and kissed her forehead. "Goodnight, Kiddo. I love you. Call for me if you need anything."

"Goodnight." She pulled her butterfly-printed blanket up to her chin.

"Need me to check for monsters?" The image of Elsey flashed in his mind, and he fought a grimace.

Glancing up, he caught sight of a drawing of a masked figure dressed in head-to-toe black standing in the middle of a darkened street. Two other figures stood on either side of them with little detail to distinguish them from shadows.

"No," Taliyah said, pulling his attention back to her. She rolled over to her side. "I know you won't let them get me."

He kissed her forehead again and crossed to the door, thoughts already working on the next step.

"Wes," Taliyah rolled onto her back.

"Yeah?" He paused in the doorway.

"You're doing a good job." She glanced away from his face. "Kade knows you're doing good."

Gripping the doorknob, he kept his expression calm. "How do you know that?"

Turning back to him, she shrugged. "He wouldn't leave you in charge if he didn't think you'd do a good job."

A tight smile inched onto his lips. His throat constricted. "Thank you. Now, get some sleep. I'll turn up the heat. It must be getting colder quicker this year." He flipped off her light and cracked her door.

Sucking in a deep breath, he shoved down any emotions before they could escape. He stopped by his room and grabbed his forest green hoodie and his phone from his bed. He had three missed calls from Charlotte. His heart jumped. His mind raced through different scenarios.

Knock. Knock.

He shoved his phone into his pocket and tossed his hoodie over his shoulder before rushing from his room. He pulled aside the curtain covering the small window in the front door. Charlotte stood on the top step. Shivering in her gray shorts, lavender T-shirt, and white sneakers. Red stained her eyes. Tears painted her cheeks.

His heart raced. He yanked the door open. "What's wrong? What happened?"

Charlotte shook her head. The breeze ripped at her wet hair. "I took a shower, and I couldn't stop thinking. My dad's working all night. I don't want to be alone. I'm sorry."

Wesley pulled her inside, wrapping her in his arms. He kissed the top of her head. "It's okay. You can stay here tonight."

"Are you sure?" She sniffled and peered up at him through her long, dark lashes.

"Of course." Keeping an arm around her shoulders, he closed the door and reached past her to adjust the thermostat. "Do you want to talk about it?"

She squeezed him tighter. "I don't know."

He led her into the living room. His eyes went to the pictures along the wall—running from the living room into the kitchen up to Kade's closed bedroom door. "Is it okay if I talk?"

Nodding, she watched him sit on the edge of the coffee table and let him pull her into his lap.

Wesley found her hand and knotted his fingers with hers. "Remember that nightmare I had?" He met her eyes. "About you dying?"

Chewing on the inside of her cheek, she nodded.

"It happened." He tightened his arm around her waist. "Tonight. It came true. The only thing that was different was you weren't wearing your mask in my nightmare. I realized it when it was happening, but I couldn't stop it. I was too rushed. I couldn't stop to think and change it. And then with the argument with Elsey, I forgot."

"Has anything like that happened to you before?"

"I don't know." He looked away, finding their darkened reflection on the surface of the television. "I don't remember it ever happening, but—"

"You dismiss things that you can explain." She itched to scrape at the side of her thumb. To distract herself, she ran her fingernails up and down his back.

He nodded toward Kade's door. "That box in his closet. I didn't look through all of it. What if there's more? He could have answers."

She shrugged and stood. "Then we'll look."

"I should probably do it alone. You had a—"

"I'll be okay." Leaning down, she pressed a kiss to his lips. "If you're there, I'll be okay."

Stealing another kiss from her, he stood and handed her his hoodie. "I'm sure you're just bribing me to get this, but I'll accept it."

She snatched his hoodie and pulled it over her clothes. "I wasn't, but I'm not turning it down."

He laughed and led her through the kitchen.

Opening the door and turning on the light shook dust free from his cracked heart. He pressed his teeth into his bottom lip. Charlotte squeezed his hand. He squeezed back.

They lingered in the doorway, taking in the bedroom that once belonged to Wesley's parents. A dresser—collecting three cameras and a cluster of framed photographs—stood beside the door. A queen-size bed with two small nightstands sat against the wall in the center. An open door by the head of the bed led to the bathroom. On the right, a closed door led to the modest walk-in closet. Stacks of boxes sat in neat rows against the wall on the left. Dates and details were printed on the front of each box in Kade's jagged handwriting. Some had locations throughout the city. Others had people's names.

"What's all this?" Charlotte walked over to the boxes. She spotted three boxes stacked on top of each other with Malini's name. A heart followed each name along with a list of dates.

"His photography." Wesley shut the door and walked to the closet. "He likes to keep it really organized."

Charlotte glanced at him, noticing his continual use of the present tense. She pointed at the boxes. "There's a lot of Mal. They were only together for ... I think a year?"

"He gets a little obsessive with taking pictures of people." He pointed to two stacks of three with his and Taliyah's names. "I don't even like my picture taken. And that's nothing. See those boxes?" He pointed to two stacks of five closest to the bathroom.

Charlotte walked over to the boxes. *Henry* was scrawled over all ten boxes. She gasped. "Why did he take so many pictures of him?"

Wesley shrugged. "I mean, they were best friends for a while and spent a lot of time together."

"Can I look at some?"

"Yeah. Just put everything back." He opened the closet door. "Kade doesn't like things being out of order."

Eyeing him again, Charlotte chewed on the inside of her cheek and decided not to bring up his use of the present tense.

Wesley stepped into the closet that had been turned into a developing station for Kade's film photography. More boxes of old clothes and memories of their parents collected dust on the top shelf. He dug behind a box marked *Mom's Pictures* and found a small shoebox. Carrying it out, he shut the door behind him.

Turning to the first *Henry* stack, Charlotte pulled off the lid. Dated folders lined the inside. She pulled out the first file and flipped it open. Finding a younger, scrawnier Henry. A version she'd never seen before. Dirty blond hair falling into his face—still finely chiseled to perfection. No trace of his characteristic smirk. A simple black T-shirt under a red plaid overshirt. She looked again at the date on the folder. *February 9, 3695.* She flipped to the next picture. She gasped. "He's wearing jeans in this picture! I've never seen him in jeans! He's always wearing some kind of fancy pants."

Wesley laughed while sitting on the floor. "He went through what I called his metamorphosis shortly before you moved here."

She sat next to him and flipped to the next picture of Henry. Her fingers went to the small silver bird charm around her throat. She squinted at the photograph. The angle had changed so she could see a faint yellow discoloration on his cheek. She held the photograph out toward Wesley. "Does he have a bruise here or are my eyes lying to me?"

Wesley glanced at the picture and nodded. "He had a bruise." He paused before explaining—picking his words carefully. "Henry used to be really clumsy or a lot more than he is now. I think he grew out of it for the most part. I've seen him walk into a door and trip over his own feet. He even fell off our steps once. Twice. Okay, it was a few times. But I think he was drunk."

"Sounds like a puppy when its feet are too big for its body." Laughing, she closed the folder and put it away.

His thoughts returned to the argument with Elsey. He recalled Henry tensing and shoving his hands in his pockets when Elsey mentioned the children she'd saved from their parents. Wesley frowned and nodded, unable to find the words to agree.

Charlotte moved over to the boxes labeled for Malini.

Flipping open the first folder, she was met with a picture of Malini's profile. Light caught the faint hues of blue and violet in her long raven hair. A small wrinkle creased her brow while she focused on something off camera. Her violet lace blouse complemented her olive-tan skin.

Charlotte glanced from the simple portrait of Malini to the more creative, stylized photographs on the dresser. Photos of blurred silhouettes, buildings patterned with odd specks, layered images with etchings in Kade's handwriting, random objects with washes of color, and trails of light cutting through darkness. "He really varied his style. The ones with Henry and Malini and the ones I have of us are all pretty plain in comparison to those."

Wesley followed her line of sight. "You'll have to ask him about that. I don't know anything about it."

Hearing his use of the present tense again, she hesitated. She returned the folder and motioned toward the boxes labeled *Henry*. "How did they even become friends? You never told me."

"That's because I don't know." He pushed the shoebox to the side, gladly putting it off. "After Mom and Dad died, Kade went to Micha Adamson's office. He knew that he was shady enough to hire a thirteen-year-old, and he got a job working at one of his property offices. The next day he and Henry were inseparable. They were like that for a long time until the end there.

"Henry's mom also died recently, so that probably played a part in it. They had something to bond over. And Kade was excessively nice to everyone, well everyone except Elsey."

Charlotte shot an uneasy glance at him, biting down on the inside of her cheek.

He caught her expression. "I don't mean he bullied her. I mean you saw him at school, he was never one of those kids. Not like

Victoria and Alexander or their gang of assholes. I don't think he really hated her. I think he was just terrified of her. He made a big deal about the rumors. So did our parents. Most parents did. They probably still do. In kindergarten, parents told their kids to stay away from her because she was a dangerous monster. They did the same thing when she returned to school in third grade."

"You remember all that?" She played with the silver bird charm at her throat.

"People made a big deal of it." He shrugged. "She disappeared when we were five after her grandparents were murdered. No one saw her or heard about her except when her dad did interviews talking about finding her covered in blood with his murdered parents. The general consensus was that she was sent away because she's the one who murdered them. When she reappeared, no one wanted her at school, but they couldn't protest or do anything because the Hallens own the city. Without them, we wouldn't even have a school. Parents just drilled it into us kids to stay away from her. Everyone got the memo except Henry."

Lines creased her forehead. She clutched the charm. "And then it happened again?"

He nodded. "Her mom's parents. Her dad announced it on the news the next morning. He found her covered in their blood. The same as before. Then she disappeared. And when she reappeared, everything repeated. Except this time, it was Kade warning me to avoid her."

Charlotte released her charm and dropped her hands to her side. "My dad told me he heard the rumors when we moved here, but Malini and Jemma made a big deal about them. They still do." She bit the inside of her cheek, debating whether she should say more.

"I was always skeptical of the whole thing. I felt bad for her." He lifted his hands in dismay. "I mean, who makes an announcement like that about their own kid? I didn't think I allowed other people to influence me. Not since I knew her in kindergarten. But now, I'm starting to if I let other people influence me more than I realized."

His memory of the earlier argument with Elsey replayed. *I am a monster. I'm the most dangerous monster there is. I'm the monster that hunts other monsters.*

"Kade was terrified of her. When she was my lab partner in AP biology, he freaked out and argued with the teacher. He was convinced that she'd hurt me." A bitter hint of guilt blossomed in his stomach. "I will say, that was the easiest class. She didn't talk much, but she did her half of the work. And we got the highest grades on everything. For a while, I was worried I'd be competing with her for the top spot in class, which could affect my chances at a scholarship to Forge Institute."

"You're not worried about that now?" She glanced at the photographs lining the dresser, spotting a single portrait of Malini wearing Kade's black oversized cardigan she now kept around her like a protective cloak.

"Not really," he said, calling her attention back. "I'm at the top spot now, and after what she said last night, I went to the school guidance counselor. I asked if there was anyone else in our grade I needed to worry about and offered some names, and she gave me a rundown of their classes. Elsey's not even taking any AP or honors classes anymore. She's only sticking to the basics and taking Humanities as an elective."

"Probably to make time for what she's doing." Charlotte sat next to Wesley. "It's probably a good thing you're not doing it anymore either then. The time it takes up could've messed with your grades."

Wesley dropped his eyes to the shoebox. "About that."

"You heard her."

"She's not the boss of me."

She frowned. Her stomach twisted. Him agreeing with Elsey on the death of their attacker weighed heavy on her heart. "Wes—"

"*Char.*" He looked at her. His eyebrows lifted. "You wanted me to do this."

"That was before we nearly died!"

"Shh. Taliyah doesn't need to overhear."

Charlotte lowered her voice. "You always said you didn't want to."

"*That* was before I knew there might be a way to find out what happened to Kade. I can find out who took him from us and maybe more about myself." Sighing, he ran his hand over his short hair. A sharp ache pulsed in his chest. "After everything he did for us and everything he had to deal with from me . . . I owe him that."

"What?" Keeping her attention on him, she scratched at the sides of her thumbs.

His eyes wandered over the room. The sharp ache pulsed again. "I was a real brat sometimes. I needed someone to blame for what happened to Mom and Dad. We didn't—*don't* know who did it. Kade was left in charge. When they didn't come home from their date at their usual time, he searched for them. He was the one who found their car. Well," he paused, nodding his head to the side before continuing, "Other people *definitely* saw, but no one stopped. They just let the car burn."

She took his hand.

"I don't know if he cried or what seeing them did to him. He never talked about it. I probably wouldn't have listened if he had." Wesley dropped his gaze to their hands entwined in his lap. "When he came home, I was waiting up in our room. I thought he was lying when he told me. Like he was playing some really cruel prank."

"He never seemed like the type to play pranks."

"He isn't—*wasn't*." The sharp ache radiated through him. The bandages plastering his heart slipped. "But I needed it to be a prank. I refused to believe him. But then he moved out of our room. He said it was to give me space since he had to be in charge. And I was pissed. Because that made it real. So, I resented him sometimes. For making it real. He was my best friend and my brother, but damn, he was only a year older than me, and he had to be my parent, too. And now I'm in the same position, and all I can think about is how much I need him here. I need him to come home and figure things out like he always did. I don't know what I'm doing. I'm going to screw up. Something will happen to Taliyah or me. Then she'll be left to starve and die like those kids Elsey mentioned.

"I used to be so mad at him. And now, he's not here, and I need to be mad at someone. I need someone to explain to me why my brother isn't coming home. He was nice. He was a good person. He was the *best* person. He cared about everybody. He went out of his way to help everyone he could. And then someone—"

Charlotte squeezed his hand.

"I need him here. Because if he's not then I'll never get to tell him

I'm sorry or that I appreciate everything he did." He sucked in a deep breath, fighting the tears he never let spill. "He did everything he needed to do without a second thought. Went to one of the sketchiest people in the city and *demanded* a job, from the way Henry tells it. Figured out how to access the bank account. Handled the money and the bills. Talked to the school and just everything. Everything that needed to be done, he just did it. I don't know how."

"It's the same thing you did when he was killed." She squeezed his hand again. "We came back here, and you wiped away your tears and put on a brave face. And you sat down and figured everything out just like you've been doing every day since."

"Yeah, but he was just a kid."

"*You're* just a kid." She jostled his hand, pulling his attention to her face. "You're not supposed to have these responsibilities. He shouldn't have had them either. But you're doing everything you need to. You're just as strong and smart as him."

Tugging her forward, he pulled her into his lap. His lips crashed into hers. He slid a hand into her damp hair. Burying all his pain inside her before it could swallow him whole. Deepening the kiss, she interlocked her hands behind his neck. Her thumbs grazed his smooth cheeks.

He broke the kiss, taking a gasping breath. His eyes met hers. Charcoal smoke meeting a forest cast in daylight. A comforting warmth coated his heart, fixing the bandages back in place. "I love you."

Charlotte's heart stuttered. Her mind spun, racing to collect itself.

"I probably should've thought about that more." Wesley glanced to the side. Heat flushed his face. His heart sprinted wildly. "I know we haven't said it yet, and maybe it's kind of soon. I mean, we've only been together since April 16th, so not even a full six months. And I don't really know how these things work. I mean, you're the only girlfriend I've ever had. I didn't even care about girls or dating or anything before. I was focused on school and work until you showed up, and I always had a crush on you. But we were friends, and I didn't think you'd see me that way because ..." He continued to ramble on, despite his brain screaming for him to stop talking. *Dear God, I'm turning back into the nerdy kid who can't speak to her again. What—*

She silenced him with a hard kiss and breathed against his lips. "I love you, too."

He caught her lips again, tangling his tongue with hers. One hand remained twisted in her hair. The other held her close to him.

Feeling him shift underneath her, a tingling warmth spread through her. She broke the kiss. Ignoring the warmth flushing her cheeks, she slid out of his lap and sat next to him. She pulled the shoebox over. "You can't avoid this now."

"I wasn't avoiding it." He caught her pointed stare. "Okay, but we can agree that I clearly needed to get all that off my chest. And if I didn't give you my full attention when you were asking questions, I would be a bad boyfriend."

"Come on." Charlotte flipped the lid off the shoebox, revealing a mound of loose papers and scraps. "I'll take the top half." She grabbed a handful of the contents and plopped them in front of her.

"Okay, just be aware there are some pictures that are really hard to see." He pulled out a few folded pages that looked like they'd been ripped from a book. He skimmed the lines.

Genetics and DNA seem to play a larger role in one's developed powers than was previously realized. Similar to traits being passed down from parents to offspring, the offspring of those with powers both supernatural and/or aethereal often carry the same powers. However, there are certain cases, like those arising in the Hybrid and Diluted populations, in which the offspring are being born with and/or developing powers that are more varied and could be connected to the randomized mix of genes at play. [For an example provided in simpler terms: in the same way that two brown eyed parents may produce a blue-eyed offspring, two people with the ability to shapeshift may produce an offspring with telekinesis in place of shapeshifting.] This phenomenon appears to have greater probabilities the more diluted the bloodline and may depend on more than genetics. Few studies have been conducted on those with the strongest powers due to the obvious problems of locating and procuring them.

His stomach churned at the use of *procuring*—a word typically reserved for inanimate objects like documents, equipment, or food when used in articles and research papers unless in reference to the topics of forced sex work or other forced lines of labor. He set the pages aside, promising to return when he didn't feel so disgusted.

He picked up the next page. An article that had been printed off from a computer. A decorative 𝒜 marked the upper corner, watermarking the page as having been printed off at Micha Adamson's office. Wesley skimmed over the page and halted when he spotted two words. *Reality Warping.*

Reality Warping, though one of the strongest known powers, is a sub-power of Absolute Will and Omnipotence. Still, many of its users (even the weakest users) have been known to develop a God Complex. Because who else but a God would have such a power? Well, that's not true. Think of Witches. They can do all kinds of things with their powers that could probably be equated to bending and shaping reality in any way they want. Same with shapeshifters. What is transforming into a lion if not a little warping of reality? Those are only two examples. Plenty of different Aetheral and Supernatural beings can have the ability to warp reality. So, what separates them from a divine being? The brain and body.

A God cannot be broken. They are immortal. If the user is not a God or doesn't have a God somewhere in their bloodline, they run the risk of letting the power literally destroy them. The risks increase greatly in Diluted bloodlines with high levels of Human DNA without any divine DNA to stabilize their powers.

The signs of their power destroying them can range from mild to severe (i.e.: breaks from reality, frequent or constant pain, partial or complete numbness, inability to control emotions or impulses, high disregard for one's own life or the life of others, self-harm and suicidal ideations, homicidal ideations, short-term or long-term memory loss, wasting away, etc.) The more the person continues to use their power, the more it will break them down until there is nothing left.

Effectively, killing themselves from the inside out.

A problem arises with the powers in that they can be highly addictive. Why wouldn't it be? To change reality in any way to fit your desires would be enticing to anybody. But the more they use it, the closer they get to the tipping point.

The pain has been known to be excruciating and to become unbearable to the point where it may be more humane to put the user down.

Wesley swallowed hard, reading the words again. He stopped on the signs and symptoms, ticking off the ones he could recognize. *Breaks from reality could be her attacks. What if the constant pain she feels isn't other people's death? Inability to control emotions or impulses? Check. Poor disregard for one's own life or the life of others? I think ... maybe yes. Self-harm.* He thought of all her scars and remembered the blood dripping off Elsey's knuckles after she repeatedly bashed her fist into the side of one of the warehouses. His stomach tightened like a fist.

"Wes." Charlotte looked up from the small slip of paper in her hands. "Did Kade ever go to the library in Brookhaven?"

He tossed the article to the side. "I don't know. Why?"

She held the slip of paper out to him. "Here's a receipt that shows someone paid for photocopies of something. I found a couple others, too."

Taking the slip, he looked over the date. April 17, 3698. "Did you find anything else?"

"No." She sifted through the papers. "The library had a watermark whenever you printed anything off because it was owned by this rich old man who insisted on putting his name on everything."

"They usually do." Wesley nodded.

"Yeah, but none of these papers have the watermark." Charlotte nodded toward the box. "Can I look through those?"

He pushed the box over to her, sitting in silence while she flipped through the pages.

She shook her head. "Nothing."

Wesley pulled his phone from his pocket. "Let me see if Kade's personal taxi knows anything."

thirteen

Pain scraped under Henry's skin. His head beat with the might of a thousand hammers. The dirt and grime shook off the memories he kept buried. Monsters cackled in the back of his mind. Taking a shaky breath, he turned off the faucet. The cold, crimson-stained water disappeared down the drain. His stomach twisted into impossible knots. Everything he'd eaten climbed up his throat.

Another shaky breath.

He stepped out of the tub, torn between gripping his stomach and holding his head.

Standing in front of the sink, he counted the minutes and hours since he'd last taken a pill. He remembered sitting in the dark of the SUV and popping them in his mouth. Just a couple of hours ago and they were already worn off. The painful effects of withdrawal clawing at him. *Fuck.*

Another shaky breath.

His stomach quaked and roiled with a vile slippery pain. The contents threatened to spill. He turned on the sink, hoping it'd cover any sounds. *If she's still here.*

Pulling open the top drawer under the sink, he grabbed the pill bottle waiting for him. He stared at the bottle and thought of Elsey sitting in his living room. *If she's still here.* Reading pieces of his heart and soul like they were sacred treasures. *Please.* Saving him just by being there when no one else was. Every single time. *Let her still be here.*

Pain tore him to pieces. *I don't want one. I don't want it anymore. Please. I just want to be here and to be with her and to just live and be happy.*

All at once the pain sharpened. As if his demons heard his pleas and decided to attack.

Grimacing, his eyes went to the mirror. The shadow of his biggest, strongest monster stared back. The monster that started it all. Every ounce of pain he'd ever felt. Every pill he'd ever taken. Every drink he'd ever consumed. He could've handled it all without that face looking back at him. He gripped the pill bottle tight. *I don't want it. I just want to be here. Please let me be here with her. Don't take this from me, too.*

Sharper.

The pain dug razored talons into his bones. Tearing at him. Peeling him open to rip out his heart.

He gritted his teeth. His throat convulsed.

He knew the signs. If he didn't take one soon—

She'll leave. She'll think I'm weak. She'll blame me. And she'll be right. It's my fault. Everything's my fault. Everything's **always** *my fault.*

Opening the bottle, he dropped one small red pill in his hand.

Just one. That will be enough. For now. I'll try again tomorrow. I'll stop tomorrow. Then I can be better.

Tossing the pill in his mouth, he swallowed it without hesitation. A buzzing warmth coated his insides. Blocking as much pain as one pill could after years of constant use. It was enough for him to breathe easier and not feel the seething hatred toward what stared back at him from the mirror. He returned the bottle to the drawer and pulled on his pajamas. Combing knots from his thick hair, he left it falling loose in his face. He dropped his blood-soaked clothes into his hamper.

Elsey still sat where he'd left her. Her eyes glued to the pages of his heart.

The chord thrummed with a vibration that sent sparks shivering through him. He smiled—a real, true smile. *She stayed.*

Shaking out his wrists and hands to get himself moving, he walked toward her. "My body and hair are clean now. My mind is a different story."

Elsey glanced over her shoulder, scanning over his clothes and lingering on his hair. A cluster of memories raced through her. She nodded toward the coffee table. "I think your phone rang."

"Oh thanks." He grabbed his phone and saw the missed call from

Wesley and three texts from his sister. He glanced at the messages without really reading them and typed a quick reply. I'm fine. Text later. Love you. "Wes called. Do you mind if I call him back really quick? He and Taliyah might need something."

"Go ahead." She continued reading the book in her lap.

Walking around Meow, who decided to lie in the middle of the floor, he clipped his shin on the edge of the coffee table. He mumbled a curse and rubbed his shin while dialing Wesley's number. Switching on speakerphone, he placed the phone on the counter. He opened the fridge, retrieving everything he would need.

"Hello?" Wesley pulled his arm out from under Charlotte's head and sat up.

Charlotte motioned for him to turn it on speaker, and he acquiesced.

"Sorry, I was in the shower." Henry opened the packages of vegetables and fruit. "El told me you called."

Wesley muted the television. "Why didn't she answer?"

"It's not my phone," Elsey said, not bothering to lift her head.

"I should've mentioned that you're on speakerphone." Henry motioned toward the produce in front of him. "I'm in the middle of fixing dinner."

Charlotte's forehead creased. "You cook?"

"Normally, yes." Henry nodded. "But I have yet to master tofu without it tasting like a soggy sponge, and I don't have many vegan recipes in my repertoire yet. And since I'm entertaining, I figured I should probably stick with something safe. You can't mess up a salad."

"Yes, you can." Wesley chuckled. "By making it."

Charlotte shook her head. "I feel like I should've known you cook. Mal never mentioned it."

"She doesn't mention a lot of things." Meow uttered a low trill and nudged Henry's leg. He glanced down. "I'm busy right now. Go bug her."

"Who's that?" Charlotte sat up next to Wesley, pulling their pillow into her lap.

"My roommate."

"His cat." Again, Elsey didn't look up.

"Anyway," Wesley said, eyeing the receipts for the Brookhaven library on the coffee table. "I had a quick question. Did you ever drive Kade to Brookhaven to go to the library?"

"No." Henry moved through his kitchenette, retrieving a large wooden mixing bowl, a glass cutting board, and a paring knife. Flipping on the faucet, he rinsed off the produce. "I never drove him to Brookhaven at all. Why?"

"I decided to look at those papers I found in his closet again, and Charlotte found a few receipts showing he'd been to the library and photocopied something there, but we can't find anything from there."

Henry heard a book shut and glanced at Elsey. Realizing she still didn't have a drink, he grabbed a glass from the cabinet and filled it with water from a pitcher in the fridge. "What are the dates?"

"There are five of them." Wesley motioned for Charlotte to pass him the receipts from the coffee table. "April 17th and November 30th of 3698 and February 3rd, June 21st, and August 20th of 3699."

He handed the glass to Elsey and returned to his salad prep. "You might want to check with his girlfriend. Maybe she knows something since she took over all my duties after she broke up with me."

Charlotte winced.

Wesley tossed the receipts on the coffee table. "Sorry, I didn't know. I never kept track of your relationship."

"I didn't either." Henry shrugged. "I just remember the day it ended."

Setting her books aside, Elsey stood. "Forward me the information for the library and I'll look into it."

"No, this is my brother." Wesley shook his head even though she couldn't see him. "I'm not backing down."

"And I'm not having your blood on my hands."

He glared at the phone. "I'm not—"

Taking his phone off speaker, Henry brought it to his ear. "Hey, let me talk to her and see what I can do."

"I'm not walking away. I need to know what happened."

"I get it." Henry sighed against the sharp knife of guilt twisting in his belly. "See you guys at school. Call me if you need anything."

"Yeah, thanks." Wesley laid back down on the sofa, pulling

Charlotte into his arms.

Henry hung up and clicked through his phone to start his favorite playlist full of classical and instrumental songs. He washed his hands under the faucet, motioning toward his small two-seater table. "We can sit at the table."

Picking up her glass, she walked over to the table. "He's not helping anymore. None of you are."

"El," he sighed. He portioned the salads out and retrieved two forks from a drawer beside the sink. Carrying the bowls over to the table, he set one in front of Elsey and the other in front of his own chair. He returned to the fridge to grab a bottle of vinaigrette dressing before sitting down. "His brother was murdered, and—"

"And he almost was, too."

"Maybe the risk is worth it to him if it means he might get answers." He watched her drizzle dressing over her salad. "It's worth it to me to be there with you and know you're safe and not alone."

"I'm not alone. I have Luci, Gene, and Tristan."

"They stay in Purgatory while you're out there risking your life. You said you keep their connection to what happens to a minimum and if something happens, Luci can wipe everything clean with a button." He took the bottle of dressing from her, not leaving her eyes. "Does Luci see all the things you see? When you find someone trapped in a basement, who hears their screams? Who deals with that? Who _feels_ that?"

Dropping her gaze, she stabbed a carrot. Ignoring the constant pain in her heart.

A hollow ache throbbed in his chest. "The cameras can only pick up so much. They can't pick up screams coming from a basement. And from what everyone has said, the cameras haven't been around for as long as you've been doing this. So, you've had to get a lot messier than what you're revealing. You've had to let yourself feel the pain and listen to it to know where to go. Like when you found that rabbit when we were younger. And you've done things that will haunt you forever."

"I don't want that for you. Or anyone else."

"I get that, but you can't do this all by yourself." He shifted in his chair, leaning toward her slightly. "You're one person, and you're trying to heal an entire city. You're also trying to solve a murder. You have people who want to help you. People who want to be there for you."

She rolled her eyes. "It's not me they're there for."

"I am. I told you I did this for you. I jumped on board to help you before I knew anything else."

Elsey looked up at him, meeting his eyes. The flame in her heart flickered.

"I would do it again, too. Even after tonight. *Especially* after tonight." He wanted to reach out and take her hand. To feel her skin against his. He tucked his hands under his legs. "That person said they were planning to kill you. I don't think they were there for the rest of us. We were just shrapnel. Whoever it was, they have some vendetta against you."

"I can protect myself." She tightened her grip on her fork. "My power—"

"Left you immobilized." Henry's mind flashed to her limp body in his arms. "You talked about not holding back if you were alone. But what would've happened if you did that? How much worse would it have been? If I wasn't there to step in front of you, what would've happened?"

She replayed the attack; from the moment the person appeared and used her powers to the end when her mind cleared for her to find Henry impaled to her chest.

"They used everyone's powers." Standing, he walked over to the bookcase and poured a glass of whiskey from the makeshift bar on top. "And it didn't slow them down when you had your episode. You can't face them alone, and you have us. We all have our own reasons for wanting to do this."

"Wesley thinks I'm evil."

"He thinks I'm an annoying imbecile." Sipping from his glass, he shrugged. "But he has a different viewpoint than us. We'll never be able to fully understand what life is like for him, and he'll never be able to fully understand what it's like for us. Dating Malini, I witnessed things and even had people offer their bigoted, unsolicited opinions. She dealt with similar things because of my sexuality. It gave us different vantage points, but it didn't change that we are two different people who have been born into two different lives with our own challenges that the other could never begin to understand."

He returned to the table. "Wesley had a loving family with loving parents who took him to church every Sunday and taught him murder was wrong. Lying, stealing, cheating, and so on and so forth were wrong. They loved him and cherished every moment they had together. Wesley was awkward and nerdy and didn't really have friends. But he had his family. Until one night his parents didn't come home. They left the oldest in charge so they could have a night out, and when they didn't come home ..."

Pausing, Henry took a shaky breath. "Kade went out. And he found them. The car was on fire. The bodies—You can imagine. Kade was thirteen and it was all on him. He didn't have any other choice. That's the way he viewed it. Nothing and no one came before his family. Not even himself or anything he wanted. He would go to the ends of the earth for his family, and he had to go home and destroy his little brother's world.

"And he had to figure out how to put the pieces of himself back together so he could keep what was left of his family together. He was one of those kids you mentioned. He decided to fight for his siblings. It wasn't an option to him. He never let them see how much it took from him or the nights that he broke down or how he was so obsessed with holding onto every single moment of his life because it might be the last."

Picking up his fork, Henry sifted through his salad. "In one instant, he had to go from being a little boy to a grown man. He didn't get a choice. It's understandable why Kade and Wesley would have different morals and views, even from each other. Kade kept attending church, but Wesley stopped. He became even more isolated, focusing on school and science and math and anything that made sense because how does a little boy make sense that their parents just aren't coming home? How does a kid keep believing in God when his world was shattered and everyone expects him to keep living like nothing happened?"

Biting down on her tongue, Elsey watched him. "Sounds a little familiar, from what I've heard at least."

A small sad smile darted over his lips. "Yeah, but this isn't about me. My point is—" He paused and met her eyes. "He needs your patience. Just like you have with me. I know it's different with me because we were friends, but he has his reasons just like me. He was taught murder was wrong, and then his parents were murdered. It was a car crash, but no one took responsibility. He had to deal with that. And then things were okay. They weren't good. They weren't perfect. But they were okay. He had a brother and a sister and a girlfriend and a promising future ahead of him.

"Then it happened again. Someone murdered his brother. Destroyed his world again. And this time there was no one there to put the pieces back together for him. Just himself. And he has someone else counting on him. He knows what it feels like to lose someone because they were murdered. Because they were taken from him. It's probably not easy to contend with that and also feel okay with that answer being used in other situations, even if he can conceivably see that it may be the only way. For him, all it's done is destroy his world.

"Wes needs something to hold onto, too. He needs people, even if he thinks he doesn't. He needs people who care about him. He needs to know he's not alone, and most importantly, at least to him, he needs to know that he's doing something to make things right." Henry took a drink from his glass and set it beside his bowl. "At least think about what I said because I guarantee you, Wes won't back down. When he has his mind made up, that's it. He's probably the only person in the world who can give you a run for your money when it comes to stubbornness."

The corner of her mouth twitched. "Tristan would argue that it's a toss-up between Luci and Gene in that department."

Henry chuckled and took a bite of his salad. "Would you like to see what I bought Wes for his birthday?"

Elsey's eyebrows rose. "You bought him something?"

Nodding, he stood and walked to his closet. He returned with a book in hand. A copy of *Cosmos* by Carl Sagan that looked to be in nearly perfect condition despite its age. "His birthday is in a couple days. I knew it would be his first year not receiving something, and I didn't want him to feel alone."

She twisted the black and clear beads on the bracelet holding her silver filigree star charm.

"He's probably already read it, but hopefully it will help the day hurt less." Setting the book on the coffee table, he returned to the table and nodded to her untouched food. "Did I make it to your standards?"

She nodded. "I was just listening to you." Pausing to take a small bite, she glanced at everything on the counters. "You remembered that I don't eat meat."

Watching her, his heart rattled. His voice dropped low, almost a whisper. "I remember everything about you."

Her eyes went to him. The urge to claw at the locked doors and to reach into the black holes of her mind—to try to remember—hit her like a punch to the gut. She shoved it away. *Don't. I can't.* "Did you buy this stuff specifically in case you could convince me to come over?"

"Yes and no." He smirked, pausing to take another bite. "I would've eaten it even if you never came over. I like to try different things, and I don't hate salad or vegan foods. They're just not my favorite."

"What's your favorite thing to eat?" She held up a hand when she noticed his smirk widen. "*Food.* Your favorite food."

"I didn't say anything."

"You were thinking it, and with you, it's safer to clarify."

"So, you *do* get my innuendos?"

"A corpse would get them."

Laughing, he picked up his glass and took a drink. "On a serious note, if they ever bother you or make you uncomfortable, tell me, and I won't say them."

She met his eyes. "Are you going to answer about your favorite food?"

His brows rose. He filed a mental note about the moment for later examination. "Will you be upset if it's an animal product?"

"No." She drank from her water. "You're free to like whatever."

"Okay, then it's hot wings." He held up a finger. "No, it's macaroni and cheese. From the box."

Her brow arched.

"It's my comfort food." He shrugged. "On nights I can't sleep, I like to fix an entire box of the cheapest, most unhealthy macaroni and cheese on the market and sit and eat it while I read until three in the morning and pass out."

Elsey looked around the apartment again. "You don't own a TV."

He took a large bite of his salad and waited until he swallowed to explain. "I don't have anything against TV or movies, I just can't focus on them. I always feel like I have to be doing something else. My brain can't stop going and going and going, and it feels like I'm stuck in a wind tunnel and can't stop. The alcohol and Reds help some, but not a lot unless I consume disturbing amounts. It can be agonizing.

"With books, I can actually focus. On the reading and the images being painted in my head. I can get lost and forget things and enjoy the moment in front of me." He took another bite, chuckling at a memory. "It gets on a lot of people's nerves. Back when I was dating Mal, Charlotte used to invite her, Ana, Jemma, Wes, and Kade over for movie nights. I was disinvited because I wouldn't stop talking or asking weird questions when everyone else was trying to enjoy the movie. Kade stopped going sometimes to keep me company, and if he didn't then I'd come back here and read, find someone to have fun with downstairs, or go annoy Alex and Victoria."

"Weird questions?" Elsey arched a brow.

He lifted his fork, flicking the tines toward her. "Okay, if I ask you one, will you actually answer?"

She shrugged. "Maybe."

Picking up his glass, he took a long drink of whiskey—eyes locked with hers over the rim. *Dammit. Temptation will be the death of me.* He set his glass down. Eyes still on hers. "If the devil promised they'd give you the one thing you wished for most in the world in exchange for your soul, would you take it?"

Elsey watched the stars dance in his eyes. Feeling her wish—the only wish she ever made—climb toward her flame to set itself ablaze. *Don't. I can't.* She took a shallow breath. It shook through her frayed threads.

She looked around her. At the apartment with all its beaten and bruised contents collected in one place and treated with reverence.

At the books she'd been offered with someone's heart beating in the pages. At the tattered tabby stretched out on the scarlet knit blanket across the back of the couch. Back to the boy across from her— watching her. Waiting to see if she would do it. If she would give him an answer. A piece of her. *But maybe I can?*

Hope shot through her like a star falling to earth. *Too much. I can't.* Still, looking at him. *But maybe?*

She dropped her eyes to her salad and stabbed a tomato. "I don't think even the devil would want my soul. It's probably not worth more than a chewed piece of gum."

He opened his mouth, preparing to argue.

"But," she said, not meeting his eyes. "If they did make the offer. I'd take it without a second thought."

Swallowing hard, he nodded. "Me too." He forced himself to eat another bite before speaking again. "Okay, maybe I shouldn't have started with something so heavy."

Sipping from her glass of water, she waited for the next question.

"What's an animal, extinct or still in existence, you would use to describe yourself?"

"Montivipera xanthina," she said without hesitation.

"I said animal, not magic spell."

A small **hmph** escaped her. Elsey covered her mouth with her hand until her flat expression returned. "It's the scientific name of an aggressive venomous serpent found in Greece and Turkey, especially in Thrace. It's also known as the Ottoman Viper. It lives in a rough habitat and prefers to avoid people, but it will not hesitate to strike if necessary."

"I can see the resemblance. Next question," he paused to hold up a hand, "and if you don't feel like answering it, you don't have to."

Taking a bite of her salad, she nodded.

"If a person had intercourse with a clone of themself, would it be considered masturbation or sex?"

Time drifted around them. Soft music traced every minute into a memory that hummed with a burning softness. Every question and laugh and word and subtle smile etched into a hopeful forever.

VII

September 8, 3699

One

"Charlotte," Wesley said, turning off his alarm and dropping his phone to the coffee table. He rubbed her back and kissed the top of her head. "It's time to get up."

"Coffee," she grumbled into his shirt.

He laughed, tossing the blanket aside. "How would I get you coffee? We don't own a coffee maker, and you're literally on top of me."

"I'm comfortable."

"I know, but I've had to pee for the last two hours." Wrapping his arms around her, he sat up. "And we have to go to school."

Charlotte glared at him. "Meanie."

"Grumpy." He gave her a quick kiss on the lips.

Stretching, she stood and walked to the front door. "I'm keeping your hoodie."

"I figured."

She stepped outside and shivered against the heavy chill on the wind. Blinking the sleep away, she let her eyes adjust to the morning light.

A familiar green car turned onto the hill leading into the trailer park. Her cheeks burned bright at the thought of her dad catching her leaving Wesley's trailer.

She sprinted down the steps and through the lawn. Her keys *jingled* in the pocket of her shorts.

Cutting over the next lawn, she glanced at the street. Her dad would see her heading straight for the front door.

Her heart raced faster.

She darted behind a neighbor's trailer and ran for the backdoor to her own.

Her foot hit the top step when her dad parked in front.

She fumbled with her keys and slipped inside, shutting and locking the door behind her.

The sound of footsteps on the front steps reached through the thin walls.

Veering into her room, she yanked the hoodie over her head.

"Mr. Marion!"

Landon heard a voice calling behind him.

Pausing with his hand on the doorknob, he twisted and saw Wesley jogging toward him—carrying a familiar pair of white sneakers. "Morning, Wes. Let me guess, Charlotte left those at your house."

Wesley took a steadying breath and nodded toward the front door. "Mind if I come in and give them to her?"

"Not at all." Landon covered a yawn with his hand and pushed the door open. A smile played over his lips. He scratched his thick, dark hair.

Struggling to hide a grin, Wesley walked down the hall. He knocked on Charlotte's bedroom door.

"Come in," she responded in gasping breaths.

He opened the door—all ability to contain himself crumbling.

Charlotte gaped. "What are you—"

Holding up her sneakers, he leaned in close and lowered his voice. "You left these by the couch. But I'm *sure* he wouldn't have suspected *anything* from you breathing and sweating like you just ran a marathon first thing in the morning."

Hot pink colored her cheeks. She took her shoes. "You really came here to return these?"

"No. Actually, I came to get this." He grabbed her face, pulling her to him and catching her lips in a deep kiss.

Tingling warmth raged through her. Curling her toes and stealing her breath. She dropped her shoes. Her hands gripped his forearms.

He broke the kiss, taking a deep breath and resting his forehead against hers. "I love you."

She gasped for air. Her body tingled with heat, and her heart quivered. "I love you, too."

Keeping his eyes on hers, Wesley snatched his hoodie from her bed. He held it up between them. "I also came to get this."

Charlotte narrowed her eyes. "Meanie."

"You'll get it back later." He pulled his hoodie on and kissed her again. "I just need it right now. It's kind of cold in the house for some reason. I might have to have someone come check out the heat."

Groaning, she tossed back her head. "Fine."

"You are *really* grumpy without coffee first thing in the morning." He spun around to leave the room.

Hearing a laugh, Charlotte peeked into the hall. Heat flushed her cheeks again. "Dad, I swear *nothing* happened."

Landon shrugged. "Whatever you say."

"I'm serious." She waved a hand. "I had a nightmare, and I couldn't go back to sleep. We slept on the couch. Taliyah's door was open the entire time. *Nothing* happened."

"Did I say anything?" He held up his hands and looked between Charlotte and Wesley. "I trust you, kids. You're smart. I gave you the money if you need to buy any cond—"

"Oh my goodness!" Charlotte slammed her door shut before Wesley could see her face turn the color of a tomato.

Torn between laughing and running from the house, heat filled Wesley's face. "I just want to say that I have no intentions of doing anything stupid with your daughter. I love her and really care about her, but I'm dealing with a lot right now. I have my sister, my job, and school. And other things. And I'm trying to get a scholarship, and I can't do that with a baby." *Dear God, I'm rambling again. Make me stop.* "And I know there are risks, even with—"

"Wes! Oh my God!" Charlotte yelled from inside her room.

Landon pressed a hand to his mouth to suppress a laugh. He motioned toward the front door. "Maybe you should go home and get ready for school."

"Yeah. Definitely. I should do that." Wishing with everything in him that he could disappear, Wesley took uncomfortably painful steps toward the front of the trailer. He paused at the front door.

"Uh, it was nice seeing you Mr. Marion."

"Wes, we've been through this. You can call me Landon."

"Yes, sir, Mr. Marion."

Landon watched the door close behind Wesley before breaking into a fit of laughter.

"Dad, it's not funny," Charlotte called.

"You're right." He nodded and continued walking into his room. "It's very immature of me to laugh at my daughter and her boyfriend being awkward teenagers in love."

At some point the brick wall outside the single window had gone from being bathed in darkness with a hint of neon to being washed in the dim light of morning.

Elsey never noticed.

Her eyes remained on the framed picture while she attempted to pry open one of the locked doors in her mind barring her from the memory that had been captured.

She was always so small it was difficult to guess her age, but from the number of scars showing in the picture, she guessed it'd been taken before she'd begun refusing to wear short sleeves. Bracelets still covered her wrists. Scars still covered her body and distorted her face, but something she couldn't remember spread across her small heart-shaped lips. A smile. The effect was something akin to staring at a stranger. If not for those fiery curls, those scars cutting into her like a river through the earth, and those unmistakable blue-green eyes, she'd swear it wasn't her.

Her. Elsey. Captured in a past she couldn't recall. Staring at a boy who was all lean legs and long arms that would take him time to grow into. Messy dirty blond hair he still let fall into his face instead of combing it back to appear more polished. Sapphire eyes that seemed to light up with stars whenever he looked at her.

Even in the picture, the effect was obvious.

They sat on a blanket in lush green grass. A short, rounded girl in the background waved to the camera. Yellow ribbons tied in her chestnut hair—not yet bleached and dyed fuchsia and teal. Her eyes glinted with a warmth from her smile that the sun struggled to compete with.

Time slipped around her in that moment while she stared at the picture, straining to decipher the puzzle it created in her mind.

An alarm **shrieked**, tearing her from the pieces before her. She ignored it.

Her eyes shifted to the other picture on the dresser. A woman with long dirty blonde hair pulled back in a ponytail. A smile stretched her lips as she stared down at the infant swaddled in her arms before she would have to return him to the NICU and leave, only to return the next day and visit for as long as she would be allowed. The edges of the picture looked charred, like someone might've ripped it from a fire before it had a chance to burn.

Still ignoring the alarm, she looked over the empty pill bottles and liquor bottles littering the top of the dresser. She lifted a bottle still half-filled with pills.

Small red circles behind translucent green plastic. A label fixed to the front of the bottle bore the name. `Petite Morte.` Little Death.

Elsey stared at the tiny pills, wondering how they could hold so much power over someone's mind.

The alarm continued to scream.

A muffled groan sounded from the bed at her back. As if from a face buried in a pillow. Blankets and sheets ruffled.

Henry lifted his hand and smacked the alarm clock. It continued to blare. He smacked it again and again. Pulling his sleep-heavy head up, he blinked and stared at his alarm. It wasn't the source of the noise. *What the fuck?* His phone lay next to it. The screen remained dark. *What the fuck?*

Rolling over, Henry disturbed the orange tabby who had been sleeping at his side. Meow grumbled and abandoned the bed to stretch on the floor. Henry's eyes landed on Elsey—still clad in her clothes from the previous day. Black top and pants crusted in their collected blood. He watched her stare at the bottle in her hands. The skin between her brows pinched together. A deep ache thrummed in his heart.

The alarm continued demanding attention. He peeled his eyes away and spotted her phone tucked in her back pocket. The screen lit up with each bellowing shriek.

Careful not to touch her backside, he grabbed her phone. She spun on him with the speed and dexterity of a skilled predator. He held up a finger—releasing a silent prayer that she would find it in her heart not to snap it in two—while he silenced the alarm.

He tossed her phone onto his bed and pulled a pillow onto his lap. "I'm surprised you're still here."

She arched a brow. "Why?"

Henry glanced around the room. From his bed that had been filled with more bodies than just his own to the couch that had seated too many people for him to count. From the closet that only ever housed his clothes to the small table by the window where he'd always eaten every meal alone. *Every meal except last night.* The chord in his heart plucked at the memory. "No one has ever stayed the night here. Not Malini or—*anyone.*"

Elsey set the pill bottle on the dresser. "You talk in your sleep."

"What?" His eyes widened. *Fuck.* "What . . . did I say?" *Fuck. Fuck. Fuck.*

"It was mostly muffled by your pillow."

His shoulders sagged with relief. "Did you get any sleep?"

"No."

"Why?"

"I needed to make sure you were okay."

"I told you last night I was okay." He questioned his words as soon as they left him despite them not sounding harsh. His heart quickened. He rushed forward to correct any damage he might've caused. "I'm glad you stayed. You can stay as long as you want. I just meant—"

"You should probably get ready for school." She grabbed her phone and crossed to the window. "I'll see you later."

"Wait." Henry threw his blanket aside and jumped out of bed. The moment his bare feet touched the cold floor, he remembered himself. He grabbed his pillow and covered the front of his pajama bottoms.

Elsey faced him again. Her sharp brow arched high at the sight of the pillow in front of him.

"Thank you." He ran a hand through his dirty blond hair, pushing the messy locks out of his face. "For staying. For last night. I had a good time, and I really hope you did, too."

She watched his eyes take on the strange depth she couldn't decipher. Her heart quivered with the flame burning brighter in her chest. *Don't. I can't.* Turning, she pulled the window up so she could step onto the fire escape. She cast a glance at him. His hair had fallen back into his face while he eyed her and plucked his bottom lip.

"Your hair looks good like that." The words stunned her. Her large, round eyes grew to the size of platters. *Why did I say that?*

Dropping the pillow, he gaped. He peered up at his hair falling into his eyes before looking back in time to see her swing over the railing of the fire escape. A faint **thud** sounded when she landed. Grabbing his cigarette case and lighter, he noticed the two books he offered for her to borrow still sat on the floor. He felt a sharp jab to his stomach and took a deep breath.

The engine of her motorcycle came to life before he climbed onto the fire escape. He watched her pull out of the alley. Perching a lit cigarette between his lips, he scolded himself for forgetting all sense of smooth ease he had around everyone else.

He looked at the bloodstain painting the pavement below and shifted his attention to the spot where Elsey had stashed her motorcycle.

A thick strand of hair fell into his face. He reached up to push it back. Redirecting his hand, he pulled the cigarette from his lips and released another smoky sigh.

Sparks shot off the chord trembling in his heart—burning low with the heat he held onto as his only hope.

three

The sun fought with thick smoke filling the sky from another fire burning somewhere on the northwestern side of the city. Heavy wind scattered leaves and crumbled newspaper across the street.

Protesters, dressed in modest clothes, rounded the corner by Trivia Reserve and made their way up the street to where they usually stood outside Purgatory. Teenagers led the younger children. A girl with caramel colored hair and dark green eyes watched Elsey steer past them.

Elsey turned onto the side street and swept into the parking lot. She parked between the SUV and Gene's motorcycle. A pack of scraggly dogs sniffed around the open trash bin.

Letting herself inside, she climbed the stairs to the black platform. Low chatter stretched beyond the gate at the bottom of the red-carpeted stairs.

She continued past the den and descended the stairs.

Tristan sat on one of the barstools. Gray paint-splattered sweatpants covered his long, powerful legs. His torso was bare. His deep skin—covered in beautiful scrolling tattoos—gleamed under the red and black lights. Gene lay on top of the bar. Snores escaped from his head tucked into his folded arms. He hadn't changed out of his cargo pants and sweater from the previous night.

Luci stood behind the bar, sweeping a pile of dust and debris. The lights washed her long silver hair and her terracotta skin in a bloody glow. She wore Tristan's distressed and stitched up asymmetrical black tee from the previous night. The long sleeves bunched at her wrists to allow her mobility in her hands. The hem stopped above her knees, revealing her bare long, toned legs. A black

T and G were inked onto the side of her right calf, laced with a black flowering vine crawling up her leg.

Arching a brow, Elsey approached the bar. "Don't you have a bed downstairs?"

Tristan turned away from his conversation with Luci. "We wanted to wait up to see how you were."

Gripping the broom handle, Luci pointed at Elsey. "Don't sit anywhere until you wash and change. You're still wearing bloody clothes."

"They're dry." Tristan gestured toward Elsey's pants. "We'd know if she got into some fun on the way here."

Elsey rolled her eyes. "It's not fun."

"Say what you want," Tristan said. "You're not cooped up babysitting a bunch of idiots in a dungeon."

"It's not a dungeon." Luci glared at him.

"If our bedroom could talk, it would disagree." He grinned, flashing sharp canines.

"Contrary to what you two seem to think, Purgatory is *not* our bedroom." Gene lifted his head. His sleep-heavy eyes remained closed. "And if *anywhere* in our apartment could talk, it'd probably ask for you two to actually use the bed like normal people for once."

"You don't want to use the bed all the time either." Luci cast him a pointed look.

"No, but first, it's rare that I feel the inclination to participate, and second——" Pausing, Gene wiped his eyes but rested his head back against his arms before continuing. "I eat on that table."

"So do I." Tristan didn't bother to hide his grin.

Letting the argument continue without comment, Elsey observed the shirt Luci wore. Her mind drifted to Henry's offering for her to wear his clothes. She bit her tongue, struggling to decipher her thoughts and feelings.

Silence settled over the trio. They watched her.

Gene lifted his head again. "What has you so confused?"

"I'm not confused." She crossed her arms.

"Then what are you?"

"I don't know." Elsey focused on the feelings inside her. Fire and aching and questions and a need or a want for ... *something*. She dug her nails into her sleeves. "Angry."

"Else," Gene sighed.

Tristan put his hand on Gene's shoulder.

"What do you want to know?" Luci asked.

Elsey shook her head, casting aside any thought of shirts and clothes and what it meant for someone to offer for her to use something that belonged to them.

Accepting that she wouldn't get an answer, Luci leaned the broom against the counter and pivoted to fix herself a glass of absinthe. "How many times have your parents called?"

"Enough." The full realization of what she did hit her in the stomach. Thoughts of the consequences she'd face attempted to materialize, but she shoved them away before the numbness could fill her. *I can't go back.* Elsey looked up. "Can I stay here?"

"Of course," they each replied in unison.

Gene sat up and swiveled so his legs dangled over the side of the bar. "The couch downstairs folds out into a bed."

"I don't do underground." Elsey focused on the conversation at hand, avoiding the thoughts clawing to the front of her brain. "Is it okay if I stay on the sofa in the den? I won't take up space. I just need to get my stuff when my parents are out. I don't have a lot."

Nodding, Gene hopped off the counter. "I'll go get you a blanket and pillow from downstairs."

Tristan stood and stretched. "And I can help you pick up your stuff after you get some sleep."

Elsey watched them walk toward the stairs. "I don't—"

"You need sleep, Else," Luci interrupted her protest. "You can't keep running on a couple of hours. It will catch up to you. It's certainly not doing any favors for your temper. Also, before I forget, Asher called to request a visit sometime today."

Biting her tongue, Elsey nodded. "I won't stay long here. Once I find—"

"Shut up." Luci walked around the bar and sat on the stool Tristan vacated. "You can stay for as long as you want."

Elsey fixed her stare on the far wall. "I might have to leave for good."

"If you go, we go." Luci leaned against the bar and groaned.

"What about Henry? You finally reconnect with him, and you're thinking about leaving."

"He almost died because of me. They all did." Elsey's persistent scowl deepened. Pinching her brows together, a strange ache pulsed off the flame inside her. "You were right. I never should—"

"*You* almost died! Are you forgetting that?" Luci **clanked** her glass onto the bar. "You didn't *have* to use that power. You could've held your own without it."

"You don't know that."

"The hell I don't!" Luci's moss green eyes flared with an orange tint. "I know how you fight! I don't know why you used it, but I don't believe for one second that you needed it. It's a crutch, and it nearly got you killed."

"They missed my heart."

"And do you think they wouldn't have if Henry hadn't been willing to stand in front of you?" Luci reached for her glass, but the memory of the panic at witnessing Elsey's near death stopped her. She faced Elsey. "I was wrong. Maybe they're not pros. But if you were alone when that person attacked ... you might not be here. Even if that doesn't mean much to you, it does to others."

Elsey's nails pressed through her sleeves into her arms.

"Who else would Tristan do crossword puzzles with or make weird clothes for other than himself? You're the only person Gene can talk to about motorcycles. And me—" Luci stopped, waiting for Elsey's gaze to move to her. "I need you here, Else. You gave me a new life. We came here for you, and I cannot even let myself think about a world where you're not here anymore."

A fistful of emotions Elsey couldn't grasp lodged into her throat. She bit hard on her tongue and focused on the pain winding tighter in her heart. Dropping her hands to her side, Elsey whirled around and stomped toward the stairs.

Luci reached for her glass, fighting a sigh. She pulled her phone from her pocket and searched for Wesley, Charlotte, Henry, and Ana in her contacts.

Stepping into the den, Elsey found her rucksack sitting on the crimson sofa along with a black blanket and pillow. A newly sewn outfit—black and white striped pants and a black stitched up shirt—

waited for her on the coffee table.

Collecting the clothes, she carried them down the stairs to the small bathroom hidden behind a flat door in the middle of the hallway under the platform. Red lights washed over her. A black cloth covered the mirror.

She reached into the tall, narrow shower and turned the water to the hottest setting.

Stripping off her blood-caked clothes, she caught sight of the newest scar added to her collection. A round knot of gnarled skin between her breasts. Just missing her heart. Another scar that would never heal no matter what.

Her lips twisted into a deep frown. Her eyes drifted over the rest of her scars. Covering every inch of skin. Stitching her into something that looked not quite right. Something more monster than girl. More artificial than real.

The flame in her chest flickered. *I'm not a book.*

Taking a deep breath, Elsey stepped into the shower. She held her knuckles—still torn from punching the storage facility until the side was a hunk of metal—under the scalding water. She let the pain burn away her ability to care until all she had left was her rage.

The small words on the page looked fuzzy around the edges. Not enough to be illegible, but enough to increase Charlotte's headache to a hard pressure against her skull.

Squinting at the page in her textbook, she pressed her forefingers into her temples. *Read. Don't think. Just read.*

Her homework from two days ago landed beside her textbook on the table as Mr. Pruitt drifted up the aisle. Noting the **86** written in red ink on top, she stuffed the paper in her binder and continued reading.

Thoughts of the previous night pushed through the text and replayed the events of her near death.

The pain still haunted her bones and her organs like a distant friend. Elsey's confessions and banning them from helping her laced each thought like a string waiting to be pulled—to unravel every thought and feeling she'd ever had about the scarred girl and the world surrounding them. Wesley's determination to continue despite the disaster—to uncover what happened to his brother—pressed even harder on her heart. Her fears about the potential clash of their morals weighed on her like a crumbling wall.

There were no gray areas in her mind. *Two wrongs don't equal a right.* Murder was murder. Even if it was to avenge her.

"What the fuck?" Victoria cried from across the room.

Mr. Pruitt groaned. "There is no swearing in this classroom, Ms. Boyer."

Thankful for the distraction, Charlotte looked toward Victoria and Alex's shared table on the opposite side of the room. A velvet plum sweater dress showed off Victoria's thin hourglass figure. Alex had his arm slung around her shoulders with his fingers twisting her long golden waves. An ivory V-neck sweater hugged his broad shoulders.

Charlotte's eyes caught the table behind them. Victoria's best friend, Rachelle, had her attention glued to the back of Alex's fluffy blond hair. She gnawed on a strand of her white-blonde hair and knotted the hem of her pleated black skirt in her hands. Her matching jacket covered her white rose-printed tank top. Next to her, Ana hunched over her textbook. Her bottom lip quivered.

Victoria held up her returned homework. "How did I get a thirty-four?"

Charlotte returned her attention to the display.

Mr. Pruitt stepped behind his desk and fixed Victoria in his glare. "You can come back to class after school is over, and we can talk about your grade then."

"We can't stay after school." Alex held up his hand. "We have an internship at HAL Tower."

"Did I say for you both to stay after school?" Mr. Pruitt crossed his arms in front of his chest. "Victoria's grade pertains to Victoria. Not you."

"Really?" Victoria dropped her paper to the table and motioned to Alex. "We do our homework together every night. It's a bit weird that our grades are different."

Red flushed Mr. Pruitt's face. "All that proves is you two didn't copy each other like most couples would." He leaned forward and narrowed his eyes. "It's a good thing you have a mind of your own. It's unfortunate, though, that your intelligence appears to have suffered."

Giggles broke out amongst the students.

Alex moved fast. Slamming his palms against the tabletop and leaping to his feet. "Don't you fu—"

A chair **scraped** the floor. Ana jumped up and bolted past Alex. She ran from the room, leaving the door swinging wide.

Victoria pulled Alex back to his chair and whispered something in his ear. He threaded his fingers through hers and kissed her temple.

Mr. Pruitt released a heavy groan. "Here I was thinking I wouldn't have to worry about the good twin pulling stunts like that."

Remembering Ana's tears at Henry's near-death, Charlotte stared at the door. Her hand shot to the air. "Mr. Pruitt, can I go talk to her? I think something upset her."

"Fine." He waved a hand to the door. "Just be back soon."

Charlotte stuffed her hands into the pocket of Wesley's hoodie and walked up the row of tables. She felt Mr. Pruitt's eyes follow her until she stepped out of the room and closed the door.

She passed an empty biology lab and closed doors to other classrooms in session. Her tennis shoes barely made a sound against the cold white tile floor. Reaching the bathroom between the science and math hallways, she heard sniffles coming from inside.

Charlotte passed the sinks tucked in a small nook. She found Anastasia sitting on the floor near the last stall. She tucked her face against her knees. Her fuchsia and teal hair spilled around her. She picked at her sheer green leggings with one hand.

"Ana?" Charlotte moved closer.

Ana peered up at Charlotte. Tears streaked her cheeks. Red tinged the whites of her blue eyes. "Sorry."

"Why are you apologizing?" Charlotte grabbed a wad of toilet paper from a stall and handed it to Ana.

"I don't know." Ana took the toilet paper and clutched it in her hand.

Charlotte sat in front of Ana, straightening the legs of her jeans and stuffing her hands back in the pocket of Wesley's hoodie. "Do you want to talk about it?"

"My brother almost died." Ana leaned back, revealing the tiny daisies covering her dress. "And it means nothing to him."

"What do you mean?"

"He's going to help Elsey again." Ana wiped her nose with a corner of toilet paper. "He's not answered a single text since she took him home except to tell me he'll talk to me later." She paused and shook her head. "Well, that's not true. He texted me this morning to talk about her and then told me he'd call me when he was ready for school. And he just never called."

Charlotte picked at the skin next to her thumb. "Maybe he doesn't know what to think. I mean, I nearly died, too, and I'm not sure what to think about anything."

"No. If you knew Henry like I do, you'd know that's not what this is." Ana tore off a clean section of toilet paper and dotted her eyes. "He's always been like this when it comes to her. Even when we were little. She could walk into a blazing wildfire, and he'd follow her without a second thought."

"Then why did they ever stop being friends?"

Ana dropped her eyes to her lap and sucked in her bottom lip. She shrugged.

Flinching against the pain from tearing a chunk of raw flesh, Charlotte forced herself to pull her hands from her pocket. "Weren't you friends with Elsey, too?"

"Not like them." Ana looked back up. "They were inseparable. Even when we first moved here, we were introduced to Alex, Victoria, and Rachelle. We all would go to the same events and things, but he stuck to Elsey. He'd only hang out with the others if Elsey wasn't around, and as soon as she showed up, it was like everyone else was invisible. Even me. I didn't get it for a long time, but I was a kid. All I knew was I wasn't my brother's best friend anymore. They tried to make me fit in, but it was still hard. It was hard for me to make other friends. Most people didn't seem to like me like they liked him. Alex and Victoria tolerated me if Henry was around. Rachelle seemed nicer, but she doesn't have much of an identity outside of being Victoria's best friend."

Frowning, Charlotte nodded. "Malini had a hard time with that, too. With all the attention he always got from Alex and Victoria's group and everyone else. She hated attending their parties with him."

"Oh, he always hated those parties. He reads and spends time in his apartment more than he hangs out with other people or spends time downstairs in Bedlam." Ana picked apart the pieces of tissue in her hand. Ripping it into strips of paper. "He still gets invited though, and people always want to be around him because he's entertaining and charismatic. Even when we were little, people were drawn to him. He's not part of Alex's posse, but they try to include him in a lot. I think they like to laugh at the guy with poor self-control getting messed up and doing something he won't remember in the morning. At least, he's been avoiding them since he's been hanging out with Elsey again."

The messages Charlotte saw on Henry's phone popped into her mind. Keeping her mouth closed, she let Ana continue.

"After we moved here from Ainsvale, I spent most of my time alone or with Dad. He'd take me with him to work or to the museum or whatever I wanted. We'd do our own thing while Henry was doing whatever with Elsey."

Remembering Elsey's request to ask Malini about Henry's dad, lines creased Charlotte's forehead. "What about your mom?"

"She loved me and spent some time with me, but she doted on Henry constantly. He was her favorite." She shrugged. "I understood that though. Henry wasn't expected. The doctors only saw me on the sonograms every time, and then Mom went into labor really early. I was born first, and then, surprise—there was a baby boy, too. But he was a lot weaker and almost died. He had to stay in the hospital even longer than I did. So, Mom was always catering to him."

Silence fell over them. Charlotte chewed on the inside of her cheek. Ana sucked on her bottom lip.

"I wasn't always the best sister to him."

"I'm sure Henry doesn't hold it against you."

"It doesn't matter. When he came out to Dad, I made excuses for Dad's reaction. Saying, Dad just didn't understand and that he didn't mean what he said and was just shocked. I've tried fixing their relationship. I mean, Dad handled it well when I came out, so his feelings must've changed. But Henry won't hear it. He won't even set foot back in the house. Between that and his substance use, I'm walking a fine line of losing him for good. And last night—" She cut herself off and dropped her head into her hands. Her shoulders shook. More sobs tore free from her.

Charlotte's fingers found the silver charm around her throat. "Elsey doesn't want our help anymore anyway."

A harsh laugh escaped Ana. She wiped her eyes. "You don't get it. For four years, he never gave up. Even before that. When she was missing, every single day, he went to her house asking to see her. When Dad or her parents told him to stop, he'd ignore it and go anyway."

"Really?" Charlotte's brow creased. "He's always seemed so laidback to me. Even Mal always made him seem like that."

"He is with everyone else. They were best friends though, and she went missing the same day our mom died—well kind of."

"Kind of?"

"If I tell you, you can't tell anyone." Ana focused her eyes on Charlotte's. "Not even Wesley."

Charlotte chewed on the inside of her cheek. *Why do I keep getting into this situation?* Taking a deep breath, she nodded.

Dabbing at her eyes with her tissues, Ana picked at the hem of her dress. "It was the same day we got the news that Mom died. We were only twelve. Henry fell apart. It was hard on me, but I had Dad and my art. He didn't have anything. Except Elsey. I remember him saying he was going to talk to her and give her a letter that he wrote. Not fifteen minutes later, he was back home telling me that Elsey's mother said she wasn't home and that she wasn't allowed to have visitors. Henry shut himself in his room and wouldn't come out. That night, I woke up to someone calling my name. I thought it was him. When he still lived at home, he had a habit of waking me up in the middle of the night whenever he had nightmares. But it was Elsey."

"How did she get in?"

"I don't know." Ana shrugged. "But she tried to give me two things. A picture of a dog that I'd never seen before and a letter. She asked me to give them to Henry. I told her that I'd go wake up Henry so she could talk to him, but she said she couldn't. Then she hugged me and told me goodbye, which if you know Elsey, you know she's not a hugger. She's not really a toucher at all. She doesn't like being touched unless she initiates it and even then ... she *doesn't* initiate it."

Flipping through her memories, Charlotte recalled Henry holding Elsey's hand during her episode from using too much of her power. No other memories of physical contact surfaced—except for moments of violence.

"I told her to at least let me get the letter that Henry wrote for her." Ana continued, "I left to get the letter. I just missed my dad going to bed, and Henry must've heard me talking to her because he was already up and throwing on clothes. He was still crying, but he came running when I told him. When we came back, she was already gone."

Charlotte cocked her head to the side. "What about the picture and the letter?"

Ana dropped her gaze to her lap and shrugged. "The next day, her dad gave a press conference announcing that his wife's parents had been killed in what they assumed was a home invasion and that Elsey had been found covered in their blood. No one saw her after that until she showed up at school freshman year."

Letting silence consume them, Charlotte stared at the stalls and replayed the story. She fiddled with the silver bird charm on her necklace and chewed on the inside of her cheek.

Ana rested her head against the white brick wall. She stared up at the lights. "Kade's the only other person I've told that story to."

"What?" Charlotte jerked toward Ana.

"Around the time that Kade and Malini began dating, he came up to me and asked questions about Elsey. He asked what I thought about her and her family and what I knew about them. I told him what I just told you."

Biting hard on the inside of her cheek, Charlotte flinched. Blood trickled over her tongue. "Did Kade say why he was asking about her?"

"No. I always thought he felt bad about what happened between him and Henry and that he was trying to fix things somehow." Ana sucked in her bottom lip and let silence settle over them. She scanned the daisies on her dress.

Charlotte took a deep breath. Something tight unfurled in her chest. "Everything seems to be connected to them. Elsey and Kade. If not one, then the other, and somehow, they're connected to each other."

"You can't mean—"

"I don't mean she killed him." Charlotte shook her head. "He was asking questions about her, then he died. She went to the morgue to find out how he died. Why?"

Ana shrugged.

"And then she happened to find out that he was killed by some murderous cult that's been killing all these other people." Charlotte strained to connect the dots. "Everything leads back to Elsey and Kade."

"And the only person who could give us answers is dead."

"Elsey could still give us answers."

"She'd have to trust us first." Ana stood and tossed her tissue into a nearby trashcan.

Climbing to her feet, Charlotte frowned. "Does that mean you still want to help Elsey, too?"

Ana sighed. "I know Henry is. I can't let him do it alone." She looked up, meeting Charlotte's eyes. "What about you? Nearly dying has to be its own kind of traumatizing."

"I haven't decided." Charlotte jammed her hands into the pocket of Wesley's hoodie. "I know Wes is insisting that he help. He can't let it go now."

"He's always been very stubborn, from what I know of him at least." A small giggle escaped Ana. "No wonder he and Elsey haven't been getting along. They probably have too much in common."

"Yeah." Charlotte's frown deepened. *That's my concern.*

Tristan's soft humming to the classical music on the radio filled the SUV, uninterrupted. He tapped out the melody on his leather pants—held together by strategically placed zippers and laces—with one hand and while he steered with the other. Plaid patches pieced together a skull on his black T-shirt, fitted perfectly to his powerful chest and arms.

Elsey focused on her book. The world around her faded to the background.

Angered by the actions of Poylphonte and her two sons, Agrio and Oreios, against humans and gods, Zeus sent Hermes to punish them. To protect his descendants, Ares snatched Polyphonte and her sons from the fate waiting for them, and with the help of Hermes, transformed them into birds. Polyhonte was changed into a barn owl, a symbol for a portent of war and sedition of mankind. Oreios was transformed into an eagle owl, which became an omen of little good whenever seen. Argios was changed into a vulture, a bird with a craving for human flesh and blood. Polyphonte and her sons had a female servant who had also been transformed into a bird—a woodpecker for—

The words died in her mind at the first sound of familiar notes playing through the radio. Jerking forward, Elsey twisted the volume dial. It snapped off in her hand.

"Um …" Tristan stared at the now silent radio.

Elsey looked between the broken dial and the radio. "Sorry. I can fix it." She held it against the radio.

Tristan plucked the dial from her hand. "It's okay. Gene can fix it later." He dropped the piece in the cup holder between their seats. "You don't like that song, I take it?"

She remained silent.

"Note to self," Tristan said with a low chuckle. "Do not show you the original version of 'Nothing Else Matters' by Metallica because I treasure my album collection. Also, I should probably advise any bands against playing covers of it at Purgatory."

"This was a bad idea." She tucked the worn-out picture of a dog between the pages to mark her spot before closing the book.

"Nah." He waved his hand. "It will be fine. You're always there anyway, except when you're beating people up."

Biting her tongue, she looked at him.

Tristan waved his hand again. "Believe me, we're okay with it. You have nothing to worry about. Nothing is changing anyway. The only difference is you'll be sleeping in the den. We know your boundaries. Nobody will cross them, just like you respect our boundaries. You've never asked me or Luci to help you with the fighting aspect of things."

"I've never asked Gene either."

"That's because you know he'd do it in a heartbeat. Give him a target, and he'll gladly take it down. Even if it meant giving me and Luci a heart attack." He glanced away from the road. "It's not that we're not concerned for you, too. We know you'll do it anyway."

She dropped her attention to the book in her hands. The worn-out cover and creased spine brought her back to Henry's apartment. To him offering for her to borrow his books … his clothes. "Why does Luci wear your clothes?"

"Because she's a thief." A throaty laugh rumbled through him. "Seriously though, she's comfortable in them, and I want her to be comfortable. So, she can wear them whenever she wants. Well, there are times I'd prefer her not to be wearing them, but I also like seeing her in them."

"Does Gene wear your clothes?"

"Not really, but they're not his style." He held up a hand. "And before you ask, Luci does sometimes wear his clothes. Mine are often more readily available. Gene's usually wearing his."

Elsey gave a single nod, still struggling to make sense of Henry's offering.

Tristan glanced at her and arched a brow, but he remained silent. His attention returned to Hallen Street as the city disappeared behind them and trees lined the road. Picking up his humming again, he bobbed his head from side to side to the tune playing in his brain.

She leaned down and stashed her book inside her rucksack with her book of sheet music. Sitting back, Elsey watched the road. Tension gripped her shoulders and tingling numbness filled her limbs. Her anger unfolded to shield her from other emotions stitching their way into her heart.

He looked at her again, brow arching higher. "Are you okay?"

Another single nod.

"No pressure or anything, but if you ever need to talk about anything ... I'll listen. We all will."

Silence.

Tristan focused his attention on the road, resuming his humming.

Elsey clasped her hands in her lap, digging her nails into her palms. All the feelings she could never name screamed to be heard behind locked doors and from the darkness that consumed the few memories that were free.

Thoughts and questions she couldn't verbalize swirled like a merry-go-round spinning off its track. Scrambling for something to hold onto to steady herself, she snatched a random thought. Plucking it and dragging it forward while the others were left to spin out of control away from her focus. "His mom died."

Brows rising, Tristan glanced at her.

"I don't know why I said that." She shook her head, frustration building and pushing her on.

Some part of her needed to scream, to release everything inside demanding her attention. From the pain tangling her heart and the pleas for help stitched into every knot to every whisper of emotion trying to drag her to a memory locked away from her sight.

She dug her nails deeper into her palms until she felt the sting of her skin tearing. Remembering she wasn't alone, she released her grip before she could draw blood. "Sorry."

"It's okay. It doesn't bother me." Nearing the walls of the Hallen estate, he veered off the road into a patch of grass. He parked next to a row of trees outlining the walls. "I do a lot of things I don't understand. I don't know why I feed the strays even though it irritates Gene. I don't know why I like making clothes. I don't know why I like our crossword competitions. You don't need an explanation for everything. Sometimes, it's okay to just do things or say things because you need to. And maybe there's a reason behind it that you don't realize yet. Maybe not. As long as it's not hurting anybody, it doesn't matter."

She arched a brow. "I *do* hurt people."

"Not how I meant." He watched her eyes lower to her hands. "You're not a bad person. You're not a monster. I know you feel like one. I know that what's said about you and to you doesn't feel good, but I promise you're not one."

Elsey replayed the argument with Wesley. *I am a monster. I'm the most dangerous monster there is. I'm the monster that hunts other monsters.*

Tristan frowned, training his pitch-dark eyes on her face. "Do you think I'm a monster?"

She shook her head.

"Gene?"

Another shake.

"Luci?"

Another shake.

"Then you're not one either." He angled toward her as much as the middle console would allow given his size. "I can't tell you that you won't hurt him. That kind of thing happens in friendships and relationships. Even with Gene and Luci, sometimes we might say or do the wrong thing even when we try not to. But we apologize and we try to make sure it doesn't happen again. Connections are uncomfortable, especially when you've had them before and you lost them. But they can be really good. You got used to me and the others being back in your life though."

"That was different."

"Why?"

She struggled to put words to the feelings. Nothing. "I don't know."

"And that's okay."

Temper flaring at her inability to express herself, she shoved the moment aside and opened her door. "Let's get this over with while we still have time."

"Sounds good." Tristan opened his door and followed her through the trees. "Gene's cooking lunch, and I'm starving."

They passed through the gaping hole in the wall surrounding her family's property and crossed the small bridge crossing the stream. They stuck to the woods edging the yard until they neared the house.

She pointed to a section of blank wall on the mansion. "There's a blind spot with the cameras, but the hidden door has a camera."

"Are there cameras inside, too?"

"Not ones that function anymore. Someone shut them down, and my father hasn't been able to get them to work since."

"Luci is a master of her craft."

"It wasn't her." The corner of Elsey's mouth twitched up. "Reality is a bitch."

Listening to him chuckle, Elsey broke away from the trees and approached the mansion. She followed a careful path to the blind spot on the side of the house. Pressing her hand against the wall, she tugged on the blue chord of power in the back of her mind. It flowed through her and into the building. With a single command, the cameras around the outskirts of the building short-circuited and died. A low buzzing hum raised in her brain.

She motioned for Tristan to follow her to the door underneath the stairs. "We have to move fast. My father might've had a system message set up to notify him if something happens." Elsey plunged her hand into the rose bush beside the door.

Tristan watched the branches unfurl, revealing the key she kept hidden among the thorns. "Why don't you just use your powers or break the knob?"

"It won't work."

He eyed the doorknob, recognizing the white iridescent metal constructing the lock. A shiver ran through him.

Unlocking the door, Elsey pushed it open. Her eyes went to the fourth bookcase against the wall. She averted her gaze and led Tristan to her bedroom.

She rushed to her trunk and clutched the lock in her hand.

Welcoming the flood of power again, the lock clicked open. She began clearing the clothes from her dresser, stacking them in the trunk on the tray covering the boxes hidden beneath.

Tristan looked around the bedroom devoid of any hint of her. "Are you sure you don't want us to set you up downstairs? We could rearrange some things and give you a room."

"No." She slammed the lid closed on her trunk and secured the lock in place. "I don't do underground."

He watched her hunch over the trunk. "Okay. If you want, we can probably do something to the den. Give you a proper room in there somehow."

"No," she said. *I can't.* "Just staying there is fine. I don't need anything else."

"Okay." He nodded. "If you change your mind, let us know."

Elsey hoisted the large trunk off the ground and carried it over to him. "Can you take this to the vehicle? I'll meet you there in a moment."

Taking the trunk, Tristan left the room.

She waited a handful of heartbeats. The tingling numbness began in her fingers and her hands. Taking a deep breath, she walked into her father's study. Her eyes went to the same bookcase with its miniature replica of the statue that topped the museum.

Crossing the room, she turned the statue to face the olive tree painting on the wall to the right. A low **click** sounded. Gears **grinded** against each other. The bookcase slid aside and disappeared inside the hollow opening behind another bookcase, revealing a small square room. Multiple layered rugs covered the floor. The walls were made of a white iridescent metal. Shelves lined the walls, holding notebooks and wooden boxes with locks fashioned of the same metal.

Her breath staggered. The tingling crept up her limbs, leaving her to feel like her hands and feet weren't her own. She took a deep breath and held it. Her anger spiked, beating back the foreign feeling in her body. Urging her on.

Elsey walked around the rugs. She grabbed the first box within reach and smashed it onto the ground. Wood splintered and snapped. She grabbed a notebook and tossed it. Paper fell out, fluttering over the floor to be stepped on.

Moving around the tiny square, she destroyed every box and notebook. Throwing them against the floor or the walls. Not giving herself a moment to watch the contents spill or shatter.

She stopped at the last box. Turning it on its side so the white iridescent metal lock faced away from her, she slammed her fist into the wood. It splintered, revealing thirteen vials full of healing serum. Elsey pulled her rucksack off her back and stashed every vial inside before sweeping the box into the floor.

Elsey left the hidden door ajar so the evidence could be seen immediately. They'd know she had been there. They'd know what it meant.

Leaving the house, she slammed the door behind her and dropped her key in the rose bush. She brushed her fingers against the petals. The thorned branches seemed to respond to her touch. Curling over the key and locking it in a deadly embrace to bar anyone else who might try to reach it without her permission.

With each step away from that building with walls of glass and concrete, her anger roared with a defiance that shook her soul. She made her way through the woods and the gaping hole she'd created many years ago.

Only remnants of chains tethered her to a past she'd believed she could never escape.

She vowed to break those, too.

The cafeteria buzzed with energy and noise.

Wesley leaned against the wall with his hands stuffed in the front pockets of his faded jeans. His navy shirt—displaying a cartoon illustration of a muscular mitochondria lifting weights—earned him questioning glances.

Spotting Charlotte wading through the crowd of students filing in, his heart took a leap. The harsh glow of the fluorescent lights caught her high prominent cheekbones and her tawny beige skin. Her soft dark hair was tied in a ponytail, highlighting her narrow forehead and chin.

She met his eyes across the room and made a beeline toward him. Jemma and Malini followed at her side.

Malini flashed a rare smile as Jemma made a comment out of Wesley's earshot. She twisted her fingers in the cuffs of Kade's oversized cardigan she wore over a black button-front camisole and a flowy raisin-colored maxi skirt with black floral detailing. In black heeled booties, she stood as tall as Jemma, who wore canvas sneakers and still towered over most other people. Jemma's black bob was pulled up into two small buns. She wore frayed baggy overalls and an oversized navy argyle sweater.

"Have you seen Ana?" Jemma asked when the girls came nearer.

Wesley pulled Charlotte into his arms and placed a quick kiss on her lips before nodding toward the hall leading to the front of the school. "I saw her go that way a moment ago. I didn't speak to her though."

Jemma nodded. "I'll be back." She spun and headed toward the hall.

Furrowing his brow, Wesley looked between Charlotte and Malini. "What's wrong?"

"Ana's upset," Malini said.

"Yeah, I found her crying in the bathroom." Charlotte shot Wesley a guarded look, hoping he'd understand.

Malini glided around the couple and walked toward the lunch line. "I ran into her in the hallway earlier, and she said she's not heard from Henry all day."

"She's heard from him."

"What?" Malini stopped and spun toward Charlotte and Wesley. "She didn't tell me that."

Picking at the skin beside her thumb, Charlotte spoke carefully. "She told me she heard from him once this morning."

Wesley lifted his hand. "What does it matter?"

"It doesn't." Malini shrugged. "I just thought maybe she was worried he OD'd or something."

"He could still—"

"He didn't." A smooth voice called behind Wesley and Charlotte.

The group turned and saw Henry approaching with Ana's arm looped through his. His dirty blond hair hung loose in his face. He wore tailored charcoal slacks and a wool pine-green sweater under his overcoat. His shiny black leather oxfords gleamed.

Walking on Henry's other side, Jemma shot irritated glances at him.

"You're here?" Malini asked.

"Unfortunately." Henry smirked. "I didn't expect you to be so concerned though."

"I'm not," she snapped, twisting her fingers in the sleeves of Kade's cardigan. "I don't see why you showed up now. It's not like you have someone at home telling you to go to school."

"That's what I said," Jemma flexed her hands by her side.

Pulling his flask from his pocket, he took a short swig. "I honestly don't know why I'm here either. I fell back asleep. When I woke up again, I was on a loop. Next thing I know, I'm in the parking lot and was like, 'Fuck it. Might as well get some lunch and enjoy my Humanities class at least.'"

Ana smacked Henry's arm. "Never ignore my texts or calls again."

"Ouch." Henry rubbed his arm. "For the last time, I wasn't ignoring you. I was distracted."

Wesley looked Henry up and down, remembering the crushed bones in his face and the metal post impaling his chest. "Are you okay?"

"I'm fine." Henry brushed off the question and dropped his flask into his pocket. "I learned I still talk in my sleep. I thought I grew out of that when I was twelve or somewhere around there."

Malini narrowed her eyes in a pointed look. "I literally told you that you talk in your sleep every time you stayed over at my house."

He held up his index finger. "In my defense, whenever I slept at your house, I had other things on my mind. Like trying to find my pants."

Charlotte raised a hand with her palm up. "Why do you think you keep getting caught napping during trig?"

Henry tossed up his hands. "Because it's the teacher's job to pay attention. Not mine."

"Come on." Shaking her head, Ana took Jemma's hand and pulled her through the group. "Let's get lunch. I feel like I can actually eat now."

"What's stopped you before?" Victoria Boyer's high-pitched voice cut through the chatter around them. Pushing her blonde waves over her shoulder, she passed the group. Her black heeled boots ticked on the floor.

Rachelle Forge clung to Victoria's side with their arms laced together. She looked between Victoria and the group but didn't comment.

Heat flushed Ana's cheeks. She stepped behind Jemma and stared at her feet.

Henry opened his mouth, preparing to speak.

"Smart move, Victoria." Jemma rolled her eyes. "Henry will *definitely* sleep with you after you insulted his sister."

The hint of a smile curled Rachelle's mouth, and she strung a chunk of hair between her lips. Hiding any smile and enhancing the baby-doll innocence in her cherubic face.

Victoria halted, spinning on Jemma. "Excuse you! I have a boyfriend."

Ana tugged Jemma's hand before the argument could continue. "Let's just go to the art room."

Jemma nodded and let Ana lead her away.

"You also had a boyfriend when Henry and I were together," Malini said, directing Victoria's attention to her. She rested her hands on her hips. "That never stopped you from trying to get with him."

Exchanging a look of discomfort, Wesley and Charlotte remained silent.

Henry pulled his flask from his pocket and held it aloft. "For the record, I always said, 'No.'"

Ignoring Henry's remark, Victoria narrowed her eyes at Malini. "Sorry, I thought you were too busy cheating on him with *my* boyfriend to care."

The chunk of hair in Rachelle's mouth hid any possible hint of expression.

Malini glanced at Henry and stormed off, disappearing down a nearby hall.

"Victoria." Henry flicked out a hand. "Why don't you do us all a favor and buy yourself a new personality?"

Charlotte fought back a grin. "What aisle would those even be on?"

Turning to Victoria's reddening face, Wesley held his hand out with the palm up. "If you have trouble finding them, I hear they sell masks in the party section. Maybe one of those could be a start."

Henry muffled his chuckle with a drink from his flask.

Scowling, Victoria's mouth opened.

"Come on." Rachelle tugged on Victoria's arm. "Alex is—"

Victoria's attention snapped away before Rachelle could finish. Her eyes locked on a target across the room. She walked away without a word, abandoning her best friend and the situation.

Rachelle gave a small wave to Henry. "I'll see you around." Glancing at Charlotte first, she flashed a tiny smile at Wesley. "See you in Mrs. Moreno's class."

He tossed her a small nod. She hurried off to catch up with Victoria.

Charlotte looked at Wesley. "You talk to Rachelle?"

"Not really." He shook his head. "She sits behind me in AP Lit, and she always attends the summer program at Forge. She's kind of quiet though." Wesley turned his attention to Henry. "Seriously, how are you feeling?"

"I'm great." Henry smirked. "My bedside nurse was a delight. How are you two?"

"Okay," Wesley said.

Charlotte scraped at the skin beside her thumb. "I'm fine."

"You sure about that?" Henry asked.

She shrugged.

Wesley frowned and slipped his hand into hers before she could scratch her thumb raw. He looked back at Henry. "Did you get Luci's message?"

"I'll be there after school." Henry nodded. "That's the other reason I drove myself. I wasn't sure Ana would be up for it anymore."

"She's okay with it ... kind of." Charlotte looked between the boys. "I ran into her in the bathroom, and we talked about it. She's upset, but she'll help."

Wesley squeezed her hand. "What about you?"

Replaying the previous night, she chewed on the inside of her cheek. The weight of their expectant stares pressed down on her, and she nodded. "I have practice though, and Mal is my ride afterward, so you'll have to pick me up when you get off work."

"I already spoke to Liev to get my hours changed today, so I can get you before heading to the house."

Henry pulled a pill bottle from his pocket and dropped two on his tongue. He swallowed them with a swig from his flask. "I'll see you guys there. Now, if you'll excuse me, I have to track down my sister and play the part of brotherly jester."

Charlotte bit the inside of her cheek. She replayed the previous night again. The sharp pain of ribs breaking and stabbing into her organs echoed in her chest. The crunch of her kneecaps traced under her skin.

"Are you sure you want to do this?" Wesley squeezed her hand.

"Yeah." She nodded, pushing against the memory of rage in his eyes when he saw her crumble to the ground. "I'm sure."

Flame-colored leaves sloshed in the water in the wake of the boat.

Asher waited for Elsey on the dock, leaning on his cane and staring at a pocket watch dangling from the silver chain around his neck.

The wind picked up when she reached North Star Island.

"I was expecting you earlier." Asher closed the pocket watch and slid it into its hiding place beneath his shirt before she could glimpse the image etched into the front. Dragging his handkerchief from the pocket of his brown slacks, he patted his brow. The bright shades of his Hawaiian shirt clashed with the season. His warm brown eyes caught the sun high in the sky.

Dropping the anchor, she slung her rucksack over her shoulder before hoisting herself onto the dock. "It would be nice if your visions were more convenient and less vague. Maybe then I wouldn't have taken a knife to the gut."

He tucked his handkerchief into his pocket, flashing a broad smile. "Are you always going to hold that grudge?"

"It's not a grudge."

"Just a gentle reminder that I'm the only one who's ever outwitted you?" He chuckled and twisted his hand around the carved triangular serpent head of his cane.

"First—" Elsey arched a brow and crossed her arms over her chest. "I could've beaten you if that was my intent. Second, you're not the only one who's accomplished that feat anymore."

Nodding, he started on the path leading to the community.

She followed him, listening to the muffled clicks his cane made against the stones. "What do you know?"

"Have you eaten?"

She rolled her eyes. "No."

"Good. We'll get lunch and have a nice chat."

Elsey resisted the urge to grumble. "Fine, but afterward, I have to see if I can get information from the men from Arnie's Deli."

"You can try, but they already told us they were hired guns," he said. Entering the clearing in front of the old prison, he tossed her an obvious look. "Mercenaries like the last bunch you brought. They're not likely to know anything."

"The chance that they might is enough for me." Stepping around him, she yanked the door open.

Asher led her through the indoor plaza. Glances shot her way. Whispers met her ears. She kept her head high.

He pushed open the door to Idalia's café and moved aside for her to enter. She ignored the stares and wound her way through the tables and chairs to stand beside him at the glass counter.

Idalia set her magazine down and stood from her stool. "It's nice to see you, Elsey."

Elsey nodded. "Idalia."

"Your usual?"

"Yes, please."

Idalia bent down to retrieve a vegan banana nut muffin from the glass case. Turning to the machines, she filled a glass with water and a mug to the brim with a dark roast blend. She set the drinks on the glass counter and picked up tongs to place two glazed donuts on a saucer.

"Thank you." Elsey grabbed her muffin and glass of water in one hand. She reached for Asher's plate and received a jab to the leg from his cane.

"I've told you; I can carry my own stuff." He balanced his mug on his saucer beside his donuts and lifted them from the counter. "Do it again, and you'll need a cane as well."

She rolled her eyes and followed him to the seating area in the back. He sat in a low-slung chair, and she took the sofa against the wall.

Resting his cane against his chair, Asher took a short sip from his coffee. Elsey broke off a piece of her muffin and popped it in her mouth.

She examined everyone and everything in the café. Idalia wiped down the counter. A young man read a book in the far corner. Two people played chess to the left. A young girl shuffled through stations on the radio by the front window. The bell chimed over the door as a man entered and approached the counter.

"Always watching." Asher set his mug on the table between them. Her eyes flicked to him. "Always observing. But what do you actually see?"

She drank from her glass. *Threats. Risks. Escapes.* "Life."

Letting her eyes return to the scene, he finished his first donut before speaking. "You're not seeing things clearly. You should know by now that not everything you see is as it seems."

"What am I supposed to be seeing?"

"I cannot tell you what you're supposed to see without being able to see the truth myself. I see what the fates will allow me to see." He watched her take another bite of her muffin. "Everything comes with a feeling. The tower came with ambition. The island came with hope. Your enemy came with desperation. *You* came with fear."

"I'm not afraid." Her words were firm.

He sipped from his mug. "Then what are you?"

Her eyes burned with a single word. "Angry."

"Anger is just a blanket to keep yourself warm when everything else has gone cold." He watched her eyes shift to her glass. "Do you remember what I said when I first told you about my vision for this island?"

"Hope lives."

"No." He waited for her eyes to level on him. "Hope is a living, breathing thing, and to keep it alive, you must fight for it. You must feed it and nurture it. Without hope, the world falls into ruin. We are in a war to keep hope alive, and if you give up chaos wins."

"I've never given up." She spoke as if she were trying to convince herself more than him.

"Because you have hope." He leaned forward, resting his elbows on his knees. "You are hope. *I* am hope. This island and your teammates . . . they're all hope. Living embodiments of what it means to fight for a new day. A better day. A day where people like us don't have to hide. Where people are not starving in the streets or killing each other to save themselves."

She stared at her muffin while her thoughts shuffled like cards.

"I can't give you the solution to your problems. I can't give outcomes. I can only tell you this: in a fight—in a war, you must find a way to use your weaknesses as a weapon." Asher lowered his voice and pushed forward on the waves in the air, wrapping his words around her. "You need to hold onto it. Don't become numb because things seem grim. You built a city from the rubble of a prison. You walk with death like you're the one he should fear. Feeling all the suffering and death in the world is not easy. It seems more like a curse than a power, but you need to let it serve you. You've not let reality break you yet."

The soft light caught on the hardened look of her eyes. She spoke with all the fire breathing life into her soul. "I don't break."

A small smile flickered across Asher's face, but he remained silent.

Gathering her hands in her lap, Elsey dug through her thoughts. She twisted the black and clear beads of the bracelet holding her filigree star. Her fingers skimmed the leather bracelet encircling her wrist like a corset. "I don't understand how what you're telling me has anything to do with what happened last night."

"I never said it did. What you're experiencing now is only an obstacle. You can let it impede you or aid you. There's more waiting on the horizon than what I've been allowed to see. You must be prepared when the time comes." Asher tapped the serpent's head on his cane. "A crutch is not a bad thing. It's simply a tool used for support. It is how we use it that determines its benefits and adequacy. It can open doors to possibilities or destroy everything you hold dear.

"There's only one way to succeed and to build the reality you want. You can either find a way to manage and use the pain eating you alive to your advantage, or you can hide from it and let it fester." Leaning back in his chair, Asher gestured toward her muffin. "Finish eating. I have a feeling you'll be needing all your strength."

Draining the last of her water bottle, Charlotte's eyes went to the dilapidated houses lining Corinth Street. Small ranches with broken windows. Two-story Craftsman with collapsed roofs. Slouching split-levels with missing doors. Signs of life still clung to some houses—someone pulling a curtain or peering out a barred window.

She recalled Elsey mentioning she'd found a body in an abandoned house, and she wondered whether it was nearby.

"You okay?" Malini glanced away from the road. Her eyes held a faint red hue from all her tears. Her nails—still ragged and unkempt—picked at the faux leather cover on her steering wheel.

"Huh?" Charlotte looked at her best friend, letting her question register. "Oh yeah."

"Are you sure?" She turned off Corinth Street and followed a sloping hill to a small patch of well-kept homes tucked behind a gate. "You're kind of quiet."

"I'm fine. Just tired." Charlotte looked at the large, picturesque houses. French country-style homes with tan stone façades. Greek Revivals with tall white columns and an air of superiority. Glass box contemporaries with clean lines and bland colors. Symmetrical Colonials that looked like anyone wearing shoes inside would be taken out back and flogged. No matter how large the houses in the neighborhood were, they didn't compare to the massive estates overlooking the city from their hill atop Hallen Street.

Following the winding roads of the gated community, the steep-pitched roof of a large Tudor home peeked over young evergreens. Malini steered onto the driveway, bringing them into the full view of the house's asymmetrical façade of dark masonry and exposed timber framing cream-colored stucco. Smoke puffed from one of three tall chimneys reaching toward the sky. An arched mahogany door and groupings of dark-framed windows with diamond-shaped panes gave the house a fairytale quality.

Malini parked in the detached two-car garage to the side and led the way to the front door.

Slipping out of her sneakers, Charlotte replayed every time she'd entered the same detailed mahogany paneled foyer. The same dark chandelier gleamed off the rich original hardwood floors. A recording of a pipe organ played a haunting circus melody from deeper in the house.

"Um." Malini slipped off her black heeled booties. "Can you wait down here for a moment? My room is a mess." Without waiting, she bounded up a stairwell on the right.

Listening to the music, a familiar chill crept up Charlotte's spine. She told herself to remain still, but the music played on. Beckoning with a ghostly hand. Her feet disobeyed her. She passed the open archways to a formal dining room and a large kitchen on the left. Ahead, the pocket doors to the den stood open. Her feet stopped at the threshold. Unable to cross into the room that seemed more like a mausoleum.

Malini's mother, Veda Nayak, sat in a high-backed blue velvet chair to the side. A small table beside Veda held a glass of cognac and a green bottle of small red pills. Memorabilia overflowed the mantel and the glass cabinets in every corner of the room. Posters, signs, and photographs lined the walls. A circular white leather sofa sat in the center of a large antique floral Indian rug covering most of the floor.

Veda stared at a framed poster above the roaring fireplace, showing a younger Veda and her missing partner, Indigo, standing together with **GILDED CIRCUS** in a bold decorative font above their heads in violet and silver.

The couple stood in front of a gray distressed wall. Indigo was tall with medium golden tan skin and delicate, fine-boned features. He wore a black suit with scrolling violet embroidery and piping. His thick curly black hair appeared to have a hint of blue and violet. In what must've been an exaggerated detail for the poster, his dark, nebulous eyes had faint blue and pink lines. Veda's tall, slender figure was accentuated in a short violet dress with sheer panels on the sides and a ruffled skirt. Small shards of mirrored glass dangled from her hair. She stood tall in heeled boots and a top hat. A devilish grin splayed on her full plum-colored lips, complementing her rich olive tan skin and dark brown eyes. A small diamond pierced the side of her perfectly straight aquiline nose.

The woman sitting in the room, staring into a past no one else could see, looked more like a premonition of Malini's future than like the woman in the poster. Distant dark eyes holding more ghosts than people. Wiry frame shriveling away with years of atrophied heartache. Long black locks growing frayed by grief.

A deep hollow pain gripped Charlotte's stomach. "Ms. Nayak."

Veda twisted. Her eyes—ringed with dark circles and tinged red—seemed to look through Charlotte. "You're here."

Charlotte scraped at the skin beside her thumb with an urgency that made her skin crawl. *Does she even see me?* "Malini gave me a ride after practice."

Veda's eyes became clearer at the mention of her daughter's name, but a haunting darkness clouded her gaze again. Her index finger circled the rim of her glass. Her dry, cracked lips twitched. She turned, staring at the poster. "I hear …"

Her words dropped off or became too low and soft. Another chill traced through Charlotte's veins. "Hear what?"

Nothing. No movement. No words.

Charlotte scraped at the side of her thumb. She took a deep breath and stepped into the room. Another step. Another. Slowly inching forward until she could see—

"What are you doing?" Malini's sharp, lilting voice called from the doorway.

Charlotte jumped and spun around. She felt Veda's eyes land on her again. She pressed her lips closed and rushed toward the doorway and past Malini.

Malini shifted her attention to Veda. "We'll be in my room until Wesley picks her up. I'll start dinner then."

Her eyes held a hint of recognition, and she nodded before turning back to the poster.

Sliding the pocket doors closed, Malini motioned for Charlotte to follow her up the stairs. "What were you doing?"

Charlotte tore a piece of her skin beside her thumb and winced. "I rarely hear her speak, but she said she hears something. I couldn't make out what she was saying, so I thought maybe if I got closer, I'd be able to get her attention and she'd answer."

Malini frowned, leading the way through the winding halls and darkened rooms left untouched by time. "She *thinks* she hears my dad."

"Really?" Charlotte's brows rose. "Is it because of the pills?"

"No." She shook her head. "She started hearing voices before she started taking them. Besides, auditory hallucinations aren't a side effect of Reds unless you take a lot."

"One of the tidbits you learned from your time dating Henry?"

Malini nodded. "He used to be a lot worse than he is now. Not all the time. He'd go through phases. But honestly, I don't know if he was ever really sober while we were together. He'd say he was. Or say he was getting sober, but it was hard to believe him. And even if he did try, it never lasted. I'm honestly surprised he didn't end up dying before."

The image of a metal bar sticking out of Henry's chest flashed in Charlotte's mind. Shaking the memory away, she glanced into a darkened room lined with shelves full of books. "Did he ever talk about why he does it?"

"Yeah."

She waited for Malini to say more, but nothing else came. Any questions about Henry died at the sight of a familiar door marked with a violet M.

Malini opened the door, and Charlotte's stomach twisted.

A single lamp cast a dim glow from the desk against the far wall. A sleeve hung over the lip of a closed dresser drawer. The bathroom door hung open, but the light was off. A box—heaped with a dried bouquet of blue asters and purple gladiolus, a bundle of dark clothes, and a couple of binders—sat on a chaise lounge between the closet and the bathroom. Clothes peeked out beneath the door to the walk-in closet. Black pillows and a leopard-print duvet covered the king-sized bed. A picture framed by violet glass sat on the nightstand.

Charlotte had seen the picture enough to recall it from memory.

Malini leaned into Kade's arms while they sat on the bleachers at school. He leaned down to kiss the top of her head. The light caught his cheekbones while Malini tucked her face into his chest. Wesley's shoulder could be seen beside Kade in the picture. It was taken before Kade had convinced him to ask Charlotte out, but he'd always come to her track meetings to sit with her friends and cheer her on. Jemma had taken the picture with Kade's camera.

Charlotte couldn't remember that particular day very well, but she remembered the picture. Malini kept it beside her bed. She had never displayed any pictures of Henry in her room.

Walking around Charlotte, Malini sat on her bed and pulled the framed picture into her lap. She ran her fingers over the glass. Taking in a sharp breath like she was fighting a fresh batch of tears.

The pain in Charlotte's heart sharpened to a point. She chewed on the inside of her cheek, letting silence widen the gap between them. "I'm sorry for not telling you when Henry found Kade."

Malini looked up with water-laden eyes.

"You shouldn't have found out from the Daily Death List," Charlotte continued. Her frown deepened. Her thoughts drifted to Wesley. "I know this has been hard on you, but it's been hard on other people, too. Kade was important to a lot of people."

Malini pulled up her knees and wrapped her arms around her legs. The photo sandwiched against her chest. "I still need him."

Sitting down, Charlotte wrapped her arms around Malini's shoulders. "I know it's hard, but you'll get through it."

"No, I won't." Malini's voice sounded like nails were scraping at her heart. "How am I supposed to get through it when he's the only person I could ever count on? I could tell him anything, and he took care of everything. For everyone. Not just me or Wesley and Taliyah."

Charlotte smoothed her hand down Malini's soft hair, ignoring the tears dripping onto her shoulder.

Malini pushed herself free from Charlotte and wiped her eyes with the sleeve of Kade's cardigan. "He always tried to encourage Henry to get sober. He helped Jemma and her mom get a new place after the situation with her dad."

"I didn't know that."

"No one else does." Malini traced his face in the photograph in her lap. She paused, biting her lip, before she spoke. "Henry's dad owns a few apartment buildings in the city. When I told Kade about what happened, he talked to Henry's dad about needing a safe place for a friend. We kept it a secret for them so the wrong people wouldn't find out where they were staying and wouldn't try to come after Kade."

Charlotte picked at the duvet cover. The mention of Henry's dad brought up her memory of Elsey's request. "Can I ask you a question about Henry's dad?"

Malini's shoulders stiffened. She fastened her hands onto the framed picture. "What about him?"

"I—" Charlotte stopped, deciding on the best way to ask the question. "You've never really spoken positively of him before."

"Because he's trash," she spat.

Her eyes widened at Malini's harsh tone. "I mean, Ana seems to like him."

"Ana likes him because she doesn't know the real him."

"And you know the real him?"

"Better than anybody. Except maybe Henry." She paused for a second and shook her head. "No, I still know him better than Henry."

Charlotte looked Malini in the eyes. A sliminess churned in her belly. "Did something happen?"

Malini stared at her with a look more haunted than her mother's.

Charlotte counted the seconds. *One ... Two ... Three ... Four ...*

Malini didn't speak.

Five ... Six ... Seven ...

Nothing.

Eight ... Nine ... Ten ... Eleven ...

Silence.

Twelve ... Thirteen ... Four—

Malini gave a firm shake of her head. "I'm fine. Don't worry about it."

Chewing on the inside of her cheek, Charlotte nodded. She stood and her fingers went to the silver bird charm on her necklace.

"Charlotte?" Malini called her attention back. "Do me a favor and stay away from him."

She opened her mouth, preparing to ask further. Charlotte replayed the conversation. Dots connected and formed an ugly picture she didn't want to see. She clamped her mouth shut and told herself Malini would open up when she was ready. She ignored the questions about what it would mean if she told Elsey what she suspected.

Avoiding Malini's eyes, Charlotte wandered around the room. She stopped beside the chaise lounge and picked one of the dried flowers from the pile on top of the box.

"They were the last thing Kade gave me. After he had to go to that benefit at the museum with Henry's dad, he came back with those." Malini sniffled and wiped her eyes again. "That entire box is stuff he left here. I thought if I put it where I couldn't see it, maybe it wouldn't hurt as much. But I can't put it away. I still need him here."

An image of Veda's tormented soul staring at the memories of her life with her partner settled into Charlotte's mind. Her stomach twisted into knots. Dropping the flower into the box, she returned to the bed and took Malini in her arms again. "You're not alone."

"It's hard to believe that when the person who made you feel whole and safe is taken from you."

Charlotte rubbed her hands in soft circles over Malini's back, remembering her own mom doing the same when she was a child. "I'm so, so sorry. I wish I could make it better. I wish I could make the pain go away."

"I just want them to go away." A sharp edge hung off Malini's muffled words.

"Who?"

"The people who killed him." Malini sniffled and wiped her tears on her sleeves. "They don't deserve to live after what they did. It's not fair that they're still living and breathing and tormenting the rest of the city when they murdered Kade like he was nothing. I need him back, and I need them gone."

Charlotte tightened her hug around her fragile friend. "I know. I'm sorry. I'm so sorry."

"It's not fair. This wasn't supposed to happen. He should still be here." Malini's shoulders shook. She buried her face into Charlotte's shirt and let painful sobs tear from her lips. "I need him back. I just need him back."

Smoothing her hand over Malini's hair again, she noticed the ragged state of her nails. Charlotte pulled back and took one of Malini's hands. "You stopped doing your nails."

"I don't really care about it anymore." Malini shrugged. "I'll just have to do it all over again. It seems pointless. *Everything* seems pointless now."

"You still dress nice."

Malini released a hollow laugh. "That's only to keep Alex away. That shark is still circling me, but if I show too much weakness now, he'll move in for the kill."

Charlotte's forehead creased. "Alex Cleary?"

Noticing Charlotte's confused expression, Malini continued. "He's the *only* one I ever cheated on Henry with. Well, before Kade."

"Why didn't you ever tell me? Why let everyone think it was so many others?"

"Because it doesn't matter who it was."

"Did Jemma know?"

"Yes." Malini leaned against her headboard. "For the record, I always felt bad. I always confessed immediately and apologized. It got to a point where I didn't even have to confess. He could see the look on my face and know what I was coming to tell him. I always hated myself for it. I knew I was hurting him, but I was hurting so much that I couldn't care until it hit me in the middle of it. By then, it was too late to take it back. That it was with Alex made it even worse for Henry."

"Why?" Charlotte remembered the text message she saw in Henry's phone and her conversation with Ana.

"From what Henry told me, when he moved here, all the families on the hill were even more closely connected. Elsey was still an outsider with everyone but Henry." Malini leaned over and set the picture of Kade on her bedside table. "Henry's dad pushed him to be friends with Alex instead of Elsey, at least until Alex's parents adopted his brother. But Alex has always been jealous of Henry. He thinks of himself as a second-rate version of Henry even though he's older and has his followers. Their similarities were what made it easy to get with Alex. Jealousy makes people do stupid things, even me. Alex has always had a thing with making Henry miserable because of it.

"It wasn't all about Henry. Alex *also* hooked up with me to get back at Victoria." Malini shook her head and met Charlotte's eyes. "That's why she hates me."

Charlotte's forehead creased. "Victoria and Alex both cheat on each other?"

"Like it's a competition," Malini said. "And it's not an open relationship thing." Climbing off her bed, she walked around her bed and crossed to her bathroom.

"How do you know all this?" Charlotte watched Malini step into her bathroom and flip on the light. She listened to the sound of drawers opening and closing.

"Henry's part of that world. Kind of. Well, he was." Malini wandered back into the room carrying a small basket filled with nail polish, remover, and cotton buds. She sat across from Charlotte and motioned for her feet.

Without speaking, Charlotte tugged off her socks and propped her feet on the bedspread.

"Also, Henry and Alex are both talkative. Henry more so, but if you give Alex a chance to talk about Victoria, he will not shut up. He talks about her like she created the universe. Hell, he was always calling her and asking her to come over before I was even out of his room." Malini set to work, painting Charlotte's toenails a pale shade of pink. "I've honestly never fully wrapped my head around either of those two. They torment everyone, and Alex's brother gets the brunt of it. But, sometimes, Alex and Victoria can be the nicest people you've ever met. Alex has let Henry crash at his house and done other things to help him, and Victoria invited me to go shopping a couple of times since we both love clothes. You never know when they'll turn. It can be sudden, and you'll have no idea where it came from."

Charlotte leaned back, pressing the heels of her hands into the bed. "You realize, this is the first time you've ever really opened up about any of this? About anything really?"

Malini met her eyes. She released a labored breath and returned her attention to her current task. "Things are different now. All I have left are you and Jemma. And Ana by association."

"You still have your mom." Charlotte looked at the picture of Malini and Kade on the bedside table. "You weren't always close to Kade though. I mean before you two dated."

"No." Another small laugh escaped her. "I'm pretty sure he hated me for a while. I wasn't his biggest fan either because of all the time Henry spent with him. Between Henry's constant presence with Kade and undying obsession with Elsey, it felt like I wasn't even part of my own relationship sometimes. And with the drugs … I didn't come second or third or even forth with him. I was dead last behind everything else."

Charlotte watched Malini, uncertain if she was aware of how much she divulged. "What changed? Between you and Kade, I mean."

Chewing on her bottom lip, Malini sat up and closed the bottle of nail polish. She replaced the nail polish in her basket and grabbed a deep plum shade. She offered the bottle to Charlotte. "How about you paint my fingernails and tell me how you knew about my affair with Kade?"

Heat flushed Charlotte's cheeks. She took the bottle and untwisted the cap, uncertain how to begin.

"We were careful not to do anything at his house. Wes never would've overheard us." Malini watched her and kept her voice measured. "We didn't want people finding out because we both felt terrible. We didn't want to hurt Henry."

"Kade told me." Charlotte took one of Malini's hands and began painting her nails. She glanced up. "He needed advice."

"About us?" Malini asked. Her voice sounded smaller with a fragile edge.

Charlotte dropped her eyes to Malini's hand and concentrated on keeping her tone normal—to make her lie believable. "Yeah."

Henry bent down to check his reflection in the side mirror of Ana's passenger door. He raked his fingers through the hair hanging in his face.

Leaning on the hood of her car, Ana watched him over the top of her sketchbook. She didn't bother fighting her giggles. "If you keep playing with your hair, you'll make it greasy. Wouldn't that ruin your whole ..." She paused and waved her pencil at him. "... thing?"

He dropped his hands and looked up. "It's hard to get used to again."

Her eyes glittered. "And why did you decide to change it back?"

"I-I-I don't know." Shoving his hands into his pockets, he sought the comfort of the pill bottle beneath his grasp.

She burst into an uproarious laugh and doubled over, clutching her sketchbook to her chest. "This is the best present ever. Someone turned *you* into—"

Charlotte's SUV turned in the driveway and parked behind them. Ana flipped her sketchbook closed and stood.

Wesley's brow furrowed with lines when he stepped out of the vehicle. "You're here, too?"

"She's still my designated driver." Henry lifted his flask to his lips and took a short swig.

"You drove yourself." Ana pointed to his cherry red roadster parked beside a black SUV.

Henry glanced at his car. "I don't know how that got here. I'm pretty certain it appeared out of nowhere. Like magic."

Charlotte shook her head. "We're not lying for you when Elsey asks."

"But I really need my kneecaps! They make my legs work, and if I don't have them, I'll be as short as the rest of you!"

Wesley held up his hands. "You're only four inches taller than me."

"It's not a competition, Wes," Henry said with a flick of his hand.

Ana swatted Henry's arm with her sketchbook. "There's nothing wrong with being short."

He rubbed his arm and glared at his sister. "You say that, but I'm certain being short means you made a deal with Satan to give up the extra inches. That's the only way to explain why every short person has a temper to match."

"Kade was short," Charlotte said. "He didn't have a temper."

"He was average height, and you *clearly* never bugged him when he was working." Henry sipped from his flask again. "For the first year of our friendship, my name might as well have been 'Stop touching that,' 'Sit down,' or, 'Do you ever stop talking?'"

Wesley chuckled and motioned toward the SUV. "I assume Elsey isn't here yet because your kneecaps are still intact."

Nodding, Henry traipsed toward the house. "The Unholy Trinity are inside."

"They asked you not to call them that." Ana followed at her brother's side.

"No, I called them the Demon Threesome." Henry lifted a single finger. "And Luci said if I called them that again, she would flambé my outsides until the only way to distinguish me from a burnt stump would be to break me open and harvest my bones. Gene and Tristan laughed."

Charlotte's brows rose. "Did they laugh at your nickname or her threat?"

"That wasn't entirely clear." Henry climbed the rotten steps and opened the door.

Lanterns hanging in the entryway cast light on the pictures on the wall. Charlotte paused to look at the missing family members. Her mind wandered to the disappearance of Malini's dad. Seeing the woman in the pictures, she thought of her own mom. Questions she avoided climbed forward. *What if she didn't just leave?*

"You okay?" Ana's voice broke into her thoughts.

Charlotte gave a quick nod. "Just wondering what happened to them."

Ana looked at the picture of a young Elsey and the long-lost boy. "Yeah, I didn't even know Elsey had a friend before Henry and me."

"She never talked about him?"

"Not to me. You'd have to ask Henry if she ever told him anything."

Dishes clanked in the kitchen, and Gene poked his head into the hallway. The lavender thread of his crochet sweater accented his small rounded amber eyes. "I'm fixing sandwiches for everyone."

"Thanks." Charlotte nodded toward the living room. "We'll tell Wes and Henry."

Turning to the living room, Charlotte found Wesley seated on the Chesterfield sofa, sifting through a box of clothes while his leg bounced in place. Luci sat on the floral camelback sofa with her attention focused on her laptop. She wore her usual all-black ensemble with the hood of her jacket pulled up over her black and silver hair. Henry wandered over to where Tristan sat on the window seat to help sift through more boxes. A pair of thick-soled black boots rested on the floor beside Tristan. Rainbow-checkered socks peeked out from the hem of his pants.

Ana walked around Charlotte and joined Luci on the sofa.

Charlotte looked between Wesley and Henry. "Gene says he's fixing sandwiches."

"Oh shit!" Henry looked up from his box filled with jeans and T-shirts in a wide range of sizes. "I forgot to eat lunch!"

Wesley glanced up from a box of more jeans and T-shirts. "How do you forget to eat?"

Henry gestured toward Ana. "My sister was upset. I had to make her laugh. It's the rule."

Leaning over to get a better look at Luci's computer, Ana recognized the images from the previous night. Her heart dropped. "What are you doing?"

"Scanning the cameras from last night." Luci tucked a loose strand of silver hair behind her ear. "I'm trying to find where that person came from and where they went when they left."

Wesley shoved a box of jeans aside and opened the next. More clothes. Light colored blouses, casual pants, and loose flowing skirts. "There's nothing here. Just a bunch of clothes."

Ana picked up a pair of jeans and began rifling through them. "Well, did you check the pockets?"

"Why would I do that?" He shoved the second box aside and reached for another box.

Charlotte grabbed the box he discarded and sifted through the clothes.

"People keep things in their pockets. Duh." Ana tossed aside a pair of jeans and picked up another.

"Not when they're not wearing them." He opened the flaps of the third box, finding a couple of folders, a handful of paperback books, and a small metal lockbox.

"You've never forgotten to empty your pockets before throwing them in the wash? Dad has had to remind me so many times to empty my pockets before giving my clothes to the housekeeper that you'd think he'd give up by now." Ana grabbed another pair of jeans. "Besides, it can be a good hiding place."

"You *do* like to snoop," Wesley said while noting the classic horror books he'd found: *Dracula, The Woman in Black, The Haunting of Hill House, Carrie,* and *The Exorcist.* He set them aside and grabbed the lock box.

"Look at who my brother is." A full laugh rolled off her lips, and she motioned toward Henry.

Henry held up his middle finger without looking up from the box of clothes he dug through. "Yes, look at me."

Chuckling, Tristan opened a new box to dig through more clothes.

Charlotte nodded toward the metal lockbox in Wesley's hands. "What's that?"

"I don't know." He grabbed the padlock with one hand. Once the boron alloy steel coated his hand he yanked.

The lock broke away, and he tossed it to the coffee table.

He flipped open the lid, revealing wads of cash. "Holy shit!"

Ana and Charlotte gasped. Tristan and Henry looked up.

Luci glanced away from her computer. "Whoever else was hiding in that attic is probably missing that."

He picked up the money and counted the stacks. "There's sixty grand here."

"That's probably enough if you need to hide for a little bit." Charlotte dug through the back pocket of a pair of patterned slacks and felt thick cardstock under her fingers. Pulling it out, she found a plain white card.

Ana flung her hand toward Charlotte. "And *that's* why I say to always check the pockets!"

"It's blank." Charlotte flipped the card over. Nothing stood out, but she could feel something embossed into the plain material. "Wait, there's something on here."

"Can I see it?" Ana took the card and ran her fingers over the surface. "One second."

Everyone watched Ana rush from the room and disappear down the hallway. She returned a moment later with a piece of paper and a pencil.

"Where'd you get that?" Tristan asked, pushing away a box of clothes and grabbing the next unopened box. It felt a little heavier.

"The study." Ana shoved the boxes aside and sat down. Placing the card on the coffee table, she laid the sheet of paper on top and began rubbing the tip of the pencil over the surface. When she finished, she held up the paper so everyone could see the charcoal imprint of a symbol. A figure eight on its side with two perpendicular lines bisecting the center. Three separate dots hung over the symbol.

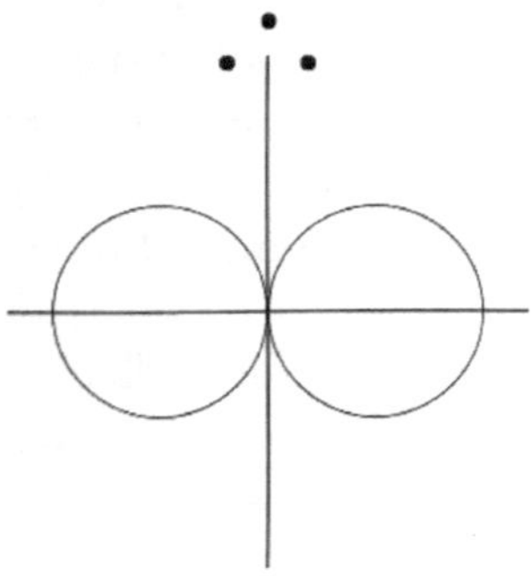

"Since when do cults pass out business cards?" Henry fished his flask from his pocket and took a sip. Grabbing his next box, he had to drag it across the floor due to the weight.

Tristan and Luci exchanged a look, but neither spoke.

Wesley shrugged. "I've never been asked to join one, so I don't know their recruitment process." He withdrew a couple of folders from his box and passed one to Charlotte. He flipped open the folder he kept and found himself peering into familiar silver eyes.

The boy in the picture looked about his age with pale golden skin. His tapered jaw and narrow forehead were framed by long black hair that grazed his collarbones. A snub nose sat above his small lips. He stood before a white wall, and what looked like a tan scrub shirt hung off his narrow chest.

Ana snatched the picture from the folder.

"Hey!"

"This is Elsey's friend!" Ana jumped to her feet and ran into the hall.

Henry and Tristan jerked their heads up.

Flipping open her folder, Charlotte recognized the woman in front of her. Honey-colored hair, plump cheeks, sharp nose, and sparkling blue eyes. A tan scrub shirt hung off her delicate frame. A white wall stood at her back. It was the woman they'd found murdered inside Arnie's house. Another spark of recognition followed. "Ana, get a picture with the whole family in it!"

"Why?" Wesley leaned over and looked at the picture. The image of the woman's dead body lying in a pool of blood filled his mind.

Ana rushed into the room, holding up a picture of the whole family. She held the picture she took from Wesley next to the image of the little boy. "It's the same boy."

Charlotte raised the picture from her folder and pointed between the woman from Arnie's house and the little boy's mother. The hair color was different. The face less full, but the resemblance was noticeable. "They have the same nose and the same eyes. They look like they could be related."

Wesley's eyes widened. He returned his attention to the folder in his hands. The symbol from the card was printed in the top right-hand corner of the first page.

He read the information aloud, "Facility Number: 218. Full Name: Carson Wei Yhu. Chip Number: 218-363. Intake Date: 10/09/3687. Birthday: 01/07/3682. Type: Immortal. Subtype:

Demigod. Level: High. Powers: healing, psionic weapons, superior strength, superior speed." The next lines were blacked out. He flipped to the next page and the next. Also blacked out. Every page was redacted.

Henry redirected his attention to opening the box before him.

Furrowing his brow, Wesley looked at Luci. "You said Immortals and Demigods were extinct."

Luci glanced at Tristan.

Charlotte read from her folder before Luci could speak. "Facility Number: 218. Full Name: Zoey Grace Angelov. Chip Number: 218-362. Intake Date: 10/09/3687. Birthday: 08/13/3649. Type: Unknown. Subtype: Anomaly. Level: Low. Powers: healing." She scanned the rest of the page. "That's the only power listed. Everything else is blacked out."

"Um … guys." Henry pulled a folder from the box in front of him. "This box is full of those files." He flipped open the folder in his hand, revealing a picture of a young woman with light brown skin and loose black curls. He began reading the information. "Facility Number: 219. Full Name: N/A. Chip Number: 219-1356. Intake Date: N/A. Birthdate: 06/30/3679. Type: Sub Immortal and Mortal Hybrid. Subtype: Supernatural Siren and Aetheral Vampire. Level: Medium. Powers: heart reading, flitting, confusion inducement, luring, sound manipulation, superior strength, superior senses, superior dexterity."

He closed the file and grabbed the next. Opening it up to a picture of an older man with pale wrinkled skin and brown hair peppered with gray. "Facility Number: 219. Full Name: Edgar Duncan Grier. Chip Number: 219-137. Intake Date: N/A. Birthdate: N/A. Type: Sub Immortal. Subtype: Elemental Master. Level: Low. Powers: electricity manipulation, technology manipulation, electrical absorption and attacks, electrical constructs."

Tossing the file to the side, Henry reached into the box and pulled out a portion of the stack. He set them on the floor and retrieved another portion of the stack from the box. "That's not even half of them." He motioned to the box beside Tristan. "What's in that box?"

Tristan pressed his lips together and pulled back the flaps, aware of Luci's eyes on him. More folders were stacked to the top of the box. He grabbed the top folder but didn't open it.

Charlotte looked away from the folders threatening to fall over in front of Henry and faced Wesley. "What do you think?"

"I don't know." Wesley glanced at the pictures Ana still held up for all to see. "But who wants to be the one to tell Elsey that her childhood friend who went missing is somehow connected to all of this?"

All eyes fixed on Henry.

He tossed up his hands. "Why's everyone looking at me?"

"She's less likely to kill you," Wesley said.

"Me? What about you?" Henry pointed at Luci.

"I don't intend to be the one who gets shot for delivering that message!"

Tristan lifted his free hand. "Everyone relax. We don't even know what's happening, and we don't have any way of knowing how Elsey will even take the news."

Henry nodded. "Thank you."

"With that said ..." Tristan swept his hand toward Henry and continued, "Henry should definitely be the one to tell her."

"Fucking hell!" Henry tossed up his hands.

Smirking, Ana set the pictures on the coffee table. "I thought you weren't scared of her."

"I'm not. That's not why I don't want to be the one to tell her." Henry snatched up a folder from the box, distracting himself from the memories of the time he spent with Elsey in his apartment. "Whatever. Someone needs to tell her, so I guess I will whenever she gets here."

Charlotte twisted toward Luci. "Any idea when that will be?"

"Well," Gene said, stepping into the room carrying two plates of food. Handing one plate to Luci and another to Ana, he brushed his hands on his green cargo pants. "The sun is starting to go down, so hopefully sometime soon."

"How do you know that?" Wesley stared at him. "All the windows are boarded up."

Gene pulled his cellphone from his pocket. "My phone has this unique invention called a clock." He shifted his attention to Tristan and the unopened folder in his hand. "Can you help me in the kitchen?"

Tristan tossed the folder into its respective box and followed Gene from the room.

Sighing, Wesley sank into his spot. "Any luck finding anything about the attacker?"

Luci looked at her screen. "Whoever it was used the same alley you and Henry hid in, so they arrived sometime after you two left and waited until someone came out to attack."

"Not someone." Henry lifted a finger, signaling for them to wait while he sipped from his flask. "They were there for Elsey."

Wesley angled on the couch to look at Henry. "They attacked all of us."

"Because we came to Elsey's defense. They said they wanted to kill her."

"We were already dying." Charlotte motioned between her and Wesley before sweeping her hand toward Henry. "They stabbed *you.*"

"We were cannon fodder."

Ana shuffled past Luci and sat beside her. "Wasn't it the same person from Arnie's house?"

"No," Henry said.

"What do you mean 'No?'" Wesley's eyes bulged. "They were wearing all black and the same mask!"

"So were you and Charlotte." Henry dropped his flask into his pocket.

"What are the chances that the day after we catch Arnie's murderer, someone in the exact same getup hunts us down to kill not all of us, but *one* of us?"

"We don't have confirmation that person killed Arnie. None of us caught them in the act."

"You cannot be serious right now! They had a bloody knife!" Wesley waved his hands. "They killed him and then they hunted us down."

"That's conjecture!" Henry flung his hands up.

"How the hell do you even know that word?"

"I read old true crime books."

Wesley shook his head. "I'm sorry, I'm just having a hard time picturing you with a book."

Charlotte stifled a laugh. "That's what I said when Mal told me."

Henry stuffed his hands into his pockets and pressed his fingers against the cap of his pill bottle. "Why is that so hard to believe?"

"Because it's you," Wesley said. "You don't focus on anything. You're impulsive. You don't really have discipline, so it's hard to picture you reading an entire book."

"I mean ..." Charlotte scratched the raw burning flesh of her thumbs. "You sleep through most of trig after the lesson, and that's only when you don't skip class."

"I don't like doing my schoolwork in front of people," Henry snapped.

Tension sizzled in the air. Luci glanced up from her computer. Tristan and Gene grew silent in the kitchen.

"Henry, they're not trying to be mean." Ana kept her tone soft. She motioned toward Wesley and Charlotte with her hand. "They're just pointing out why they thought that. You can't really blame them for thinking that based on the way you take advantage of how easy we have it. You get let off the hook for everything at school because Dad—"

"Don't you dare bring him into this!" Henry's stomach churned with violent disgust. "Do you really think Dad makes things easy for me when he's so fucking ashamed of me being pansexual that I had to get a girlfriend for him to pretend I'm straight? Do you think it was easy when I realized that still wasn't enough? Or that it never even mattered because I'll always be a disappointment to him? Or how about all the people who have no problem saying shit to my face because I'm not exactly the most intimidating person? Do you think I have it easy with them?"

Silence carved itself into the cracks of everyone inside the house.

"I know I don't have things as hard as other people." Henry's voice—normally smooth and soft—trembled and splintered. "But I have had to learn not to give a shit because otherwise, I wouldn't fucking be here."

Watching her twin brother with wide eyes, Ana plucked the hem of her dress—undoing the stitches. She struggled to think of the words to correct her misstep in front of an audience.

Charlotte looked at the ground, remembering her conversation with Malini.

Wesley sucked in a deep breath, wishing he could go back in time to erase his joke that sent the conversation onto its current trajectory. His assumptions about Henry's relationship with his dad sent his stomach into knots.

Luci bristled, waiting for someone to speak.

Realizing the effect his reaction had on everyone, Henry pushed his hair out of his face only for it to fall back due to the lack of product. He avoided meeting anyone's eyes. "Sorry. I'm sorry."

Henry traipsed around the piles of folders and made his way outside, shutting the door behind him. He sat on the first step that wasn't broken and stretched his legs in front of him. Digging in his pockets, he retrieved his cigarette case and lighter. He perched the first cigarette between his lips and lit it. Inhaling and exhaling. Trying to release the painful emotions peeking out beneath his mask.

Shadows in his mind peeled back. All his monsters rose with a cackle rattling all the fractured pieces of his heart. Shoving his hand into his pocket, he grabbed his pill bottle. *Buzzzzz.*

The chord of his heart thrummed a soft note, sending a shiver of sparks through him. He pulled out his phone, finding a new message from Victoria. Feeling the disappointment bite down, he ignored her text. He started to shove his phone into his pocket but stopped himself. Breathing in a deep gasp of smoke, he typed a message to Elsey. How are you?

Hearing the door creak open, Henry dropped his phone into his pocket.

Tristan sat on the rickety step beside Henry, shooting a concerned look at the rotting wood before turning to Henry. "You okay?"

"I will be."

"Okay." Tristan nodded. He rested his elbows on top of his knees. "Listen, if you ever need a place to go or need to talk or anything ... you can come chill at Purgatory."

Henry glanced at him. "I thought Luci said she didn't want us there."

"She's not our boss. We're partners. We all get an equal say, but we respect each other's boundaries. And well, she'll understand." Tristan paused before adding, "Also, I'm pretty sure Wesley and Charlotte would understand as well, if you ever need more people to talk to."

"I never really had a friendship with them. I was friends with Wes's brother." He kept his attention focused on the moment, away from the tangle of emotions and memories.

Tristan arched a brow. "Friends?"

"Yes," Henry spoke firmly. Puffing on his cigarette, he stared at the dying overgrown grass surrounding the house. "You mentioned before that you don't like going to the store. I'm guessing you deal with it, too."

"Have you looked at me?" Tristan gestured to himself. "If people have the balls to say shit to me, they have issues beyond just my sexuality. And they're always hoping they'll get a reaction out of me so they can make me look like the bad guy to all their clan members. The people who don't have anything to say to my face, usually stare and whisper. That itself is exhausting and dehumanizing, so I usually stay home. People still say things to Gene or Luci, but I'd rather spend my time in a positive environment than waste energy dealing with negativity. For the most part, the people who come to Purgatory are usually open-minded and friendly, but sometimes we get shitheads who need to be escorted off the premises. Even people harassing the protesters have to leave. Luci and Gene both have tempers though, so they're usually more comfortable handling that stuff than me."

"You don't have a temper?"

"I don't get to have a temper," Tristan said. "People can get as ugly as they want with me no matter how it makes me feel, but if I react——"

"Then you're the bad guy."

"Yeah." Tristan stretched out his legs and leaned against the railing. "Gene and Luci deal with that too, but to a lesser extent. I've always been more laidback than them anyway. Maybe because we had different upbringings, kind of. I mean, we grew up together in a way, but we—Before we met—"

Listening to Tristan stop and start, Henry released a soft exhale of smoke. "You don't have to talk about it if you don't want."

"I know." He stared at his hands, running his eyes over the lines in his palms. "Elsey mentioned that your mom died when you were younger."

Henry cocked his head to the side. Sparks flared in his chest. "She talks about me?"

"Sometimes. She mentioned it today. I think partially because she might've wanted some insight, and she thought I'd be able to offer something since my parents died when I was younger, too."

"I'm sorry."

"It's not like it's your fault." Tristan curled his hands into fists and cast Henry a glance from the corner of his eyes. "Besides, I can tell that her death isn't the only thing you're trying to bury."

Henry pinched the filter of his cigarette. He jammed his free hand into his pocket and retrieved his flask. "I don't know what you're talking about."

"I figured that'd be your response." Tristan looked at the trees, zeroing in on the birds and chipmunks bringing life to the wild around them. "Anyway, I just want you to know that you're not alone. I know what it's like to feel alone and to feel like you need to belong somewhere whether that's due to being judged or other reasons. If you ever need a place to go. To talk about things or just to get away, our door is open."

"Thanks." Henry swigged from his flask.

"You're welcome. Also, I don't know if I should mention this, but I'll deal with the shrimp's wrath if not. Elsey moved out of her parents' house and will be staying in the den at Purgatory for the foreseeable future."

Henry jerked toward Tristan. "Really? Why?"

"That, I don't know. She's very vague, but I thought you might want to know because you never know who could be at Purgatory if you do come hang out." Standing, Tristan motioned toward the door. "I'm heading back inside."

"I'll be in, in a moment." His head spun with thoughts of Elsey talking about him and moving out of her parents' house. Catching on a question, he swiveled in his spot to face Tristan before he could open the door. "Why are you being so nice to me?

"Because I'm a nice person. Besides, Elsey cares about you. If she cares about you, that's all I need to know."

Henry plucked at his bottom lip, thinking over how his relationship with Elsey had changed since she returned four years ago. Since he—

"Just so you know," Tristan said. "Elsey doesn't care about you being pansexual."

"How did you know I was thinking that?"

"Easy guess. Hell, if she knew people said shit to you, or even to the *Unholy Trinity*," Tristan chuckled. "She'd make it her mission in life to bury every single person responsible. Same with everyone in there. She may seem distant and cold, but she gets attached to people quickly if the situation is right. You give her an inch, she'll give you her life. She'll go to the ends of the earth for people who don't treat her like she's a monster. And to be honest, I think you're the person she'd go the furthest for."

Henry faced forward, studying the smoke curling off the tip of his dying cigarette. "It doesn't feel like that."

"I know. But trust me. Everything she does has your name on it." Tristan twisted the doorknob. Stopping, he spun back. "One more thing, you asked if I could take your dad in a fight."

"Change your mind?"

"I don't think I'm the one for the job. You might be though."

"I wish."

"Don't sell yourself short. We're the only ones who can defeat our own demons. Just something to think about." Tristan opened the door and disappeared inside.

Henry inhaled what was left of his cigarette and stamped it against the porch railing.

Buzzzzz.

Another spark flew off the thrum of the chord in his heart. He pulled his phone from his pocket.

A response from Elsey waited for him. Same as always. How are you?

Typing a response, a small smile curled his lips. Better now.

A beep sounded in Elsey's ear. She ignored it and focused on steering the boat through the bay.

The colors of a late sunset painted the sky in a gradient of sunlit amber rising to rich tones of blue-violet and cobalt. She pulled her mask down, covering the top half of her face. Her mind fixed on Asher's words, questioning whether he spoke about the attack from the previous evening, her move from her parents' house, or something else altogether.

The beep sounded again, but she continued to ignore it. She compartmentalized her thoughts. Her attempt at a conversation with Tristan. Her interactions with Henry. Her attempt to put together a puzzle while missing more pieces than she previously realized. The complications with trying to be normal enough to think people could see her as more than all her stains and scars.

She dropped the anchor when she reached the dock. A long beep sounded in her ear.

Stepping into Purgatory's den, Luci set her laptop on the coffee table. "Goddammit! Stop ignoring me, you stubborn ass!"

Giggling, Ana glanced at the large trunk beside the sofa and accepted the laptop Gene passed to her.

The bitter claws of anger hooked into Elsey. She rolled her eyes and climbed the dock. "I hate it when you override—"

"Then answer when I beep in," Luci growled. She marched over to the bar cart to pour herself a glass of absinthe. Remembering the events of last night, her hand halted on the bottle. "I don't always have eyes on you to make sure you're not dead."

Ana remained silent, focusing on getting her laptop set up for the evening.

"Is it an emergency?" Elsey rolled her eyes again. Rats and feral cats watched her traipse through the lot to her motorcycle.

"No, but you didn't know it wasn't. What if someone was being attacked?" Luci took a long drink from her glass.

"Then you could've sent the other three." Tension seethed in her voice.

Luci swallowed hard. She looked at Ana.

Ana shrugged, holding up her hands in confusion.

"That's what you did, right?" Elsey mounted her motorcycle and roared it to life. "You went behind my back and made a decision that I explicitly stated I didn't want *after* you initially lectured me about putting them at risk."

"How did you——"

"You don't giggle." Rolling her eyes again, she sped out of the lot and onto the road. "Hi, Ana."

"Hi." Ana picked at the frayed stitching at the hem of her dress. "Henry and the others are waiting for you at the house. They have stuff to show you."

Abandoning the bar cart, Luci sat in front of her laptop and pulled up her screens. "It's for the best. You're only one person, and you need people who can be out there to have your back."

"No!" Elsey's temper flared with the memory of the previous night's attack overtaking her thoughts with full technicolor blood stains. "I need *not* to have more death on my fucking conscious." She yanked the communicator out of her ear and tossed it in her path. Her front and back tires crushed the plastic earpiece.

Tearing through the street, she headed toward the heart of the city. The realization of her rage-fueled actions smacked her with the wind hitting her face. *Fuck.*

She forced her attention on the task at hand, deciding how to handle the others waiting for her at the house.

The sun dipped beyond the horizon, painting the heavens in deep blues. Thick black smoke curled toward the sky in the distant northwestern area of the city. She cut across the sidewalk to turn onto Boyer Road. The pink and blue lights from Bedlam washed over her as she passed. Nearing a section of the street with factories and abandoned homes, streetlights flickered above. The soft white glow of HAL Tower's illuminated letters called like a beacon in the distance. People crowded the streets. Someone wailed in the distance. A loud pop echoed.

Someone glided into the street. The wavering streetlights caught them in a dying flicker. A tall figure dressed in black. A black mask covered their entire face.

Elsey sucked in a breath.

Stooping to the ground, the person pressed a hand to the road. The asphalt crumbled away to stretch in long, jagged terrain rolling toward Elsey.

Pedestrians screamed and ran.

Elsey swerved around someone darting to the side of the street to look for cover. Hunks of asphalt punched up in front of her. Her front wheel caught on the uneven stones, pitching her and her motorcycle through the air. Her hands slipped off her handlebars, and she flew overhead.

Her eyes widened at the fast-approaching ground. Shooting her hands out before her, she pulled on the sapphire essence at the back of her mind. It flowed through her with a speed that almost seemed like it held a sentient understanding of the situation. The second her fingers lighted against the surface of the road, the asphalt melted to a cooling tar.

She landed with a heavy **plop**.

With her hands still in the tar, she pushed the essence to return the tar to its hardened asphalt state. The hum in her brain crept forward.

Catching a glimpse of her motorcycle lying in a battered heap on the side of the road, every ounce of rage Elsey held back begged for release. She climbed to her feet and watched people scatter around them.

"Impressive." The attacker advanced. Their sharp voice was low and muffled beneath their mask. "What are you going to do without your backup here?"

She whirled toward her attacker. "I *was* just planning to kill you for what you did to them, but now, I'll make your death extra painful for massacring my bike."

Somewhere in the back of her mind she remembered Wesley's words. *We need their information to find out what's happening. We can't get information from a dead body.* Irritation scratched at her instincts. She tried to shove his words away, but they remained fixed. Waring with the endless rage eating her alive.

If this person had something to do with the deaths of Kade, Arnie, or any of the bodies she'd found, they'd have vital information.

"You seem to have very violent tendencies." Their voice carried a lilt to the edges, as if they were smirking beneath their mask.

"My apologies." Elsey gestured toward her motorcycle. "I didn't think you wanted to be friends."

"I don't. I want to kill you." They stepped forward again, standing nearly a foot taller than her.

Elsey released a haughty ***hmph***. "Good luck with that."

They charged forward.

With no time to settle the war building inside, Elsey's impulses took over. Driving her on instinct.

She ducked under their fist, grabbing their arm and kicking herself overhead. Elsey dragged them down to the ground with her. Their other fist connected with Elsey's chin. Snatching their wrist, Elsey twisted it and punched them in the face.

The attacker stumbled but recovered. They pivoted and kicked out. Elsey caught their foot and yanked them toward her. Seizing their throat, she squeezed. They reeled forward and bashed their face into Elsey's.

Crunch. Warm blood dribbled from Elsey's nose and seeped out beneath her mask to roll over her lips.

She tightened her grip on the attacker's throat. They coughed and dug at her hand. She tightened her hold more. Feeling every ridge and crevice of flesh and muscle protecting bones. She could crush it to nothingness. With one swift close of her fist, their life would be over.

She'd done it before. The number of times was a blur now.

Elsey tightened her fist more. More.

Their ragged nails dug into her hand. Plum colored polish flaked away while they clawed for freedom.

Staring at their dark eyes beneath their mask, Wesley's words replayed in her mind again. *We can't get information from a dead body.*

Logic and bloodthirsty instinct tore at each other inside her mind. Locking her up and splitting her focus from the moment at hand.

A fist rammed into Elsey's jaw. Pain shot through her face. Another punch jostled her hold on her attacker's throat. Another. Her teeth bit down on her tongue. The salty copper taste of blood fed her anger.

The attacker grabbed Elsey, wrapping their arm around her throat and kicking her feet out from under her. Her knees hit the road.

They pressed their arm against Elsey's windpipe. "I should've stayed last night and made sure you and your partners were dead. I won't make that same mistake again."

Images of the previous night flashed through Elsey's mind.

Charlotte lying a few feet away. Internal organs pulverized and pierced with broken ribs—fighting to hold onto her last breath. Wesley lying even further away in a pool of his own blood. Bones crushed and ripped through his skin. Death hovering over him until he healed. Henry's body impaled to hers. His blood mixing with hers. Painting the road while he clung to the sliver of life he had left.

Rage tore free inside her. Wings unfurling in her chest and talons shredding every bit of her restraint to confetti.

Slamming her hand into the asphalt, Elsey let her power surge through her.

Asphalt crumbled apart. Curling up like fingers, it wrapped around the attacker's shoes. Ignoring the humming that built in her mind, Elsey elbowed them in the stomach. She leapt and spun out with a kick aimed at their head.

Ducking low, the attacker pressed their hand to the asphalt shaped fingers holding them still. The asphalt crumbled away, and they stumbled backward.

Righting themself in time to catch Elsey's fist, they twisted and kicked back. Elsey hooked her elbow around their calf before their foot could connect with her ribs. Slamming her boot into the back of their knee, Elsey dragged them down.

Elsey kept their foot locked up, pressing her hand against the road. The asphalt heated up and melted into a warm tar. Thick-bodied black serpents writhed to life in the oozing muck. Elsey ignored the hum taking on a sharper sound in her brain.

The serpents slithered over the attacker's hands. Coiling around their wrists. They thrashed their arms and yanked one free before it could slide around their throat.

The serpent warped into a hot iron poker in their hands. Elsey caught the poker before it could bash into her face. Gritting her teeth against the heat scalding her hands, she jumped up and kicked her attacker in the chest. They flew backward and skidded across the tarred pavement. Elsey let the iron poker crumble to dust in her grasp.

Sounds swam in and out. Everything blurred. Her head felt like it would split in two.

She fixed her attacker in a barbed glare that promised more than death—total obliteration. Kneeling, she pressed both hands into the tar. The road returned to hardened asphalt only to begin cracking open further. With a shudder of pain coursing through her, the ground gaped wide like a sea being parted. So deep, a layer of solid black iridescent metal could be seen beneath the road. A deafening *sccrrk*—like paper being torn—echoed over the city with a rip tearing through the fragile tapestry of reality above the split in the road. Revealing only pitch-dark nothingness. The atmosphere trembled. Buildings took on wavy edges, making room for the tear. White flakes fluttered through the rip and caught on the autumn wind.

Gasping, the attacker touched a ripple that seemed to breathe through the space in front of them. Their fingers passed through what felt like the most delicately woven fabric.

A high-pitched ringing blocked any sounds from reaching Elsey's ears. Darkness flickered over her eyes, making her oblivious to the approaching SUV. She blinked and continued to push forward.

Rage fueled her determination to erase the attacker from existence. To erase the memory of Henry impaled on top of her in a pool of their collected blood with Charlotte and Wesley's broken bodies lying out of reach.

The attacker stumbled back, rushing to escape the tear splitting toward them. They tripped over their own feet and fell. The gap in the road slipped under them. Their hands caught the sides, and they held on. The tear in reality cut toward them.

The SUV slammed into park. Gawking beneath their masks, Henry, Wesley, and Charlotte jumped out of the vehicle.

"Holy fuck!" Henry pulled his flask from his pocket and took a drink. "This is a terrible time to start hallucinating."

"You're not hallucinating." Charlotte shook her head.

"What is she doing?" Ana gaped at her computer screen. In black and white, she saw the lines around the scene blur.

Wesley stared at the dark tear in the atmosphere. "It almost looks like a black hole or something like it. How is that even possible?"

Henry pointed to the white flakes on the air. "Is that snow?"

Catching a flake, Wesley watched it crumble to gray and black dust. "I think it's ash."

"She's pushing herself too far!" Luci pressed her hands onto either side of her face. "Someone needs to grab her!"

Darkness blanketed Elsey's vision. The ringing sharpened in her ears like someone flipped the switch on an electric saw. Her breath caught in her throat. Pain cut through her scarred flesh and tore through her bones. She clenched her teeth against any scream that might escape. Wobbling on her legs, she collapsed in a heap.

"Fuck!" Henry ran toward her.

The attacker pulled themself from the wide splinter in the road. Pressing their hands against the asphalt, the ground and the fabric of reality melded back together. The waves on the atmosphere curving the buildings flattened as if no one had started to pull back the shroud of the universe. Turning their attention to Henry, they charged.

Luci stared at her screen with wide eyes. "Guys, Charlotte's faster. Get her an opening to grab Elsey and get her out of there!"

Wesley ran toward the nearest alley. Finding a fire escape outside an abandoned apartment building, he wrapped his hand around a bar beneath the lowest step. His skin morphed with the iron alloy. He yanked hard and broke the metal bar free. Gripping it tight, he dashed toward the street.

Pulling on the scarlet essence flooding his mind, Henry placed himself in front of Elsey and gave a hard shove. The air punted forward, and the attacker soared back.

Wesley caught them in his free hand. Before they could get their ragged nails around him, he flung them into the picture window of a decrepit house.

Henry gave another shove on the atmosphere. The attacker's hand shot up with their own shove. The waves crashed into each other and rebounded, sending everyone to their knees. The window behind the attacker shattered inward. They grabbed a piece of glass on the ledge, and the glass covered their skin.

Wesley and Henry jumped to their feet. Wesley dashed forward, swinging the metal bar. The attacker caught the bar in their free hand and kicked themselves off the ground. Wrapping their legs around his neck, they tried to jam one of their glass thumbs into the eyeholes of his mask. Wesley seized their wrist.

A heavy blast came again on the atmosphere, knocking them both back. Releasing the piece of glass, the attacker grabbed the metal bar in Wesley's hand. The metal coated their skin, and they both landed with a heavy ***thud***.

The person yanked the metal bar from Wesley's grasp and swung at him. He ducked low and shoved them off him to regain his footing.

"Charlotte, get Elsey out of there now!" Luci shouted into their ears.

The attacker leapt toward Wesley again. He jumped backward, catching a glimpse of Charlotte running to Elsey's side.

"Wesley! Watch it!" Ana yelled.

Wesley spun in time to catch the metal bar before it could connect with his face. He tightened his grip and welcomed the iron transforming his skin to an unbreakable barrier. Planting his feet against the ground, he captured the person's foot when they kicked at his stomach. He tossed a sidelong glance to Henry. "Can you destabilize this situation?"

"Are you sure?"

"Yes!" Releasing the metal bar, Wesley gave the attacker a hard push. Sending them to the road. The bar flew from their hand and ***clanked*** into the base of a streetlight.

Raising his hands, Henry pulled more of the essence in his mind forward. The ground quaked.

Wesley darted toward the metal bar.

Henry's gaze went over his shoulder to Elsey being dragged to the side of the road by Charlotte.

The rumbling grew more violent. Sending cracks through the road once more. The attacker leapt to their feet but struggled to remain standing. Wesley barreled into them, knocking them to the ground. He lifted the bar overhead. Pulling their knees up, the attacker slammed their feet into his chest and seized the metal bar in their grasp. Kicking Wesley overhead, they jerked the bar from his grasp. His skin returned to normal before he crashed into the street on his back. Pain flared in his body.

Leaping up, the attacker ran toward Charlotte and Elsey.

Light flickered before Elsey's vision. Sounds returned in chunks. She gasped for air as the pain eased.

Charlotte scrambled to shield Elsey while she was still coming to consciousness. Henry swept his arm wide. The attacker smashed into the side of a building with a blast of wind. They dropped the metal bar at their feet and copied Henry's move, knocking him to the road. Grabbing the metal bar again, the person let the metal roll over them while they raced forward.

Meeting them halfway, Charlotte caught the metal bar in one hand and held on with all her strength. The person kicked out. Charlotte twisted to the side. She ducked and dodged their fist. Stepping into the attacker, Charlotte hooked her leg behind their knee. Henry jutted out his hand. The road rolled, and the person fell backward. Charlotte landed on top of them.

They both grappled with the metal bar. Charlotte's eyes went to the attacker's hands and the deep plum polish covering ragged, raw nails. Recognition sparked in her, catching her off guard. The attacker yanked the bar free and swung. Charlotte reeled to the side before the metal bar could connect with her face.

The attacker leapt to their feet and launched toward Elsey. Landing on her, they swung the metal bar. Elsey's hand shot up and caught it.

"Holy—" Ana gasped.

Wesley ran to Charlotte's side. Henry lifted his hands.

Charlotte jumped between Henry and the attacker. "Don't!" She spun to face the attacker. "Malini, she didn't kill Kade!"

Wesley and Henry froze. Realization washed over them.

Luci and Ana stared wide-eyed at their screens, uncertain if they heard everything correctly.

"What?" Malini jerked back.

"Mal, it's me." Charlotte motioned toward herself. "Charlotte."

A garbled gasp choked free beneath Malini's mask. "No. Char?"

Charlotte nodded. "Yeah."

"No. No." Malini shook her head. "I didn't know! I swear I didn't know!"

Wesley held his hands outstretched. "Do you really think I'd be helping anyone who killed my own brother?"

Malini turned to Wesley. "Wes?"

"Yes!" He tossed up his hands. "Why would I help anyone who hurt him?"

"No." She gasped. Her voice trembled under her mask. "I didn't know. I didn't—"

Elsey rolled her eyes. She slipped her legs out from under Malini and wrapped them around her shoulders. Shoving, she rolled them forward until she was straddling Malini's chest. She jerked the metal bar from Malini's grasp and tossed it aside before standing. "I didn't kill Kade."

Marching over to her motorcycle, Elsey pressed her hand to the distorted body. She let the power surge through her and returned her motorcycle to its proper condition.

"She's been helping us find out who did," Charlotte said.

Wesley looked at Charlotte and then at Malini. "We didn't tell you because you've been so distraught, and you weren't thinking clearly at times. Like this, right here. You were accusing everyone."

"Not everyone." Charlotte shot a pointed look at Henry. "Just two people."

"Me?" Henry's brows rose behind his mask. He looked at Malini. "What the fuck? Why would you have sex with me if you thought I killed him, which by the way, I didn't. We were friends."

"Until I broke up with you." She yelled.

"And what? You thought I'd tell you the sordid details of how I committed murder when we were in bed?" He retrieved his flask from his pocket. "I may be dramatic, but I have some sense."

"That remains to be seen." Wesley scoffed.

"Hey! I was right! I told you that she couldn't be the murderer, but no one wanted to listen to me." He took a quick swig. "I'm an addict. Not an idiot."

Malini motioned toward Henry's flask. "That's actually how I knew it was you helping Elsey."

Henry looked at her with narrowed eyes. He put the flask to his lips and drained it in one long gulp. Wiping his sleeve across his mouth, he returned his flask to his pocket.

Gesturing toward Elsey, Malini looked at Charlotte. "What did you mean she's been helping you find out who killed Kade?"

Wesley nodded. "She has a lot of—"

"Don't." Elsey's hands tightened into fists.

Hearing the cold tone in her voice, everyone twisted toward Elsey.

Charlotte chewed on the inside of her cheek.

Wesley nodded again. "Yeah, we should get out of here before someone sees. You can follow us to the team house."

"No," Elsey's voice became colder, harsher.

"What?"

"I don't want her there." Her nails dug into her palms.

Henry lifted a finger. "I'm not a big fan of her joining our super-secret club either."

Wesley groaned. "Well, do either of you have somewhere else we can all go?"

Henry looked at Elsey.

She paused. Her gaze fixed on Malini with frost lacing her eyes. "Fine, but it doesn't mean anything."

"You okay?" Henry whispered to Elsey. He shut the door and switched on the lanterns in the hallway. With the light, he could see the remnants of blood streaking her nose, lips, and chin from where she tried to wipe it away.

"No." Elsey let her eyes flit to him before stepping into the open archway to the living room. She folded her arms in front of her chest, digging her nails into her arms.

Henry leaned against the wall on her left.

After turning on the lanterns in the living room, Wesley sat on the Chesterfield sofa. Malini wandered over the room, taking in the mismatched furniture and the boxes of clothes and folders scattered about from the earlier investigation.

Charlotte sat next to Wesley. She scratched at the sides of her thumbs, unable to release the sinking feeling that she wouldn't be able to avoid the inevitable.

"How did you know about Elsey?" Wesley asked.

"Kade left a box of stuff at my house." Malini looked at him. "Things he asked me to hold onto for him. I thought it was just a gift he didn't want you to find before your birthday. Then when he—"

She blinked up at the ceiling to stop her tears. Taking a deep breath, she turned to Elsey. "I found pictures of you dressed like this and beating up people in the street."

Henry's shoulders tensed. He glanced over at Elsey. Her gaze remained hardened like ice.

"That's why I thought you killed him. I thought he saw you do something you didn't want him to see." Malini dropped her eyes.

"That and the rumors. That's why I confronted you at school."

Elsey arched a brow but didn't speak.

"She started all this." Charlotte motioned toward Elsey. "Wesley and I ran into her saving someone, and then we ran into her again but that time she was with Henry."

"Did you know Kade had powers?" Wesley watched Malini for any hints to determine the truth of her responses.

"He had powers?" She jerked back.

"He must've had them if I have them."

"No, I had no idea." Malini shook her head.

Charlotte focused on Malini. "How did you get powers?"

"My dad was a Brithel."

"A what?" Wesley and Charlotte echoed each other.

"Brithels are considered distant relatives of Aetheral Witches and Fairies." Malini gestured with her hands as she spoke. "My power comes from auras. I can see everyone's aura at will. For the people with powers, there's a vibration in their auras. It can vary. Sometimes it's stronger than others. Other times it's strong, but it's not all free flowing. I can pull on that vibration and use whatever powers are at my reach."

She motioned toward Wesley. "I didn't feel yours until the moment you used your power. When we were fighting, I was still able to pull on it even if you weren't actively using it, but it must lay dormant when you're not in the mode to use it frequently. So, assuming Kade's worked the same way, he never used his powers around me, at least not while I was using mine.

"At the funeral, I could see Henry's aura had changed and that he had powers now." Malini directed her attention to Henry and continued. "When I realized you would've gone to Elsey, that's when I had my suspicions of you working with her. I couldn't tell Charlotte or Wesley the truth without telling them I knew you had powers or how I knew. By the way, care to enlighten me how you got powers?"

"I was blessed for performing a good deed." He pressed his thumb into the ridges along the cap of his pill bottle in his pocket.

Malini released an exasperated sigh. "Care to be more specific?"

"Not after you tried to murder me."

She shook her head, failing to keep the irritation from her tone.

"Your powers are characteristic of some Aetheral Witches, Demons, Fairies, and Elves. You can't just be given those powers. Even to be gifted like that, you would have to have one of those in your ancestry fairly recently in order for it to be strong enough for you to absorb any abilities. But your aura was always in line with an average Human."

"I don't know what to tell you. You should know I've never been good with average." A smirk curled his lips.

"So, have you seen if other people we know have powers?" Wesley leaned his elbows on his knees.

"Alex Cleary." Malini tore her gaze away from Henry before she could catch his expression. "I don't know what his powers are though. The vibration in his aura isn't free flowing, so I can't access anything."

Charlotte fiddled with the silver bird charm around her throat. "Does Jemma know about you?"

"Yes." Malini nodded. "I told her when I was little before I understood the danger. When my mom was still lucid, she taught me to keep them secret so the same thing that happened to my dad doesn't happen to me."

Charlotte thought of Malini's mother staring at the portrait of her missing partner. Shaking off a shudder, she looked between Malini and the rest of the team. "We've been trying to find out who killed Kade. We found—"

"Don't." Elsey's voice was deadly sharp.

Charlotte's eyes dropped to the floor.

"What?" Wesley asked.

"I don't trust her." Elsey's nails cut deep through the sleeves of her shirt.

"You don't trust anybody." Wesley motioned toward Malini. "She could help."

"I don't want her on the team." Elsey's eyes flared with anger.

Malini shifted on her feet. She kept her gaze on the coffee table.

Charlotte scraped harder at the sides of her thumbs, peeling raw shredded flesh.

Waves of uncertainty bubbled up inside Henry.

"Elsey," Wesley kept his voice steady. "I know she accused you, but—"

"Tell them." Elsey's eyes never left Malini's face. Her voice sharp as a blade ready to slice into supple skin. "Tell them why I won't work with you. Tell them why I don't go to school anymore."

"We've seen you at school." Wesley's forehead creased. "We were lab partners."

"Freshman year." She pushed against the rage crackling inside her. "I have not set foot inside a classroom in two years. I haven't stayed inside that building or on the grounds for longer than fifteen minutes after the final bell for the last two years. And it's because of her."

"Elsey—" Malini opened her mouth.

"Tell them," she growled. "Kade's not here to tell them what he saw you do."

"What?" Wesley and Henry echoed each other with wide eyes.

Something inside Elsey broke under the pressure of all the anger that filled her for so many years. For so many years that she didn't know what it was like to feel anything else.

Her rage took on a life of its own. Spreading darkened wings and hooking talons into her.

Any inch of forgiveness she had been working on crumbled.

"Or maybe you want to tell them how I got the scar on my forehead instead? If you won't, maybe Charlotte will." Her eyes sliced to Charlotte. "You were there for that one, weren't you? You didn't join in, but you didn't do anything to stop her either, did you?"

"What happened?" Wesley twisted toward Charlotte.

Resisting the need to flinch, Charlotte flung a hand outward. "I said something to her about it afterward! You can ask her!"

"That makes it so much fucking better. You stand there and say nothing while someone gets tormented for no fucking reason, but suddenly because you scold her behind closed doors, it's supposed to make everything okay?" Elsey's gaze cut to Malini. "You don't want to tell them? Fine. I will.

"When I finally returned to school after—" She stopped herself and amended her statement. "When my parents allowed me to return to public school, I found Henry in the halls. Malini and Charlotte were there. Henry and Malini had just started dating. She dragged him off before we could talk.

"Later that day, Charlotte found me and said that Henry wanted to talk to me. I went with her to a classroom. Only Henry wasn't there. Malini was.

"She said that he didn't want to be seen talking to me because I was an ugly freak and that I was crazy. I told her that Henry was my friend. She told me things changed while I was gone and that Henry told her I scared him because bad things happened around me, and he was worried about what I'd do if he told me to stay away from him. But she thought I deserved to know so I wouldn't make a fool of myself."

Malini could feel Henry's heated glare even without looking his way.

"And then she shoved me," Elsey said in the same frosty tone.

"You didn't move!" Malini flung her hand's up. "I thought you were going to attack me!"

"I couldn't move!" Elsey stepped forward. "I knew you never liked me. I know no one likes me. But I still couldn't believe what I was hearing. Henry was my friend. The one person who ever gave a shit, and I was told he hated me just as much as everyone else. I didn't know what to do."

Malini looked down at her hands and then back up. Her eyes landed on Henry. A mix of pain and fury twisted his face. She looked at Elsey.

"You shoved me," Elsey repeated. "Hard. I fell wrong and hit my head on a desk, so hard it gouged my forehead open. And then you and Charlotte left. I lay there, hoping that if I waited long enough, I'd bleed out and die. But I didn't want to make trouble. I called my father's driver and told him I had an emergency and needed to be picked up. While I waited for him, I used my jacket to mop up my blood on the floor. And then I left. I didn't tell my parents who did it.

"When I returned to school with stitches, no one asked how I was. No one asked me what happened." Elsey's eyes stung, but she didn't cry. "No one gave a fuck. Instead, they decided to give me a fun new nickname. And the rumors about me got worse. They weren't quiet. I heard the giggling and the laughs and the people calling me an ugly freak. I kept to myself. Retaliation was never an option. I didn't want to make trouble. But that never stopped anyone from making my life a miserable hell. Then you did it again."

Malini's eyes dropped to the floor. Tears slipped down her cheeks.

"I got sick of hearing about you cheating on Henry, so I confronted you before school started. You were walking with Kade up the steps. I didn't know you two were having an affair until he reacted when he tried to get between us and went off on me. Then you pushed me. Again."

Shooting a look at Henry and Wesley, Malini dragged in a deep breath. "You didn't move!"

"I *couldn't* move." Elsey's shoulders tensed, but she didn't elaborate. "Kade tried to catch me, but he wasn't quick enough. I fell down the stairs. My chin smashed into the cement. Then I heard the laughter. Everyone outside saw what happened. They stood there laughing even though I was bleeding everywhere.

"You went inside. Kade was the only one who came over and helped me. And he did the one thing no one else has ever done. He apologized. He sat with me and waited until Luci, Tristan, and Gene got there. Tristan stitched me up that time." Her hand went to the scar on her chin, still feeling the stitches like a phantom thread lacing her up.

"The next day, I returned to school. The rumors were worse. Someone said I attacked you. No one asked my side of the story. No one gave a fuck about what happened to me. The only person who asked if I was okay was Kade. But it didn't matter. No one else was done having their fun. So, I left. Every day, I tried to return. But they never fucking stop. Now, I stay long enough to get my schoolwork for the day. Then, I leave and beat the living shit out of people who hurt other people for no goddamn reason."

"How are you still in our grade?" Wesley asked.

"I was homeschooled." Elsey looked at him, finally turning away from Malini. "I'm far ahead of what they teach in school."

"Why even go then?"

"I like learning. It gives my brain something to do. I also *liked* being around people. I wanted to make friends. I wanted to fit in somewhere." She shrugged. "Now, I know it's hopeless."

Henry stepped toward her. "Why didn't you ever tell me?"

"Weren't you listening?" Elsey threw out her hands. "She told me you didn't want to be my friend. That you thought I was an ugly, crazy freak. That you were *scared* of me. I was gone for two years. I didn't think you'd give a shit! You saw me when I returned to school with stitches both times, Henry. You saw me, and you did nothing. You said nothing."

Wesley shifted beside Charlotte, a hollow ache growing in his chest as questions hung over them.

Taking a pained breath, Henry looked between Charlotte and Malini. "Why would you do that?"

Malini opened her mouth, but Elsey let out a disturbed rasping laugh. "You guys don't get it! You'll never get it because you don't have to get it. I'm not one of you. I'm not like you. I never have been."

"What do you mean?" Henry asked.

"I've never been one of you beautiful fucking people! I'm the village monster. The ogre. The boogeyman parents use to scare their children. You think I don't hear the shit everyone in this city says about me?" Elsey's chest ached, and she knew that if she touched something, she'd destroy everything around her. She kept her hands to herself. "I've *always* had my scars! I've *always* looked like this!"

"That's not why." Malini shook her head. "I would never—"

"You called me an ugly freak." Elsey dropped her arms to her side and balled her hands into fists.

"I was scared of you!" Malini tossed up her hands. "Everyone knows you were the only one there when your grandparents died. Both sets of them. That you were found covered in their blood. Everyone knows you're dangerous. You literally stare at people like you're studying them and waiting for them to make one wrong move so you can snap their neck!" She took a breath and lowered her tone. "And I was jealous of you."

Elsey rolled her eyes.

"I still am." She looked at Henry, noting his shoulders tense again, and she faced Elsey. "You have everything, okay? You do. You have both of your parents, and neither one of them walks around like a zombie every day. You don't have to live in the city and breathe in the fires and worry that someone will kill you so they can live in your house. You have so much money you've never once had to worry what will happen when it runs out. You've never had to worry about *anything!*

"Everyone knows you have powers. Everyone knows not to mess with you! Do you know what it's like to know that there's a whole part of you that you can't share or else you risk being killed just for existing? Especially when that very thing probably happened to one of your parents? I've lived my entire life being afraid and hiding who I was, and you get to live without any fear about ever experiencing even a fraction of what the people like us face."

"Jealousy is stupid." Elsey's nails cut into her palms. "Most of the time you're jealous of your own perception, meanwhile you have no idea what you're truly jealous of."

Malini's smooth brow creased. "I don't understand what you mean."

"I mean this in the nicest way possible," Elsey arched a brow and added, "but I hope you never really do."

Henry watched Elsey, glimpsing the soft features between every crack and crevice marring her skin. Charlotte kept her eyes on her hands, aware of Wesley shifting beside her with unanswered questions drawing lines between them. Wesley brought his hands to his face and attempted to pick apart everything that had just happened.

Malini looked around the room, first at each person individually and then as a whole. "I want to help."

"No." Elsey and Henry spoke in unison. She looked at him, catching his eyes for a moment before tearing hers away.

"I can help!" Malini gestured out with her hands. "I *need* to help."

Wesley breathed a deep sigh and looked at Elsey. "I think we should let her."

"No." Elsey shook her head. "I don't trust her. I don't want her on the team. Are you forgetting that she nearly killed you and Charlotte?"

"The whole reason she did this in the first place is because Charlotte and I didn't tell her about you." He flung up his hands.

"If we did, none of this would've happened."

"Fine." The cold stare returned to Elsey's eyes. "If she's on the team, then I'm out."

"What?" Henry stood straighter.

Elsey spun to leave.

The front door opened.

A figure crossed the threshold.

The glow of a lantern caught onto silver eyes. Stepping into the light, Elsey could see long black hair framing a tapered chin and narrow forehead.

She glanced at the pictures lining the hall and back to those silver eyes.

Her breath stole from her lungs. "Carson?"

December 5, 3697

Silence filled the car with a tense spark. A chill gust of wind blew in through Kade's open window, rolling off the bay—dragging fluffy white flakes of snow with it.

"Can you roll that up?" Henry dusted the snow off his dashboard.

Ignoring the snow melting into his dark wash jeans, Kade closed the window. He kept the channel to his emotions closed so he wouldn't be dragged down by the darkness eating Henry alive. "At least it got you to talk to me. What's your deal today? You've not made a single joke. Are you mad at me?"

"No," Henry said too quickly. He tightened his grip on the steering wheel. "No. I'm not mad. I told you I understood. I'm tired. That's all."

"You usually talk more when you're tired." Kade's brows pushed together. "You just make less sense."

"Yeah, well maybe I got sick of being told by everyone to shut up." Henry took a deep breath. He rubbed his eyes and refocused on the road, turning off the bridge and onto the street that would carry them to the school. "Sorry, I'm—I don't know. Mal stood me up again last night, and she waited until three in the morning to call and tell me what happened."

Kade forced his eyes to the bald trees. "What did she say?"

"Same thing she always says." Henry glanced at him. "She got busy helping her mom and didn't realize what time it was. I can't really be mad at that, but it's the same thing she'd say whenever she was with Alex. Except I was at his house, so I know she wasn't with him."

Reaching up to scratch at the part between two of his braids, Kade kept his gaze fixed on everything else. The cracks in the road. The snow blanketing the trees and lining the street after being cleared. The clouds covering the light blue of the morning sky. Everything except Henry. He reminded himself to keep his breathing normal. *Things will be okay soon. He'll understand.*

Henry turned into the school parking lot, following the cars to his reserved spot near the front. Ana's vehicle was already in her spot beside his. He looked at the first spot near the stairs, finding it empty. The bitter chill of dread sunk into his stomach. He jammed his hands into the pockets of his wool overcoat, seeking his pills and flask as a reflex only to remember he'd been trying to remain sober.

Kade looked in the opposite direction, spotting a familiar violet sports car park six spots away. His heart kicked into a quicker pace, and he reminded himself to breathe normal. *Act normal. It will be okay soon.* "It looks like Mal just got here, too."

Jerking his attention away from Elsey's designated parking spot, Henry looked past Kade to see Malini climbing out of her car. He suppressed a groan and took his cue to do the same.

The cold hit him in the face and cut through his gray tailored slacks. Henry stuffed his hands into his coat pockets and walked down the rows of cars.

Malini met him halfway. Snow dusted her long raven black hair and blue and purple knitted hat. She managed to look chic even dressed casually in jeans, boots, and a dark purple coat. She greeted him with a smile and leaned in to kiss him. "Sorry again about last night. I really let time get away from me."

He nodded, repressing the emotions straining his resolve. "It's fine. How many times have I gotten distracted anyway? Want to go out tonight to make up for it?"

She opened her mouth to respond. Glancing over his shoulder, her words caught in her throat. Malini closed her mouth and gave a short nod.

Henry twisted to see what captured her attention. His eyes landed on Kade walking in their direction with his hands shoved into the pockets of his puffy black coat. He faced Malini and gave her another quick kiss. "You want to help me track down my sister?"

Malini's eyes darted over his shoulder again. She looked back at him. "I'm waiting for Jemma and Charlotte."

He grasped his phone inside his pocket, desperately needing something to fidget with. Desperately needing to distract himself from the urge to track down someone who could make his thoughts and feelings disappear behind a burst of colorful stars and fizzling warmth. Henry forced himself to nod and spin away.

He paused and looked at Kade. "You coming inside?"

"Nah," Kade said, motioning with his elbow toward the cars still turning into the parking lot. "Wes and Charlotte should get here soon. I want to make sure they dropped Taliyah off all right."

"Right." Henry gave another short nod. He tightened his grip on his phone and strolled toward the school.

Watching Henry trail up the stairs, Kade and Malini didn't speak until they saw him disappear inside.

Kade faced her, unphased that he had to look up at her more than usual since her chunky brown boots added to her height. His heart skipped a beat. Aware of all the people walking around them, he reminded himself to keep his hands in his pockets. To resist every temptation to reach for her.

He always kept the channel to her emotions closed, the need to allow things to organically blossom outweighed his burning curiosity. "We need to tell him."

Malini shook her head. "Not yet."

He thought of the brief conversation in the car. "He's going to figure it out, and it will be a lot worse when that happens if we don't tell him first."

"He's sober right now." She shook her head again. "Telling him something like that so soon might send him off the deep end."

Kade sighed. His breath a visible puff of white in the air. "I don't like hiding it from him. He doesn't deserve that."

"I know. But you don't know him like I do." Malini bit her bottom lip, struggling not to think about the night her life shattered.

Recalling how she had to find out how to put her pieces back together while dancing around a boy who never knew what it was like to have his pieces together in the first place. "The only way it would make sense to him is if we told him everything. He wouldn't understand unless he knew why, and that would destroy him."

"What about you?"

"I'm okay." She forced a smile to her lips, ignoring the taunting fear in the back of her mind. "I promise. You helped me be okay. I just can't make that change now. I want to. I do. I want things to be different. I don't like the secrets. But I know what it would do to Henry if we don't handle it right. We need to give him a little more time to be okay. Let him get a little more stable, and then we can talk to him."

He pressed his lips together and nodded toward the school. "Let's get out of the cold."

"What if he sees us? We said we were waiting for other people."

"It's snowing. Just start shivering and he'll forgive you for changing your mind."

A loud rumble smothered Malini's laugh. Elsey passed them on her motorcycle and parked beneath the stairs.

"How the hell can she even drive that thing when the weather is like this?" Malini asked, falling into step beside Kade.

He fixed the redhead in a hard glare. "It's probably easy when you already have a heart like ice."

Malini chewed on her bottom lip. She shot another look at Elsey when they walked past, noticing the girl's eyes following her with a calculating glare. Malini tugged on the violet essence coiling through her, opening up her mind to see what she always saw when inspecting Elsey. An aura of reds and blues wrapped in darkness—pitch black. A steady stream of energy swirled around a heavy pulsing vibration of untapped power. Beneath the aura large black leathery wings like that of a dragon spread out against Elsey's back. Black scales and hooked talons covered Elsey's hands. Not a girl. A monster.

Forcing herself to mount the first level of stairs, a deeper chill settled into Malini's bones and sent a shiver through her stomach. She walked closer to Kade. Hoping his warmth would stave off the cold sweat of fear springing to life from the eyes burning holes into her. They started to climb the second row of steps. She kept her attention on the building ahead. On the chance to disappear among the students. To erase the feeling inching over her spine.

"Malini." A serrated voice called behind them.

Her heart sprinted. She took a breath and held it, forcing her head to remain high as she turned. Kade stopped and turned with her.

Elsey stomped up the stairs toward them. A glare hotter than the fires of hell fixed on Malini.

Kade found Malini's trembling hand—lacing their fingers together. It wasn't until he began moving in front of Malini that he froze, realizing how his actions would read.

Elsey's glare fixed on both of them.

He still wanted to move in front of Malini, telling himself the risk was worth it. But his feet remained glued in place. His heart pounded hard enough for him to feel it in his throat.

Elsey halted in front of them. Her eyes darted to their entangled hands.

Malini squeezed Kade's hand and stared Elsey down. "What's your problem?"

Crossing her arms, she looked up at Malini. "My problem is that I continue to hear rumors about your involvement with other people despite your exclusive relationship with Henry. He deserves better than that." Elsey shifted her gaze to Kade. "From both of you."

All Kade's memories of Henry talking about how much he missed Elsey and wanted her back burned away the feeling of the cold. He dropped Malini's hand and did his best to mimic Elsey's glare. "You think you have any right to lecture anyone about what Henry deserves? You abandoned him."

"I didn't abandon him," she spat.

"Really? Because ever since you came back from wherever the heck disappeared to, you have had nothing to do with him. What did he ever do to deserve that?" Kade's emotional channel ripped open against a heavy force.

His temper rose with incredible speed. Something seemed to push him further, urging him to a point of destruction.

Not his own.

Someone else's.

A tremor of fear and confusion flashed through him. *Something's wrong. What's happening?* The anger continued to rise, to unfurl into a rage of darkened wings and hooked talons.

He recognized the emotion wasn't his own, but it grabbed him in a sharp grasp—demanding ruin and devastation. Clamoring for vengeance and war. Pain and death.

Knowing the source of the beast of blood and rage all at once, he stared at the girl.

A monster within a monster.

He pushed, but its grip didn't loosen. The talons hooked into him harder. Compelling him to say the worst things he'd ever thought about her. Things he'd never say aloud. "All he ever did was be your friend when no one else cared about you. He cared about you and spent every waking moment wanting to be around you when no one else can even stand to look at you. He's the only person who never cared that you have blood on your hands. And in return, you turned your back on him and act like you can't be bothered to give him the time of day. You don't deserve him anyway. You really are crazy if you think you do. He would've given the world for you, and all you've ever done is hurt him."

Another emotion bloomed beneath the rage.

A hollow aching pit of the deepest pain.

Feeling all the rage tumble down toward the pit, Kade recognized the emotions.

A heart of shades of blue and red wrapped in gray and black. He'd seen it before.

The rage caught onto the pit of despair, hooking its talons onto the rim and refusing to let go entirely—lacing everything with a constant unbreakable burn. Pain screamed from the darkness, and he realized everything he said too late. That he couldn't take it back.

He scrambled for an apology.

Malini looked between Elsey's narrow-eyed glare and Kade. Her heartbeat raced. All the rumors—the cold-blooded murder of Elsey's grandparents—ricocheted off her mind. Her lungs struggled to take in air. She glanced at Kade and saw horrible mental images of blood and a broken body. She looked at Elsey and her hardened gaze. Malini's panic reached a breaking point. She could see it—wings and talons. The monster underneath the façade of a girl.

Elsey shifted. Just an inch.

Jumping in front of Kade, Malini's arms shot out, and she shoved Elsey.

Trying to catch hold of the railing, Elsey stumbled. Her boot slipped on a patch of ice, toppling her balance even more. She plunged down the steps.

Kade dashed around Malini to catch Elsey, but he couldn't move fast enough.

Elsey hit the landing between both sets of stairs with a hard **crack** from her chin smashing into the pavement. Bright crimson blood gushed forward.

Kade spun on Malini. "Why did you do that?"

Gawking, she shook her head. "I didn't mean to! I don't know what happened! I was scared! I thought—"

Laughter erupted around them. Everyone who had been outside was staring. Victoria and Alex pointed at Elsey kneeling in a pool of her own blood while they laughed and made rude remarks, urging the crowd to join them.

Kade choked on his breath as he felt the hollow aching pit of pain open wider, threatening to consume him. He hurried down the stairs to kneel beside Elsey. He held out a hand to her to help her up but noticed her fumbling to remove her coat. Her eyes fixed on the blood painting the pavement. "What are you doing?"

She didn't reply. Yanking her arms from her coat, she dropped it and began pulling her sweater overhead.

"Whoa! Hey!" Kade grabbed her arm, but she jerked herself free. "It's freezing out here! What are you doing?"

Again, she didn't reply. As if the only thing that mattered was her blood painting the landing. She ripped her sweater off and pressed it into the blood.

"What? Elsey, no! Stop!" He grabbed her arm again, but she yanked out of his reach. His stomach twisted—a feeling he recognized as his own—beneath the hollow ache. He seized the sweater and yanked.

Holding onto her sweater, she spun on him. "Let go."

He held firm. "You don't have to clean this up. The school will clean it. It's okay."

"No, it's not."

"Yes, it is." He took a deep breath and plunged forward. "I'm sorry for what I said. I shouldn't have said it. I know it was mean and hurtful. I'm sorry. I'm really sorry."

Elsey's round eyes widened. She loosened her grip on the sweater.

He motioned to the blood on the stairs. "You don't have to clean this up. The school can get someone else to do it. You're bleeding really bad right now."

She released her sweater with one hand and pressed it to her chin. Pulling her hand back, she saw all the blood. "Facial wounds always bleed worse."

Telling himself not to stare at the rest of the scars carved into her face, he jostled the sweater. "Maybe press this to your chin for the moment." He looked around and saw everyone had gone inside. *Dang.* He glanced over his shoulder to her motorcycle. "You probably shouldn't drive yourself to the hospital like that."

She balled up the sweater and held it to her chin. "I can't go to the hospital."

"You need to. You're bleeding a lot. You probably need stitches." He nodded toward Henry's car. "What about Henry? I can call him. He'd take you."

"No." Elsey grabbed her coat and tossed it over her shoulder. Standing, she walked around him and marched down the steps.

Kade hurried after her, holding up his hands in a plea. "I said I'm sorry. I really am. I didn't mean what I said. But you really need to get that looked at."

Pulling the sweater away from her face, she saw the blood pouring down her chin and painting her black T-shirt. *Fuck.* She retrieved her phone from her pocket.

"What are you doing?"

"I'm messaging someone to pick me up. Is that okay with you?" She selected Luci's number from her contacts and sent a quick text. **Had an accident at school. Need stitches and a ride.**

Holding her phone in one hand and pressing her sweater to her chin with the other, Elsey sat on the bottom step.

Kade sat next to her.

She arched a brow. "What are you doing?"

"Waiting with you." He shoved his hands into his pockets.

"Why?"

Kade looked at her. He searched for the words, but all he could think of was the ache radiating from the pit inside her. He settled for a shrug.

She didn't respond.

Silence settled over them. Snow fell around them with the passing minutes.

A black full-size SUV turned into the parking lot at a dangerous speed. The vehicle whipped around the cars and parked in front of the stairs. Gene, Tristan, and Luci piled out of the SUV. Elsey tossed her keys to Gene. Catching her keys, he offered her a nod and mounted her motorcycle.

Luci pulled the sweater from Elsey's hands and examined the damage. "Shit!"

Tristan eyed the pool of blood on the landing. "Who did this?"

Elsey stepped out of Luci's reach. "Nobody. I fell."

Kade's eyes bulged. He strained to get a grasp on the newcomers. All he could feel were Elsey's emotions fighting to drown him.

Tristan and Luci exchanged a look.

Gene paused before turning the key. He lifted his hand. "I'm sorry, did you say *you* fell?"

Luci fixed her attention on Kade with narrowed eyes. "Who are you?"

"Uh … I'm Kade." Uncertain what to say, he caught Elsey's eyes and read the hardened look coupled with the emotions swelling inside her. He motioned toward her with his elbow. "I saw her fall, and I told her I'd sit with her until someone got here."

Luci, Tristan, and Gene stared at him. He kept his face blank and his breathing normal.

Returning his attention to Elsey's motorcycle, Gene revved it to life. "I'll head back."

Luci nodded toward the SUV. "Come on, Else. Let's go."

Elsey followed her.

Waiting for them to climb in, Tristan turned to Kade. "What really happened?"

Kade stared up at Tristan, recognizing he was taller than Henry—possibly even taller than Henry's dad. He thought about Elsey's decision to lie and about all the pain and rage he felt living inside her. The inkling of a thousand questions rang in his mind.

He shook his head. "Nothing. She fell. I saw it."

Tristan stared at him for a second longer before nodding and turning to the SUV.

"Hey, wait!" The questions rang louder. Kade stepped forward. "Who are you guys? I thought she was messaging her parents. You're not her family."

Pausing by the passenger door, Tristan glanced at Kade. "Blood isn't what makes a family."

Kade waited for him to say more, but Tristan climbed in the SUV and shut the door. The vehicle hurried out of the parking lot just as fast as it had arrived. Kade stared after it, his mind swelling with questions.

CHAOS
PLAYLIST

I put together this list of songs that relate directly to **CHAOS** in some way or inspired me while writing. The songs are in no particular order.

The playlist can be found either on my website at https://cydneydaemon.com/chaos_series/chaos/playlist/ so you can find the individual songs to add to your preferred music streaming platform.

Alternatively, the playlist is available on YouTube labeled **CHAOS** Soundtrack for you to listen at your leisure.

The QR Code below will take you directly to the playlist on YouTube.

ACKNOWLEDGEMENTS

First and foremost, the biggest thank you goes to my mom for reading me books of all kinds as a child whenever I would visit her, including books she wrote herself. Without her, I probably never would've even realized that I could write my own books.

I also wouldn't have gotten this far if not for my best friends: (in alphabetical order) Kelsey, Samantha, and Shae.

Kelsey for being there for me every step of the way ever since we met and wanting to devour everything I write while not being afraid to give me honest feedback. Also, for designing the indicator for the past scenes.

Samantha and Shae for putting up with me telling them every single story and dream I've ever had, in great detail, every time we rode the bus to or from school.

Samantha for continuing to provide a motivational boost whenever we talk.

And Shae for continuing to want to read everything I write, being real with me when I need to hear it, and helping me so much with advice, marketing stuff, and so much else.

The best cheer team ever! I love you all with every fiber of my being!

I also want to thank all the friends I've made on social media who have been supportive and friendly, especially since I'm extremely anxious when it comes to interacting with people. And a special thank you to the people who were kind enough to beta read and sensitivity read for me: Bryanna, Bradley, Erika, Kristy and many others. (I only listed the names of those who provided permission.)

This book also wouldn't have been completed to such quality without the help of the creative team I hired.

Editor, Belle Manuel, for understanding and respecting my vision and catching how many times I excessively used the word "grabbed" and "slammed" in fight scenes.

Dan, part of the kingkrd team on Fiverr, created the font used for the title, volume numbers, and drop letter at the beginning of each scene, and many more accents. He also created and the font used for my author name, volume dates, the scene headers, and many more accents. I love the fonts so much. They look so amazing with the book and the standard fonts I've used throughout. I couldn't imagine what this book would look like without them.

Cover artist, Clint Lockwood, for being just an amazing artist who was patient with me and worked to make my vision come true. I appreciate you all so much!

I also want to say thank you to anyone who has decided to read CHAOS, whether you loved it or not. I have stitched pieces of my heart and soul into the words of CHAOS, and it means the world to me that anyone would give it a chance.

And last, but definitely not least, thank you to my fur babies: Tapiocca, Leia, and Holly for just being you. I can't express how much I love my girls, but yes, they get appreciation too because without them, I wouldn't be here, and this book never would've been finished.

Thank you to everyone from the bottom of my heart. I appreciate all the support.

I hope you stay with me for whatever comes next.

x Cydney Daemon

ABOUT THE AUTHOR

Cydney Daemon, first and foremost, is a human being.

She is definitely not a demon of chaos taking human form in order to collect as many books, black cats, and items of gothy wonder as possible.

When she is not hyperfixated on writing whatever has possessed her brain, Cydney can be found arguing with her dog, playing referee to her two house panthers, consuming media things meant to scare her for fun, and testing the limits of Dr Pepper consumption on the human body. Alternatively, if spotted in the wild instead of in her cave of darkness, she may be seen rambling to herself about anything from book ideas to how many times she had to walk down that aisle before remembering to grab the damn chips she came here for.

Prior to becoming a published author, she worked in customer service—which was a grave mistake on everyone's part—and a freelance writer, writing the session notes for mental health professionals.

With an origin story that includes poverty and severe childhood trauma, mental health and empowerment for everyone has always been extremely important to her.

Cydney seeks to write books that have their own heart and soul and that can help those in the way books helped her growing up, whether that be by providing an escape or an inspiration.

Threads: @CydneyDaemon
Instagram: @CydneyDaemon
Website: www.cydneydaemon.com

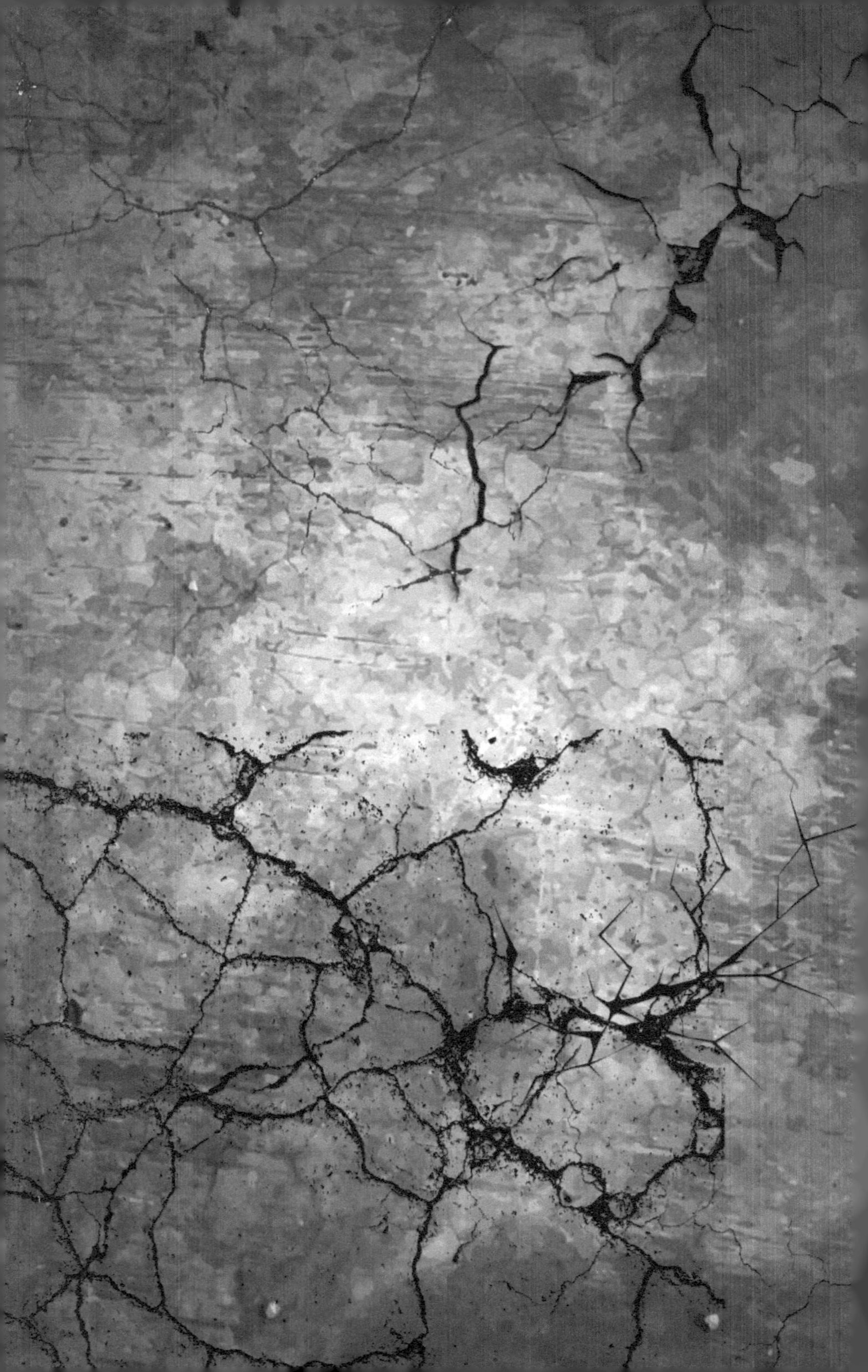